"I was utterly transported by *Moth*. In exquisite prose, Melody Razak takes us right to the heart and the heat of Partition-era Delhi—a fracturing city, a fracturing nation and a family attempting to hold themselves together when everything threatens to tear them apart. *Moth* is a rare, winged delight—able to stare unflinchingly into the darkness, while always illuminated by a fierce love for life. A stunning, powerful work by a brave new voice in British fiction."

—Anna Hope, author of *Expectation*

M O T H

M O T H

a novel

Melody Razak

HARPER

An Imprint of HarperCollins*Publishers*

MOTH. Copyright © 2022 by Melody Razak. All rights reserved. Printed in Canada. No part of this book may be used or reproduced in any manner whatsoever without written permission except in the case of brief quotations embodied in critical articles and reviews. For information, address HarperCollins Publishers, 195 Broadway, New York, NY 10007.

HarperCollins books may be purchased for educational, business, or sales promotional use. For information, please email the Special Markets Department at SPsales@harpercollins.com.

First published in Great Britain in 2021 by Weidenfeld & Nicholson.

FIRST US EDITION

Library of Congress Cataloging-in-Publication Data has been applied for.

ISBN 978-0-06-314006-6

22 23 24 25 26 FB 10 9 8 7 6 5 4 3 2 1

For my mother and sister.

I shall not commit the grievous sin of losing faith in Man. I would rather look forward to the opening of a new chapter in his history after the cataclysm is over and the atmosphere rendered clean with the spirit of service and sacrifice. Perhaps that dawn will come from this horizon, from the East where the sun rises. A day will come when unvanquished Man will retrace his path of conquest despite all barriers to win back his lost human heritage.

—*Rabindranath Tagore*

PROLOGUE

Lahore, Pakistan, May 1948

IN A MAKESHIFT sling across her chest, she holds a sleeping baby. A swaddled baby who drinks in her mother's scent, the promise of milk, and moves her mouth in quiet sucks like tight petals blooming.

In the dark corridor, she slips a hand into the sling, grips through the cotton the steel of a paring knife. Next to the knife is a vial of rosewater, next to the vial, a newspaper twist of turmeric.

She wishes she hadn't promised. Only, the birth had been so hard, with the old stitches unravelling, and the girl had thought she would surely die. She had not known that the child pressed to her chest could be so warm.

She clutches the baby now and walks outside, stands on the garden path. It is raining.

I was not expecting you, says the girl to the rain.

I'm here for you, says the rain. *I'm not supposed to be here at all. This will confuse everyone.*

Thank you for coming.

The rain is as good as her word. Hot rainwater falls so fast and thick, she can barely open her eyes. Puddles of mud swell in every hole and dent.

The hibiscuses are flowering. She has waited nine months to see them open, and now that they have, she walks past them, doesn't see the petals like ripped hearts beckoning. Misses in the dark the red warning.

She walks confidently. Relishes the smell of wet earth and knows the path. She is not afraid of the dark. The rain pushes her forwards. She lets it take her by the hand, by the elbow.

You should sing to her, you know, says the rain. *It will help with the rebirth.*

Yes. Sing, says the wind just arrived.

What should I sing?

Sing the ancient myths. Sing to Kali. Sing to us.

She presses her lips to the baby's head, in a low voice sings a poem that Ma had sung to her when she was small. She holds the baby closer. Once, there was a sister, she had sung to her too, swaddled her in white cotton with embroidered birds across the folds. When no one was look-ing, she had fed the baby sister Nestlé straight from the tin, licked sweet condensed milk from the spoon.

Yesterday, the mali gave her a small lump of opium. Crumble this, he said, into the milk and feed it to her in a baby's bottle. I can't bear that she might suffer.

The girl nodded slowly, throat tight and eyes burning.

The mali was as gentle in his ministrations as if the baby were his, as if the baby were theirs. He stroked the baby's cheeks, her nose, her petal mouth, her tiny hands and feet, the hollow of her downy head.

Except that he didn't. The baby was in the zenana and he, untouch-able servant, was not allowed in the big house.

The girl walks past the guava tree, now bereft of fruit. The leaves whisper and rustle. She will not listen to them. Those leaves will try to dissuade her. She walks past the dark of the mali's hut. The palm frond door is closed.

At the end of the garden, she sits down in the wet dirt beneath the mango tree, its boughs heavy with fruit that is almost achingly ready. She is thoughtfully tender. Doesn't want to make a mistake. She unties the sling. Lays the swaddled baby on the wet earth, uncorks the vial, and douses her with rosewater. Dips her finger into the powdered turmeric and smudges it across her daughter's forehead. Yellow to repel the evil eye, rosewater to claim the goddess's good grace.

The girl unsheathes the knife. Stolen from the kitchen along with the turmeric. It smells of yesterday's sliced onions and the cumin that was crushed to dust with the width of the blade. She should have washed it. That the knife is dirty, that she did not think to clean it, upsets her and her eyes begin to swell.

It's all right, says the rain. *Put the knife down. I will wash it for you. Pick a mango leaf off the ground. Rub the leaf between your fingers to release the oils. Use the leaf to wipe the knife. The oils will smell sweet, and the knife will smell sweet, and the blood too will smell sweet when the blade cuts through the skin.*

She listens to the rain and cleans the knife. Yesterday, she threaded yellow marigolds that she picked from behind the mali's hut. She puts her hand now into a cavity of the tree, pulls out the sodden garland. Places it around the baby's head.

The baby soaked in rainwater is heavy. Her face is blue-grey and cold. The girl places the flat of her palm against the small cheek, and there is something about the small cheek blue-grey and cold that feels unreal, as if the baby were already dead.

Is a sacrifice a proper sacrifice if the sacrificial being is already dead?

I think I gave her too much opium, she says to the rain, stomach curdling.

It is better this way, says the rain. *Slit the throat first, then break the skull to release the spirit.*

The girl takes the knife, now clean, and holds it to the baby's throat.

Part One

1

Delhi, early February 1947

THE DOGS OUTSIDE are fighting and the gutters on Nankhatai Gali are overflowing.

In Pushp Vihar, the House of Flowers, Alma sits up in her Sunday dress and leans against the bedstead. From her bedroom on the first floor, she can hear the jingles on All-India Radio from the courtyard downstairs. This means that Bappu is either awake and listening, or asleep on the swing with his head fallen into his chest.

Alma is fourteen. She will be married-soon and she will be an exemplary wife. She hugs her knees tightly. To be married-soon is like snow. Alma has never actually seen snow, but has come to the conclusion—after examining the diagrams in Volume Seven of the *Encyclopaedia Britannica*—that snow is a miracle of nature. Snow is like putting your feet in the icebox, drinking nimbu pani as fast as you can, with the fan set on six and blowing straight into your face.

Alma has only ever had glimpses of her husband-to-be, at his house first and then at Pushp Vihar, when the two of them had mostly stared at their feet. For a minute, she had caught his eye, the ghost of a smile soft on his mouth, and of course, she had smiled back. He was so fair she could hardly believe it. It was as if Kamadev himself had stood behind her and struck her with one of his arrows. "Would you like some chai," she had asked, averting her eyes, and "Yes," he had replied, "yes, I would." She was like a gopi bathing unclothed in the lake, all hot and cold at once. Glancing down she had peeked at the boy's feet. He wore clean socks and proper shoes, chocolate-coloured and laced.

Alma's grandmother, Daadee Ma, who had made the match in the first place and organised the horoscopes and set the date, is very keen. Questionably so in fact. Daadee Ma told Dilchain-ji, the family cook, that she had never seen such an auspicious horoscope and the quicker Alma was wed the better. That it will be a small wedding can't be helped. A small wedding is in keeping with the climate. Alma will invite a few of the girls from school and Sister Ignatius and Mary. Mary is new and not necessarily the kind of girl that Alma would be friends with, but Mary has a secret and secrets are always interesting.

Outside the bedroom window, the night sky is thick with lilac-grey mist that Bappu says is the smoke of wood-and-mud huts burning all the way from West Punjab. Alma had asked Bappu if they would come here, those people that burnt down each other's homes; he had reassured her they would not.

Inside, Alma leans across the tin chest of extra winter bedding and lights the stub of a candle with the one match left in the box. There has been a shortage of matches recently and Dilchain-ji has rationed each family member to two matches a day. Alma turns to prod her sister and tug her plaits. "Wake up," she says.

Roop squirms sleepily and kicks her.

There are three long-legged beds in a row, but Roop is always in with Alma. The third bed belongs to Bappu's dead little brother and is never slept in.

"Roop," Alma pokes her sister, laughs quietly to herself. "Do you remember that time, when you slept in the third bed and woke up in the middle of the night and I asked you. What did you say?"

Roop giggles sleepily, her back still turned, naked but for white knickers. "I said I felt a bit pe-cu-liar." She says the word slowly as she has been taught to do. Bappu says speaking slowly and repeating is the best way to learn. "And then we put the bowl of kheer under the bed for Bappu's dead little brother's ghost, in case he was hungry."

Alma hugs her rosebud pillow. Everyone knows that spirits don't need to eat, but the gesture of friendship had been there. "Dilchain-ji found it. It was blue-black-green, and all those ants stuck in the middle squashed in the sweet milk and rice."

"They were dead!" says Roop, turning to face her sister. "Squashed," she says, pressing her little palms firmly together and nodding. "A family of greedy ants. Dilchain-ji said I wasn't allowed to cremate them and then she smacked me with the broom. On the bottom. Oh, it was so funny."

"I'm too excited to sleep. It's boring being excited alone," says Alma sitting up, sucking the inside of her elbow.

"Why?"

"It's better when you're awake too. Sit up and I'll tell you where the little mouse lives?"

"Where? I love little mice."

"In the courtyard."

"Where exactly in the courtyard?"

Roop sits up and rubs her eyes. A mouse in the courtyard will need a trap. A steel catch on a spring mechanism that will ping forwards and cut off its head. A mosquito buzzes by her ear, she claps her hands and stumbles off the bed. "Got it. Look!" she says, showing Alma the smear of juice and blood on her palm.

Alma pulls a face. "I'm getting married in this many weeks," she says, holding up five fingers. "Look."

On her wedding day, Alma will wear silver shoes with pearl buckles made to measure by the cobbler with the henna beard who sits on the far corner of Ballimaran Lane. Alma points her toes and slips on her imaginary shoes. The imaginary pearl buckles glow resplendent in the imaginary moonlight. At her wedding party, she will dance and dance and her husband will dance with her.

"What are you doing?" asks Roop. She is not at all impressed that her sister is getting married soon.

"Trying on my silver wedding shoes. When I'm married you can come to my house every Friday for jalebis and I'll let you eat as many as you want, hot from the pan."

"They won't be as good as Dilchain-ji's though, will they?"

Roop picks the wings off the mosquito and inspects them for translucency. She licks the mosquito pulp off her palm, wonders if "when I am married" is the most stupid thing she has ever heard her sister say. "Why are you wearing that in bed?" she asks, pointing to Alma's frock.

Alma arranges the creamy frill of her Sunday tutu like a fountain's spray around her. Recently, she has started to wear her best-occasion frocks—those meant for Sundays, holidays, parties, and trips to the Royal Cinema at the Queen Victoria Circle—every day. She won't leave the house without a red apple clip in her hair.

When Bappu had teased her about it, Alma replied that you just didn't know who would pass you in the street, and by who, she meant her husband-to-be or "the so-fair-boy" as she had started to call him. "You should always look your best because first impressions count for a lot."

When Bappu said she was right, first impressions did count for a lot but there was more to it than that, she asked if she could start wearing lipstick. He laughed. Absolutely not.

"Lucky for me you're such an intelligent girl," said Bappu, tweaking her plait. "Otherwise, I would disown you."

"I should disown you," said Alma, putting one hand on her frilly hip and scrutinising his khadi trousers, his khadi shirt, and the thin-rimmed glasses that he cleaned so fastidiously. "Bappu, you are so beige."

"I am, aren't I?" he said, looking down at himself and laughing. "Too much colour terrifies me."

Alma looks at her sister now, says in a gravelly voice, her plait held across her top lip, "I am a fierce Pathan warrior. Come down from the tallest mountains to save your humble people. See how fine my mustachios are?"

"Are you a Pathan from Kashmir?" says Roop, forgetting the whys of the Sunday dress.

Ma is from Kashmir. That means that they too are half from Kashmir. Although they have never been there, they have heard Ma talk about it. When Ma talks about Kashmir, her pale blue eyes steam as though someone has reached into her face and lit a match behind the irises.

Alma shakes her head, says in the same gravelly voice, "I am a Pathan from the Afghan mountains. I have come to put an end to the fighting in Bengal and Punjab. East and West."

"How will you do that?"

"Jadoo. I will put a spell on the nation, bring the misplaced people to their senses."

"Mis-pl-aced?" says Roop.

"Lost-absent-gone astray."

"Where have they gone?"

"They haven't gone anywhere," Alma concedes, "not yet, but they have lost all their good sense. That's what Bappu said."

"What religion are you?"

"Irrelevant," says Alma with a hand held up in protest.

"Pathans are actually Muslim, which means you can't be one. Fatima Begum's great uncle was a Pathan. She told me herself."

"Pathans are Muslim. It's true," admits Alma, "but a real warrior is brave no matter what. It's the bravery that counts not the colour of the god. Gandhi-ji says so and so does Bappu. Independence from the British will bring freedom, and with freedom comes equality. Pandit Nehru said it on the radio. I heard him."

Alma touches her heart when she says the Mahatma's name. She tries to imagine the biological diagram of the oval-shaped organ, and the muscles clenched around it. She can't believe her heart would look like that or that it would be there, when it feels like it might be in her brain, her stomach, or even in her throat.

"Equa-li-ty," says Roop, touching her heart in imitation of Alma. "Equality like Kwality?"

"Kwality. Purveyors of Modern Confectionery. Sweet Making for a Free India," says Alma in her best radio announcer's voice. "No. Not like that at all."

"What then?"

"It's very modern. It means that in essence, in our hearts, we are all the same."

"But some are better than others. Does Daadee Ma know about equa-li-ty?"

"No, and you better not tell her. She won't like it. Promise me—cross your heart, hope to die, stick a needle in your eye—and then I'll give you a story."

"I promise," says Roop, making the sign of the cross as she has seen the sisters do. "Tell me the one about the man who was tied to the tramlines. That's my favourite."

"Lie down next to me then. Put your head on the pillow," Alma lowers her voice. "During the riots in August last year . . ."

"Direct Action Day," says Roop promptly and sits up. "When the Muslims killed the Hindus. They burnt them alive, didn't they?"

Alma nods solemnly and pushes her back down. "Yes, but the Hindus did exactly the same in return. Lie down, I said."

"Co-py-cat kill-ings. I heard Ma say so. That's what Bappu said, and then Ma said, 'Does fasting count if you kill a man whilst you are doing it?' Because it was Ramadan. That's why."

"Do you want the story or not?"

Roop sucks on her thumb and nods.

"Hush then. In the city of Calcutta, in the East of India, in the middle of all that rioting—"

"And looting, there was looting too."

"Shh. A man was tied to the connector box of the tramlines—"

"Because in Calcutta they have trams, don't they?"

Alma nods. "This man had a small hole drilled right into his skull and he was left to bleed to death, drip by drip."

"What did they make the hole with?"

"A screwdriver?"

"How long till he was dead?"

"A few days I think," whispers Alma, her hand cupped to her sister's ear. "It's called torturing."

"Tor-tur-ing?"

"To inflict pain as slowly as possible. Now go to sleep."

"Oh," says Roop, eyes wide. She tries to picture the pool of blood, its size and colour, spreading around the dead man's feet. "Can you tor-ture a mouse?"

"Shh. Close your eyes. I mean it."

"Can you torture insects?"

"Probably, but you mustn't. Baby Jesus would not like it one bit. Let's go to sleep."

Alma blows out the candle and turns her back. Eventually, she falls asleep with the distant lullaby of the muezzin singing the azan. She dreams of the river Jamuna flowing the wrong way and on its sandy shores stands the so-fair-boy. He looks up at her and waves.

. . .

Bappu listens to the news every day. Obsessively so, in fact. The Emerson Radio Model 517 has been taken out of his study and placed on one of two teak tables in the courtyard. The tables, a low table and a dining table, are made from British Burmese teak by an Indian carpenter to European specifications, "Made-in-India" is scratched into the underbelly of each one.

When he goes to work at Delhi University, Bappu listens to his colleagues. Every day at noon, the male teachers sit down at the canteen's communal table for a lunch of rotis-dal-sabzi. Some eat with their hands, others use a tin spoon bent out of shape. They pass round a steel pitcher of water.

Ma, also a teacher at the university, eats her lunch in a separate, windowless room with those nominal female students who are allowed, by the grace of their generously wealthy families, to attend. Both Bappu and Ma agree that the situation is unfair.

In the main canteen, the Congress-supporting Mr. Viamika, a muffler round his neck, comments one late February Monday, between mouthfuls of dal scooped up with a roti, that albeit Pandit Nehru is doing the best he can, he shouldn't be trying to please everyone. "It is a question of loyalty," he says, loud enough so the students will hear.

"Haan ji," agrees his close colleague, passing the chilli, the red thread of several pujas tied to his wrist, "all this pandering to the League haramzadas, when they are butchering our brothers."

Professor Singh stands to attention, holds up a finger, and lisps, straight from Tara Singh's mouth: "If the Muslim League want to establish Pakistan they will have to pass through an ocean of Sikh blood first. Our people will not forfeit Punjab without a fight," he adds, mumbling and swallowing. "Punjab is blessed land, richest agricultural soil on the subcontinent."

"Hear, hear," shout a few of the students, clapping and stamping their feet.

"Do not think for a minute," says the usually calm professor of Botanical Studies, Mohammed Ghualam, now incensed, "that we will stay in a country where we are clearly a minority and treated as such. Pakistan is a holy land. It has been promised to us by Allah and it will be delivered."

Mohammed Ghualam is one of five Muslim teachers in the predominantly Hindu—but proudly open-minded—institution.

Mr. Viamika slams his fist on the table. "All this rioting and raping," he glowers. "Your people are butchers. Do not think for a minute we have forgotten the events in Calcutta."

"We have not forgotten those in Noakhali," retorts Mohammed Ghualam, standing up quickly, spilling hot chai all over his trousers.

Bappu rubs his eyes—they always sting nowadays—adjusts his glasses, and passes his handkerchief to Mohammed Ghualam. He wishes Ma was sitting next to him. "We are old friends and colleagues," he says, looking from one teacher to the next. "We have worked together for years. We can't fight amongst ourselves. Not now."

"When these meat-eaters learn their place," retorts Mr. Viamika.

The students stop eating, one or two of them smirk. A boy named Arun throws a cup of water at Mohammed Ghualam and hoots with laughter when the water splashes the teacher's robes. "Pakistan murdabad," Arun shouts mockingly, lighting an imported cigarette and smoking it with defiant pleasure.

Mohammed Ghualam pushes his tin thali aside. He spits and walks away. "I resign," he shouts back.

· · ·

Bappu, home earlier than usual, the last class of the day cancelled, sits on the swing with Ma. He tells her about the tension in the canteen and the resignation of Mohammed Ghualam. "Soon there will be no Muslim teachers left," he says.

"I know, my love," she replies. She takes Bappu's hand, squeezes his fingers, and wraps her arm around him. The heat from his body is a tonic and she could lose herself in it. She presses her nose to his neck.

"Alma asked me if the troubles in Punjab would come to Delhi. I said no," says Bappu. "Was I wrong?"

"What else could you say? How do you put into words what we feel, what we smell is coming?"

Bappu nods and cleans his glasses; they are always so dirty, the air so dusty. "Can you smell it too then?"

She nods. "Sometimes, I sit in the courtyard, I try to read but I'm distracted by the cumin frying in the kitchen, and the gutters overflowing outside, hot milk and my own sweat and all of it feels so close, and then there is the radio always in the background and the news never good. There is no peace anymore."

"I can't work out where the tide is swelling, but I know it's growing faster than there is space to hold it. India will collapse and Independence will come too late." Bappu rubs his eyes, so she takes his hand, presses it to her mouth.

Ma pushes her bare toes against the low teak table. The swing sways, backwards and forwards in a soothing, cooling rhythm. Her anklets chime and she picks star-shaped jasmine from the tree behind them, crushes the white flower between her finger and thumb. "Smell this," she says to Bappu, and he does. "Some things will always be constant. Jasmine will always smell sweet, and when it is pushed to your nose like this, you would almost forget the gutters outside. Listen to this, my love, and tell me who wrote it: 'If your prayers are potent, Mullah, move this mosque my way. Else have a drink or two with me and we'll see its minarets sway.'"

"A Shayaris by Mirza Ghalib."

"With poetry like that, how can hate prevail?" she says to reassure and reward him.

Bappu remembers the day he met her. Her rose-dipped voice. She had rubies and pearls in her ears. The stones of sorrow, his twin had said.

"I haven't the heart to discuss wedding plans tonight," he admits.

"Nor I. Lakshmi will be here soon. She will help."

"Thank god for my twin," says Bappu.

He agitates the branch behind them. Star-shaped blossoms fall across Ma's shoulders and face and she lifts her head, laughs at the tickle on her skin.

. . .

Alma and Roop skip around Bappu at least once a day, pleading for his attention. Bappu, me! No me! I am the favourite. I am the eldest. They pinch each other out of the way.

Roop, who likes the jingle of the radio adverts, hears that Horlicks Overcomes Weakness and that the Lovely Leela Chitnis uses Lux soap. She runs to Dilchain-ji demanding that both be purchased at once. "Dilchain-ji, please," she pleads, "we need them for the state of the nation. You know there might be an actual war soon—Sister Ignatius said so—with rationing! Well then, let's go to Chandni Chowk, let's go! That's where all the important things are sold." Dilchain-ji is busy and shoos her off, so Roop runs to her ayah, Fatima Begum, who always agrees.

Alma likes to listen to the news with Bappu. After school one day, wedged next to him on the swing, her leg in his, she asks outright if he is a communist.

He looks at her serious expression and tries not to laugh. "Where did you hear that?"

"At school. Ruby Patel said that her second cousin who was a communist was shot in the head."

"I went to a few meetings. Read some pamphlets when I was a student. It was a long time ago now."

"But why?"

"You know how I feel about the caste system?"

"It divides our society. That's what you always said," she says, looking up for his approval.

"It's a cruel system. When I was a boy, older than you, communism offered an alternative."

In Bappu's first week at university, a student at a rally had handed him a home-printed pamphlet. Something about the tilt of the boy's head, the red bandana across his forehead: Bappu had accepted the pamphlet at once. It wasn't so much that he wanted to be friends with the boy, more that he had wanted to *be* the boy. Less sensitive. Bolder. Brighter.

"But you're not a communist now, are you?" says Alma. "I don't want you to get shot in the head and I don't want the boy's family to hear rumours that might put them off."

"Quite right," says Bappu laughing. "No one wants a communist in the family."

"Seriously Bappu. It's not funny."

"No, it's not and I am not."

"Promise me?"

"Yes. Hand on my heart. To be honest, Alma, I can't condone extreme beliefs anymore, no matter how I might try to understand them. When explosive ideas are no longer just ideas, yet they become the foundation for new political parties, they can feel quite dangerous. Do you understand, my love?"

"Do you mean like the HRWP?" asks Alma. She smoothes down the tulle layers of her lilac tutu. The so-fair-boy is standing on the shores of the Jamuna, and she can tell by the tilt of his head he's impressed by her questions. "I've seen them walking round, all puffed up and slinging their guns."

"The HRWP claim to be defending our Indian humanity, our pride and independence, but really?" He shakes his head.

"They're modelled on fascist soldiers, aren't they?"

"How do you know?"

Alma looks down sheepishly. "I might have read it in *The Times of India*: 'cloaked in nationalism but inciting hatred,'" she quotes.

"Should I be impressed or worried that you know that?"

"Impressed, of course," she says, looking up and smiling. "So what do you believe in now, Bappu?"

"Ahimsa."

Ahimsa, Gandhi's policy of non-violence, is something Alma thinks about often. Is it like turning the other cheek? She worries that if pushed too far, she would hit back. "I believe in it too," she says now, for Bappu's sake, and presses her body to his, rumples his beige shirt with her hands. "Bappu, when I am married, I can still come home, can't I? Once a week? On Sundays for kheer, and Fatima Begum will still do my hair?"

"It depends," he says slowly. "You might be needed in your new home. Your mother-in-law and husband will have lots for you to do."

"But then you will have to come and see me?"

"You might not want us to; you'll be so busy being a new wife."

"Don't be silly, Bappu, I will always want to see you." She observes him carefully. "Bappu, you don't seem very happy I'm getting married?"

"It's not that." He looks up at her with a rueful smile. "It's just that it's all happening so fast."

He can't bring himself to tell her that he is ashamed for agreeing to the wedding so quickly. That for a moment, encouraged by Daadee Ma, losing sight of rationale and logic, he was caught up in the terror that the things happening to girls throughout the nation—abduction-rape-murder—might happen to her. That she would be safer, after all, with a husband than without.

"Who will look after the flowers when you go?" he says instead, feeling wholly inadequate and small.

"Don't be silly, Bappu. I will show Roop how to do it. You can't be upset about that, surely?" She is quiet for a minute, mulling it over. "You're nervous about Independence Day, aren't you? But, Bappu, it's not for another year. And, you're worried that the troubles in Bengal and Punjab will come here." She looks at him straight. "There's no point hiding it from me, I've been listening to you and Ma talk."

"I know you have," he says.

"Well?"

Bappu shrugs his shoulders. He takes off his glasses and puts them down on the teak table. "I just don't know," he says, "about any of it. Everything feels so uncertain."

"Unstable?" she suggests. "Like it could tip either which way?"

"Exactly. When did you get so clever?"

"I have always been like this, Bappu. Did I tell you that I overheard Sister Ignatius speaking to the sisters about me becoming head girl next year? She also said that rats are known to eat their own tails before they die of starvation. Did you know that?"

"No, you didn't, and I had no idea."

"Don't you think then that perhaps rats are more intelligent than humans?"

"I don't doubt it," says Bappu, smiling despite himself.

2

Mid-February 1947

DAADEE MA'S ARTHRITIC knees hurt more than ever. Briefly she wonders if the pain is a forewarning for her meddling ways. She did interfere with the horoscope, but what choice did she have? She did what she had to do. It was a question of honour.

Daadee Ma was very careful to meet Astrologer Uncle at his office, on the third floor of the dentures-fitting unit behind Chaori Bazaar. No one saw her dictate the date and time of birth, or hand over the envelope of baksheesh. She had to do it. The girl's horoscope was shocking. It makes Daadee Ma queasy to think of it. Who would marry a girl like that? No one, that's who, and the family name soiled, stinking of mutton fat, and everyone talking. For shame. The wedding will be rushed, when everyone knows that a tip-top, Class-A wedding takes time to plan.

Daadee Ma's shrine is set up in the tubers of the young peepul tree growing in the centre of the courtyard and up through the open roof. At 5:00 a.m., when the rest of the household are asleep, she is awake and bathing her gods. Portly Ganpati Remover of Obstacles; Hanuman the Warrior and bringer home of Sita; blue-skinned Krishna, the flute of seduction to his lips; and the black marble lingam of Shiva-Supreme-Lord. Daadee Ma has been in love with Shiva since the day she was born.

She washes the gods with real cow's milk, rubs ghee and honey into their crevices, and douses the tops of their heads with sandalwood oil. She hangs marigold-jasmine-rose garlands around their necks. Offers sweet prasad, puffed rice, lights a stick of incense and seven ghee lamps with matches that she hides in a padlocked box. She rings a small brass bell seven times, holds her hands over the flame of the seven ghee lamps seven times, and praises the deities seven times. Seven is the most auspicious number of all.

She asks to win the next round of poker at the Gymkhana, for the shit on the streets to be cleaned, a Class-A tip-top wedding, protection against the evil eye, for Bappu's pa's soul to dissolve into the ether and stop sitting in judgement against her.

She asks most of all for a Pure Hindustan.

"It's about time, don't you think," she mouths, "for that fatty ayah to go?"

She tells the gods of the HRWP soldiers, parading each morning along Nankhatai Gali in starched brown uniforms. Fine Hindustani boys, not a crease or a stitch out of place. Shiny shoes and neat laces. She beams and caresses the black marble lingam in her hand. The regimented lines of the HRWP are nothing if they are not shipshape.

. . .

It's Sunday, and Dilchain is making parathas for breakfast. Alma and Roop skip around her. They take it in turns to listen out by the door. Daadee Ma does not approve of the girls idling in the kitchen. "Their mischief-making," she says, "will leak into the food and make it bitter."

The kitchen walls are painted with an indigo wash to keep the flies out and the cool in. Brahmin blue. Shiva blue. Pious and practical blue.

MOTH

Dilchain chose the colour herself. A long slate countertop runs the length
of one wall and the shelves are stocked full of good things to eat.

"Ooh, a green fly," says Alma, pointing to the insect hovering above
the muslin-covered jaggery. She lifts her hand and lilac glass bangles
plink up and down her arms. Her lilac ruffles sashay around her calves.

Dilchain in her floury apron laughs and pulls a lilac ruffle out of
shape.

"Let's catch it and squish it dead," suggests Roop, reaching up with
a ready clap.

"No!" says Dilchain. She catches the fly in her cusped hand and
guides it out the window. "That fly might be someone's pa," she says.
She turns to Roop, pinches her lightly on the arm. "Little brute, where
are your clothes?"

"Too hot," says Roop. She picks an old scab off her knee and eats it.
"Dilchain-ji, I know where the mouse lives. I'm going to catch it and then
I'm going to tor-ture it," she says proudly.

"What mouse? What torture?"

"Don't listen to her, Dilchain-ji. She's full of nonsense," says Alma,
pulling her sister's plait hard.

Dilchain sits on her haunches and holds a pot between her knees.
With a coconut husk, salt, and half a lemon she scrubs the pan until the
copper shines like a wet orange.

"Look," she says to Alma, "this is how you clean a pot."

"But Dilchain-ji," says Alma, looking at the pot and Dilchain-ji's calloused hands, "there will be a cook to do this sort of thing. I won't have
to do it. Ma doesn't clean pots."

"Acchaa, but your ma works at the university. She is learned and
clever."

"I am learned and clever too," protests Alma.

"Acchaa, but you should know these things. Mothers-in-law are not
easy. My mother-in-law was awful," confides Dilchain.

Alma gives her an anxious look. She's heard all about Dilchain-ji's mother-in-law. "How awful?"

"A witch."

Bappu says that, though Pushp Vihar belongs to them, the kitchen is Dilchain-ji's to do with what she will. Alma points to a corner where the ghee, milk, and curd are kept in steel pails, and whispers to Roop, "Dilchain-ji was born right over there. Dilchain-ji's daadee ma had all the secrets and she passed the secrets to Dilchain-ji's ma, who finally passed them to Dilchain-ji."

"Where does she hide the secrets?" Roop whispers back, scanning the shelves.

"See that stone over there? The one she uses to pound the spices?"

Roop looks at the stone and nods discreetly.

"There. That's the Philosopher's Stone."

"What's that?"

"It means that everything it touches turns to gold."

"I don't see any gold."

"The gold is actually in the chai. You don't see it, but you drink it—and then your stomach grows a gold lining."

"When you die, and they cut you open, will your stomach be made of gold then?" asks Roop.

"Exactly. It's been passed down all the generations in Dilchain-ji's family."

"How did they die? Her daadee ma and ma?"

"They wasted away," whispers Alma.

Dilchain, listening to the girls, smiles with dimples. Her English is bad and she has only understood half of what has been said. Will they still speak English when the English Sahibs have left, or will the English Sahibs take their words with them? Words like pyjamas and toffee, tip-top and shipshape. Will they take the Horlicks and the Cadbury's? That would be a shame.

. . .

When Dilchain was just a year older than Alma, she too had got married. At first her husband had liked her dimples, but once he had had a drink, two drinks, three drinks, the bottle and then some, he changed his mind. She was married for almost a year until he beat her almost to death, at which point, drunk on cashew-nut toddy, he accidentally set himself instead of her on fire. She watched him for a whole minute before throwing a bucket of water on him, and by then it was too late. The internal organs had sizzled.

Brahma, before he was Bappu, hearing the news from Dilchain's ma, went to fetch her at once.

"I've come to take her home," he said. And he said this to the grieving in-laws in a move that was unusually bold for Brahma, who much to his own shame was shy of confrontation, and more so if the confrontation was with someone of the lower castes. "It makes me feel like a bully," he later confessed to Tanisi, his wife, before she was Ma.

The in-laws stared at the Mughal Arts lecturer in his pressed khadi clothing, who wore thin-framed glasses, as if he were an apparition. What, what? Who's he, they muttered amongst themselves, faces stuffed full of Dilchain's kachori chaat, date chutney dribbling like incontinence from the corners of their mouths. They sniggered at Brahma's beigeness.

They stopped sniggering when they saw the fat red-and-gold envelope of cash in his hands. Red and gold were wedding colours. The envelope was a dowry envelope. Brahma liked the subtle dig, but feared the in-laws just didn't get it.

Dilchain, hiding in the kitchen with two panda eyes, the faint shadows of which would stay with her forever, had an ear pressed to the door. Her head was as bald as a freshly boiled egg. Her in-laws had demanded it be plucked rather than shorn for greater suffering, feeling she was somehow responsible for the death of their beloved son-nephew-grandson-uncle and that if he was a drunk, well then, she had led him to it. When Dilchain heard Brahma-ji's voice, she packed her meagre possessions into a sheet at once. She had known he would come for her.

"No. Not possible. No way," said the mother-in-law, who had got used to her daughter-in-law's exceptional cooking and shrewd household management. "Over my dead body." She stuffed another kachori into her mouth.

Brahma had come prepared. His ma, who had given the cash to him herself, knowing this sort of thing might happen, had insisted that he buy Dilchain back immediately. Bribe-baksheesh-persuade.

"These low, no-moral types," she had said. "Slick their hands and they'll give you anything. Don't you dare come home without her."

Under any other circumstances, Brahma's ma would have insisted that the girl stay with her in-laws and carry out her duties with no arguments. Two black eyes aside, it was a matter of honour. But it was different with Dilchain. Not only was Dilchain an exceptional cook, she was an exceptional Brahmin cook.

Dilchain had grown up with Brahma and Lakshmi, listening to them speak, even adopting some of their ways and ideas. After she was rescued so gallantly by Brahma-ji, she looked at him in the way any girl age seventeen and two months might look at her spectacle-wearing rescuer, with an exposed and suggestible heart. That he was married to blue-eyed Tanisi, jasmine in her hair and a baby in her belly, seemed not to matter. Dilchain kept the infatuation to herself and stored it in a jar of unrequited love, stacked next to the pot of precious saffron. Every now and then, she would open it for a sniff. Unrequited love smelt like a too-ripe Alphonso mango.

· · ·

Roop sits cross-legged in a corner of the kitchen and squashes ants between her fingers. Knowing she is not being watched, she lays trails of grain pilfered from an open sack. She is practising the best way to catch a mouse.

Dilchain shows Alma how to measure two cups of wheat flour. She drizzles a tablespoon of oil, explains what is meant by a pinch of salt, and demonstrates how to crush the salt into a fine dust between dry palms. She kneads and pummels the dough, passes it to Alma to knead and pummel too.

"Knead until your face is pink and hot," advises Dilchain, whose own face and cheeks are always pink and hot. "When you can't breathe, then you know it's ready. Saraswati Madam is very strict."

"Ooh. Do you know her?" asks Alma, of her soon to be mother-in-law. She presses close to Dilchain and pulls her hand. "Have you met her?"

"No. But I know her cook and her cook says Madam-ji is very stern and no-nonsense talking and Sir-ji is diabetic, so there is no sweet-making or eating in the house."

"Oh," says Alma. "No kheer?"

Roop, who has been listening, looks up from the ants in horror. No kheer?

"None," says Dilchain. "No English talking either." She sticks out her tongue and flicks flour on Alma's arm. "No more kheer or jalebis for you."

Alma flicks flour back and laughs when it lands on Dilchain's chin.

"The water will be here in a minute," says Dilchain, glancing up and wiping her face on her apron. On cue, there is a familiar tap-tap on the door.

Varuna Bishti, the water carrier, and his grey donkey, Nel, stand on the other side of the door. Dilchain lifts the metal chain and pushes the heavy door with her shoulder. She places a large earthenware pot on the threshold and holds a clay cup of cow's milk at arm's length. She is careful not to touch him.

Varuna Bishti greets her, drains the milk, and smashes the cup on the pavement. A mangy cat appears and laps up the milky residue.

Dilchain asks after his ma, his pa, his brothers-sisters-aunties-uncles-cousins, the neighbour with the peg leg, and Varuna Bishti replies that his father has a terrible cough but the rest of the family, god bless, are well.

"If you touch an untouchable, the cockroaches that live on his body will crawl into your ears and nest in your brain," whispers Alma to Roop. "That's what Daadee Ma told me."

"Where are they?" says Roop also whispering. "I don't see them."

"They live under his skin."

"Would I die if I touched him?" says Roop. "He's very dirty," she adds, looking him up and down approvingly.

"You go mad first from the disgrace and then you die."

"How do you die?"

"From the pollution."

"Shame on you," says Dilchain, who overhears as she closes the door. "You don't go mad and you don't die."

"Daadee Ma said it. I don't actually believe it," says Alma contritely, poking the paratha dough with her finger. "Don't tell Bappu, will you?"

Dilchain shows Alma how to stuff and roll the parathas. She hands her the rolling pin. "Your turn," she says encouragingly. From the corner of her eye, she spies Roop cross-legged on the floor coaxing and squashing ants. She smacks her on the head. "Kill one more and no more kheer all week," she warns.

Dilchain heats a drop of ghee on the tawa and shows Alma how to fry each paratha until caramelised spots bubble on the surface, and then how to flip them.

Roop, drawn by the scent of hot bread, stands up to watch.

"Shall we have one warm?" says Dilchain, covering the final layer with a dampened cloth.

"So hot it burns our mouths?" says Alma.

Dilchain nods. She tears a paratha into three and giggles softly when the steam burns her fingers.

Dilchain sets the teak dining table for breakfast. There is triangular toast on the rack, butter in a lidded dish, kumquat marmalade in one jar, and carrot chutney in another. She puts the warm parathas in the centre of the table, brings hot coffee in a porcelain pot, and hands each person a matching cup and saucer. She pours the coffee.

The coffee pot and cups are from Japan. They are glazed with whorls of cerulean blue and white. A gift from the head of the university, now retired, to Bappu and Ma on their wedding day.

"This shade of cerulean blue," Ma had said to Bappu as she lifted the delicate china and pressed it for a thrill against her warm lip, "is the bold blue ache of loss." And she had said it as simply and deliberately as if it were a fact.

"What have we lost that it should ache so deeply?" Bappu had asked, entranced by his bride. They had been married for seven weeks and three hours.

"Nothing yet," Ma had said in a moment of rare melancholy, and then, to compensate, she had held him and kissed him hard on the mouth, met his tongue with her own. She had tugged at his ear lobes with her teeth, guided his hand inside her, rocked and arched against his fingers. My love, she had whispered, push there, and she had smiled to his smile.

She blushes now to remember it: the sweetness, the sort of intense closeness that came with its own fragility. She looks up to catch her husband's eye, to reveal somehow, with a covert look, the contents of her mind, but his face is beind *The Times of India* already. She drops an extra sugar cube into Daadee Ma's cup and stirs to dissolve it. "I'll need help with the wedding trousseau this week," she says, handing her the cup. "I have made a nightdress and half a kurta pyjama set. There are still yards of cotton and silk left, but I have lectures now until the end of term. The students have exams coming up, as do Sahib Ali's two boys. It's all such bad timing."

That Ma loathes sewing is something she keeps to herself. "Why couldn't we have just gone to a tailor at the Darziwali Gali," she will later say to Bappu. "It's so archaic that she expects me to do it all."

Daadee Ma sips her coffee and looks at Ma with well-practised reproach.

Alma stops chewing and listens. Her leg jiggles under the table. That Ma has mentioned the Muslim widower, Sahib Ali, will irritate Daadee Ma no end. That Ma is a private tutor for his two little boys is already a point of still-to-be-discussed contention.

"We can either take the material to the Darziwali Gali—though it's probably too late by now—or Lakshmi could help me when she gets here?" says Ma, drumming the tips of her nails on the tabletop. She pauses, talks quickly, "Fatima Begum has offered to help. It would make her so happy to contribute." She raises her voice a little and glances across at Bappu, who looks up and catches her eye.

Bappu puts down his paper. He winks at Alma, who is looking anxiously from one to the other. "Fatima Begum practically raised Alma," he adds.

"Daadee Ma?" says Alma carefully. "Fatima Begum embroidered a beautiful shawl last year at Eid, by hand, for her niece. You should have seen it."

Daadee Ma lifts the coffee to her lips, blows on the hot liquid, and sips. She makes a face and pushes the cup to Alma, to pass back to Ma with the instruction that more sugar is necessary if the coffee is to be palatable.

"Unless she is trying to ruin my breakfast," she mutters peevishly before turning to Bappu. "Have you forgotten our respected family name? You are asking for polluted hands on our cloth and you want me to sit here and be quiet like a mouse?"

"Fatima Begum is very clean," says Ma, meeting Daadee Ma's glare and staring right back. "She washes herself at least five times a day. In fact, each time she prays."

"Fatima Begum is family," says Bappu. "You know that. She has been here since Alma was a month old."

"I love Fatima Begum the most," says Roop, with a mouth full of paratha, half a keen eye on the mouse hole. "She smells of cake."

"Why don't you turn up the radio?" says Daadee Ma. "Go on. Turn it up. All day long, every day, the numbers of dead are reported alongside the cricket score. Our brothers and sisters are butchered like pigs in the middle of the night, in their beds, and those meat-eaters are drinking their blood and whatnot."

There is silence around the teak table. Daadee Ma sips the coffee that is finally sweet enough. She dips in her buttered toast and sucks the soft crust, glad she has spoken her mind. Too often she will sit on her hands and say nothing.

"I listen to the same radio that you do," says Bappu. "There is killing on both sides and we are all to blame."

"Copycat killings," says Roop, interrupting proudly. "I know what that means. Shall I explain it to you?" she says to Daadee Ma.

"Shh," says Alma. "Let Bappu talk."

"We can't believe everything we hear. Our journalists have no moral compass. How can we trust their reports?" says Bappu.

"There is a lot of propaganda," agrees Ma. She looks at Alma and Roop. "And it is difficult to be who you are, whoever you are. My loves, you must remember that."

"I know about pro-pa-gan-da too," says Roop. "It means lying."

"Misinformation," corrects Bappu. "Not exactly lying, but as good as."

"They started it," replies Daadee Ma. She crosses her arms in front of her chest. "What can we do but defend ourselves? How can we forget the Ramayan? For the sake of one woman kidnapped by Ravan, the whole nation took up arms and went to war. Our sisters have been sold in bazaars and whatnot has been done to them. As descendants of Ram, we have to avenge every Sita. It is about honour and duty." She looks at Ma. "Enough of this politics chit-chatting, you are ruining my breakfast. Lakshmi can help you with the sewing."

Honour and duty, she says firmly to Bappu's pa's spirit, in case he has one ear to the door.

3

Late February 1947

"Don't move," says Ma.

The air in the bedroom is still and there is no fan because the power has been cut.

"I'm hot," says Alma. "It's sticking to me. I have homework to do and I'm sure you've got papers to mark. Can't we do it tomorrow when Cookie Auntie gets here? You hate sewing and she'll know how to do it properly." Alma stands with her feet apart, a hand on her waist, impatient for the fitting to be over. "Anyway, don't you have to go to Sahib Ali's soon? Those little boys will be waiting for you."

They are in Ma and Bappu's bedroom, and Alma stares at the tiles on the floor.

Diamond squares alternately ink-blue and rust-red with bronze edges and yellow gold-starred centres. Each tile a toffee wrapper. A pin sticks into the soft of her thigh and she yelps.

"Sorry," says Ma, flustered. "Yes. I do, but not till later."

It's three weeks until Alma's wedding. Five weeks until Easter, when Jesus was pinned to the Cross. One whole year until Independence Day.

Alma fidgets against the silk that Ma is trying to tuck and pleat against her waist.

Alma has never worn a sari before. Ma has never made one. The silk is turquoise with dark blues and bright greens that swirl across it like the sea. Ma says it's the colour of a Kashmiri lake after the storms. It's not that Alma doesn't want to be fitted for the sari—she has been waiting to wear a sari since she was twelve, when she had asked Bappu, and he had laughed and flicked her ear. "No," he had said, "only married women wear saris."

No, it's not that at all. The so-fair-boy raises his palms. What then? Two spots flush his cheeks. He has been standing on the shores of the Jamuna so long, freckles have peppered his nose.

"I'm sorry," says Alma, half to him and half to Ma. "I'll try to keep still."

Ma looks at the silk draped across Alma's chest, and puts down the pins she's holding in her mouth. "Tomorrow will be fine, my love. Go on," she says with a reluctant smile. "You can put your Sunday dress back on."

"Don't be sad, Ma," says Alma, in her white knickers and vest, a love-heart motif on the cotton, a red apple clip in her hair. "After I am married, once I move to England, you and Bappu can come to visit. Roop too. By aeroplane or on a ship. Until then, I'll come home once a week. Dilchain-ji has promised to make kheer every Sunday especially for me."

Ma folds the silk away. She presses carefully, the fabric cool against her skin; it makes her feel uncommonly wistful. The boy is fair and soon he will be a doctor and move to England. His family are good-in-name, but does that make him good-in-person? Will he be good to Alma? Is a boy still a boy at twenty-two? Alma is still a child at fourteen. Ma wants to sit her down, caution her: love is intricate enough, without marrying someone you don't even know.

"Ma?" says Alma impatiently tapping her foot. "Ma, have you told Sister Ignatius about the wedding? You know I will need time off school."

Ma bites her lip. She swears under her breath and turns to Alma, "Oh god, it's not that long now is it?"

"Twenty-one and a half days," says Alma, hand on her hip.

Ma never swears. She clearly has not told Sister Ignatius about the wedding.

. . .

When the girls get home from school the next day, there is no Cookie Auntie waiting for them as promised. Ma and Bappu are at the convent, having tea with Sister Ignatius. Sister Ignatius, who is married to Jesus, will be so disappointed to hear that Alma is getting married to a real person.

Alma waters the pots of star-shaped jasmine in the courtyard. Watering the plants is her designated job, handed down by Bappu's dead pa, who loved flowers so much he was called an anthophile. Alma had looked it up in Bappu's Dictionary. A book so heavy she had to hold it with both hands.

Once she has finished, she sits at the teak table and makes a list. Getting married. Cookie Auntie coming to stay. Independence Day. Free India. Azaadi. She chews the end of her pencil and underlines "Azaadi." What does it even mean to be free? Her idea of freedom would be different, say, to a chamar's or a shopkeeper's. How would they do that then? Deliver freedom to everyone. Please everyone?

In the middle of the courtyard, Roop catches a large moth. She puts the insect under a glass jar pilfered from the kitchen and whoops in delight. "I have to keep it in here for as long as possible," she explains, turning to Alma and pointing.

The moth has large wings, delicate and lovely, their useless fluttering drumming against the glass.

"Are you trying to suffocate it?" asks Alma, still chewing her pencil. She draws a small heart by "getting married" and colours it in.

"What's a suf-fo-cate?" says Roop.

"To cut off the air supply so the moth dies."

"I am trying to suf-fo-cate it," says Roop. She looks longingly at the small hole in the far corner of the room. The crumbs of jaggery she put out have disappeared, but the mouse is nowhere to be seen. She lies belly down on the stone floor and peers closely as the insect beats frantically and then suddenly just stops, limp and exhausted against the glass.

"Fatima Begum?" Roop asks when her ayah comes into the court-yard. She pushes the glass jar behind a pot of star-shaped jasmine. "Where's Cookie Auntie? She's so late."

"She'll be here soon," says Fatima Begum, lowering herself into the swing and motioning with a hairbrush that Roop should sit. She oils and plaits Roop's hair as she does every afternoon, slaps her playfully when she squirms. "Ladoo, ladoo I could eat you," she says, kissing Roop's cheeks and laughing. "How are you always so sticky?"

A jingle comes on on the radio and Alma turns it up.

"Our favourite song! From *Dil Ki Rani*," says Roop, wriggling loose. "Do you remember, Fatima Begum, when we saw this at the cinema?"

"I remember," says Alma, tapping her feet. "We drank mango sherbet really fast through a straw."

"And it fizzed up our noses," says Roop, who has started to cart-wheel across the stone floor.

. . .

"No, you can't have any more money," says Cookie Auntie to the tonga driver with a hard look. "I don't care that it's three a.m. This was the price we agreed on."

She knocks and Dilchain is up at once to open the door. They kiss each other warmly on the cheek, Dilchain rubbing her eyes and yawning, Cookie Auntie's gold bangles chiming up and down her arms. Husband-ji appears with the luggage behind them. His hair is slicked back and brilliantly shined, a firoza peacock brooch on his lapel.

Daadee Ma rises at once to greet her daughter. She leads them into the courtyard.

"Are you tired, Ma?" asks Cookie Auntie after she has kissed her. "Can we talk?"

"I am awake now and Dilchain will bring chai," says Daadee Ma, making herself comfortable on the swing and patting the cushion so her daughter should sit next to her.

In the kitchen, Dilchain pounds spices with her grandmother's stone. She boils tea, sugar, and fresh milk, adds the spices, and spoons rose-scented kheer into crystal bowls and sets up the tray.

"Dilchain-ji," says Cookie Auntie when she is handed a crystal bowl, "you know, don't you, that you are the best cook in the country?"

Dilchain laughs with deepening dimples. "My ma taught me everything," she says. "I used your pa's roses, from that pot over there, and left them in the hot milk over night."

"Well, I will relish each mouthful. It is a treat to be given rose-scented kheer at three in the morning. I will eat it slowly and it will help me forget the country is turning to shit."

Dilchain ducks her head modestly and wishes them goodnight.

"It is true. She is the best cook," ventures Husband-ji once Dilchain has gone back into the kitchen. He drains his chai and pours another. "Our servants are very bad. They never listen, complain every day, and now they have started forming secret socialist-type unions. They don't know what's good for them."

"This democracy-hypocrisy, it is confusing everyone. Full of empty promises. Pah. As if any of that nonsense can hold," says Daadee Ma, blowing on her cup. "Purity and a belief in the old systems. That's how to progress."

"Ma! Those things are the exact opposite of progress," protests Cookie Auntie.

"Bombay is full of tension," says Husband-ji, crumbs in his moustache.

"Everyone threatens everyone else and police intelligence is poor. I have close friends, you know, connections in Congress, I give them money to expand and develop so we are always in the loop. Independence Day will come and go, and then what?"

"Do we really have to talk politics?" says Cookie Auntie, looking at him with a slight frown.

"We have friends in the League too," admits Husband-ji, talking over her, his mouth full. "It's a tactical sort of friendship." He pauses, spoon halfway to his mouth. "This kheer is excellent. We really must get the recipe before we leave."

Cookie Auntie slaps his outstretched hand and pulls the plate away. "Leave some for tomorrow."

"There was fighting on our train," says Husband-ji, eating more kheer.

"And gunshots. We were held at gunpoint for twelve hours. We were lucky to be in the first-class cabin with two armed guards and enough cash for baksheesh. Who knows what could have happened otherwise?" says Cookie Auntie.

"Every man, no matter his social standing, has been collecting weapons or making bombs. There is a lot of ammunition left over from the war," says Husband-ji.

"It is not just that ammunition has been left over from the war, but that it's being distributed to all the wrong people," says Cookie Auntie. "Every amateur goonda suddenly has a gun and an elevated sense of his own power." She looks at Daadee Ma. "Anyway, I don't want to talk about that. I want to hear about this boy you've found for Alma."

"Very nice Brahmin boy. Postgraduate. Neat and tidy. Hair always spick and span. Only twenty-two years of age and soon to be a doctor. Very good teeth."

Daadee Ma ticks the boy's attributes off on her fingers as though she is personally responsible for them all.

"Why so soon though? She's only fourteen. Even I didn't get married until I was nineteen. I hope she's allowed to finish her education? I'm sure Bhai will insist on it. My nieces are too bright to be married off like this."

"Acchaa, it has been agreed she can finish the school year. After that, it's up to them. All this reading will get her nowhere if she can't please her husband."

"Shame on you for saying things like that. I'm astonished Bhai is allowing this."

"Your brother can see the situation with his eyes wide open. In times like these, a young girl, unmarried, is a target for unmentionables, what-nots, and so on. If anything should happen, no one would marry her and the family name would be dishonoured."

"Oh, come off it. These notions of honour are so archaic."

"Maybe in Bombay, but the rest of the country, thanks be to god, is not so modern. I consulted both a priest and Astrologer Uncle. Every-thing is aligned as it should be."

Daadee Ma crosses her small hands defiantly. She can feel Bappu's pa's spirit hovering. "Alma has an excellent horoscope. Her horoscope specifically says that this boy is her perfect match."

"I hope you're right, Ma," says Cookie Auntie.

4

1 March 1947

ALMA LIES ACROSS Ma and Bappu's bed, her white school socks pulled up to her knees and a red apple clip in her hair. She props her face in her hands and watches Ma and Cookie Auntie sew. Cookie Auntie has been there for a day and a half, but already she has taken them all in hand, and finally, to Alma's relief, the wedding trousseau is under way.

Afternoon light floods the bedroom. The wooden shutters open into the courtyard below and the scent of star-shaped jasmine and condensed milk fills the air. The shutters were a present from Bappu's pa to Ma on her wedding day, commissioned to imitate those that had hung in the harems of Shah Jahan.

"For you," he had said, presenting them, "for your love of all things Mughal."

"As fine as lace," she had replied, rubbing her palm against the grain of the dark wood. She had not known what to say. The shutters were so intricately carved that a simple "thank you" would not suffice.

Red-poppy curtains pleat across the shutters and drop to the floor. There is a rosewood four-poster bed in the room and across the bed an embroidered cloth of Rabari hook-and-chain stitch, in indigo and black, with silver threads and tiny mirrors pulled through it.

"We are lucky to have this, my love," Ma had once told Alma, when Alma had asked where the embroidery had come from. They had been lying across the bed, Ma reading Urdu poetry and explaining that it didn't matter if Alma didn't understand every single word, it was about rhythm and sound, to which Alma had nodded emphatically, that yes, the melodies were beautiful. "The Rabari tribes are nomadic," Ma continued. "They never embroider to sell, or give away."

"Why do you have it then?" Alma had asked.

"It was a present from my uncle. He was friends with a tribesman and commissioned this for my wedding," said Ma. "He wanted to give me the night sky when the night sky is seen from the desert."

"What was he like, your uncle?" Alma asked curiously.

"He was like Kashmir," Ma replied with a fresh glaze in her eyes and two bright spots on her cheeks.

What did it even mean for a person to be like a place and for that place to be home? Alma couldn't work it out at all. "Have you seen the night sky from the desert?" she finally asked. And then, because Ma looked so forlorn, Alma held Ma's hand in her own and stroked it the way she had seen Bappu do.

"Yes. When I was a girl, I went to the Thar desert with my uncle."

Was the night sky from the desert the most expansively open sky there was, then? The sort of sky where you could lose yourself, and then find yourself on the other side of it, a different person altogether? Alma looked at Ma for an answer, but Ma said nothing, she just hid her face in Alma's long hair and sniffed it. "Alma," she said, her voice muffled, "you smell of apples," and Alma could not tell then if Ma was weeping or not.

Now, Ma and Cookie Auntie sit on the opposite side of the bed, a pile of sewing between them: silks and scarves and spools of thread. Cookie

Auntie's high-heeled shoes are kicked to the floor. She squints as she tries to thread a length of silk into the eye of a needle.

"I love the curtains you made," she says, looking up from the thread to admire the block-printed muslin.

"You say that every time you're here. You just can't believe I made something," says Ma. She makes a face at them both. "I only printed the cloth though. I sent them to the tailors to be hemmed." She puts a finger to her lips and whispers, "I deplore sewing, but don't tell Bappu."

This makes Alma laugh a lot because everyone knows that already.

"Ma printed those, when Roop was in her belly, as small as a cashew," says Alma to her aunt, showing the size of a cashew with her finger and thumb. "Was I ever that small, Ma?"

"Smaller. You began as an idea. A sense of meaning."

Alma loves it when Ma says things like this. She repeats it to herself when she is alone, "a sense of meaning"; that she should be such a thing to Ma and Bappu makes her feel very valuable. She doesn't tell Roop, in case being born second is not as good. She would hate Roop to feel neglected. "What did you eat when I was in your belly?" she asks, knowing the answer but infatuated by the tale. "Tell me again. Do you know?" She turns to her aunt, who laughs and nods with a mouthful of pins.

"Of course I know."

"I ate as much sour fruit as I could," says Ma. "Poor Dilchain had to go to the market every day and find me all that sour stuff—and her with such a sweet tooth."

"How sour?" says Alma, biting her finger trying to imagine all that sourness.

"Lemons and limes, pith and skin intact. Green mangoes and guavas, amla and tamarinds still in the pod."

"Oooh," squeals Alma, her toes in her socks clenching and curling.

"Your Daadee Ma said it was my sour-fruit obsession that invited the evil eye into the house," says Ma, the corners of her mouth twitching.

"She wanted a grandson. Said it was my fault a djinn had crept into my belly and changed you from a boy to a girl. Under her own roof."

"Imagine that? Only a djinn would have such gall," says Cookie Auntie.

"Did you?" asks Alma. "Want a boy?" And then, "Djinns can't do that, can they?"

"No, and I wanted only you."

Ma's features are delicate, sketched out on good paper with a sharp pencil. Sometimes, she will have a faraway look on her face, and this faraway look will be so subtle that Alma will almost not see it. It is a look that gathers momentum around the mouth, paints the cheeks, before flickering behind the eyes.

Cookie Auntie always wears gold bangles that tinkle up and down her arms. Alma admires the cerise lips tinted to match the cerise nails and the pale silver sari that folds and shimmers. Cookie Auntie has short hair set in waves. Alma has never seen a woman with short hair before, unless of course the woman is a widow, and a woman who is a widow is hardly a woman at all.

"Beta, what did you learn in school today?" asks Cookie Auntie, still trying to thread the needle, despite the needle's eye being smaller than the thread.

"Sister Ignatius taught us about the Greek goddess Psyche. She was married to Cupid. Cupid is the God of Love. He carries arrows on his back like Kamadev."

"As if we don't have enough of our own gods, they have to bring those Greek ones in too," says Cookie Auntie. She finally pulls the thread through the eye and deftly knots it.

"The syllabus will change after Independence," says Ma, looking at Alma. "Imagine, if schools started to teach Indian history and Indian mythology, Indian literature and Indian poetry? Tagore rather than Keats."

"I would like that," says Alma.

"Me too," says Ma, and smiles at her daughter. "I would love it if everyone would just quote Tagore all the time. 'Faith is the bird that feels the light when the dawn is still dark.'" She puts a hand to her heart and falls back on the bed.

"I know that one," says Alma. "I wrote it in my notebook."

"What," says Cookie Auntie, "and not indoctrinate our children in the superior ways of the British? But we are mere savages. Oh for the shame."

"For the shame," echoes Alma, looking between them both. "Cookie Auntie, or Ma, what does it mean, Psyche? I know it means butterfly in Greek, but does it mean anything else?"

"Psyche is the Greek symbol for the human soul," says Ma, sitting up and spooling a length of thread back round its wooden drum.

"Like Alma?"

"Exactly. Imagine you cut a chrysalis open, what do you find?"

"A caterpillar?"

"A rotting caterpillar. The process of transformation starts with decay. Most people don't think about that."

"And then you have something beautiful?" asks Alma.

"But first you have something ugly, my love. Foul and fair always live together," replies Ma.

"And then you will have a butterfly who, for all that struggling to get out of the chrysalis, for all its beauty, will only live for a few days," says Cookie Auntie.

"Beauty is ephemeral," agrees Ma, stroking the pale cream silk on her lap.

"Ephemeral": short-lived, brief. Alma considers it. "But beauty will exist for the person who sees it. And after they have seen it, the person will not forget having seen it," she says dreamily.

"Beauty can live on. In a memory or a story, in language and words, in music," agrees Ma.

I know, says Alma to the so-fair-boy standing on the shores of the Jamuna. *I remember your face exactly. Do you remember mine?*

The so-fair-boy has a sunburnt nose. He looks at Alma and shrugs. No, he seems to say, or is it yes? She can't quite tell.

Ma reaches over to the bedside table and picks up two glasses of watermelon sherbet. She passes one to each of them and takes the third for herself.

"Cookie Auntie?" Alma sips her drink through a straw. She blows bubbles into the pink liquid and giggles softly. What she really wants to know is what it feels like to kiss a boy on the mouth and who should kiss first, the girl or the boy. And, after the kiss, what then?

"Yes, jewel-of-my-heart?"

"What shampoo do you use?" She is suddenly too shy to ask.

Ma smiles. "Is that really what you wanted to know, my love?" She leans over to smell Cookie Auntie's hair. Ah, she exhales with pleasure. "I know that smell."

"Himalaya Herbal Remedies. Do your locks lack shine? Is your husband bored? Himalaya Herbal Remedies. The magic to every marriage," says Cookie Auntie in a singsong voice. "Made in India, no less."

"But some good things have come from England, no?" says Alma. "Horlicks and Cadbury's?"

Alma tried Horlicks once when she was invited to take afternoon tea with Sister Ignatius. She had liked the hot malty drink, though it had needed several spoons of sugar-adding and Sister Ignatius had said, oh my, in a slightly shocked but indulgent tone of voice, as if that much sugar-adding was a sin.

"Gordon's Gin," says Cookie Auntie promptly.

Ma brings a finger to her lips in thought. "Avoid failure by avoiding bad breath. Colgate. Proudly British." She takes Cookie Auntie's wrists, lifts them up to her nose. "You always smell so good," she says.

"How else do you think I've been married these twenty years? French perfume. Guerlain." She looks at Alma, "Seriously, beta, you will need to know so much more than sherbet making if you want a happy husband."

Alma nods. Exactly. So tell me, she wants to say.

Standing on the shore of Jamuna, the so-fair-boy, hands on his hips, eyes her up and down. *It's true*, he says. *You'll have to know every trick there is to keep me happy.*

Alma looks at her aunt. "What do I need to know?" She chews her lip and busies herself with a square of fabric.

Cookie Auntie reaches into her handbag, pulls out a small bottle of Johnnie Walker Black Label Whisky, and splashes a little into her drink. She reaches over and splashes a little into Ma's glass too. Ma tries to protest, but she does so in a very half-hearted way.

Alma watches them. She did not know that women could drink, that Ma could drink.

"What do you think? Is she old enough?" says Cookie Auntie.

Ma shakes her head.

"If she were my daughter," says Cookie Auntie, tapping the side of her nose with a cerise nail.

Cookie Auntie doesn't have any children because Husband-ji's sperm is only semi-conscious even at the best of times. That's the sort of thing that happens if you marry for money. Alma looks at the whisky and pulls a face. She can smell the liquor and it stinks like a dawa from one of the hakims behind the Jamma Masjid. "I don't want to drink it anyway," she says.

"Old enough to get married, but not old enough to drink. Tell me how that works?" asks Cookie Auntie, adding another capful of whisky to her glass. "I remember Bhai getting blind drunk when he was younger than you are now."

"No!" says Alma. "I don't believe you."

"It's true. He bribed the dhobi for his whisky. The man was a drunk. All our clothes used to come back dirty. Somehow, Bhai had found out about some tawdry secret of his and in a move very unlike himself—himself being always-so-good—he threatened to tell. He drank the whole bottle, neat, in one sitting. I found him passed out in the courtyard. 'Ah ya Bhai,' I said, holding my nose. I hid him under a sheet in the bedroom and forced him to chew mint. I told Pa he had a fever from eating too many grapes."

"Bappu!" says Alma. "What was the dhobi's secret?"

"I tried to get it out of him, but he kept his word. Probably saved the man's job. Twelve years old and he was more worried about the man's low caste than he was about the whisky."

Ma holds the petticoat she has been hemming up for inspection and frowns.

"Bappu believes in equality," says Alma.

"Bhai does, doesn't he?" says Cookie Auntie, taking the petticoat from Ma and unpicking the hem.

"Did you know about the time when Gandhi-ji made his wife clean the latrines in the ashram? She refused and he forced her to do it in front of all the other workers," says Alma.

Latrine cleaners, chamars, and road sweepers have filthy hands and black nails. The dirt is actually in their skin, in between all those fine lines. If you share food with them or sit next to them, then you will be dirty too. That's what Daadee Ma says, and though Alma doesn't believe her entirely, she does wonder where all that dirt goes.

"Poor woman," says Cookie Auntie. Her pink sherbet finished, she drinks directly out of the bottle, passes it to Ma, who does the same. "Imagine how she would have felt, humiliated like that in front of everyone?"

Alma shrugs, disinterested. "I'm so bored of politics, Cookie Auntie, that's all anyone wants to talk about. Can you help with my hair? Make waves like yours and cut some off?"

Alma picks up her plait and waves it in front of her face. The plait is long and thick and stretches down to her waist. The so-fair-boy looks on approvingly.

"Just for the wedding or forever?" says Cookie Auntie. "Once it's been cut, it will take a long time to grow back."

Alma uses her hands to demonstrate, lifts her hair, doubles it up, and tucks half into the nape of her neck. Up to here, she indicates firmly.

"There is a lady in Karol Bagh who is very good with hair," says Cookie Auntie. She has started to assemble a nightdress. She holds the pins in her mouth and joins the edges neatly. "You won't be able to wear those hair clips anymore. Not when you are married."

"Why not?"

"Because overnight, you will go from being a girl to being a woman."

Oh. Alma frowns. *I'm not sure,* she says to the so-fair-boy, *if I'm ready for that.*

Tough luck, he says. *I don't want to marry a little girl.*

. . .

Later, Ma will tell Bappu when they are together and alone in the half-light, when no one else can hear, her head on his shoulder, that she almost cried when Alma asked if she could cut off her hair. "I know it's only hair, but still."

. . .

Ma drinks a capful of neat whisky and it goes straight to her head. She downs another and closes her eyes, composes herself, and then opens them again. The red apple clip has melted into Alma's dark hair. "Dear daughter," she says, sitting up, her irises glittering, "we might as well get on with it?" She looks at Cookie Auntie and mouths, "Am I drunk already?"

"Yes," Cookie Auntie mouths back and grins. Her eyes are also whisky-lit, but differently so.

"These are the principles of a happy marriage," begins Ma in an odd and formal voice. She could almost be giving a lecture. She would like to give a lecture on the subject of marriage, and if candour were allowed, truly allowed, she would have a lot to say.

Cookie Auntie puts up her hand. "May I add, this list was composed by a man?"

"Surely a given?" says Ma.

Alma giggles and sips.

"True. Nevertheless, for the record: a pious Brahmin priest, elderly and bad-tempered with no sense of humour." Cookie Auntie puts down her sewing. "Please continue. Oh. Let me add that these particular rules only apply to women in India. Everything is easier if you come from the West." She nods to Ma: Go on.

"You must welcome your husband home every evening by standing up when he walks into the room. Lower your gaze when you speak to him. Sleep only after he sleeps. If your husband cannot sleep, you cannot sleep. Rise before he rises. Eat only after he has eaten. Drink only after he has drunk."

"But you don't do those things for Bappu," says Alma. She sucks the pink liquid loudly through her straw. "You're making fun of me, because I want to get married and you don't think I should, but it's your own fault for agreeing to it in the first place." She looks at Ma with reproach.

"You're right," admits Ma. "But I'm not making it up, you know. The list of rules is real. They might not apply in this household, but everywhere else, they do."

Alma looks at them both and sticks out her tongue.

"We are so backwards in this country," says Cookie Auntie. "Positively prehistoric." She lifts the whisky to her lips and drains the bottle, licks inside the neck. "India is the nation of sati, of child marriages, of widows who must stay widows forever. Look at Dilchain: she will never remarry, never have a child—and her with such a lovely face and so gifted, so intelligent you would never know she hadn't been educated. I don't think these 'laws' will change that easily, not even after Independence." She picks up a length of khadi cotton and begins to hem the edge, squints at the fabric and thread. "I might be too tipsy to sew," she says with a laugh. "Imagine, how backwards a country is when a woman like Dilchain, with dimples like that, can never remarry, but a man can marry a tree?"

Alma giggles softly. She has heard of the men who marry trees.

5

2 March 1947

THE NEXT MORNING, Cookie Auntie insists that Ma must spend the day with her. She wants to buy jewellery for Alma, and she would like Ma to help her choose.

"We'll go early while it's cool," she says, kissing Husband-ji on the forehead. He is lying across the swing, legs dangling off the edge, sipping coffee and smoking a cigarette. "I expect you'll be here all day," she comments, and he nods that yes, indeed he will.

"I'm taking your wife for the day," she says, turning to Bappu. "To the Old City. To see Ali Ahmed Abed. If you insist on marrying my niece so young, then let me at least buy her some jewels."

"Is it safe?" asks Bappu. "To go that far into the labyrinth?"

"I know my way round, and most of the shopkeepers. Anyway, it's quiet in Delhi at the moment," she replies.

"Roop?" Cookie Auntie looks at her youngest niece, who is naked and squatting on the stone floor, sprinkling a line of rice outside a hole in the wall. There is a glass jar with a dead moth next to her. "Where are your clothes? What are you up to? What's in that jar?"

"Too hot. I want to see the mouse that lives there," Roop explains, pointing. "When it comes out, I'll catch it. This is mine," she says, picking up the jar and holding it behind her back. "For school," she lies.

"What will you do with the mouse?" asks Cookie Auntie carefully.

"Kill it," says Roop, calmly concentrating on the hole again. "Maybe I'll suf-fo-cate it? Or, chop off its head?"

"Chandrarupa, you mustn't. Promise me you won't?"

Roop tilts her head to one side and looks at her aunt. She won't promise anything without a bribe.

"I'll bring you a butterscotch Amul ice-cream?" says Cookie Auntie, well tuned to her niece's inclinations. "They'll be marrying you off next," she teases, pinching Roop's chin. "Be careful."

Roop looks at her aunt with disdain. "No way. And I like Nestlé best. Chocolate," she adds quickly.

"Okay, but promise first. Pinky-shake." Cookie Auntie extends a jewelled hand and sticks out her little finger. Roop slips her own into it. They lock fingers and shake.

. . .

"How much to Chandni Chowk and then for the rest of the morning?" Cookie Auntie asks the tonga driver when he pulls up outside.

"Best morning price," he reassures her. He sticks up half a thumb. Grins with a mouthful of bad teeth.

"And you will wait for us outside every shop and stall until we are finished?"

"Theek hai, Madam-ji. Anything doing for having such tip-top ladies in my carriage."

The driver manoeuvres the tonga through the coiling lanes. The fragrance of mutton stewing in spices, masala milk rolling to a boil, griddled rotis, and steamed rice saturates the air. An elderly man on a battered bicycle, wearing a grey karakul hat, nearly collides with them. He raises a bony arm and shakes his fist.

"Infidels," he cries. "Kafirs!" He spits on the wheels of the carriage.

"If Pa hadn't raised me to respect my elders, imagine the curses I could throw back at him? It was him, silly old fool, that got in our way," says Cookie Auntie.

"He's angry with the world," says Ma, "not us."

The tonga skitters to a halt outside Abed Jewellers, Finest Purveyors of Handcrafted Silver-Gold-Gems. Ali Ahmed Abed, the proprietor, is an old family friend.

"Let me spoil her," says Cookie Auntie, stepping out of the carriage and standing in front of the shop.

"She's infatuated by his face," says Ma, looking up helplessly. "I have no idea what to do with a restless adolescent daughter. I was so different when I was her age, living on the houseboat with only old servants for company."

"A beautiful boy is a tricky thing when you are only fourteen, I have to agree with that. And were you really that different? I mean, really? I know I wasn't."

"Perhaps not," says Ma. "It was such an unusual life back then, you can't imagine the solitude. And suddenly, out of the blue, you're thirteen years old and everything that was once familiar is now mysterious, full of a strange sort of excitement."

"You don't talk about it much—your girlhood. Your dashing uncle. I was quite taken by him when he came to the wedding," Cookie Auntie admits.

"That is a story for another time," says Ma. "Shall we go in?"

They step into a room furnished with a white bed and a wooden cabinet with a set of scales, weights and measures on it.

"Alma's too romantic." Cookie Auntie takes off her shoes and sits on the bed. "It is not good for a young girl to be so in her own head. She forgets reality."

Ali Ahmed Abed comes in from the back and claps his hands to see them. His tangled beard is brilliantly white and his bony hands speckled. He calls out to his wife, Luijiana Begum, that Alma is to be wed. The little girl who used to sit on his knee with a fistful of stories. What an imagination!

"Be comfortable. Please. How is my niece, Fatima Begum?"

"She's well. I have never known her not to smile," says Ma. "I would be lost without her. The girls adore her."

"She was always the niece with the biggest heart. Tell her to come and see us. It has been a while. We will cook her something good to eat. A mutton biryani. Tell her that. What can I do for you Memsahibs today? What fine jewels will you allow me to show you?"

"Show us your best of course," says Cookie Auntie. "Show us those secret boxes only your favourite customers are allowed to see."

Ali Ahmed Abed laughs throatily. "Your dear papa's daughter." From a drawer in the wooden cabinet he pulls out a glut of gems and displays them on the white sheet. Bangles and anklets are passed round. Clasps are unhooked and necklaces lifted to the neck, earrings to the ear. Everything shines.

Ali Ahmed Abed brings out his scales and weighs, with good-humoured bartering, the selected pieces of gold.

"I would have it all if I could," says Cookie Auntie, looking at Ma teasingly, "only I know how upset you'd both get."

"It's not that," says Ma, and she reddens, because she would get upset and Brahma would too. "It just seems indecent for a girl so young to be given so much gold."

"When others are starving?" says Cookie Auntie, gathering their treasures and hiding them in her handbag. "I know how you both think."

"What will you do, Daadaa-ji?" asks Ma as they prepare to leave. "Will you stay in Delhi?"

"Beta," he says, twisting his fingers into a knot. "I am too old to go anywhere. We have lived in this mohallah all our lives. I was born in that room behind the shop. I have gone to the Jamma Masjid every Friday for my prayers since I was old enough to walk there. Karim Bukhari has made my mutton koti roll every week. Extra coriander and chilli, pinch of sumaq, just how I like it. Who knows if they will make kebabs that delectable in Pakistan? An old man like me cannot lose these small pleasures. In Pakistan, my mouth will water for the kebabs of Old Delhi. That's just how it is. Send my niece here. Tell her she has been neglecting us, and we being so old and not long left."

"Daadaa-ji, you will live to be a hundred. I'm sure of it," says Cookie Auntie, kissing his hands.

"If you need our help, you will ask won't you?" says Ma. "If you are threatened or told to leave?"

"If the chaos comes to Delhi, send my niece back? She will only be safe if she is amongst her own. I wish it weren't like that, but it is."

"We would look after her, you know that don't you?" says Ma, startled at the request. "But as you wish, of course."

"Do you think it is prudent having a Muslim ayah? We asked our Muslim servants to leave and they were glad to go," says Cookie Auntie to Ma as they leave the jeweller's and walk towards the flower market.

"Fatima Begum has been with us for fourteen years. I'm not sure I could cope without her," says Ma.

"They say the animals sense it first. I've not slept through the night since I've been back. It's like I am just waiting for bad news."

"The dogs are keeping us all awake."

"I really think you should let the ayah go, as much for her own safety as yours. What if something should happen to her?"

"I know, but I don't think I can. She practically raised them both. Without her to look after the girls, I'd have to stop working."

"If you weren't like my own sister, I would say you were being selfish."

"I am being selfish," says Ma, shrugging her shoulders, "but what choice do I have? Roop is so attached to Fatima Begum, how could I separate them?"

"I am surprised my mother has allowed it for so long."

"Oh she's tried, but your brother insists that Fatima Begum must stay. 'My girls will grow up to be free and liberated women in a free and liberated India. Ours is not an exclusive way of living.'"

"He actually said this? My timid twin?" Cookie Auntie slips her hand into Ma's and holds her tightly.

"He did. He's very protective of Fatima Begum. I feel so proud when he's like that."

"Bhai is a dreamer. I often wonder if he dreamt you into being. How else did he convince Pa to let you and your flawed Pir Ali lineage into the fold, and with all that ancient Muslim blood running through you?"

"I read your father poetry," says Ma wistfully. "Mirza Ghalib and Tagore. He told me I would have to live in Pushp Vihar, just so he could be read to every day. I never knew my own pa, so to have yours for a year was a gift. One of the many reasons why your mother dislikes me so much."

"He chose you over her. That would have been hard for any wife to take," says Cookie Auntie with a dry smile.

They are nearly at the confectioner's now. The roads narrow and lead into a covered space. Here, colour and noise, human bodies pressed one against the other, spill out in a flood of lively profusion.

"This azaadi we are all grasping for, this ideal of freedom, do you think you might have a measure of it already?" says Ma as they walk in. "I sometimes think that you are the most unrestricted person I know. I envy you that."

"Don't. It is only because I am very wealthy. Take away my money and you take away what little true freedom I have," says Cookie Auntie.

At Kwality Confectioners, at Cookie Auntie's insistence, Ma eats two plump gulab jamuns. She tucks small mouthfuls into her cheeks and the soft sponge dissolves.

"It tastes," she says, "like stolen time. Why do I feel guilty?"

"Don't. There's plenty of time for guilt yet."

Cookie Auntie orders boxes of mithai. A selection of everything for wooing the in-laws. She gives the confectioner a list of addresses for delivery. Ma ticks them off on her fingers: grandparents-parents-aunties-uncles-cousins-neighbours-brothers-sisters-first-in-law and twice-removed, of the groom.

"Have the boy's parents been in touch much?" Cookie Auntie asks curiously.

"No. I don't think so. Or only with your mother."

"Don't you think it's strange?"

Ma shrugs. "I hadn't thought of it, to be honest."

"Thank you," she adds, once they are back in the tonga. "I'm not sure I could have managed this without your help. I've lived in this city for years and I still get lost in those lanes."

"Bhai and I used to run around here as kids, looking for hakims to buy dawas from. We'd invent all manner of ailments."

"I longed for a playmate when I was a child. I had to make them up. Hold conversations with my own reflection in the lake and give her a name."

"That is why you are a true poet," says Cookie Auntie. "Solitude breeds creativity."

The tonga threads its way through the lanes. Dogs biting their ticks, cats and goats, emaciated cows eating yesterday's headlines all crowd in and slow them down.

"Look," says Ma, pointing to the blue-grey pigeons in the sky. There are diamond kites up there too, vying for attention, tying each other up into knots. "When you look at the light at this time of day, you might almost be fooled into thinking the world is a good place."

"The golden hour when everything is blessed."

"I have to be at work soon."

"But it's Saturday?"

"I'm expected at Sahib Ali's at 18:00 p.m. The boys have exams coming up."

"I didn't know you were still tutoring?"

Ma nods guiltily.

"Your daughter is getting married in a week and you, mother-of-the-bride, are going to work on a Saturday afternoon?" Cookie Auntie shakes her head sternly.

"May I add, I have been indoors for two days, with the sewing that you should have done by now? Though god knows why we couldn't have just got a tailor?"

"Three weeks," says Ma. "She's getting married in three weeks and of course thank you for your help, both Alma and I will be forever grateful. I did ask if we could go to a tailor but all the really good ones are Muslim, and if they haven't already left, they are packing up to leave. And then of course there is the issue of your mother."

"Polluted hands on our clean cloth?"

"Precisely."

"Well, I'm glad to help. You know I am."

"And I know it's bad timing, but I'm so dedicated to those two boys. They're so earnest and the eldest, Husain, is set on being an imam."

"It will cause quite a scandal, you know, your spending so much time with a widowed Islamic cleric. And don't look so shocked: you're naïve if you think people won't talk. They'll say you are having a liaison. They won't care that you go there to work."

"How awful the way people gossip." The tonga lurches forwards. Its wheels catch on a stone and Ma almost loses her balance. "Brahma will be so upset if he hears this nonsense."

"Don't worry. The husband is always the last to know. I'm just saying, be careful."

"He is not for Pakistan you know, Sahib Ali. We are made to believe all Muslims are, but that's just not the case. His family lineage is firmly in Old Delhi. He will not leave."

The azan drifts across from the Jamma Masjid. The sunset tinged with mauve.

"Listen," says Ma. She brings a finger to her lips.

"Ah, yes. I've always loved the sound. As children we would wake up to it. I can't remember a morning without it," says Cookie Auntie.

"When the Muslims leave, they will take the Urdu language and poetry with them. That's why I need to keep a trace of it alive: teaching it, passing on the knowledge is the only way I know how. Our literature and poetry, our vocabulary: it will be a tragedy if we lose all those layers of richness. It's awful. My colleagues are starting to disappear. No forwarding addresses. Nothing."

6

August 1946

M A STARTED HER new job as a private tutor one week after the Direct Action Day riots in Calcutta. The University Board of Male Superiors had recommended her as the only teacher suitable for the position. Not only was Ma's knowledge of Urdu poetry and language more advanced than her peers', but in that politically charged time, when others had refused, Ma had said yes.

The well-known Islamic cleric and intellectual Sahib Ali was already a benefactor of the Urdu department and his two small sons were in need of grooming for their mapped-out careers. The Supervisors had cleared the matter with her husband. Did Miss Tanisi comprehend the importance of the task ahead? they asked in unison. That she was a woman could not be helped. The Supervisors did not come right out and say this, but Ma knew anyway.

There was a lot she could have said at this point, but she had decided against it.

That first Saturday, after she had marked her papers, she gathered her things and checked the address. She hailed a tonga and agreed a price with the driver. The lanes narrowed the further in they went. The skin-and-bone nag skittered on the paving stones. The driver, a man with jittering eyes, whipped the animal with such malice that Ma demanded he stop and let her down at once. She would rather walk. When the driver asked for more money, for having come so far into enemy territory, Ma said no. When he called her a Muslim-fucking-whore and spat in her face, she stood her ground and told him that his own mother would be ashamed of him. She kept her voice steady, but her hands and knees were shaking. She ducked into Hakim's Lane, led by the reek of camphor and the line of druggists, and stopped to catch her breath.

An urchin offered her a cup of goat's milk, which he claimed had been blessed by Hazrat Nizamuddin himself. "It will cure your leprosy," he said, looking her up and down, scanning what skin he could see for the tell-tale lesions. "It's in your eyes," he said finally, fixated by the milky blue.

Ma shook her head. No, she was not a leper. She pulled her dupatta over her face and walked away quickly, counting each step as she went. She could smell gasoline and boiled mutton.

She asked directions from a man with a shock of orange hair beneath a white taqiyah, and was pointed the right way. Head down, she ducked into a cul-de-sac, checked the address, and saw it was straight ahead, a grand haveli worn around the edges. Watermarks greyed the surface of the outer walls. The wooden shutters were tightly closed. The name on the black marble plaque read *Hafiz Manzil*. Home of Hafiz.

Ma reached out and pulled the frayed rope attached to the bell. She could hear dogs fighting and a man shouting. A blue diamond kite flew above her head.

The peephole opened and a pair of myopic eyes stared out.

"Yes?" came a suspicious voice.

"Assalaam o Alaikum," said Ma, hesitant but only for a second, determined to show mettle. "My name is Miss Tanisi. I am the new tutor."

The door opened and Ma went in. She could smell orange blossom water and strong black tea. She slipped off her shoes and waited to be shown in.

. . .

My heart is mine
I have sold it to none
Be it tattered and torn and worn away
My heart is mine.

"Who wrote that?" asked Ma, her dupatta pulled over her hair, a makeshift hijab tucked behind her ears and drawn tightly under her chin.

She sat cross-legged on an intricately woven Persian rug, on a stone floor at a low cedar table. Two small boys sat opposite and stared at her with wide eyes. Miss Tanisi was an unknown, a mysterious quantity, a female tutor with a rose-dipped voice. They had not seen one like her before.

Sheets of paper and pencils were laid out in front of them. Kidskin reference books open on select pages. There was water in a brass jug, a sprig of green mint floating on the surface like a lone lily, and cups to drink from.

The eldest boy squinted beneath his round spectacles. His long eye-lashes, magnified, flickered quickly. In time Ma would learn that this was how Husain focused his thoughts into deep concentration. Eventually, he raised his hand and waited to be called upon.

"Miss Tanisi-ji? Rabindranath Tagore, Bengal, born in 1861," said Husain, after Ma had nodded with an encouraging smile.

"See? You knew all along and I knew that you did. Tagore was a poet inspired by nature. He wrote about expansive tropical skies and the wash of a monsoon rain. He saw beauty in the sweeping line of a coconut grove and the loneliness of the noon sun."

"He was inspired by Allah, you mean, who created the Universe?" asked Husain.

His eyes were so long-lashed, he could almost be mistaken for a girl. His younger brother nodded in agreement. The natural world would not exist without the grace of Allah.

"By a power greater than man, yes. But also, by an expansion of man's own consciousness when he suddenly stumbles upon a great truth," replied Ma, smiling at them both.

Sahib Ali, standing in the doorway, curious to hear what this new tutor had to say, was astonished to hear Miss Tanisi speak. He had not heard a woman speak like this before. Truthfully, he had not wanted her at first, but after Direct Action Day in Calcutta—when Jinnah had confused the Muslim masses with his words and twenty thousand Hindus had been slaughtered—the mood in Delhi had changed. No other teacher would accept the post or risk travelling so far into a Muslim mohallah. Just yesterday, Sahib Ali's cook went to the Sabzi Mandi for apples and came back with a purple eye. The one sly vendor who had called him over when the others had turned their backs charged him triple. Just a few days ago, the words "Mussalman Murdabad" had been painted in orange across the walls of Hafiz Manzil. The letters had been cleaned off and his boys had not seen them, but still. The sentiment was clear.

Sahib Ali came into the room and without introducing himself began to speak. Hearing Miss Tanisi had stirred something in him, a readiness and excitement for debate.

"As Muslims, we don't think like that," he said, sitting down drawing his boys close with an animal instinct to protect them. "You see, in Islam we love equilibrium and order. You've seen the precision of the

Mughals? The Red Fort? The Jamma Masjid, Humayun's Tomb? You've been to Agra?"

Ma nodded. Of course she had. She had memorised their lines.

"Within this symmetry, impulse is crushed. And so it must be as we submit to the higher edict of Allah. Impulse brings passion. With passion comes the end of order. With the end of order comes chaos. And with chaos, well, you know what happens next."

"Of course," said Ma. She could feel her cheeks grow warm, her reflections unsteady. Here was the kind of conversation that could yield a friendship of sorts, of the kind that she knew, instinctively, would not be countenanced and which she craved. "Islamic purity of form, especially architecturally, is a wonder," she said carefully. "Poetically too, the Urdu language wraps sound and meaning into perfect syllables, both in the ear and on the page. It is a joy that something so precise can be so ethereal. Nevertheless."

"Ah," said Sahib Ali. He grinned. "There is always a nevertheless. I live for it. Please, go on. Speak freely."

"Nevertheless," Ma returned the smiled, "the human mind, the imagination can expand beyond its boundaries, beyond form and precision. It is capable of so much if we allow it the space. This is why I admire Tagore so much."

"Some would argue that that much freedom of imagination and thought would lead to madness."

"Perhaps. But wouldn't it be worth the risk?" said Ma. "To be that much closer to the essence of your own truth and worth?" She saw Husain staring up at her as she spoke. He had left his father's side and inched closer, mesmerised by her voice. He looked down at once when she caught his eye.

When Ma's two hours were up and she was by the door—a hand on the wall as she slipped on her shoes—Husain ran up to her.

"Miss Tanisi?" he asked.

"Yes?"

"Do you have children?"

"Two girls."

"I don't have an amma. She died."

"Oh. You must feel so sad."

"It's OK."

"Actually," Ma knelt down to meet his eye, "I don't have a ma either. Or a pa. They drowned when I was a baby."

"Oh," said Husain. "So you are like me and my brother and my father too? You have lost?"

Ma nodded. She had lost. "Like you," she said softly.

Sahib Ali approached them and shooed Husain out of the way. "Go upstairs. I would like a word with Miss Tanisi."

"Miss Tanisi, may I be frank?" he said, once the boy had gone.

"Please," said Ma, standing to face him.

"I understand how you think, but my boys are too young for that much intellectual freedom. Husain has a religious calling, I think. Whether it is an instinct embedded in the boy himself, or whether I have unconsciously been mentoring him as my own father mentored me, I have yet to work out. He wants to be an imam and he is quite staunch in this desire. I am hoping the poetry, as appropriate, will open his mind to beauty and greater devotion. The work you do with him must be applicable."

"Of course," said Ma. "He is a remarkable boy. Terribly wise at such a young age."

"Yes. I have always thought so. He seems to see right through a person when they speak. Right down into the heart of them."

Ma was curious. "Can I ask you, if it's not too forward, what your plans are? I imagine after what happened in Calcutta, that your position here will be compromised? Will you stay in Delhi? Are you not frightened?"

"My family has lived in this house for seven generations. I presume it is the same with yours?"

"On my husband's side."

"My great-great grandfather, seven generations ago, was a Hafiz. How can anyone else live in Hafiz Manzil but his kin?"

"Don't you want to move to Pakistan? Is Pakistan not the dream?"

"When the League invoked the notion of Pakistan, they did so without the compliance, without even—in more remote places—the awareness of many Muslims. What would you do in my position, Miss Tanisi? Would you abandon everything to follow blindly a paradigm that has no roots?"

"It would be like moving to live in a house that had no roof," says Ma.

"You understand me exactly."

. . .

The next time Ma went to Hafiz Manzil, once her two hours were up, Sahib Ali invited her to take tea with him and his boys. Ma hesitated but then she agreed.

"Please, Miss Tanisi," said Husain, "come and sit here." He motioned to the cushion he had brought over especially for her.

"Yes," echoed his little brother Mohammed, "sit here. Near us."

"My sister, Shahnaz Begum, will join us, for propriety's sake," said Sahib Ali. "Don't be alarmed by her. She has been raised to speak only when spoken to. She is shy and not much of a conversationalist."

Shahnaz Begum, dressed in a black niquab, poured the tea and offered sugar. She dropped a cube into each glass with silver pincers shaped like a heron's long legs. She did not speak once and she avoided eye contact even when Ma said *salaam*, how are you, and then yes, no, and *shukria*. Though she did not show it, Ma was aghast—not for her own sake, because of the implied rudeness—but for Shahnaz Begum, whom she feared had been deprived of her voice since birth.

Once the tea had been served, Shahnaz Begum took her place in the far corner of the room. Ma would glance up every so often and smile in her direction, determined but failing to inspire the slightest bit of warmth.

The two little boys pressed against their father, one on each side, and not once did they take their eyes off Miss Tanisi.

. . .

Weeks later, Bappu was at the breakfast table reading *The Times of India* again, the coffee cold again. They were always at the breakfast table reading and discussing the news lately, as though this were the new pattern of their lives, their food untouched.

In response to Direct Action Day, there had been trouble in the east, in Noakhali in Bengal. Not the sort of trouble that was passionate, unruly, a moment of madness that would dissipate, but a new sort of strategic, systematic, well-thought-out, and carefully executed trouble.

There had been mandatory public conversions to Islam. Hindus had been collected and force-fed beef. Their idols were smashed, their temples violated, their mothers-wives-sisters-daughters raped. The men, who had been forced to watch their mothers-wives-sisters-daughters being raped, were slaughtered by the same cleaver that had been used to butcher the beef.

How-now-brown-cow, said Alma to herself, listening to Bappu read. She didn't care what the men did to each other, didn't really understand anyway—Bappu was mumbling, leaving out entire words. The men were stupid, but the cows with their soft hides and long lashes, their slow, languorous gaits, suckling calves, and bellies full of milk, she cared what happened to them.

The announcer on All-India Radio announced: Lock up your mothers-wives-sisters-daughters. Your mothers-wives-sisters-daughters, distant cousins, aunties near and far have become the soil. Defile the body of your enemy's womenfolk and you will defile your enemy's. This was not exactly what the announcer said, there being strict guidelines for what could be said "live-on-air," but this was what Bappu and Ma heard.

Alma heard it too but it seemed so far away to her, this spoiling of the female body and honour such an abstract concept, because how would a body spoil, if not with liver spots like fruit left out in the sun, and no one would tell her anyway, not even Dilchain-ji. So, she thought only of the how-now-brown-cow and the milk and the cream and the kheer.

"Like rabid dogs on heat," said Ma in a low voice, turning her head aside so that Alma and Roop would not hear. "They should all be lined up and shot."

Daadee Ma, alarmed at the panic in the radio announcer's voice, the implications of dishonour to the family name, could feel the twitch of the evil eye giving her all manner of dirty looks. Alma, who smelt suspiciously like a ripe guava, would need to be wed as soon as possible. She was twelve going on thirteen but still, these things took time to organise. Daadee Ma made a mental note of five potential families with five potential sons and started to divvy up the copper pots, and the gold-silver-gems as dowry. She would call their mothers in the morning and bribe them. They would need a horoscope.

Alma, who had no idea she was being examined, ate her toast-butter-jam, drank her milk, and kicked her sister's short legs under the table.

. . .

A few days later a telegram arrived, addressed to Bappu as head of the family, with news of a distant, but no less regarded cousin, twice removed on Daadee Ma's side. A cousin whom Bappu had not seen since he was a boy and a cousin whose face he couldn't quite recollect, but a cousin he remembered playing dice with in the courtyard one summer.

The cousin had lived in a small village on the edge of Lahore and she had had a fondness for pineapple jam, having once tasted Dilchain's ma's recipe. Once a year, Daadee Ma would ask Dilchain to make up a few jars of pineapple jam and they would send these to her with a courier. There would always be a letter of "thank you very much" in reply.

In the telegram addressed to Bappu, words were typed in English capital letters to the effect that this distant cousin twice removed had had her unborn baby carved out of her stomach at 4:00 p.m. on Tuesday, week just gone. She was penetrated by four men, one of whom calculated the activities of the group on the stop clock of his new watch. It was a very fine watch, a Made-in-Switzerland watch, with handsome silver hands. Her ordeal was over in twenty-five minutes and five seconds according to the Made-in-Switzerland watch. She was dead by the time her husband came home from work. The four men left her husband a note outlining their activities. They signed their names. Two signatures in Urdu, one in English, and one smudged thumbprint.

Leave, said the note. *Or we will come back.*

Bappu deduced this from reading in between the lines of grief, and confirmed it later when he spoke to her husband on the telephone. He called his twin in Bombay, and they talked for a long time in thick voices.

Daadee Ma, though dry-eyed, having spent all her tears on a lifetime's worth of forfeiture, spent two sleepless days bathing and honeying her gods.

. . .

Ma went to tutor that evening and, after the lesson had ended, once the tea had been poured, she told Sahib Ali about the rape of the distant cousin twice removed, and of the fissure like a tiny crack that had appeared in the walls of Pushp Vihar. She didn't say the word "rape" out loud but only mouthed it, and not even then directly. She did not want the boys to hear.

"Fissures like that grow you know, all the way to the roof," she mumbled.

"I know. We have our own. Over there." Sahib Ali pointed to a visible crack on the wall. "That came after my wife died," he said.

"How did she die?"

"She was pushed over by a mob. She cracked her head. We were visiting family in East Bengal last year. She was in the Sabzi Mandi buying figs, because I had told her just that morning I was craving them."

"Oh," said Ma, her eyes prickling, a hand to her throat, "how awful."

. . .

Dilchain stayed up through the night and stirred a pot of pineapple jam, which she jarred whilst still hot and buried in the roots of the peepul tree. Daadee Ma helped her. They lit seven candles and kept the fires burning for seven nights. Alma and Roop took it in turns to stir the jam and keep vigil over the flames. Dilchain remembered the distant cousin's face well. They had sat on the swing together and Dilchain had plaited her hair. They had been the same age when they had met. They had been nine years old.

7

5 March 1947

"You MAKE BEAUTIFUL plaits," says Alma in English, watching Fatima Begum oil and braid Roop's hair for school. "There's a new girl at school," she adds. "Mary."

The so-fair-boy stands on the edge of the shore with freshly washed feet and sandalwood paste on his forehead. Three stripes to show his allegiance. Shiva. Vishnu. Brahma. *Who's Mary?* he says.

"Mary is a converted Christian." Mary, Mother-of-God.

Not my god.

"Oh," says Fatima Begum with a slight frown. "Converted from what?"

"Mary has a djinn," mouths Alma with a hand held out to her lips. She doesn't want to tell her ayah that Mary used to be a Muslim. "I overheard her talking about it last week."

"Oh, a djinn?" says Fatima Begum, also whispering as she threads and twists Roop's hair. Fatima Begum is excellent with secrets.

"What are you talking about," says Roop, wriggling. "I can't hear when you whisper."

"Exactly," says Alma with half a smile.

"Very good, but speak in Hindi," says Fatima Begum, hairpins in her mouth. "All this English talking is no good."

"Bappu says we should speak Urdu with you. To practise," says Alma.

"Mashallah," says Fatima Begum. "Even better." She pins the second plait into place and ties the ribbon swiftly. She holds Roop tightly and kisses her cheeks, pulls Alma to her and embraces her too. "How quickly you both grow," she says.

. . .

When Alma was a month old, Ma's milk dried up. On recommendation from Ali Ahmed Abed, the family jeweller, whom Bappu valued as an old friend of his pa's, he hired Fatima Begum.

Fatima Begum's husband had recently died on his way to the Friday namaz. A tonga swerving to miss a crate of apples had dragged him under its wheel, mangling his body and brain. Fatima Begum mourned him for propriety's sake, though she did not mourn him for love.

Her baby had died in her arms a week later. The little girl, named Azizaam, which meant "my dearest," had a weak heart and one day, when she was exactly one month old, her weak heart just stopped.

Despite Fatima Begum's grief there was a warmth to her that Bappu liked at once. Ma agreed. When Roop was old enough to talk in sentences, she told everyone who would listen that her ayah was made of cake. A melt-in-the-mouth vanilla cake, best consumed with lashings of hot milk.

Ma said it would be complementary to have an Islamic influence in an otherwise strictly Brahmin household and Bappu agreed. Hiring a Muslim ayah felt like progress.

Daadee Ma was livid. But, she was also wary of displeasing Bappu's pa, who was dead less than a year. It was not often either that Bappu was so firm. His was a natural male authority she could not go against. She simmered down, but insisted that she would starve herself to death if there was to be any co-dining. If Gandhi-ji could do it, all stick-and-bone, so could she. She sat on her charpoy, crossed her small arms, and pinched her lips, her short legs dangling off the edge.

There was a servant's quarter at the back of the haveli with enough space to set up a small cooking area, and Fatima Begum would live, wash, and eat there. Daadee Ma missed five meals and refused chai. Being so slight anyway and still in her widow's white robes, her head a mass of tufts, she was forced to take to her bed. That she secretly ate jaggery when no one was looking was something only Dilchain knew about.

Bappu, feeling guilty, agreed that they could make that small concession. Ma, feeling that Daadee Ma was manipulative and sly, but out of deference for Bappu's pa, of whom she had been so fond, said nothing.

That Alma had been born on the same day as Azizaam was further proof of Allah's clemency and wisdom. Alma Azizaam, Fatima Begum would say, throwing the baby up into the air and catching her with a light touch. Alma, my dearest.

Fatima Begum had milk to share. She suckled Alma every day for a year, and later when Roop was born and the milk just flowed, rich and sweet and creamy, no one questioned it.

. . .

Mohammed Reza Sir and Betty the nag are waiting to take the girls to school. When Roop, weighed down by layers of school uniform and her enormous satchel, complains of the heat, Mohammed Reza Sir shakes his head morosely.

"It will get much worse than this. Astrologer Sahib, he is saying hot hot no rain all summer. Everyone is cooking."

At school, Alma is distracted from her lessons all morning. She thinks about Mary and the djinn, and she thinks about the so-fair-boy standing on the shores of the Jamuna. He has not moved from his position for days.

Jesus died on the Cross for our sins, she says to the so-fair-boy, repeating after Sister Ignatius, *and then he was resurrected. Did you know that?*

Yes, he says, *I did. Judas betrayed him.*

In the margins of her notebook Alma sketches the djinn. She draws an outline of his shape, his nose-eyes-mouth, his enormous girth.

Alma stares at the drawing of the djinn and colours his eyes in. Dark irises and darker pupils. She coils a snake around his neck and gives the djinn a deliciously forked and intrusive tongue. A slippery-slidey clean-out-your-insides and hot sort of tongue. She tries to imagine her wedding night, and though she is not sure what exactly will happen, not really, she does know they will sleep in the same bed and that they will possibly be wearing no clothes.

She recollects a statue of Kali she saw as a child in a temple in Benares. Bappu told her that Kali was to be revered, that she granted her worshippers release, rebirth, but with her open mouth, the lolling tongue, the crossed eyes, Alma wonders now if the djinn and Kali are kin.

She looks up and surveys the classroom. All heads bent, all hands taking notes. No one has noticed her red cheeks.

The so-fair-boy has noticed though, and he looks up in surprise.

What? She kisses the flat of her palm and blows it across to him.

At break time, when the rest of the girls are queuing for milky tea and Marie biscuits two apiece, Alma stands at the edge of the playground, which is just a patch of dusty ground, and pets the how-now-brown-cow that lives outside the gate.

Once, Alma overheard Sister Ignatius discussing the size of the playground with Father Patrick, in private, when Sister Ignatius thought that no one else could hear. The Mary and Joseph School, she had said, was clearly not designed for this many ribbon-headed girls, wanting to hop-skip-jump as much as possible. The diocese had run out of funds by the time the nuns realised that Delhi was not as small as they had hoped, and gave them only a patch of dusty ground that was not the convent's to take, but which the convent, in the name of the Lord, laid claim to nonetheless.

She looks around now for Mary. Mary is standing with three other girls. The girls are on the charity quota and their shoes are scuffed. They take it in turns to skip with a thinning rope. Four more skips and the rope will break. The other girls are converted Christians too. Alma can see the shine of the tin crosses beneath the buttons of their off-white shirts.

On Sundays the converted Christians go to the St. James's Church near Kashmere Gate and they sing hymns from a small leather-bound book. They sing about lambs and then they eat them. After they eat the lambs, they stretch and tan the skins to make covers for their Bibles and hymn books. It is actually barbaric.

Alma remembers the time she peeked through the railings of the St. James's Church. She had thought then that the church, with its pale yellow dome resplendent against the bright blue sky, was the most beautiful building she had ever seen. It shimmered like a mirage in the dusty city.

"Mary?" says Alma. She walks up to Mary, takes no notice of the other three girls. "Can we talk in private?" she says.

Mary, tongue-tied, nods. She follows Alma to a corner of the playground. The other Christian girls stare at Mary's back with wide and curious eyes. It is not often that a Brahmin girl will speak to one of them. Their families, having forsaken one god for another, are openly looked down upon. *They* are openly looked down upon. They take it in turns to stare at the red apple clip and nudge one another.

Alma looks at Mary. Mary looks at the dusty ground.

"I like your clip," says Mary, still not looking up.

"You should come to my house for dinner one day."

"Oh." Mary looks up in shocked surprise. Obviously no one has ever invited her over for dinner before. "Is it a trick?"

"No," says Alma, "of course not."

There is an awkward pause.

"Mary, I overheard you the other day, by accident, saying you were possessed by a djinn? Is it true?"

Mary looks up and realises that Alma has been listening to her conversations. It makes Mary feel important, Alma can tell. The bell sounds a loud crack, and the girls jump apart.

"If I tell you, promise not to tell anyone?" says Mary.

"I swear on my ayah's life," says Alma.

"Yes," Mary whispers. Her plain face is lit. "Amma says there is a djinn living inside me."

"In your body?" asks Alma. She desperately wants it to be so, wants Mary to convince her. But she is not convinced: Mary looks perfectly common to her.

Mary has a wet nose and thin lips.

"Yes." Mary moves closer and Alma takes a step back. Mary puts a hand on her heart and then a hand on her mouth, in here, in here. She touches her head and says in the same quiet voice, "and sometimes in here."

Mary is a bit odd.

"Here, have this," says Alma, thinking quickly. She takes off the red apple clip, pushes it into Mary's hand.

Mary clutches the clip tightly in case Alma should change her mind. She puts her clenched fist straight into her torn pocket.

"It's a present. You don't have to give it back. I have more at home," says Alma.

Sister Ignatius appears out of nowhere and claps them apart. Sister Ignatius does not under any circumstances approve of girls, one rich one poor, whispering in corners.

8

7 March 1947

IT IS STARTING to get light when Daadee Ma reaches the foot of the banyan tree growing in a cul-de-sac off Nankhatai Gali. Prospective weddings are the banyan's speciality and the seventh day of the month is an auspicious day. She puts down the heavy jute bag and lifts out a copper vessel of water. She takes off the lid, pours it slowly on the roots and into the earth. She smears sandalwood paste on the bark, across her forehead, and lights a nub of lotus incense.

She circles the tree, counts each round on her rudraksha beads, and loops white thread around the bark. There are one hundred and eight rounds to complete. As she goes, she tucks a coin or a square of coconut barfi amongst the tubers.

Daadee Ma stops midcircle to massage her knees and take a breath. She slips a coin into the bark. For Ambika, who was two, she says. Another coin for Raju, three months old. One more turn and she places a sweet in one of the gnarled roots. Gullu, four years old only and cholera out of the blue. The indent of his small body still stuck in the mattress on the third long-legged bed. Another for Baluka, who stopped breathing after a week. Another coin for Tara, who was born still, eyes closed and feet turned inside out. Not even a day in the world. Dilchain's ma had helped her each time, pressing cold herbal compresses on her forehead and feeding her sugared water with a spoon.

Her own ma, a much beaten and berated woman, had stirred bitterness into all her cooking. Bitter gourds, bitter unsalted aubergines, burnt garlic-cumin-asafoetida, sour green tomatoes for the gravy, undercooked dal and overstewed tea with a tight-fisted sprinkle of sugar. She couldn't help herself. Bitterness leaked out of her and she wanted her daughters— Daadee Ma and her two sisters—to have the same. Why should they have a better life?

Daadee Ma breaks at fifty rounds, out of breath. There are three more babies to remember. Three nameless foetuses that poured out of her child's womb, each so squashed it might have been stamped on by a soldier's boot.

She cried only the first time it happened. She was chasing a chicken in the courtyard, desperate for a pet, when the invisible punch knocked her down. Hot tears on her face and bile in her belly. She vomited all over herself and curled into the ground.

When they found her, they called the doctor. The doctor wore a white coat, said it was a miscarriage, her body too skinny, too young.

"But what of the chicken?" she had asked tearfully. The chicken had discovered a fortuitous gap in an open door and had made its escape. She cried for the bird first, and then for the baby.

Daadee Ma will not cry now. It would be inauspicious to mourn the long-time dead, and the spirit of the tree would not like it at all.

She completes the last round and places her palms in prayer. For a Class-A tip-top wedding. For the evil eye above Alma's head to just go away. For a Pure Hindustan, she slips in for luck.

. . .

In the kitchen, Dilchain lights a ghee candle and places it in front of the goddess Annapurna that used to belong to her ma. Dilchain knows all about the seventh day of the month. In one sandalwood hand, Annapurna, goddess of food and nourishment, holds a sandalwood bowl of sandalwood porridge that Dilchain smears with honey from the northern Himalayan valleys. She tears the petals off an orange marigold and throws them at Annapurna's wooden feet. Where the honey is smeared, the petals fall and stick.

"For Alma," says Dilchain and raises her hands in prayer. Jai Hind.

. . .

In her designated chambers, Fatima Begum fills a small metal bucket with water from a larger earthenware jar. She sets her intention with a silent prayer: Bismillah ar-Rahman ar-Raheem, and prepares to perform wudu. She washes her hands and wrists, brings a palmful of water to her lips, and rinses her mouth. She brings a palmful of water to her nostrils and sniffs the water in and then out. She washes her face from the top of the forehead to the bottom of the chin and then washes her arms from right to left. She does everything three times and then wipes her wet hands across her hairline from front to back and then she cleans inside her ears. Finally, she washes her feet.

She unrolls her prayer mat, which she has had since she was four years old, brings her hands to her ears, and begins to pray. She doesn't know about the seventh day of the month, but she prays for Alma today as she has done every day since the wedding was announced.

"Pakistan Zindabad," she says at the end when she rolls up her mat.

. . .

At night, when they are in bed and Fatima Begum has left the room, Roop and Alma, heads touching, whisper into each other's ears. Alma tells Roop about the djinn living inside Mary, though Alma pulls a face. She can hardly believe it herself.

"She looks too ordinary," says Alma, "with a wet nose and thin lips. I'm not sure that a djinn, who could choose any body to possess, would necessarily choose hers."

"I don't think a djinn would care about things like that," says Roop. "Djinns are made of fire. Fire that has no smoke. Fatima Begum told me."

"Sometimes they are as beautiful as a pari," says Alma.

"Actually, they are mostly ugly."

"A churel is a djinn who is beautiful and ugly at the same time," says Alma.

"How?"

"In the *Kashmiri Folktales*, on page twenty-one, it is written that if a lady dies when she is pregnant, or even worse if she dies on the day the baby is born, her djinn will come to life as a churel."

"Is there a lot of blood when the lady dies?"

"So much blood."

"Show me how much with your hands."

"This much blood." Alma stretches her arms out as far as they will go. "You can't even imagine it, and not just any blood, but impure blood. Churels are very malignant."

"What's a mali-g-nant?"

"Hateful-wicked-full of spite. From the front, the churel is as fair as a rose, but from the back she is black, and her feet are turned the wrong way round. Heels in front and toes behind."

"Swear to god?"

"Swear to every god. Shiva, Allah, and baby Jesus. Heels in front and toes behind. At night, because the churel is so beautiful from the front, she likes to charm her way into the lives of young men."

"Handsome ones?"

"The most handsome ones. She carries them on her back to the kingdom of all djinns and offers them delectable tiffin. Such tender morsels you can't even begin to imagine it."

"Kulfi and kheer and jalebis?"

"And samosas with green chilli chutney and unlimited mango lassi . . ." Alma stops, lifts a stern finger to her face. "But when the handsome young men partake of the tiffin and drink the lassi?"

Roop draws a finger across her neck. Everyone knows that humans must never ever partake of food or drink in the fairy kingdom. No matter how hungry you might be. You just have to abstain. Ab-stain. To hold back. Everyone knows that.

"Exactly. She keeps them there. Prisoners in her kingdom. And when they are old and grey and have lost all their beauty, so that no one will marry them, she sends them back. It's actually very sad."

"It's actually their own fault. They're too greedy."

"One boy managed to escape though."

"How?"

"The churel was sitting on a cemetery wall at dusk, and because the boy was friendly, he said namaste. When she said namaste back, her voice was like warm honey and her eyelashes so long and her hair curled like this," Alma pulls a ringlet through her hair.

"What happened?" says Roop, chewing a nail.

"He was much cleverer than all those other boys."

"The greedy ones?"

Alma nods. "He looked carefully and saw her feet. Heels in front and toes behind. He said no when she wanted to give him a kiss. She screamed and screamed such abuse at him, but he ran. Fast fast all the way home."

On the shore of the Jamuna that is flowing the wrong way, the so-fair-boy whose features are a little hazy today asks Alma to show him her feet. She kicks off her slippers, rolls up her pyjamas, points her pink-polished-toes.

You have long toes, he says.

I have Bappu's toes, she says proudly.

One foot faces the so-fair-boy and the other is turned inside out and back to front. He looks at her and points. She looks at him. Neither of them says a word.

9

COOKIE AUNTIE'S VOICE is stern as she fits the turquoise silk around Alma's waist.

"Move and I will stick this pin right through you," she says.

Alma does as she is told. She practises her soon-to-be-married smile, and lowers her eyelids to half-mast. Cookie Auntie catches her and smiles.

"Go on," she says, when she is satisfied with the length. "I can see that you're dying to run away."

"I am," Alma agrees. "I have to water the flowers."

She fills the watering can from an earthenware jar in the kitchen, douses the star-shaped jasmine. There are rosebuds growing too. In less than a week they will bloom. When she is finished, she runs up to Bappu's study and brings down Volume Four of the *Encyclopaedia Britannica*, turns to page two hundred and twenty five. "Djinns." She fetches a pencil and a notebook, looks out of the window into the courtyard, chews the end of her pencil. She can smell the milk boiling.

She writes "how to catch a djinn" as neatly as she can. Underlines it. Twice. She writes "Kali?" with a question mark and underlines that too.

Daadee Ma is helping Dilchain-ji in the kitchen. There is a vat of sweet milk to reduce for the wedding and they are taking it in turns to stir it. There will be enough sweetmeats to feed the entire neighbourhood, Dilchain-ji had said that morning when Alma had snuck into the kitchen before school to dip a spoon into the hot milk and taste it.

Alma chews the end of her pencil. The question is how to convince Mary to let Alma extract the djinn and then how to coax the djinn into a bottle. She makes lists and draws diagrams. She will need to make a sacrifice. A proper sacrifice that requires fresh blood.

. . .

"Bappu?" Alma asks later, voice conspiratorially low. "Quick, come over here."

"Yes?"

"Will you tell me about Kali?"

"Kali? Oh." Bappu looks at her in surprise. "Why are you interested in her? What are you up to?"

Nothing. Alma shrugs sheepishly. "Can a goddess be a demon? Is a demon the same as a djinn?" she demands.

"Kali is a manifestation of the Goddess Durga, consort of Lord Shiva."

Alma nods.

"Kali drank the blood of the demon Rak and it made her wild. She danced on the world, stamping on it with her feet, until the world shook. Shiva had to throw himself beneath her feet to stop her. She was on her way to destroying the entire Universe."

"Is she bad?"

"No. Kali destroys the world so that the world may be rebuilt. She purges evil to make room for good. She does not destroy for destruction's sake alone."

"Should I be afraid of her?"

"No."

"But she likes blood, doesn't she?"

"Yes, but she drank Rak's blood to prevent more demons springing forth from it. She drank it to protect us. This created her bloodlust. Sometimes the good things we do have unforeseeable consequences. And always remember, Alma, without Kali there is no rebirth, and therefore no life."

. . .

At school the next day, at first tea break, Alma finds Mary. She links arms with her and suggests they walk around the playground.

"But the biscuits?" says Mary. She looks in the direction of the queue. The other three Christian girls look back at her. They make eyes. They have saved her a place.

"Don't worry," says Alma. "You can have mine. Anyway, they won't run out. The biscuits have been counted." She pulls Mary away and Mary follows her. Walking, unlike standing still whilst whispering, is encouraged.

"How do you know?" says Alma. "That you have a djinn living inside you? What does it feel like?"

"Like a light that spins me round and round until I get so dizzy, I fall. I don't remember what happens next, but Amma says I shake. She says I foam at the mouth. She says that my eyes cross."

"How horrible," says Alma, wincing. "I saw a dog once, foaming at the mouth. It had rabies. Its eyes were blood red. The dog catcher came and shot him in the head." She talks quickly. Poor Mary. Mother-of-God. No one will marry her with an affliction like that.

"I am not a rabid dog!"

"Oh no. No, of course not. I'm sorry. I didn't mean it like that."

Mary crosses her hands over her chest and stands with her legs apart. She purses her thin lips in much the same way that Amma does. Alma has seen Amma waiting for Mary after school. Mary's amma wears an enormous tin crucifix and tries to hide her one leg shorter than the other with her sari.

"I am not a rabid dog!" says Mary again and louder.

Sister Ignatius calls over, "Is everything all right, girls?"

"Yes, Sister Ignatius!" Alma calls back. She grabs Mary's shoulder and takes them back into the walk.

"I'm sorry," says Alma. She reaches out for Mary's hand, abashed to have been so insensitive. This is not how she had planned to approach it at all. "You will come for dinner soon, won't you?" she says by way of an apology.

"I'll ask Amma if I may," says Mary stiffly, but relenting.

"We could do an exorcism?" suggests Alma. "I'll ask Fatima Begum to get us a vial from the Jadoo Wallahs Lane, it's near her uncle's shop, and then—" she stops midsentence. Oh.

Mary is staring at Alma with narrowed eyes. No, she shakes her head. No.

"But don't you want to get rid of it? We could trap him in a bottle? Fatima Begum, my ayah, she would know how to catch a djinn."

No. Mary puts her hands on her hips again. Purses her lips so they disappear into her face.

"Oh," says Alma, taking a step back. She doesn't even particularly want Mary to come for dinner, but she is desperate to see the djinn. Somehow she feels that the djinn is a kindred spirit. "You should still come for dinner. We can have ice cream? Pinky-shake on it?" Alma puts out her little finger with the pale-peach-polish, and Mary hesitates but eventually offers her own.

. . .

"Roop, come here," says Alma after dinner, when the teak table has been cleared and the adults have dispersed. They sit cross-legged in a corner of the courtyard with their backs to the room. "Shall we catch a djinn?"

"Yes!" Roop whispers loudly. "How? What do we do?"

"It has to be a secret?"

"Cross my heart, hope to die, stick a needle in my eye."

"Bad things will happen if you tell anyone else—you will go blind."

Roop nods. She knows about secrets.

"I've collected some things to help us lure him in. Lure means tempt."

"Lure," repeats Roop in rapt attention, hands clasped to her chest. "Go on."

"Djinns have debauched appetites. I read about it in the encyclopaedia."

"What's a de-bau-ched?"

"Easy to lead astray."

"Oh. I don't know about that one. What's my job then?"

"To prepare the sacrifice," says Alma. "I've given you the best job."

"The moth? It's under the bed."

"No. It wouldn't work. Blood is essential—that means very important. Without fresh blood, the djinn might never come out."

"The mouse?" says Roop, following Alma's gaze and glancing surreptitiously at the hole in the wall.

"Good idea," says Alma, who has been angling for the mouse all along. "How will you catch and kill it?"

"Not sure."

"Maybe you should suffocate it? It will hurt the least and you know how to do that now."

"OK." Roop chews her nail.

"Don't worry. It won't be a sin. God loves you."

"Because I'm a child?"

"Exactly," says Alma, and pats her encouragingly on the arm. "I'll give you some chocolate too, but only when you're done."

That night, Roop crouches outside the mouse hole when everyone else is asleep. Daadee Ma is watching from the charpoy, pretending not to, but Roop can see the whites of Daadee Ma's eyes like slivers of moon.

When the mouse finally comes out, its pink nose twitching for the kheer left out by the hole, Roop is wide awake and ready with a jar and a lid. The mouse might be fast, but Roop is determined. Hiding behind a chair, she is totally still, holding her breath and watching as the mouse sniffs the kheer, its whiskers so fast she can hardly keep track of their shivering. The mouse picks up a crumb in two tiny hands, sits up and nibbles. Roop, well versed on the magic of Dilchain-ji's kheer, inches forwards slowly and places the jar, very fast and neck down, over the bewildered creature.

"Got you," she whispers.

She sits for a while on the stone floor, holding the jar down as firmly as she can, using her legs for extra support, watching the mouse scramble in panic. She is fascinated by the animal's fear and the way the jar is juddering under her hands, but she holds it anyway and counts to ten, to twenty and so on until the mouse, having run out of air, is finally still. She counts to three hundred, doesn't once look away. The mouse must have very tiny lungs indeed. She screws the lid on quickly and takes the jar upstairs to bed. She can't wait to show Alma her prize.

In the morning, she is surprised by the softness of the limp thing she holds in her hand, how easy it had been to kill it. The tiny head is bloodied from where the mouse knocked it over and over again as it ran into the glass. Roop puts the creature in a box, strokes the matted fur with her finger as gently as she can, kisses the tiny head, and hides the box under the third long-legged bed next to the moth in the jar. She is proud of her collection.

. . .

For her part, Alma has collected and stashed the following items in their room. She makes a list of them in her notebook.

She has collected seven ghee lamps. She has stolen matches from Dilchain-ji's stash, and from Fatima Begum, a dusty vial from the Jadoo Wallahs Lane, in case the djinn is pure smoke; she is determined to catch him. From Ma and Bappu's bedroom, she has taken a volume of Mirza Ghalib, in case the djinn needs sweet words to lure him out; a vial of attar of roses, in case the poetry doesn't work; and failing these options, she has decanted a quarter bottle of whisky into a small copper urn. She found the whisky in Cookie Auntie's handbag and topped up what she took with water, hoping Cookie Auntie would be too preoccupied to notice. Alma is confident the djinn will not be able to resist.

10

"BE CAREFUL," SAYS Alma. "We mustn't keep the door open, or the dust will get inside and then Dilchain-ji will be really cross." She looks at Mary. "Is it the same at your house? Does it get very dusty?"

"I think so," says Mary.

"Come on." Alma takes Mary's hand, it feels clammy, warm, and she pulls her in, talking quickly. "Ma and Bappu are at the university. Daadee Ma is at the Gymkhana. Cookie Auntie and Husband-ji are out for dinner. Daadee Ma would not approve of you. She is a fascist." She stops and looks at Mary. "Do you know about fascists?" she demands.

"No," says Mary.

"Oh," says Alma. "Never mind. Let's go and sit in the courtyard." Alma takes her shoes off by the door and Mary copies her. "Dilchain-ji will bring us some snacks. She's the only adult here."

In the courtyard, Mary sits on the swing and sneezes. Her nose begins to run.

"Oh dear," says Alma, who has never seen such a wet nose. She pushes the swing backwards and forwards with her foot, and looks at Mary with a sideways glance. "Mary, have you seen the djinn recently?" she asks.

"Oh yes," says Mary brightening up. "Just a few days ago, I was dizzy and fell over, and then he came out of my mouth, and he stood in front of me and was enormous and terrible."

"Do you think we could see the djinn tonight?" asks Alma, eyeing Mary up and down doubtfully.

"It depends."

"On what?"

"If I get twitchy. Amma says the djinn feels what I feel. When I am twitchy, he needs to leave my body to breathe."

"Do djinns need to breathe? I thought they were alive with fire and smoke, not human breath?"

"Amma said so," says Mary, her thin lips drawn in a line.

. . .

For dinner Alma has talked Dilchain-ji into making a feast. She wants Mary to have a Class-A tip-top dinner. It is easier to coax a person into doing what you want them to do if they are given good things to eat.

On the dining table, Dilchain-ji lays out potato pakoras with green chilli sauce, ghee-drenched rice, rajma with caramelised onions, and creamy shahi paneer. There is a plate of warm rotis, a bowl of curd and another of sour pickle to complete the meal. Alma has convinced Ma and Bappu to allow her to use the second-to-best china from England, the one with the pink rosebuds around the rim.

"Don't you think Dilchain-ji is the best cook?" says Alma to Mary, when they are seated around the teak dining table and the food is glorious in front of them.

"Yes," says Mary.

Mary obviously doesn't sit down to eat at a table that often, with cutlery laid out in a row or Made-in-England china plates with rosebuds around the edges. That there are no adults in the room clearly makes her nervous. She looks at Alma's hands, at the pale-peach-polish on the smooth nails.

"I have some polish in my room," says Alma, following Mary's gaze. "We can put some on later, if you like? I have four different colours to choose from. Peach-lilac-pink-silver. Cookie Auntie brought them for me from Bombay."

When Mary is too shy to help herself, Dilchain-ji keeping an eye from the kitchen, comes in and fills her plate. She smiles her warm, dimpled smile. "Use your hands. I always eat with my hands," she says. "Or just the spoon. You don't need the fork."

"It will be Easter soon," says Roop, speaking through a mouthful of food. "Will you go to church and sing hymns to baby Jesus?"

"Yes," nods Mary, who is careful to swallow before she speaks.

"Will Jesus, as a grown-up, come back from the dead? Will you see him?"

"Yes," says Mary. "He will. It's called the Resurrection. At Easter we are allowed to eat sweets."

"Only at Easter?" says Roop, cramming half a roti into her mouth and then choking.

"At Christmas too."

"Oh. That's too bad. We are allowed to eat sweets every day," says Roop, kicking the table leg with her foot.

"Jesus was put on the Cross because Judas betrayed him," says Alma, daintily licking the back of her spoon. She can tell that Mary is impressed. "Judas was a very bad man. That's what Sister Ignatius said."

"Judas was bad, but Jesus forgave him. The forgiveness part is important too," says Mary, copying Alma and licking the back of her spoon.

"I love baby Jesus," says Roop. She can't take her eyes off the tin figure around Mary's neck. "When you die, Mary, can I have your Jesus-on-the-Cross?"

Alma covers her mouth, giggles softly into her hand.

Mary does not reply.

"Why don't you write a note and sign it? You could bequeath it to me? Be-qu-eath means to give," says Roop, pleased with her choice of word.

Dilchain hears Roop's question from the kitchen, swallows her own laughter, and smacks Roop on the back of the head when she comes in to clear the table.

"Kheer!" shouts Roop, forgetting the cross, and banging her spoon on the table.

When the oval dish is brought in from the larder, and the top muslin peeled off to reveal the sugar-cracked, cardamom-infused rice pudding beneath, Roop and Alma clap their hands.

"Thank you, Lord, for all we are about to receive," says Mary to herself, lips moving slightly. Mary lifts a spoon of kheer to her mouth. She is so serene there is a halo above her head. Her toes curl in and out. Mary has evidently never eaten such good kheer before.

Alma watches Mary from the corner of her eye. She sees the halo, the curling toes, the tiny sigh of contentment. "Let's go upstairs, Mary?" she suggests. "Once you have finished eating. It's much nicer upstairs in my bedroom. Dilchain-ji, we are going upstairs on secret business. I don't want anyone to disturb us."

"What business?" says Dilchain-ji.

"The sort that is not your concern."

"Tell me, or I'll come upstairs and sit with you."

"If you must know, I'm going to paint Mary's fingers and toes with peach polish. Like mine, see? If you disturb us and we have to move, the polish will not set and it will crinkle." She holds out her hands and points her toes. "See? Come and sit with us if you want, but it will just be boring for you."

Dilchain, who knows nothing about the art of applying nail polish, but does know when not to trust Alma, looks at Mary sympathetically. She too sees the halo illuminating the plain face.

"Go on," she says, "but if there's any nonsense, I'll be straight up."

Upstairs, Mary stares at the three long-legged beds made up neatly with pretty cotton sheets and pillows. Alma tells Mary to sit on the third bed. That the third bed belonged to Bappu's dead little brother and is generally not sat on is not mentioned. Alma is certain that the djinn is more likely to respond if there is another ghostly presence close by.

"Like responds to like," she had explained to Roop, when Roop had voiced her misgivings.

Alma lights the ghee lamps and places them on the tin chest closest to Mary. She arranges the lamps carefully in a circle. Circles have protective qualities. It's not that Alma is overly concerned about protecting Mary, but she would not like to explain it to Bappu-Ma-Sister Ignatius if something untoward should happen.

Something untoward happening would be exciting, of course, as long as Alma was not held culpable and no one died. That the mouse died does not count.

Roop sits on her own bed and looks at Mary's halo in awe.

"I've lit the candles in case of a power cut," says Alma to Mary, who is more startled by the minute. "Here. Take this." She gives Mary four bottles of polish to choose from. "Do you like poetry? Shall I read you some?" She opens the volume of Mirza Ghalib, and in her best imitation of Ma's rose-dipped voice, begins to read.

Mary looks around the room.

"Smell this, Mary," says Alma, uncorking the attar of rose and rubbing a little on Mary's wrists, on her temples, and behind her ears, just as she has seen Ma do. "Now, inhale. It's attar of roses."

Mary inhales and sneezes. "Oh dear," she says with an overly worried look. "I don't like this smell."

"Why not?" asks Alma, curiously sniffing the bottle. "Ma likes it."

"Amma says that attar of roses stinks of sin." Mary blushes. "She says that it is sent from Lucifer to lead us into temptation."

"Who is Lucifer?" asks Roop.

"Sheitan," explains Alma.

"Sin takes you straight to hell. I don't want to go to hell," says Mary.

Alma and Roop exchange looks. Roop holds the vial and waits. She fiddles with the cork stopper impatiently, but knows not to open it.

"Why don't you try this special drink?" says Alma. She jumps off the bed and brings out the copper vessel of whisky. Knowing the whisky to be unpalatable, she has added water, sugar and lemon. Also a strand of saffron, which she stole from the jar, and a sprinkle of unrequited love from the pot next to it, not knowing that unrequited love was what she was adding, only that it smelt as delicious as a too-ripe Alphonso mango.

"What is it?" says Mary, sniffing.

"Oh, just a special sherbet that Cookie Auntie brought from Bombay. It's very sophisticated."

"I don't I like it," says Mary, wrinkling her nose.

"But you must. After all, you've had a good dinner, haven't you? It would be ungracious not to," says Alma firmly.

"It doesn't smell very good," Mary points out.

"Hold your nose," says Alma. "It tastes better if you can't smell it. Take a big mouthful. It's like dawa, but of the good sort. Cookie Auntie, who is the most sophisticated person I know, drinks it all the time."

The so-fair-boy is standing on the shores of the Jamuna. He shakes his head in silent admonishment. *No*, he says, *no*.

Oh, go away, says Alma, pulling a face. *You're not my husband yet.*

Mary takes a long draught of the proffered liquid and because her mouth is lined by milky sweetness, the whisky too must taste sweet. She clenches her little body and exhales sharply as though fire were running through her. Her toes curl and uncurl quickly and she shivers.

"Drink more," demands Alma.

"What about the mouse?" mouths Roop, looking at the box under the bed.

Alma brings a finger to her lips. In a minute.

Mary drinks more. She feels a little bit sick so she covers her mouth in alarm. She giggles loudly, hiccups, and falls backwards on the bed.

"Jesus is love," says Mary in a high voice. She puts both hands on her heart and sighs. Her halo shines brighter than ever.

Look! Roop points to Mary's halo and Alma nods. They have never seen a girl with a halo before.

"Tell the djinn to come out," says Alma. "Tell him I will get him more to drink if he comes out. Tell him I will find him a cigarette."

Mary hiccups loudly and laughs. She closes her eyes and concentrates, hiccups, and laughs again. "He just doesn't feel like it," she says teasingly and boldly drunk.

"Tell him I'll give him some blood. Sacrificial blood."

"From where?" says Mary widening her eyes.

"I'll get it," says Roop, scrambling under the bed. She pulls out the box and takes off the lid.

"What is it?" asks Mary, sitting up and craning her neck to see. She wipes the snot off her upper lip with her hand, wipes her hand on her school uniform skirt.

"It's a mouse," says Roop, showing her the limp ball of fur. She cradles the dead mouse in the palm of her hand. "I have a knife."

"Oh no," says Mary sniffing nervously. "I don't think you should do that."

"Don't worry," explains Roop. "It suf-fo-cated last night. It's actually already dead."

Roop looks to Alma, who nods silently. She reaches beneath her pillow and pulls out a small paring knife.

"It's Dilchain-ji's," she explains as the other two girls stare at her. "I borrowed it. From the kitchen."

"How will you do it?" asks Alma, suddenly a little uneasy. She has never killed a thing before.

Mary whimpers.

"Shh. Be quiet," says Alma, and then to Roop. "Go on. And be quick about it."

Roop nods. She puts the ball of fur back into the box and puts the box on the floor. She kneels down beside it.

"Are you scared?" whispers Alma.

"No," whispers Roop, shaking her head, eyes fixed in concentration.

She grips the knife in her hand as though it were a pencil and very quickly drives it down into the soft belly of the creature. Bright red blood shoots all over her hand and it makes her shiver.

"I did it!" She picks up the wet mouse and shows Alma. "Look!"

"OK. Good. Now smear some of the blood on Mary's forehead," says Alma.

Mary backs herself into the wall. "No," she says. "I don't want you to. I'll scream if you come near me."

"Mary," says Alma sternly. "You have to do what you're told. This is my house."

"Mine too," says Roop.

"No," squeals Mary, when Roop with blood on her fingers reaches over to touch Mary's face. "No!"

Alma jumps off the bed and pinches Mary hard on the arm, she wrestles her still so that Roop can reach over and smear blood on Mary's cheeks.

Mary, full of whisky fire, sits up and pushes Roop to the floor. She turns around and pinches Alma back. "Get lost!" she says. She grabs the whisky off the tin chest and drinks to finish it. It makes her retch.

Alma slaps her on the cheek and then on both arms and Mary slaps back on Alma's cheek and Alma's arms. Mary falls back giggling, slightly hysterical. She is not sure if this is a game or not.

Roop grins. She had not known that her sister could be so mean.

Mary hiccups again. She starts to cry this time and the halo dims.

"Mary, you are such a baby," says Alma, with her hands on her hips. Really, if she had known Mary would behave like this, she would not have invited her over at all.

There is a knock on the door. The girls jump a little.

"It's Ma and Bappu!" says Alma. "Mary, stop crying at once. Here, use this handkerchief to clean your face. If they see you crying, we'll all be in trouble, and then I won't do your nails, and you'll have to return my red apple clip and go home in disgrace. Is that what you want?"

Mary hiccups and does what she is told.

"Wipe your face," orders Alma.

When Bappu and Ma come in, the girls are sitting on the bed looking at the floor.

"Namaste, Mary. Welcome. Oh my dear," says Ma. She looks at Mary's blood-smeared face and eyes. She smells whisky. She looks at Bappu. He can smell whisky too. She sees the dead mouse in the box on the floor and sharply inhales.

Mary stares at Ma, transfixed. She has never seen an amma as lovely as Ma before.

Ma kisses Mary on the cheek, asks her if she has eaten enough. Has she enjoyed Dilchain-ji's cooking and of course the famous kheer? Was it as sumptuous as she had expected? She does not mention the smell of whisky or the blood on the girl's cheek or the dead mouse in the box on the floor.

Mary nods shyly and her halo glows effervescent.

Alma watches Mary from the corner of her eye. She can see by the fizz of the halo that Mary is in love with Ma, and it annoys her because Ma is Alma's. It annoys her so much she sits on her hands and counts to ten to hold her temper.

. . .

What Alma doesn't know yet, is that on the second of September 1947 at five minutes past noon, Mary and her entire family will be set alight.

There is no reason for this setting of a family on fire, only that they are in the wrong mohallah at the wrong time. The man who lights the match, and his comrade-for-a-day who pours the kerosene, are drunk on cheap feni, laced with amphetamines, a gift from their otherwise tight-fisted landlord. Taking the landlord's matches and following his instructions, they don't stop to question the tin crosses that Mary and her family wear around their necks.

. . .

"Mary," says Alma, suddenly spiteful because Ma has reached across and is holding Mary's hand. "Tell Bappu and Ma about the djinn. Is it true or did you make it up?"

Mary doesn't answer.

"Jesus doesn't like girls who lie," says Alma softly.

"It's true," says Roop earnestly. "Baby Jesus doesn't like liars at all. Sister Ignatius said so."

Mary shifts uncomfortably and stares at the floor.

"Go on. Tell them," says Alma.

"Mary has a djinn," says Roop promptly. She squeals as Alma reaches over and pinches her thigh. "In her ribcage. We've been trying to get him out," she explains before pinching and kicking back.

"Oh," says Ma, followed by Bappu. Oh.

Mary has closed her eyes and is holding the tin Jesus so tightly, her knuckles have gone white along the bone.

"Well," says Ma after a pause, her rose-dipped voice sweeter than ever. "It must be a terrible and wonderful thing to have a djinn living inside you."

Mary opens her eyes and looks at Ma gratefully. She doesn't let go of the cross.

"Tell Ma," says Alma, unrelenting, "what you told me. Go on."

Mary starts to cry. She cannot stop no matter how many times she wipes her sleeve across her face. "I want to go home."

"Alma," says Ma, "this is not how we treat our guests. You will need to apologise to Mary at once."

"Why are you still crying?" says Alma irritably. She will not apologise. "For goodness' sake. Stop it now. Jesus does not love girls who cry over nothing."

"There is a djinn and he does live inside me," says Mary to Ma in a low voice, each breathless word caught in a sob. "Amma said I mustn't tell anyone. If Sister Ignatius finds out, she will say I am full of sin and she will ask me to leave. Sister Ignatius doesn't like me because I am bad at my lessons. I'm bad at algebra and reading and writing and everything. I am a disgrace."

"Do you know what, Mary?" says Ma. "I'm really bad at algebra too."

Mary looks up at Ma with shy pink cheeks.

"Mary, would you be gracious enough to accept Alma's apology?" says Ma. "I'm sure she didn't mean to blurt out your secret, and we won't tell anyone, so don't worry."

Alma can feel Bappu's eyes on her. She looks at Mary and is about to offer a half-hearted apology, but something makes her start. "Mary!" she exclaims.

Ma and Bappu follow the panic in Alma's voice. Ma brings a hand up to her mouth. "Oh," she exhales softly.

Mary has seen a point of light on the wall, and she rises off the bed to touch it.

She babbles incoherently and her eyes cross. She spins around herself in slow motion transfixed by the invisible light. She falls down and hits her head on the floor before Ma scoops her up. Mary's shoulders jerk with sudden odd movements. Rivulets of white foam gather around her mouth, and then she is eerily still.

"Is she dead?" whispers Roop.

"It's the djinn," whispers Alma hopefully when Mary's leg jerks.

Ma, who has seen this sort of thing before, is quick to act. "Call Dr. Biswas," she says quietly to Bappu and then mouths, "I think Mary is epileptic."

Dr. Biswas, who lives around the corner and is just about to start his evening puja, comes round as soon as he is called.

Ma cradles Mary's head in her lap. She puts a finger in Mary's mouth.

Alma and Roop are sitting on the floor. Pressed together, they can't take their eyes off Mary.

"Is she dead?" says Roop again in a whisper. She looks longingly at the glimmer of well-worn tin around Mary's neck.

"I can see her breathing," says Alma.

Dr. Biswas talks to Mary in a soothing voice. He confirms Ma's diagnosis.

When Mary eventually opens her eyes, she stares at Dr. Biswas in fright.

"Don't be afraid, Mary," says Dr. Biswas. "This has happened before, hasn't it?"

Mary looks up at Dr. Biswas. He is so kind and she is so ashamed.

"Don't be scared. It's a medical condition, that's all," he says. "I can take you home, speak to your family, and prescribe the right medicine."

"No," says Mary. "Amma wouldn't like it. My brothers wouldn't like it. They will beat me if I come home with a man."

"You will be sensitive, won't you?" says Ma quietly to Dr. Biswas. "I don't think her mother realises. It would be hard for her to accept an illness of this sort."

"Perhaps you should go with Dr. Biswas?" Bappu says to Ma in a low voice.

Of course. Ma nods and collects her things at once.

Alma and Roop sit in silent awe.

"Was the mouse a Hindu, do you think?" whispers Roop, suddenly worried in case the mouse was a relative.

"Animals don't have a religion," Alma reassures her.

"But what about cows? They're Hindu, aren't they? Can we cremate the mouse tomorrow?" asks Roop, speaking directly into her sister's ear so that no one else hears.

"Yes," says Alma just as quietly. "And then we'll bury its ashes under the peepul tree." As an afterthought, she adds, "and it won't be a wasted sacrifice, we'll offer the mouse to Kali."

. . .

When Ma comes back from Mary's house and everyone else has gone to bed, she asks Bappu to sit with her on the swing. Beneath the star-shaped jasmine, the night scent is heady and thick. There is a thermos of hot chai on the low teak table, and a plate of butter biscuits. She pours them each a small glass, breaks a biscuit, and offers half to Bappu. She sits across from him and puts her bare feet on his lap.

"Mary's amma screamed in horror," she tells him. "She blamed herself and then she blamed Mary. I'm sure she would have beaten the girl if I hadn't been there. It was truly awful how miserable their home was. Six of them crammed into one room." She gestures around her. "We have so much here. I feel so humbled."

11

11 March 1947

MA AND SAHIB Ali are sitting on the floor, drinking black tea from a silver-rimmed glass, a plate of dates on the low cedar table between them. The lesson is over and they are talking companionably.

Husain and Mohammed are arranging the pieces of a jigsaw on the floor. When the puzzle is complete it will say "Allah Is Great" in gold calligraphy against green mountains and blue sky.

"Pakistan," Husain will whisper to his brother when the last triumphant piece is pushed into place with the soft pad of his thumb. "That's where it is."

"Can we go?"

"Inshallah, we will go soon."

Shahnaz Begum sits in the corner of the room and observes Ma silently through the gap in her niquab. She is not sure how she feels about her nephews' tutor, or her brother having a woman for a friend. That little Husain is so fond of Miss Tanisi irks her the most. Shahnaz Begum will discuss this unsureness with the other women in her mohallah, and the other women will not like it at all.

. . .

"She has blue eyes," she will say later when they ask. "Unearthly eyes."

"What do they do?"

"They drink tea and talk intimately."

"Intimately how?"

"With secret looks and unsaid words," she will say. Shahnaz Begum has not actually seen these secret looks or heard these unsaid words. She has just imagined them into being.

"Don't trust her motives. Don't take your eyes off her for a minute. Her mother was a dog," they will whisper. "She goes to work every day. It is not normal for a woman with a husband and two girls to go to work every day."

"You will report her to the university," the boldest of the other women will say. "Put her back into her rightful place. Only Sheitan has eyes that colour."

Shahnaz Begum is startled at the suggestion. "But," she begins, "how would I?"

"I will do it then," says the boldest woman decisively. "I will tell my husband and he will report her. The university superiors will listen to him."

. . .

"Should we be worried?" says Cookie Auntie to Ma, steering her into a private corner of the courtyard. It is 8:00 a.m. the next morning, the girls are eating breakfast, and Ma is sorting through papers for work.

"About the state of the country? Yes," says Ma. "We should be very worried." She ties a pile of exam papers with string. Her students have not done as well as she would have liked.

"About the wedding! It is unseasonably hot, and what with all the power cuts the fans keep stopping. I almost can't bear it. It makes thinking so difficult."

"It is hot," says Ma, still distracted by the papers in her hand.

"There's been no word from the boy's family, not even a thank-you for all the mithai we sent out last week. We should have received Alma's wedding trunk by now. At least. Tanisi-ji, are you even listening to me? Put those papers away."

"We could send them a telegram?" Ma wraps her dupatta around her head and tucks the edges behind her ears. More often now, she has been leaving the house with her hair covered. "Has your mother not been in touch with them?" She looks across to the table where the girls are engrossed in their breakfast, hopes Alma can't hear.

"It is not the done thing we should chase them. Who do they think they are?"

"They think they are the chosen ones. Chosen for the merits of their accomplished son," says Ma, tapping her foot, glancing every now and again at the girls. "Let's talk in the corridor," she says nervously, pulling Cookie Auntie's arm.

"I think we have a problem here. Have they been given a portion of the dowry?" Cookie Auntie is insistent now and walks quickly ahead. She stands tetchily in the corridor.

"Your mother gave them a purse of gold coins when the date was set," says Ma. "I've had so much on my mind I've lost all track of time." She looks at the papers in her hand.

"I think we should pay them a visit," says Cookie Auntie, "as soon as you get back from school today? I'll send a boy up ahead, so they know to expect us."

"A friendly visit?" says Ma, steering Cookie Auntie towards the front door so she can put on her shoes. "Promise me?"

"Of course. I'll be very polite."

. . .

Fatima Begum is having a late lunch with Ali Ahmed Abed and Luijiana Begum at their small house behind Abed Jewellers in the Old City.

The mutton biryani is so delectable Fatima Begum eats twice as much as she should. She goes out for a walk to help digestion and ambles towards the Jamma Masjid. The early evening light is kind on her face and the azan is rich in the air.

She is lost in a daydream, of celebration feasts and stories told, of Pakistan, when someone rushes past and pushes her to the ground. She grazes her knees-elbows-cheeks. Someone else runs past and kicks her. Someone stands on her. Her left shoulder is bruised and she has no idea what's going on, only that men-women-children are starting to run in both directions, they are screaming, and lying on the floor she is an easy target for their feet. She lifts both hands and covers her face. She balls herself up as tightly as she can, starts to pray.

She wonders if this is the end of all existence, asks Allah to save her from terror and keep her from harm. Her hands are bleeding.

A crowd squeezes round her. Black veils and niquabs billow on all sides, her lungs scream, and all she can smell is warm milk as vats are overturned and creamy rivulets gather into her curled feet. She has lost her chappals.

A neighbour spots her and runs across the street to pull her back up. He guides her to safety.

"Go home to your uncle," the neighbour says. "Walk as fast as you can, and once you are there, shut and lock the doors. Shut and lock the windows. Stay indoors."

"What's happened?" she says panting, her back and armpits drenched.

"Murder," the neighbour says, and runs off with a length of lead pipe tucked into his trousers.

Fatima Begum in her daze doesn't go back to her uncle's. Not straightaway. She follows the tide of hot bodies and is led to the steps of the Jamma Masjid. A huge crowd has gathered. There is shouting and there is blasphemy of the kind Fatima Begum did not even know could exist. Haram. To say that in the name of god. She elbows her way to the front of the crowd. She is sweating of course and flushed with fear but curiosity propels her to the front. For the love of Allah, what is it?

Her hands and nose are bleeding.

"What's happened?" she calls out to passers-by as they push and shove her. She holds her hand up to her nose, uses the edge of her hijab to stopper the red flow.

A devotee in front of her, robed and washed for the Friday namaz, trips up over the guts of an animal, not realising what has caught his foot, until there is a snub snout in his face, and by then it is too late. He screams in disgust. A pig. His bare feet dipped in pig blood walk red footprints up and down the steps.

Fatima Begum backs away at once. A dead pig on the steps of the Jamma Masjid will bring reprisals of a terrible sort.

"Where are your chappals?" Ali Ahmed Abed says softly when Fatima Begum is back. "Your poor feet."

"I lost them. I don't know how."

"Stay with us tonight?" Ali Ahmed Abed pleads after they have tended to her cuts and grazes.

Fatima Begum, in her shock, cannot speak but she nods that, yes, she will stay. In her sleepless fright, she eats all the biscuits in the house, brews several pots of chai, and uses up all the sugar.

The doors and windows of Abed Jewellers, Finest Purveyors of Silver-Gold-Gems are boarded tight and will stay boarded for months to come. The sign is removed from the door.

. . .

The next day, when Fatima Begum is back at Pushp Vihar—despite Ali Ahmed Abed's protestations that she should stay—she tells Ma and Bappu the details of what she saw. She shows them the bruises on her face and the scratches on her hands and feet.

Alma and Roop sit on the top steps and listen.

"We heard about the pig last night. It was a senseless, stupid, provocative act. We will look after you," says Bappu. "You are home now."

"No one will harm you whilst you are with us," says Ma. She puts her hand reassuringly on Fatima Begum's shoulder.

Ma and Cookie Auntie did not make it to the boy's house last night, though they stood on the corner of Nankhatai Gali for an age, holding hands and not knowing why the city was so quiet. There were no tongas anywhere, no drivers fool enough to take them across the Old City. Even before they gave up, before the news had spread, the curfew was announced by a man in a truck screaming through a faulty microphone.

· · ·

Alma and Roop sit on the bedroom floor by candlelight. They take it in turns to blow on each other's faces and fan cool air with an old school notebook.

"There's a dead pig," says Alma, "and a curfew. That's why Fatima Begum didn't come home last night. That's why she got beaten up."

"I thought she fell over?" says Roop.

"It's the same thing."

Roop thinks longingly of the mouse. They had cremated it in a secret ceremony, with a tiny jasmine garland and a pyre made from old matchboxes. "What does a dead pig smell like?" she asks.

"Rotten I bet, and covered in flies," says Alma.

"How many flies exactly?"

"Maybe a million? More."

"Does a dead pig smell like the white chickens?"

Alma nods. The white chickens live in cages on Butchers' Lane behind Chandni Chowk. The white chickens have to sit next to the carcasses of their killed cousins-siblings-friends and know they will be next. Chicken meat tastes of anxiety and those who eat it will always be anxious. That's what Dilchain-ji once said, and she would know. The butcher wears a blood-spattered apron and holds a cleaver in his hand. There is blood and feathers everywhere. Alma and Roop have seen it for themselves.

. . .

The next day at school, the ribbon-headed girls skip rope in the dusty playground and whisper about the dead pig. The how-now-brown-cow walks past in long-lashed innocence, with no inkling that she will be next.

By the time the girls have finished their ruminations, the now giant pig has several heads, multiple trotters, piglets strewn half born all across the steps of the Jamma Masjid.

"Baby pig foetuses," whispers Mary to the other Christian girls, "covered in pig jelly."

Mary will not talk to Alma or even look in her direction.

The man who did it has not been caught. It is rumoured he has gone into hiding in the jungles of Lanka, where he is plotting more heinous crimes, the Hindu girls say over egg sandwiches at lunch.

He eats insects and worms. He shimmies the palms, drinks fermented coconut water, and his eyes, like this—the Muslim girls demonstrate—are always crossed.

"He is neither Hindu nor Muslim nor Christian but a hybrid of all three," says Alma, who really should know better but is enjoying the tale. She dips a Marie biscuit into the milky afternoon tea and offers it to the how-now-brown-cow.

12

14 March 1947

THE LECTURE THEATRE is almost empty. Ma is not surprised. Since the pig was found—and a day later a cow slaughtered in reprisal—a new hush has taken over the city. There is an eeriness in the halls and classrooms and the canteen is closed. Ma walks past a group of male Brahmin students loitering and whispering. Among them is Ma's student Arun, who licks the corner of his wet mouth in a way that makes Ma feel nervous. Her palms are clammy, so she wipes them on her dupatta and walks past him quickly.

She is called into her superior's office at midday. She knocks and stands by the door until he is ready to admit her.

"Enter," he calls out.

He has kept her waiting on purpose, through spite, she can tell.

The superior of the Urdu Department is a small man with weasel eyes buried deep into his forehead. He coughs to clear the phlegm in his throat. His tiffin tin is empty. Streaks of oil and crumbs soil the napkin next to it. He spits red betel-nut juice into a filthy spittoon.

Ma shifts her weight from one leg to the other. There is a greasy fingerprint on the corner of his left spectacle lens. His office is bare. There is a desk, a chair, a stool, a pile of books, and a stack of papers. A framed script of Arabic calligraphy, a holy quote she cannot read, is pinned to the wall.

"Madam." The superior has a clipped voice. He doesn't offer her a seat, though there is an empty stool by his desk.

"Sir?" Ma is polite. Reserved. "You asked to see me?"

"Yes." He coughs again. Spits again. "It occurred to me, after this business of the pig . . . You have heard of the incident, to be sure?"

"Yes, sir," says Ma. The entire city has heard of the incident and is talking of nothing else but the incident.

"Then you will understand the wider implications?"

"Yes, sir."

"Then you will cooperate with my suggestion that you reconsider your place at this institution." He doesn't look at Ma when he speaks but fixates instead at a stain on the wall.

"As if I were the stain," she will later tell Cookie Auntie and Bappu.

Ma stares at him. He is an odious man. She has always thought so. She looks at the taqiyah on his head. At the delicate net that someone, perhaps his wife, or one of his daughters, spent hours weaving with wooden bobbins and a length of thread pinned to a cushion.

"I don't understand, sir, why the situation should affect my teaching?" says Ma.

"The university is a place of debate and learning, is it not?"

"I still don't understand?"

"As I'm sure you are aware, I have never thought it to be a place for women, but I have had to adapt my beliefs according to the times. That you were appointed was never my choice." The superior allows the words to settle. "You are lucky to have married into a distinguished family. Without the pulling of strings by your father-in-law, you would never have got a job at this institution. Not on your own merits."

"No, sir," says Ma, eyes burning, incredulous.

"Debate and learning are set to take on a new fractured note, reflective of the divisions forming in society. Political divisions that are beyond feminine intellect. Do you not wonder, madam," says the superior, "that you are going against god and all that is good by neglecting your family like this?"

He looks up to catch her eye for a second, and she knows then that he despises everything about her. He snorts with a self-satisfied sound, pleased to have finally said what he has wanted to say for so long.

Bad woman-bad wife-bad mother. Infidel. Kafir.

"Sir, with all due respect, there are no Urdu language teachers left. They have all gone. I am the only one in the department now. My students have their exams soon. Who will see them through?"

"Madam." He is cold. "It is a question not just of your inferior sex, but a religious one too. Urdu poetry should be taught by a Muslim teacher. Surely I don't have to explain this to you?" He looks at her face and then he looks at her shoulders and then at her breasts where he stops, her stomach, her thighs—he stops again—her legs. In between her legs. He stares until Ma crosses her hands in front of her chest. "You are dismissed," he says, with a wave of his hand. "Please leave my office at once."

Ma, not sure how to react, but sure that she does need to leave the small room at once, turns around. She walks clumsily to the door, her arms knock into her body.

"Madam," he waits until she has reached the door, and then calls her back. "Do not think, for a moment, that the nature of your relationship with Sahib Ali has gone unnoticed. Nor that we are unaware of the tutoring sessions that have extended to tea drinking and talking. Have you no shame?"

"Sir! I am the boys' tutor. Recommended to be so by this very university. How dare you question my position." Ma raises her voice, can feel her entire body shake with rage and humiliation. How dare he. How dare anyone.

The Supervisor stands up. "Lower your voice. What kind of woman are you? Where is your sense of propriety?"

Ma turns and stumbles out into the corridor.

She gathers her things as quickly as she can. She drops her papers, picks them up, shoves them into her bag. She drops the bag and needs to sit for a minute on the steps outside. She is dizzy, pulls her dupatta over her head; the cool cotton rests on her cheeks and hides her hair and face. Her legs are shaking, she is not sure she will be able to walk. A group of students pass by and she ducks her head into her lap.

This is what it feels like to be vulnerable. Her breath is rapid and short and her head so light she can hardly focus her eyes.

The boy Arun stops directly in front of her. She doesn't look up, wills him to move away but he doesn't move, he just stands there and stares at her until she shifts in discomfort. Designated spokesman for the rest, he sits next to her, closer than he should. He places a hand on her knee, moves it up an inch towards her thigh.

Ma flinches and slaps it away. She moves further along the steps and puts her bag between them. He doesn't care, moves closer. There are encouraging hoots from the watchful crowd. There are no women amongst them.

"Teacher-ji," he says, fixated on her face.

The boy is handsome and self-assured, well brought up and well mannered.

Ma knows his parents. Brahmin blue. Pious blue. His mother goes to the Lakshmanji Temple every day. His sister is in the same class as Alma.

"Why so far?" says Arun, mocking and cool. "We are friends, are we not?"

"Arun. What are you thinking? I am your teacher," says Ma. She speaks with as much composure and authority as she can, but her rose-dipped voice fails her.

Arun brings his hand closer: it could almost slip in between Ma's legs with inquisitive fingers. She slaps it away again, tries to stand up, but he reaches over with one hand, holds her tight with another, flicks with a casual movement the tip of her nipple through her kurta and dupatta. He laughs, and his friends laugh with him.

Ma pushes hard now, and he almost loses his balance. If he were to fall and crack his head and die, she would not care. Suddenly, she understands how violence begets violence and the horror of this, once gleaned, stuns her. She stands up quickly and straightens her kurta, grabs her bag, but he snatches her hand and pulls her in. He is rough and she stumbles.

"You may want to consider the company you keep, Teacher-ji," he says. He stands up now, they are at eye level and he lowers his voice, digs his hand into her arm.

Arun drops her hand, dusts himself off, motions to his friends that the amusement is over. "Nothing to see. A little skin-to-cloth contact is hardly a crime," he says. He swings his bag over his shoulder and saunters away.

. . .

"I've been suspended from the university," says Ma, markedly flat.

Cookie Auntie takes her hand at once. "Why?"

"What happened?" says Bappu.

"God, how awful," Cookie Auntie mutters, looking at Bappu. "How awful."

Ma nods, picks a blossom from the tree and crushes it between her fingers. She inhales the heady, broken softness.

Ma and Cookie Auntie are on the swing. Bappu is sitting on the stone floor at the low teak table in front of them. There is sweetened milk coffee in the pot. Three empty porcelain cups sit on three porcelain sau-cers. Ma can't take her eyes off the cerulean blue. There is an unforgiving sharpness to its hue she had not seen before. She wants to smash one of the cups, to fling it against the wall.

Bappu looks at her sympathetically. "Tanisi-ji, I'm so sorry," he says in a low voice. He is shocked, there is no doubt to it, and it is heartfelt, but what will he actually do? Ma watches him, curious.

"Were you threatened?" asks Cookie Auntie.

"I have been suspended because the superior believes my place is at home. He said as much when I was called into his office," says Ma, avoid-ing Cookie Auntie's penetrating glance.

"The superior of the Urdu department is a horrid weasel-eyed man," says Cookie Auntie. "He was an old acquaintance of Pa's. I never liked him."

"Half my students don't come to class anymore," says Bappu, rub-bing his eyes, his face. "Those that do are so frightened or unsettled by something they have read or heard, they are ready to fight at the slightest push. Everyone is confused. The superior is panicking. His po-sition as a Muslim teacher in a predominantly Hindu faculty is on edge. His own dismissal is inevitable. Someone is picking on him, and so he is picking on you, as the most vulnerable member of staff."

Ma stares. She should have known he would rationalise it, but part of her had hoped he would fight for her. She does not want calm reassur-ance. Not now.

"I'm sorry," he says again, failing again somehow. "Please tell me what I can do?"

Ma arranges the semblance of a smile on her face. She wants to say the ceiling is pressing down on her head. That she is scared. "He looked at me with such distaste. I don't think anyone has ever looked at me like that before," she says instead.

"It is a cowardly way to fight," says Cookie Auntie. She looks pointedly at Bappu. "And you. Is that all you can say? Make excuses when your wife is humilated?"

"What can I do? If teachers are not being dismissed, they are leaving. I sat in an almost empty canteen yesterday and ate lunch in silence. Dr Singh asked me to pass the pickle and that was it."

"What has that go to do with anything?" says Cookie Auntie.

"Only that eventually, once all this, this"—he motions helplessly with his hands—"is over with, after Independence," he looks at Ma, "you will get your job back. I know it. I promise."

"Oh, for god's sake," says Cookie Auntie.

"It is a whole year until Independence," says Ma, as evenly as she can.

"The superior is just one man and there are others above him," says Cookie Auntie. "We could file a written complaint?" She looks at Bappu. "You can do that much surely?"

"Of course," he says.

Ma holds her face in her hands and rubs her forehead. Something is irritating her beyond measure. Bappu's sympathy. She feels small and incapable. An errant child that can be petted and wheedled into favour.

Cookie Auntie takes Ma's plait and curls it round her hand like a rope. With her other hand she lights a cigarette, and this she balances between her lips.

"I stole this from Husband-ji," she says. "I don't usually smoke, but I'm feeling tense. He told me it would help, and then he gave me the whole damn packet. All he does, all day long, is lie across the swing and dangle his legs in the air. The man is idle, but I am grateful for this." She takes a long drag. "It's that bloody radio. Bhai, must it be on all the time?"

"I can't turn it off," says Bappu. "I'm sorry. I just can't not know."

"It's not healthy," says Cookie Auntie. She taps the ash off the cigarette and offers it to Ma.

Ma pulls hard on the cigarette. The smoke in her lungs and the lightness in her head are calming. She closes her eyes, savours the rush. "The superior demanded I stop teaching Sahib Ali's boys. The whole time I was in his office, it felt like he was punishing me for the incident with the pig. As though, being a Hindu, I was personally responsible for dumping the carcass at the Jamma Masjid."

"Do you know what I think?" says Cookie Auntie. She takes back the half-smoked cigarette and inhales. Coral lipstick smudges the filter. "I think a Muslim killed the pig. As a way of inciting further hatred."

"You don't really think that, do you?" says Ma.

"I do," she says. Cookie Auntie looks at them both and shrugs, hands the cigarette to Bappu.

"Everything is so strategic now," he agrees, smoking. "Anything is possible. Nothing a surprise."

"It doesn't seem right, the wedding," says Ma. "A celebration in the midst of all this."

"No, it doesn't, does it," says Cookie Auntie. "Whilst our fellow countrymen murder each other, we will wear our finest silks and feast on Dilchain's superior cooking."

"A telegram came from the in-laws this morning," says Ma. "At least."

"I read it. Their manners are appalling. Not a word of thanks for all the gifts we sent them. What does it even mean, they've been held up? With what?" Cookie Auntie pauses. "I'd like to make a suggestion?"

"Go on," says Ma taking the cigarette. She takes a long drag before stubbing it out.

"I don't think you should tutor Sahib Ali's boys anymore. After all that trouble with the pig, it's not wise to go into the Old City on your own." Cookie Auntie pushes her feet against the table and the swing moves slowly.

"But they depend on me. I can't not go," says Ma disconcerted. "I've made a commitment."

"Actually, Tanisi-ji, you *can* not go," says Cookie Auntie firmly. "You can send a note with a message that your eldest daughter is getting married. Sahib Ali is a family man. He will understand. There's still so much to do. Have a few weeks off. Wait for Alma to be married, and then decide? Your head will be clearer by then too."

"Is my head not clear?"

"No. You are upset by the dismissal. Understandably so. Bhai, what do you think?"

"You know I would never tell you what to do?" Bappu looks at Ma and reaches for her hand. She moves it out of his way.

"But now you will." Ma shakes her head, does not want anyone to touch her. What would he think of her—what would any decent person think of her—after the way the superior had spoken to her, looked at her? And then there was Arun, his hand across her clothing, fingers touching the tip of her nipple, on her legs, in between her legs, and all the time, on the surface of her skin, that hot flush of shame. That she is so quick to blame herself hits her hard, leaves her dizzy and reeling. She had not known this of herself, that she would react like this, until now.

She puts a foot on the floor to halt the swing and stands up. The air feels so thin. "If I have to stop teaching them, I will have to go in person. A telegram will not do."

"I will come with you," says Cookie Auntie. "I'll wait outside in the tonga until you are done."

"I'm tired," says Ma. "I want to go to bed."

"Have something to eat?" suggests Bappu, and he stands up to face her, to offer succour, his arm, and there is that familiar thing in his voice, a desperation to make amends.

"I'm not hungry. Things are always better in the morning. Aren't they? That's what they tell you. That's what you're supposed to believe," says Ma. She refuses his arm with a slight shake of her head and moves towards the stairs.

13

THERE IS A folded note addressed to Miss Tanisi on the table in the corridor where the letters are usually placed. Ma sees it when she comes down in the morning. It is still early and she cannot sleep. No address, just her name, slotted in under the heavy front door.

She leans against the wall to read it. Her legs give way and her back slides down, but the wall is there to hold her. It is a cool stone wall, painted saffron, the exact shade of the crocuses at the edge of Nigeen Lake.

Whore, says the note, among other things. *Veshya.*

She recognises the swoop of the cursive script across the page. She has marked papers written in this hand. Papers that were always a day late and later discussed for their merits. She was a generous marker, valuing passion as much as technical skill. She should have failed him.

She looks at the note carefully. "Whore," like "vulnerable," is an unfamiliar word. She supposes she is lucky. It is only a note. It could have been so much worse than pen on paper, than the flick of a nipple with a forefinger and thumb. It's humiliating, that's all.

This is what she tells herself, as she sits with her back to the wall.

She folds the note into small squares. With each fold, she presses the fresh pleat with her thumbnail, so the edge is sharp. She turns it clockwise, folding and pressing so that by the time she has finished, the note is a trim square in her hand. Almost, but not quite, negligible.

She looks at the square for a long time, is glad Brahma and the girls are asleep. That no one is there to see her read the note, or watch her slump against the crocus-yellow wall. Painted to remind her of the spring in Kashmir.

. . .

A few hours later, Daadee Ma, Alma, and Roop are at the Made-in-India teak table eating toast-butter-jam and drinking hot chai.

"It was your Mahatma Gandhi," says Daadee Ma. "He's the one that told them to do it. If you want to blame anyone, blame him." She takes dainty sips of tea and her small feet dangle off the chair.

Alma looks at her with irritation. She can feel her temper rising. Daadee Ma wouldn't dare talk like this if Bappu were in the room.

"Daadee Ma, those women jumped into the well of their own volition," she says heatedly. She uses "volition" because Bappu would say "volition," and to say what he would say brings him almost into the room. "It's not like Gandhi-ji pushed them in, is it?" She moves her toast-butter-jam to one side.

Ninety-three Sikh women from the village of Thoa Khalsa in the district of Rawalpindi, dead in a well. Their bodies piled one on top of the other. Some held suckling babies to their breasts. All but two suffered death-by-drowning. These brave women acted for the good of their community when their homes were raided by a Mussalman mob from the surrounding Pathan areas.

A moment of silence for their lost lives.

"Bravo," said the voice on All-India Radio, earlier that morning when the sixty seconds were up. Bravo.

It has a ring to it. Like a song you might sing to your children to scare them into going to bed. Ninety-three women jumped into a well, says Alma to herself over and over again.

"He didn't need to do the actual pushing," says Daadee Ma insistently. She drops another sugar cube into her tea. "It was his sneaky lawyer-way of talking. He's the one that said wives-sisters-daughters should always put their morality first. He said it, at his own prayer meeting. He said drink poison, or bite your own tongue if you have to. As you should."

"He did not say any of that," says Alma, suddenly confused in case Gandhi-ji did say something like that. Sometimes Gandhi-ji did say strange things.

"He did. He said suicide is preferable to loss of honour. Sati is saint-hood. All good ladies and girls should learn from the example of Sita," says Daadee Ma, looking pointedly at Alma. "Our godly Sita walked on hot hot coals when her chastity was questioned and after the soles of her feet were blistered, she exiled herself into the forest." She nibbles more toast, drinks more tea.

Alma kicks the table leg. "I don't want to be a good girl then," she mutters. Sita and Sati. Sati and Sita. "Daadee Ma, stop looking at me like that," she says crossly and turns her face.

"How did they all fit," asks Roop, wanting to picture them but not knowing how. "Was it a very big well?"

"It must have been," says Alma quietly.

"Families who martyr their girls keep their honour intact," says Daadee Ma. "Their communities celebrate them and the girls who die become godlings. If anything should happen you must do the same, otherwise you will bring shame to us all. Your husband's family would disown you, and we would certainly not take you back. Rat poison is best. There is always some in every kitchen."

"I will not," says Alma. "How dare you say that to me? I'm going to tell Bappu every word you've just said." She pushes her chair away from the table and stands up.

"Ha! What can he do? Soon you will be married and then your Bappu can't say anything at all."

"Daadee Ma! Just shut your mouth."

Roop stops chewing and listens. Dilchain, hearing the raised voices, comes and stands by the kitchen door.

"When you are married and forced into your wifely duties, then you'll see. Wifely duties are painful. Imagine that done by a meat-eater with dirty hands and a filthy so-so? You'll be grateful for the rat poison then. You'll be thanking me for it."

"What are wifely duties?" says Roop, looking from Daadee Ma to Alma.

Dilchain comes into the courtyard, throws a ladle on the floor, and bangs a tray on the teak table to signal her displeasure.

"You're talking nonsense. As usual." No one had warned Alma it would be painful and she is suddenly queasy all over. "This is why all your babies died," she says finally, staring back at Daadee Ma and refusing to look away. "As punishment for being so wicked."

Dilchain stands next to Alma and grips her hand in her own. "Alma," she says quietly. "Let's go upstairs and get ready for school."

"Pah. Call me what you like. I don't care. You have impure blood in you, and there is an evil eye above your head. Bad things would have happened if I hadn't spoken to Astrologer Uncle and if I hadn't thought to find you such a fine match. And this is how you thank me? Like a spoilt baby."

"What do you mean?" says Dilchain. "What did you say to Astrologer Uncle?"

Daadee Ma averts her eyes at once. "Nothing," she says defiantly.

"What?" says Alma.

"Everything I do, I do for the best. For our family name. Nasty un-grateful child."

. . .

Weeks later, a female cousin of Pandit Nehru will say the following, and it will be quoted in *The Times of India*, which Alma will read aloud at the breakfast table.

"It was eighteen days after the incident that we arrived at this sa-cred spot. The bodies of these beautiful women had become swollen and floated up to the surface of the water. Their colourful clothes and long black hair could be seen clearly. Two or three women still had the bodies of infants clinging to their breasts. We thought of it as our good fortune that we had been able to visit this site and worship these *satis*."

Sati and Sita. Sita and Sati. Alma will feel the morning's toast-butter-jam rise up her throat as she reads. It doesn't help matters that Pandit Nehru's pretty cousin will speak so elegantly and wear such a fine sari.

. . .

Ma gathers her legs into her chest, holds her bare feet in her hands. She can feel the tautness in her limbs, the dull ache of clenched muscle. She is on the swing and Cookie Auntie is next to her. Bappu is sitting on the stone floor and Alma beside him, her head on his lap, one leg dangling above the other.

The evening's news announcement is over and Alma is listening to the adults talk. She is hoping if she is quiet enough, intelligent and mea-sured enough, she will not be sent to bed. Cookie Auntie flings Bappu a cushion and she tosses it so irritably it almost hits him on the face. Her bangles chime noisily up and down her arms. She swears under her breath. A lot.

Dilchain-ji comes in with a tray of coffee. Bappu pours it and they drink it in silence. Even Alma is allowed coffee today.

"Don't you wonder," says Ma, breaking the silence, her voice so unforgiving that Alma flinches at the thought of what she might say, "because I wonder, I can't stop thinking about it in fact, whether those women, all ninety-three of them, walked up to that well and jumped into the water because they wanted to. They actually believed death was the only option, that their babies too should die." She looks down at the stone floor as she speaks. "Is that not murder?" She wraps her arms around her shoulders and neck, shrinks back as if to disappear.

"Perhaps death was the only option," says Bappu carefully. "If they were going to be murdered by the mob anyway? I read that the decision to jump was made as much by the women elders as by the men. I'm sorry."

Cookie Auntie lights a cigarette and pulls hard. Her hands are trembling and there is no colour in her face, even her lips are drained of paint. "Honour," she says, then glances at Alma and stops. The sight of her niece, legs childishly in the air, feet kicking out; Cookie Auntie exhales sharply: that she should have to hear this. "Purity. The family name. It all comes down to this, doesn't it? Our lives have no value. None. It is the great tragedy of our nation." She shakes her head morosely, smokes deeply. "I am so sad, Alma moon-of-my-heart, that you have had to learn this today. But perhaps you have always known it? If so, I am sad for that too."

Alma nods, can't quite bring herself to speak. She could almost weep at this ember of shared understanding. She looks at Ma, who nods.

Alma scans the shore for the so-fair-boy.

You wouldn't, would you, she wants to ask, *make me jump into a well? You wouldn't push me or try to convince me, because if you did try, and I believed you, what then?*

She shakes her head quickly to dislodge the thought.

"Those women are martyrs now. The village elders feel important," says Bappu.

"To hell with the elders," says Cookie Auntie. "God, I despise their sanctimonious ways. I've spent my whole life trying to get away from the village elders."

"People have lost everything. Their homes, their lives, their families," says Bappu.

"And?"

"People are furious," says Bappu. "I don't think we can overestimate the pain and rage. We can't imagine what it feels like to lose everything. When you have lost everything and you are grieving for it all, and there is no dignity left, you will seek solace however you can."

"Solace," says Ma, shaking her head in disgust.

"It is hell," says Cookie Auntie. "There is no rational explanation you can give me, Bhai, that I will accept."

She offers him a fresh cigarette when he asks, and lights it for him too.

"The last match," she says, striking it against the box. "Look at the propaganda, even on this stupid matchbox." She shows them the box before throwing it against the wall. On the box is a map of India with a cleaver through the top, where Benares is, and a single drop of blood in the South.

Alma listens and watches them smoke. She is confused and there is a topsy-turvy feeling in her stomach. She can't see the so-fair-boy on the shore, though she cranes her neck and looks for him everywhere.

I don't care, says Alma to the empty space, *if you are not there*. But she does care and her belly pines with longing.

Ma inhales the smoke deeply, holds it in her lungs, feels the sharp edges of the folded note scratching at her brain like a paper cut on the thumb, slight yet sharp. She should have thrown the note away. She doesn't know why she didn't. Or why, instead of throwing it away, she tucked it in amongst her silver-gold-gems as though it too were something semi-precious.

"So much grown-up talking today," says Cookie Auntie, looking at her niece.

"I understand most of it," says Alma, because she really does want to understand and to be allowed to sit with them. She gets up, lifts the porcelain cup to her lips, blows softly, the tepid liquid ripples like loose skin folding in on itself, a concertina of miniature waves. A milky Kashmiri lake in her cup. The coffee is at once sweet and bitter, bitter and sweet.

You can't back out now, she says to the mist on the shores of the Jamuna. *In a few days, I'll be your wife and you'll be my husband.* She thinks she sees his chocolate brown shoes on the shore. Neat laces undone.

14

16 March 1947

THE NEXT DAY, when Alma comes home from school—where the other girls talked of nothing but the drowning in Thoa Khalsa—she puts down her satchel and unbuckles her shoes.

Pushp Vihar is unusually quiet. Alma stands in the crocus-coloured hallway in white school uniform socks, a red apple clip in her hair, and listens. Something has come undone, but she is not sure what. She imagines it is some insignificant thing, a cat has slipped in through the back door and spilt the cream, but of course she knows she is wrong. The reek of star-shaped jasmine makes her feel light-headed. She walks up the stairs two by two, quickly. She stands outside Ma and Bappu's bedroom, rubs her head. The door is closed. She hesitates. She knocks and enters.

Ma and Cookie Auntie are sitting on the rosewood four-poster bed. Beneath them the night sky in the desert sparkles. They are passing a quarter bottle of whisky between them, taking small sips and sharing a cigarette. They don't even try to hide it anymore, as if cigarettes and whisky are now also normal and acceptable. They stop talking the second Alma walks in.

"What?" she says, suddenly self-conscious.

"Sit down," says Cookie Auntie, and she pats the bed.

"Sit down," says Ma.

"No," says Alma. "Just say it. I know already anyway."

"What do you think you know?" says Ma. She speaks in the same soft voice she would use when Alma was small and ill, and the sound of it now makes Alma bristle. A soft voice cannot compensate for what she knows will come.

"I'm not sure," says Alma, swaying slightly on the balls of her feet, so dizzy she has to clench her hands. She knows the so-fair-boy has left the shores of the Jamuna, but she doesn't want to say it out loud, because to say it out loud might bring it into actual existence, and to not say it might keep it where it is.

"Sit down. Next to me," says Cookie Auntie, gently demanding.

Alma perches uncomfortably on the edge of the bed. She takes off the red apple clip and holds it tightly in her hand. The hard plastic cuts into her palm.

Between them, they tell her the wedding has been called off. The so-fair-boy is going abroad to study in a school that is better than the schools in Delhi. Neither Cookie Auntie nor Ma mention the money wasted on mithai and flowers, nor the time spent on the trousseau. Nor do they mention that Alma's reputation is mud. Thick and dark and filthy. No one will marry her now. She crosses her arms and arranges her features to sit in the coldest way she knows how. She is tempted to hold her breath, just to see if her skin will turn blue. It would serve them both right if she fell off the bed and cracked her head.

"I have asked Ma and Bappu if you might come and stay with me in Bombay. After Independence Day next year," says Cookie Auntie, overly bright. "Would you like that?"

"Would I be allowed?" asks Alma, staring at them both. "Or are you making a promise you can't keep?"

"We can talk about that later. Closer to the time," says Ma evenly. "In a way, I am relieved. I wasn't quite ready to lose you to someone else's ma just yet."

"You can finish school. Go to university and when the time is right, together, we will find someone for you, or you might even find him yourself," says Cookie Auntie.

"Once the disappointment has worn off, you will forget all about him," adds Ma.

Chocolate-coloured shoes with laces. Fair of face. Soon to be a doctor. He had caught her eye, smiled at her. It wasn't much, but it was all Alma had. She will not let go of it.

"It won't affect your reputation. These are difficult times and the normal rules do not apply," says Cookie Auntie.

"Bappu will be so pleased not to lose you, though of course he will be disappointed for you too," says Ma, careful with her words. "England really is so far away, my love."

"And the food is terrible. So bland. How much better it will all seem in a year or two, when you're older? Three more years of being a young girl, and then you can get married. It's much more modern that way."

Alma looks at Ma. Perhaps she is being unfair, but she doesn't care. "Other girls' ma's would have double-checked all the details first," she points out savagely. She kicks the edge of the four-poster bed with her foot. "They would never have let this happen."

"Yes, you're probably right," says Ma, picking at a thread on the indigo bedspread and prising it out.

Alma stands up to face them both, shifting her weight to her hip. Her entire body trembles. "You were both against the wedding. You probably made this happen. What did you say, Ma? Were you rude to his parents?"

"Alma," begins Cookie Auntie. "Sit down, moon-of-my-heart, let's talk about this. I understand that you're angry. I would be furious, too."

"You don't actually understand anything. You are just as bad as her!" Alma raises her voice, thrusts an indignant finger in the air. "You think that just because you live in Bombay and have so much money, that you can lie to me in this way. You think that I am stupid, but I know the truth." She kicks the edge of the bed again and the force hurts her toes so she limps a little but refuses to sit down. Her eyes fill up and her nose runs. "You are never on my side," she almost shouts.

"What truth is that then?" says Cookie Auntie evenly. She grips Ma's hand and presses against her. "Please tell us."

"That no one will marry me now!"

"Alma, my love," says Ma. She stands and moves towards her daughter.

Alma puts out her hand. "I hate this, I hate this and you." She lifts the hem of her school skirt and uses it to wipe her eyes and to blow her nose. She sobs into it for a minute, wretched. "I just want to go to my room," she says. "I want to leave this house. I don't want to live here anymore."

"Oh my love, you will break my heart crying like that, talking like this," says Ma, and she moves forwards again, tries to hold her daughter.

"No," says Alma and shrugs her off. "I'm fine. I'm fine." She backs out of the room, unsure of where exactly to put her feet. She sways for a minute in the doorway. "Please, may I be excused," she finally says.

"Of course," says Ma. Her arms still held out, she lets them drop feebly to her side.

. . .

What Cookie Auntie and Ma don't mention, but which they will later discuss with Bappu behind closed doors, is the tampering with Alma's horoscope.

Alma, who knows they are talking about her, presses her ear to the door and listens to every word.

"How could you?" Cookie Auntie demands of her mother. "You should have known they would want to check the dates and times. It was a stupid thing to do."

"How did I know Astrologer Uncle would accept their baksheesh? Or that after all the gold coins I gave them, they would behave like this? Like commoners."

"Oh? So it's their fault?" asks Cookie Auntie. "For having the nerve to question your flagrant deceit?"

"I had no choice. Her real horoscope was terrible. No decent family would accept her with a horoscope like that."

That bad? How bad? Alma wants to see the real horoscope for herself.

"I did it for her own good," says Daadee Ma, folding her arms. "She is a bad stinking egg. Now, you just wait and see."

"How dare you say that," says Ma. She steps forward, almost as if to strike Daadee Ma, who shuffles back in fear.

"Don't you come near me," Daade Ma shrieks now, high pitched, and stamps her tiny feet. "Terrible things will happen now. Shame to the family name. Whatnots and so on. It's your fault," she says, giving Ma a dirty look. "All that sour-fruit-eating whilst you were pregnant. Bringing the evil eye into my home."

"My fault?" says Ma in a furiously cool voice, her body rigid. "That you are a meddling old witch, who cares more about the family name than you do about your own granddaughter?" She does not blink or look away. "To hell with the family name."

"I never wanted you in the first place," answers Daadee Ma, her feet firmly on the stone floor. "Dirty Pir Ali," she mutters. "Filthy mother's dog."

"It was never your choice," says Ma.

"Do you have any idea the damage that will be done by this?" says Cookie Auntie to her mother. "I'm just so glad Pa is not alive to witness this shame. He would be sickened."

"I am glad he is not here too," says Bappu, quietly shaking.

Daadee Ma comes forward, she stumbles and clutches her knees in a show of pain.

"Please don't speak to me," says Bappu. "I don't want to hear it. I am sorry," he says, turning to Ma, who is still rigid. "I am sorry that this has happened. That I was not more aware."

"Pah!" says Daadee Ma in a high pitched voice. "Pah!" She shoos them away with her hands held out in front of her. "You will see, that I am right. Go! You are all godless children. Leave me in peace to sit at my shrine. Do not forget that I am the elder of this house. Your pa left me in charge. I can throw you all out onto the street if I want to."

Under the tree, she mutters firm words to Bappu's pa's spirit. *This is your fault*, she says. *You allowed a Pir Ali into our household and then you died and left me to deal with it. I will never forgive you.*

. . .

Daadee Ma refuses to speak to anyone for days. She sits beneath the peepul tree and fasts until she falls over and then she lies in a ball on the floor, exhaling and inhaling with soft animal moans. She lifts her head a little, and every now and again, she looks around to make sure that someone is watching. Bappu gives in eventually and takes her a thimbleful of chai.

. . .

"Your mother is manipulating us all," says Ma boldly, first to Bappu and then to Cookie Auntie and then again when they are all in the same room together. "I've seen her fast and eat jaggery when she thinks we can't see. How dare she. Let her starve herself to death."

. . .

"It's my fault," says Bappu to his twin. "I should have checked the horoscopes. I should have checked everything."

"You should never have agreed to the match in the first place," she agrees. "And you should have listened to me when I asked you to question it. Bhai, you are an idiot. Can you even imagine how ashamed Alma must feel? She will take it to heart."

Bappu says nothing.

"She will think it is her fault," says Cookie Auntie, pushing him.

"I feel a bit sick," he mumbles.

"You'll have to make it up to her. You are to blame for this. Letting our deranged mother have her way all the time."

He looks up at his sister. "What should I do?"

"Alma can come and live with me in Bombay for a while, just until things calm down. She needs to get out of Delhi. I think it would be for the best. However much we play it down, incidents like this tend to stick."

"Will she be ruined, do you think?"

"Temporarily. Bombay will distract her. God knows I have plenty of room. There's a wonderful school nearby and you know I will take care of her. She is like my own."

"But how can I let her travel? It's too dangerous. Every other passenger train is ambushed and set alight."

"I will send a chaperone, of course, and even a policeman if need be. And we can wait until after Independence Day, when the country is tired of fighting. Who knows, Bhai, we may all be brothers and sisters yet."

"You will spoil her."

"Bhai, you are a fool if you think that. She is already spoilt. She can talk you into anything. I've seen her do it."

. . .

Alma sits on her bed in her favourite lemon-yellow dress. She refuses to come down or go to school. She knows everyone is talking about her.

"Give her a few days," advises Cookie Auntie, when Bappu and Ma exchange worried looks. "She's sulking. You can't blame her. Don't make her do anything she doesn't want to do. Take her good things to eat and plenty of sweet chai. Promise her a trip to Bombay. She will get over it."

After three days of sitting in her room, the boredom kicks in and Alma comes down and goes into the kitchen.

"Take this," says Dilchain-ji, passing her a ladle, "and stir. Don't take your eyes off it for a minute, if you do the milk will stick and burn."

"No one will marry me now," says Alma, feeling sorry for herself and for the silver shoes with the pearl buckles at the cobblers. They will be ready tomorrow.

"Sing to the milk." Dilchain-ji brings her head closer to the pan of boiling milk and hums a tune. "Go on. Try it."

Alma copies her. "What will it do?"

"Make the milk so sweet you will never taste anything so good."

They stir and hum together. Dilchain-ji sings a wistful melody and Alma imitates so that for a moment they are in harmony.

"You have a lovely voice," says Alma, pressing her body as close to Dilchain-ji's as she can, threading her loose arm into hers, feeling the warmth of her skin. "If I could sing like you."

"You are singing like me. Alma, shall I tell you a secret?" says Dilchain-ji, impulsively hugging her.

"If it will make me feel better?"

"The goddess of rain is your friend. She isn't everyone's friend, but I know she is yours."

"How do you know?"

"She told me."

"She speaks to you? The rain has never spoken to me before."

"She will. When you need her the most, she will come. The rain spoke to me, when my drunk husband tried to set me on fire."

"What did she say?"

"She asked the wind to blow the fire away from me and towards him."

"And did the wind do it?"

"That's why I'm still here."

"What else did she say?"

"That death is a whimsical thing."

"Yes. That's true," says Alma, humming and stirring, thinking about the ninety-three women dead in the well, and the distant cousin who had liked pineapple jam. "Death is a whimsical thing."

15

Late March–August 1947

"Will you wait for me?" asks Ma as the tonga comes to a halt outside Hafiz Manzil.

"Of course," Cookie Auntie nods as gently as she can. "Take your time."

They are both wearing dark hijabs, on Cookie Auntie's insistence, borrowed from Fatima Begum. It would have been foolish any other way. It was difficult finding a tonga to take them into the Old City. If it weren't for Fatima Begum asking Ali Ahmed Abed and him in turn bribing his nephew, they would have had to stay at home.

The streets are quiet. There is an eeriness as people go about their business, heads down, eyes drilling the pavement. The incident with the pig is still fresh.

Ma stands in front of the grand haveli. It looks more dilapidated now than she has ever seen it. There are marks on the walls as though someone has thrown mud at the stone and there are streaks of rust red, faded now, of blood or paan. There is no frayed rope anymore, so she balls her hand into a fist and pummels the door.

Shahnaz Begum's myopic eyes stare out of the peephole.

"Let me in," says Ma. "Please? I don't have a lesson planned for today, and I didn't send a telegram, but I have come to see the boys." When there is no answer, just the shutting of the peephole, Ma bangs on the door again. "Please? I have come to say goodbye."

The door opens slowly, as if the door too is afraid, and Ma walks in.

"My brother is not here," says Shahnaz Begum. It is the first time she has ever spoken to Ma. "You didn't come last time?"

"No," Ma replies. She takes off her shoes. "Assalaam o Alaikum," she says with a friendly smile. "Can I see the boys?"

Shahnaz Begum doesn't greet her back. "My brother is not here," she repeats.

Before Ma can answer, Husain runs up and Mohammed follows. They are quick and loud, excited by Ma's presence.

"Miss Tanisi. Miss Tanisi," they call out, each grabbing an arm, pulling Ma into the room where they normally have their lessons.

"You didn't come last time," Husain tells her sternly. "We waited."

"I'm sorry," says Ma. She sits at the cedar table, it is bare today, and the two boys sit with her. "I couldn't."

"But why?" asks Mohammed.

"Shall we have chai?" asks Husain, remembering his manners. "Baba is not here." He runs up to the door where Shahnaz Begum is loitering and pleads for chai and biscuits.

"Why didn't you come?" he asks, sitting cross-legged in front of Ma, his eyelashes flickering. "We have exams soon."

"My daughter, Alma, was getting married and before that . . ." She hesitates.

"The pig," says Husain. "It wouldn't have been safe."

"No."

"It's still not safe, is it?" he asks in a small voice.

The chai arrives in three glasses. There is no pot to refill and no bowl of extra sugar cubes on the table. There are however three malt biscuits laid out in a fan. One apiece. Shahnaz Begum gives them each a glass and positions herself at the back of the room. Ma has never minded her presence before, but today it makes her uneasy. There is a strange look in the woman's milky eyes. A hard look.

"Here," Ma breaks her biscuit in two. "Have mine as well," she says, giving one half to each boy.

"You're wearing a proper hijab today," says Husain. "I can't see any of your hair."

Ma touches the edges of the black cloth. "I'm glad to meet your approval."

They sit for a minute in silence. Ma blows on her tea.

"You can't teach us anymore, can you?" says Husain awkwardly, breaking the silence. "You are a woman and a Hindu. You're not allowed."

"My family don't think it's a good idea for me to come so far into a Muslim mohallah."

"Oh," says Husain. "I suppose you have to listen to them. If your husband said so, he would know best."

"I'm hoping that, once all this is over, we can start with our lessons again."

When Ma has drunk her tea, she stands up and proffers a hand to each boy in turn.

"We will go to Pakistan soon," says Husain.

"Really?" asks Ma. "I didn't think your pa would leave his home."

Husain considers it. "No," he concedes, "Baba doesn't really want to go. Delhi is Home, but Pakistan is the Land of the Pure. It has been promised to us by Allah. It is our duty to go."

"A dilemma?" suggests Ma.

"A dilemma," agrees Husain. "Miss Tanisi, before you leave?"

"Yes, Husain?"

"I remember what you said last year, about Tagore being inspired by nature. Tropical skies and the monsoon rain. The beauty of a coconut grove and the loneliness of the noon sun. I thought you were wrong. I thought there could be no great truth without Allah. I still believe that, but I think I have worked something out."

"What have you worked out?"

"That love is a kind of truth. Don't you think? Perhaps stronger even than the words of the Holy Book?"

Ma looks at him in pleasure. Yes, she nods. Yes. "You will make a fine imam one day."

"Khuda-hafiz, Miss Tanisi," he says. His bright eyes watch her leave.

. . .

Alma, at the teak breakfast table with a by-now cold glass of chai, stares at the black-and-white photograph on the front page of *The Times of India*. In it, the well-dressed figures of the new Lord and Lady Viceroy are stepping out of a Sunbeam-Talbot, their golden visages shining through despite the colour restriction, hands waving. On the one hand Alma is enamoured, on the other she is not impressed at all. The so-fair-boy comes to mind. He too was very good-looking, with the sort of sheen that hints at nobility, but now he was over the water claiming the better life that was his to take, leaving her in Delhi, stranded and bruised.

A truly noble soul would have seen the essence of her soul, and would have married her no matter the horoscope.

Alma wants to hold a grudge—she wills it with all her might—but she can't because she had never even known him in the first place. Instead, not knowing how to react, not having a marker by which to measure the required reaction, she decides to hold a grudge against herself.

What would those women have done? The ninety-three women dead in the well? She can't very well throw herself into a well now, can she, and nor does she want to. And then there are the two women who had survived. They had floated to the top with not enough water to fill up their lungs. Imagine that? She doesn't want to be them either. Half in and half out of the suicidal well, one lung full of water and the other full of air.

. . .

Bappu and Ma, and by extension Alma, already know something of the word "Partition," but then, one day in early June, it is confirmed. For a word to be confirmed on All-India Radio as the only feasible alternative to an already diabolical situation does not make it any less of a filthy word.

"What does it mean, exactly?" asks Roop, lying across the stone courtyard floor playing cards by herself.

"Par-ti-tion. To divide-separate-divvy up," says Alma. She has a bottle of lilac polish in her hands and is carefully painting each toenail. Now there is no school, and no real outings either, she paints her toes and fingers at least once a day.

"Independence is now on the fifteenth August, this year," she says. "That's a whole ten months earlier than planned. They just said it on the radio."

"Daadee Ma said there would be free sweets at Independence," says Roop, lying on her back cycling her legs as fast as she can until she collapses in a sweaty exhilarated heap.

"Shh," says Alma, reaching across to turn up the radio. "They're talking about it now."

"If Ma finds out, she'll send you upstairs."

"Shush, then." Alma listens carefully. "He said moth-eaten," she finally says.

"Who said it?"

"Jinnah. About Pakistan."

"What does it mean?"

"It means full of holes. Listen," and she strains but doesn't understand it herself. How can a country that doesn't even exist, not yet, how can it already be full of holes?

On All-India Radio, Pandit Nehru announces the proposal again, as he does every few hours, and will do so for days, with "no joy in my heart but clarity in my mind." Words that Alma will repeat for days, and Roop will pick up, and which eventually Ma and Bappu will hear like a refrain. Jinnah follows suit. His dissatisfaction seeps through. "Pakistan Zindabad," he says to bring false jubilation to the hearts of those who have listened and not understood. Lord Mountbatten ends the programme by maintaining, hand-on-heart, that his personal preference is for unity.

Alma draws her breath in disgust. This is an outright lie. What does he care, all medals and white-pressed Captain-of-the-Navy uniform, about India—her India? And then he says the "but," which Alma had known would come. She leans forward to catch every word, her hands sweating.

"But there can be no question of coercing any large areas in which one community has a majority to live against their will under a government in which another community has a majority. And the only alternative to coercion is Partition."

. . .

"The Viceroy might be charming but he is also naïve," mutters Ma quietly to Bappu later that evening. "How can he say people will stay where they are? If they stay where they are and if where they are is the wrong place to be, they will get killed."

"What does it mean, naïve?" Roop whispers to Alma.

"That he's basically stupid," says Alma, cupping her hand to her sister's ear.

They are sitting in the far corner of the courtyard, pushing the pieces of a jigsaw round and round, so the pushing itself has become the game and the puzzle forsaken. They are too hot to do anything else.

"The flow of migration has already begun," says Ma, sitting at the table, talking into her hand and pouring them each a cup of strong coffee. "Families have started to walk across the country in kafilas, carrying everything they can. All the trains are dangerously overflowing."

"What about their homes and their things?" mutters Alma, not daring to ask, her back turned to the table and to them. She will hear about it later from Dilchain-ji. The giving of keys to trusted neighbours, the burying of valuables in back gardens. Always that tragic hope of coming home.

"Will we have to go?" asks Roop, standing up, unable to keep it in any longer. "I don't want to leave," she adds, suddenly tearful.

"No," says Bappu firmly, looking at Ma, sighing, putting his paper down. "Shh now. Pushp Vihar is our home."

"Be quiet, be quiet," says Alma and bundles her sister away.

. . .

Bappu's words stick to Alma like glue on her fingers and she can't shake them off, much as she wants to, because she is still furious and though she might act like she's forgiven them all, she hasn't. Pushp Vihar is not her home. Not anymore. Not after she was so ready to leave. To be married. She can't very well stay here forever. An unwanted spinster. Spinster, she decides, is a horrible word.

Soon, now that Independence Day has come forward a whole year, she will go to Bombay and Bombay will be home. She overheard Bappu and Cookie Auntie discussing it after the un-marriage and she could tell Bappu felt guilty, as he should. Ma will not want her to go, of course, but Alma doesn't care. They have failed as parents and they know it.

. . .

The following morning, Bappu reads *The Times of India*, but he reads it quietly, half to himself and half to Alma, rather than aloud to Ma, which is his usual habit.

They are sitting on the swing rather than at the breakfast table because Ma has not come down for breakfast and it feels strange without her. In fact Ma does not come down that day at all.

"On eighth July 1947," he reads when prompted to do so by Alma, who pleads and promises not to tell Ma, "the large Sikh community of Western Punjab, proud of their fertile soils and deep rivers, put down their tools and padlocked the shutters of their businesses. They wore matching black armbands and gathered in Gudwaras to pray for the sustained unity of their kinship. They did not want their ancient homelands to be divided. They did not want Partition."

"The Sikhs have not forgotten the ninety-three women dead in a well," says Alma, when he has finished reading. Alma has not forgotten the ninety-three women either. She has started to give them names and faces, birthmarks and laughter lines.

"No," says Bappu. "They have not."

Ma sits on the Rabari bedspread, the starry desert sky beneath her, and reads *The Hindustan Times*. She has a fresh note in her pocket, and for the life of her she can't work out how and when these notes are delivered and how so strategically placed so that only she will find them. She wonders if he is outside and, if so, if he is watching the haveli? So far, she has received five notes. Five pieces of paper with the same message that she has folded and refolded and tucked into the drawer of her jewellery box.

There is a law—unwritten, unspoken—that Ma had not understood before. Women cannot confront their male persecutors. Neither can they look them in the eye or report them. If they are being persecuted, well then, they only have themselves to blame.

Ma, too, cannot stop thinking about the ninety-three women dead in the well.

. . .

"Absolutely not," says Ma, unwavering. She is sitting on the starry desert sky and Alma has come into the bedroom to sit with her.

"But you promised," says Alma. "I heard you."

"I only said what had to be said at the time because the news was so awful and because I thought Independence Day would come next year."

"You lied, then."

"Alma. You read the papers every day when you think we can't see. You've seen the pictures of the trains, full of refugees piled up on the roofs and coming out of the windows. You've heard stories of the trains that are stopped, every person inside shot. How can I let you go?"

"Cookie Auntie will pay for me to go first class. It's different in first class. There are private berths and it's civilised."

"Even Cookie Auntie was on a train that was held up for twelve hours on the way here, and again on the way back. Don't you remember?"

"So it took four days, but she got there in the end, didn't she?"

"No," Ma crosses her arms on her chest. "It doesn't matter what class you sit in, when a train is ambushed, everyone is game."

"Cookie Auntie said she would send a chaperone and meet me at the other end."

"I don't care."

"She said she would provide a police escort. I'm going to ask Bappu. Bappu will say yes."

"Bappu will not. He knows better than all of us how dangerous it is."

"Cookie Auntie will be so upset. Is that what you want? After everything she's done for us?"

"Your aunt is a sensible woman. She will get over it."

"Ma, you are being selfish! As usual you are only thinking about yourself!"

"No. Alma, no. You cannot go to Bombay. Don't ask me again."

"You are a terrible mother." Alma stands up from the bed and puts her hands on her waist. She is wearing a pink ruffled dress and matching socks. Fatima Begum has laced a red ribbon into her hair. "The worst. You pretend to be open-minded but you're actually just like the others. A hypocrite." She pronounces hypocrite very deliberately, having looked it up in Bappu's Dictionary earlier that day. Hyp-o-crite: a charlatan and a fraud. That is exactly what Ma is.

"Say as many nasty things as you want, but my answer will always be no. One day, when you are a ma, when you have a daughter, then you will know."

"I will be a much better ma than you have ever been," says Alma, turning her back haughtily and slamming the door for effect.

. . .

When Alma asks Bappu, he pales and sits down at once.

"I can't let you go," he says, flinching at the solemn, awful thing she is saying. "I can't let you go."

"But she's your twin. She's never had her own children, and you know how I love her so."

"It's not safe. What would I do if something, anything happened to you? How would I live with myself?"

"But Bappu." Alma stands in front of him, her finger pointing in the air, and she is so like Daadee Ma in this gesture, in her stance and grit, that Bappu almost smiles. "You agreed to the wedding and then you did nothing when you found out that Daadee Ma had fixed my horoscope."

"Oh. So you know about that?"

"Of course I know. I'm not stupid. How can you expect me to stay here, with her looking at me all the time, after she did a thing like that?"

"Oh." Bappu breathes into himself, into his hand and then into his elbow, which he brings up to his face. He is intensely nostalgic, locked as he is in this moment, for that time when Alma had just been born, when he had not yet failed her. He knows he will never inhabit that place again.

"If I stay here, no one will marry me. You know that everyone is already talking about me. Saying all sorts of terrible things. All those awful women at the Gymkhana. It makes me sick just to think of it. I want to go, Bappu. You're always talking about freedom and choice and yet you're so quick to take away mine."

"I can't."

"Fine. I will starve myself then. If Daadee Ma can get away with not eating until she faints, then so can I. If I become sick, it will be your fault."

. . .

"You can't let her go," says Ma to Bappu late at night, when neither of them can sleep and the sheets are damp with their own sour sweat.

"No," he agrees, "but I feel so guilty. She will despise me. She will despise the both of us if we keep her here. It will be calm after Independence Day. People will be too busy celebrating to think of how much they want to kill each other. It will be a good time to travel. The only time."

"No," says Ma, "it's just too dangerous."

"How can we say no to her? After what happened?"

"You'll have to take her then. If you're both set on it, then I can't think of any other solution."

"Really?"

"Yes," says Ma. "Go with her. Protect her. That's your job." She thinks of the notes. Neatly folded, sharp edges, one on top of the other.

. . .

"What are you saying?" says Daadee Ma, astonished, when Bappu tells her. "You, man of this house, standing where your pa would stand—god bless his soul that he will die a second time from shame—shirking your responsibilities, leaving us ladies, alone, to get murdered in our beds?"

"That's not exactly what I'm doing, is it? I'll be gone for a week."

"You might as well take the knife and slit my throat yourself." She stares at him.

"You are being unreasonable."

"Don't you read the papers? Don't you listen to the radio? Go then. Chutiya! Don't talk to me. I am disowning you. When you come back, I will be dead." Daadee Ma mutters under her breath, strikes her chest several times, and hits her own head until Bappu reaches over and takes her hand.

"Don't you dare touch me. Bad bad son." She picks up a lopped marigold head from a bowl, threads it on a garland with the others. "Your pa's favourite flowers were marigolds," she sobs in a forlorn voice just loud enough to be heard. "What kind of man leaves his family to be butchered by the wolves?"

. . .

Bappu passes the telephone to Alma, who is standing expectantly next to him. They are in the study and they are alone.

"Talk to her yourself," says Bappu. "It's your aunt."

"I know," says Alma. She holds the receiver close to her ear, cradles it against her face. She talks in a low, secretive voice. *Yes*, she says over and over again. *OK*, and then, *thank you. Thank you.* She passes the receiver back to Bappu, who rubs his eyes, exhausted. "You don't look well at all, Bappu," she says.

Bappu talks to Cookie Auntie in the same low and secretive voice that Alma had used, only that his aches with sorrow. He puts the phone back in its place. "I miss you already," he says.

· · ·

On 16 August, the day after Independence Day, Alma will catch a train to Bombay. Cookie Auntie will book her a first-class ticket on the 16745 Bombay Express leaving at 16:50 p.m. She will send a trustworthy chaperone to accompany them, and Bappu will go too.

"Thank you Bappu," says Alma quietly. "You will see that it's for the best." She imagines that although it will be hard to say goodbye, and Roop will hate it, once she is on that train moving forwards and not standing still, that everything will bloom. But of course it will not. She knows it even herself.

16

14 August 1947

THE WOODEN SHUTTERS in Pushp Vihar are closed. The poppy curtains are drawn. Even in the half-light, the sun banished, the air is still so warm, the dampness on the skin so sticky it itches.

Dilchain has managed to find a lump of ice, which she is jealously guarding in an earthenware urn. She breaks off small lumps with a mallet and holds one up to her cheeks. The rest she distributes among five tall glasses with a squeeze in each of lime and a sprinkle of sugar and salt. She slips a hand into the hollow of her armpit and brings the moisture to her nose. She sniffs and sticks out her tongue.

"I stink of overripe bananas," she tells the goddess Annapurna.

Dilchain is waiting for Varuna Bishti to deliver the water. She clicks her tongue and glances often at the door. He has never been late before.

The rains are overdue. The underground water tank will soon be empty. She has not told Bappu that the tank will soon be empty or that she has started to move certain items, a stool, a tin spoon, a metal plate and gas lamp into its damp confines. Her ma had always said that a good servant should be prepared for anything.

Tomorrow is Independence Day. A whole year earlier than planned. At midnight, India will be free.

The mood at Pushp Vihar is glum, but Dilchain is determined to bring some small joy to the day. She will make a biryani, use her grandmother's clay pot, leave the rice with cinnamon and cloves on hot coals overnight. An event is still an event, no matter the conditions that surround it.

She drums her fingers on the slate countertop, and jumps when there is a knock on the door. Varuna Bishti! She is so glad to see him—because anything could have happened—she pushes two cups of milk across the threshold and a small box of Kwality Biscuits. For your family, she tells him. Happy Independence Day to you all.

. . .

Bappu and Ma sit on the swing beneath the jasmine tree.

"If it doesn't rain soon the flowers will die," says Bappu, cleaning his glasses with the hem of his shirt. He puts *The Times of India* face down on the floor. "I can't bring myself to read it today."

"Nor I," says Ma, turning her head. Her hair is freshly washed and sits in tendrils on her shoulders. Her face is thinner than usual. She doesn't look well.

Ma has not gone to work since March. Since March she has sat at home like a dutiful wife and penned letters and telegrams to her uncle in Kashmir. Letters and telegrams that murmur discontent and that, because there is no post, have not arrived. *I want to come home*, she has written over and over again.

The day after tomorrow at 16:50 p.m, on the 16745 Bombay Express, Alma will leave Pushp Vihar and them.

"I'm not sure how we're supposed to celebrate," says Bappu, holding his face in his hands. His shoulders are slumped into his chest.

"Nor I," says Ma.

Bappu picks up a glass of water and drinks it. "The water is warm," he says, and folds his hands neatly on his knees, awkward with his own ineptitude.

"The air is warm," says Ma, restless and sharp. And suddenly she can't bear his proximity, can't bear her seat on the swing and the cushion with its pattern of feathers, its gaudy colours. She stands up with clumsy legs that buckle. She is trying not to shake and she's not sure if it's rage or fear.

There have been new notes pushed under the door, and Ma, recognising the script, is quick to pocket them at once. She reads each one when she is alone and then like the first, she folds and refolds the paper as tightly and as neatly as possible, drawing her thumbnail across the crease. She is curious to know how many variations on whore, in how many languages and dialects, there can be. She almost wishes she had done more than talk and drink tea so the notes and her shame would be justified, but then she is full of shame of a different kind, for even considering deceiving Brahma.

Lately, in the news, there have been rumours of a different kind. Gandhi-ji, unclothed, has started to sleep next to his young niece, also unclothed, every night as a measure of celibacy. The experiments are called Brahmacharya, and Gandhi-ji's intentions are pure. And it's not that Ma doesn't believe him, she does, but that doesn't stop her fury swelling. That he would do that, use his young niece in that way. She remembers the flick of Arun's finger on her nipple through her kurta. Her burning skin.

. . .

When Brahma saw Tanisi for the first time it was in the university canteen. He stared, and his twin, who was standing beside him, pinched his arm; when that didn't work, she used the back of her palm to slap the top of his forehead.

"Bhai! Don't stare like that," Lakshmi admonished him. She felt embarrassed for him and then for herself that he was her twin.

Brahma looked at his feet. His chappals were scuffed from the morning's walk through the dust. It was nearly May and there were signs that the Loo was coming in from the deserts of Rajputana.

He saw Tanisi in the canteen every day for a week and each day there was a bit more dust in the air but not enough to keep the students at home. He noticed she read a lot, that her gait was slow and dreamy. He noticed she wore plain khadi kurta and pyjamas in washed-out colours. The only jewellery she had on was a pair of ruby and pearl studs, shining pearlescent blood through her loose dark hair.

"Rubies and pearls help overcome sorrow," said Lakshmi. She remembered reading it to him when they were children, ill together and home from school. *The North Indian Compendium of Folktales*: "The Pomegranate Princess. Do you remember?"

Brahma nodded.

Tanisi had blue eyes. Pale blue, washed-out-blue, drowning-in-a-lake sort of eyes.

"You have death-by-drowning eyes," he would later tell her, and the expression would stick.

"That makes sense," she would say in return, "my ma and pa drowned in a lake."

"Bhai, you're really taking this too far," Lakshmi said. "Eyes are eyes." But she smiled that her twin was so-besotted. It suited him to be so-besotted, and once again she thanked her namesake, with a thousand thank-yous and a box of ladoos, that she was her own person and not like her twin at all.

He learnt that Tanisi was from Kashmir. She was in his Urdu poetry class. She was a brilliant student, so brilliant in fact that the teacher compared her to the Koh-i-Noor, the largest diamond in the world. The diamond, the teacher informed them, belonged to the Nizam of Hyderabad, the richest man in India, who used the gem as a paper-weight.

Brahma, who in his entire life had not felt jealous yet, felt jealous now.

"Jealousy," he said to his twin, "is a dark and enormous emotion. It takes over completely. I never want to feel that way again. There is no empathy in it. No reason or logic."

"Oh Bhai, you have a lot to learn."

"It still irks me that the teacher used a compliment like that when I would have liked to use it myself."

"Really? *That* is why you're jealous?" His twin looked at him as if he were an idiot.

"Her name is Tanisi," he said, foolish under scrutiny.

Tanisi for the Goddess Durga.

"She doesn't look like much of a warrior to me," said his twin, flicking the corner of his ear with her finger and thumb.

This was all the information he had managed to gather in a week. His twin teased him and in the end, because she loved him and because she just could not bear the bovine look in his eyes, she offered to introduce them.

Brahma looked at her in amazement. "Do you mean you know her?"

"Of course I know her. We have the same miniature drawing class. I like her very much."

"You have known her all this while, you have seen me pine and you have not said a word," he said.

"Well, these things are not to be taken lightly. What if she doesn't want to meet you? What if she's been engaged since birth to marry a distant cousin? You can't just go in there and demand her attention. Women have rights too, you know." She was stern when she spoke, as though she had given the matter a great deal of thought, which she had.

He looked at her in surprise. He had never heard his twin speak like this before.

"Close your mouth," she said. "You look like a fish."

He closed his mouth and glared at her. He wanted to hit her but knew she would hit him back—and harder. Once when they were children, squabbling over a square of milk cake, he had dared to kick her in the shin, grab the last piece, and stick out his tongue. She broke his nose with the tightness of her fist. She was sorry for it of course, and sacrificed all her sweets for a week, but by then it was too late. He had a bony bump on the bridge of his broken nose and one black eye.

"It's called feminism," Lakshmi explained to him. "It's from England. Someone gave me a pamphlet and really we are so backwards in this country. You should read it. Everyone should read it." She lowered her voice to a whisper and pulled her brother close. She spoke into his ear. "Women can feel desire in their bodies. Like men."

Brahma was shocked, but more than that—more than the initial shock that his sister should speak so plainly about a subject as taboo as desire—he felt a sense of elation. He felt heat. Women could feel desire in their bodies like men.

"Bhai, if you want to woo this girl, you'll need to read the pamphlet. She's read it already. All the girls in my class have."

Brahma read the pamphlet. He sat in the outdoor latrine and swatted at the flies that they should leave him in peace. He read every word slowly and then he read it again.

The next day, he approached Tanisi himself. He asked her her name, though he knew it already, and introduced himself. He asked what she was reading and she showed him the cover of her book. They discussed the poetry of Mirza Ghalib, and agreed that Dal Lake was the most beautiful place in the world. They had been to the lake as children, he on a family trip, and she when she had lived with her uncle in a houseboat on the water's edge.

Brahma hadn't really seen Dal Lake on a family trip, he had never even been to Kashmir, but he had researched it and he had seen a photograph that although sepia-coloured was suitably dreamy. Mirza Ghalib was his favourite poet, so that at least was true.

She told him she liked he was one of a pair. A twin. Her ma had been one of a pair too.

Brahma left it at that. The next time he saw her, he would kiss her. It would be a light kiss, a dusty, Loo-filled kiss. More a brush of skin on skin than an actual kiss, but it would be enough to charge everything that was otherwise ordinary with a new kind of grace.

. . .

Fatima Begum has asked if she may spend a few days with her uncle and Luijiana Begum. Independence is a time to be with your own and Ali Ahmed Abed has killed two goats. There will be a long metal table in the middle of the street and everyone will eat together. She doesn't want to eat in the back room on her own.

At ten minutes to midnight, Cookie Auntie is on the telephone from Bombay.

The lines are jammed. When she finally does get through, she is connected for seconds before the operator on the other line shouts "Pakistan Zindabad" over and over again. Another operator who has somehow connected himself to their call shouts "Jai Hind" in angry retaliation. Bappu hardly gets a word in before the line goes dead.

"At the stroke of midnight, when the world sleeps, India will awake to life and freedom," says Pandit Nehru on All-India Radio.

"This is not freedom," says Ma. "This, is a wooden loaf."

Alma shuffles closer to Dilchain-ji and takes her clammy hand in her own even clammier one. She is wary of Ma's storm-lit eyes, doesn't like the way Ma is talking. What does it even mean, a "wooden loaf"?

Daadee Ma lights a candle.

Roop, who has been pretending to be asleep, creeps down the stairs and listens. She is holding a squashed cricket in her hand. The cricket is as green as a stripe on the national flag. "Jai Hind," she whispers to the dead insect.

Five, four, three, two, one.

It is the stroke of midnight.

There are fireworks, guns, jubilant laughter and shouting. There are brass bells and conch shells, cymbals and wooden sticks banging on plates-walls-other people's front doors. The whole street comes to life in one fell movement of sound.

"Let's have a look," says Alma, tugging Dilchain-ji's hand. "From the roof?" Alma would like to go out and into the street. To get lost in the crowd and to be pulled from here to there, buoyed by pure exhilaration, but she knows it would be forbidden, this stepping out of the safety of the haveli, when joy could so easily cross into fury.

"Me too," shouts Roop, and runs downstairs quick and loud. She throws the squashed cricket up into the air. Jai Hind! "Let's go." She grabs her sister's hand and pulls her, two by two, back up the stairs leading up to the roof. "Hurry. I can hear fireworks."

"I want to see," says Dilchain and follows them. "Come," she says, holding out her hand to Bappu first and then to Ma.

From the roof, they see the surge of revellers like a river, like the Jamuna after a heavy monsoon. Bodies fill Nankhatai Gali and are carried forwards. Someone fires a gun into the sky. Someone else copies and so on until gunpowder lights the night. Fireworks explode. Paper effigies of King George VI and Churchill burn to ash in the air.

Alma stands and looks down at the street, breathless. Despite Bappu and Ma's reservation, she feels a flicker of anticipation for the shift to come. In two days, Alma will go to Bombay. In Bombay, there is no Jamuna flowing the wrong way. No empty footprints of the so-fair-boy on

the sandy shore. In Bombay there is an entire ocean swelling and expanding, roaring like a wild tiger, throwing its cool froth into her hot face.

"India is free!" She throws her arms up, pirouettes around herself,
lilac ruffles floating in the air, until she is dizzy and falls over in a fit of
soft giggles. India is free. We are free.

Roop, encouraged, does the same. She whoops and cartwheels and
somersaults until she too falls over and laughs hysterically. "India is
free!" she shouts into the night sky lit up with flame.

Dilchain watches them with pleasure, her dimples sinking into her
cheeks.

She would like to cartwheel and shout too. She presses her fingers
into the soft pads of her palms and clenches her body tight and close.
"We are free," she says in a whisper to herself alone.

"I have a surprise," she says, and runs down the stairs. She kisses
Daadee Ma who can't climb up for her knees, on both cheeks. "I have a
surprise for you too," she tells her, and comes out of the kitchen with a
dish of saffron jalebis. "Look," she says proudly, "like my ma would have
made. Two each and still warm."

"Dilchain-ji. You are a jewel," says Daadee Ma, biting into one and
beaming.

"But where did you find so much sugar?" says Roop, following Dilchain into the kitchen. She crams a jalebi whole into her mouth and almost chokes.

"I have it in a secret place," says Dilchain, pulling Roop's plait. "And
you will never find it."

When everyone else goes to bed, Bappu and Ma come into the courtyard and sit on the swing. Ma pushes her jalebi aside and wraps her
arms around herself. "Have I told you, I've seen some of my old students
parading round in the uniforms of the HRWP, and they look so proud.
These are the same boys who were running after a ball in the games
fields last year."

What Ma doesn't say is that her old student Arun, now a member of the HRWP, has taken to standing on the corner of Nankhatai Gali. He leans against the wall, smoking one imported cigarette after another and watching Pushp Vihar. Sometimes she will see him from the corner of her eye, and pull her dupatta over her face, walk quickly. More and more, she stays indoors.

"How will they do it?" says Bappu. "Cut a sacred river in half and cork the flow?"

"I don't know," says Ma, "how that man's conscience has allowed him to draw those lines. He has not once left Lutyens' Delhi."

"He has never leant out of a train," says Bappu. "He has not smelt our air. Half the country don't even know what's to come. They don't know that in a few days their homes will no longer be their homes. Where will they go?"

He is tense now and exhausted too. He takes off his glasses and holds them in his hand, blinks rapidly, adjusting to the blur. He remembers a train journey with his pa when he was a boy. The first time he had left the city. From Delhi to Madras. How he had leant out of the open door, wind striking his face and body, exhilarated by the speeding landscape of temple town and market. Sacred shrines and connecting rivers. Buffalo submerged in muddy waters and rows of dusty cornfields. Holy cows tethered. He had known then the value of his ancient homelands: that India was many complexities of tribe and dialect and ritual woven together, an inextricable fabric of pulsating life. How could anyone put borders on that?

17

"Do you know what happens when a tiger dies?" says Alma to Roop in a whisper.

They are in bed. There is no fan and the air is so thick the sheets stick to them in a tangled sweaty mess.

"No," says Roop. She sucks her thumb and turns her back. On reconsideration, she turns around, hits her sister in the face.

"Oww. I won't tell you if you're going to be like that," says Alma, shielding her face with her hand.

"Tell me or I'll hit you again," says Roop.

"No."

"Tell me, or I'll bite," she growls and bares her teeth.

"Dead tigers are full of jadoo. The fangs, claws, and whiskers are made into amulets to protect the wearer against death and disease. They sell the amulets at the hakims behind the Jamma Masjid."

"Fatima Begum will take me," says Roop, sucking her thumb.

"These are for you." Alma sits up and takes three coins out of a drawstring purse, which is on the top of her packed tin trunk. The tin trunk has been emptied of the extra winter bedding and filled with layers of folded Sunday dresses, socks, knickers, and cotton pyjamas. The silver wedding shoes with the pearl buckle, still unworn, are also in the trunk. Alma's collection of bangles and hair clips are slipped in among the layers. Her name and address, and that of her destination, are printed on a label attached to the front.

"There is enough money here to buy a tiger's claw amulet from the hakim who sits on the kerb outside Best Paper Products, next to Zakim the horologist, just behind the road to the left of the Jamma Masjid. Do you know which one I mean?"

Alma talks quickly without pause for breath and then she holds out the coins.

Roop nods. She takes the coins, clasps them so tightly, they are still in her damp fist in the morning. They are still there at midday and they will be there until the time when Dilchain gives Roop the assuaging bar of Cadbury's chocolate, the unwrapping of which will require both hands.

"Did you know that tiger fat can be rubbed all over the human body to help with aching joints and stiff legs?"

"I knew that one already," says Roop, unimpressed that her sister is leaving in the morning.

"If you eat a tiger's heart when it's still warm, it will give you the courage and strength of a warrior."

"Do Pathans eat tigers?"

"If they can get them. In Kashmir, there is a tiger that lives in the mountains. If you see him, and say 'Uncle-ji' and put out your hand, he will let you pet his head and he won't eat you. It's true."

"Uncle-ji?" says Roop. She turns around and looks at Alma with scorn. "I don't believe you. Any respectable tiger would want a better name than 'Uncle-ji.'" She kicks Alma's leg. "You are stupid and ugly! I don't care that you're going to live in Bombay, because I am going to Kashmir.

Ma will take me. We're going to live on a houseboat and you can't come."
She pinches her sister's arm as hard as she can.

. . .

Tomorrow, when Alma is on the train, sitting on the lower berth playing
cards with the chaperone, eating a cream horn—before the thing that
happens, happens—the pinch will bruise indigo sky and plum in perfect
Roop-size fingerprints.

. . .

Dilchain layers hot roti in cloth with pats of ghee, trapping the steam to
keep the bread warm. She ladles dal in the first compartment of the steel
tiffin; she used to fill it for Sunday picnics and outings. Where would
they even go for a picnic or an outing now?

In the second compartment she ladles green sabzi. In the last, rice
cooked with ghee-fried jeera to mark that, although sad, the occasion is a
good one too. Forwards motion is always heartening. She snaps the com-
partments shut and wraps the rest of the saffron jalebis in yesterday's
newspaper, all jubilant headlines and flags.

She packs it all carefully in a small cloth bag, adds a newspaper twist
of pickle, two oranges, water, and a bar of Cadbury's chocolate. She packs
enough for Alma and for the chaperone. The bar of Cadbury's chocolate
is a present from Ma, bought on the black market for a very high price.

"How much?" Dilchain had exclaimed when Ma had given her the
two bars, with instructions to keep them cool.

Ma had looked sheepish, embarrassed even. "I thought it would be
a treat for her to find when she unpacked her lunch. And for Roop after
her sister has gone."

"It will melt," said Dilchain with a displeased frown. It would take more than a bar of imported Cadbury's to make up for the no wedding, but she took the chocolate anyway and put it next to the ice.

. . .

Alma stands by the front door in her best lemon-yellow dress. In her hair there is a red apple clip. On her arms, she wears glass bangles that chime up and down each time she moves. By Alma's feet is her tin trunk, and on top of the tin trunk is the cloth bag of lunch.

Roop is upstairs and refuses to come down. She has pushed the third long-legged bed to the door so that no one can come in. "Leave me in peace," she shouts when anyone knocks on the door. "Go away! Your ma is a dog and your pa is the son of an owl."

She holds the jar with the dead moth still trapped inside it, and inspects the insect's wings. Alma had said they were beautiful. Trans-lucent. Like fine paper held up to a flame. Roop unscrews the lid fiercely and empties the moth on the floor. It tumbles out soundlessly. Light. Like dust. She pokes it with her finger, pulls off a wing and then pulls the other.

She strikes a match on a box stolen from Dilchain-ji and sets fire to one wing first and then to the other. She burns the body next, riveted, watching closely all the while. A cremation for a pagan god or a djinn. When she has finished with the moth, she burns strands of her own hair and watches the satisfyingly quick crinkle.

. . .

Daadee Ma is at the Lakshmanji Temple. She is so pleased the evil eye is leaving with Alma that she has taken the deities a large vessel of milk and another of grain. Good riddance, she says, and prostrates herself to Shiva. Thank you, she murmurs as she kisses Shiva's stone feet.

. . .

Fatima Begum holds Alma as tightly as she can and kisses her eyelids, her forehead, cheeks, ears, the tip of her nose, and the rose of her mouth. "Oh my dear," she says. "Alma Azizaam. How I will miss you." She wipes her eyes with her hijab. "Telephone as soon as you arrive?"

Alma nods.

"Even before you take off your shoes? As soon as you walk through that door?"

"Yes," says Alma in a tiny voice.

"Let's shake hands?" suggests Dilchain, thrusting out her hand, though she has never actually shaken hands with anyone before. They shake, and the formality makes them giggle. "See? It will be OK."

Alma nods.

When Alma, Bappu, and Ma step outside, Nankhatai Gali is quiet. There is no one else on the street, not the dry-biscuit bakers, not even a chaiwallah. It is so serene, so still, they are momentarily baffled.

"Are you sure you want to go?" says Bappu. He knows that stillness this serene can only be a prerequisite to chaos.

"You can change your mind?" says Ma. She will not look at Bappu or speak to him. She is pale with seething anger ever since he wavered and decided not to go on the train, talked out of it by Daadee Ma.

"Oh no," says Alma, swallowing hard. "I definitely want to go. Cookie Auntie is sending a policeman with a rifle to stand guard. I will be perfectly safe."

"I suppose the city is sleeping off yesterday's festivities," says Bappu, picking up the tin trunk.

Ali Ahmed Abed has arranged for a cousin to collect them in his tonga. A fair and trustworthy man.

In the carriage, Alma focuses all her attention—because her eyes have started to sting, and she does not want to cry—on imagining Cookie

Auntie's cream bathroom with the rose-embossed tiles and the taps that run both hot and cold.

After two sleeps, she will be walking on Chowpatty Beach, wearing the silver buckle shoes, eating bel-puri from a paper cone, the sea will be on her face, and her lips will taste salty.

. . .

When they have left, Dilchain and Fatima Begum take the second bar of Cadbury's upstairs. They smell the singed hair and decide with an exchange of looks to say nothing. Plenty of time for reprimands yet.

"I have chocolate," says Dilchain. "Open the door or we'll eat it."

Roop opens the door by a fraction and looks at them suspiciously. She rubs her red eyes and holds out her hand.

. . .

The railway station is chaotic with the din of distressed chatter and the stench of ripe bodies. There is hardly any room to move. When a how-now-brown-cow ambles past, all-bone, Alma, despite her focus on the cream bathroom with the rose-embossed tiles, feels the morning's toast-butter-jam curdle and rise.

Sandwiched between an armpit and a sweat-drenched back, pressed so she almost can't breathe, and then stood on and pushed, she calls out to Bappu, who grabs her arm and pulls her to him.

She stands next to him, her hand in his hand, on platform five, outside the carriage where her allocated seat is marked with a bronze plaque, her name printed on the reservations chart, and suddenly she doesn't want to go.

It is so hot and the station fans are not working, even Bappu's immaculate creases are rumpled dark and his armpits sharp.

The chaperone, a small woman in a lime-green sari that clashes with Alma's lemon-yellow, is waiting inside the carriage. She has a kindly face and a brisk manner.

"Come on," she says to Alma. "Come and sit next to me. We can play cards. I have cream horns, made with fresh cream. There's a policeman too," she adds kindly to Bappu and Ma, "who will keep watch outside our door. So you see? We are perfectly safe. I myself would not have risked it otherwise."

"She said she would send one," says Bappu. "When I told her I might not come."

"Do you have children?" Ma asks the chaperone quietly.

"I have four naughty boys," she beams. "The policeman is very kindly and he has a gun," she says in a confidential whisper to Alma as she takes her hand.

"A gun," echoes Alma, but she is not convinced. The station is a horrible place and she thinks she might want to go home. Her breath comes quick and shallow. She clenches the chaperone's hand.

"It is safer in Bombay than it is here," says Bappu to Ma. "There is less fighting. Less chance of rioting."

Ma looks down at the ground when she speaks. The station floor is grimy with discarded food and wrappers. As though people were animals and not civilised at all. "It's not Bombay that worries me," she says. "It's the train journey to get there."

Ma doesn't know how to say goodbye. She bends down and kisses her eldest daughter's cheeks with awkward politeness-contrition-shame and then of course she can't let her go and Alma has to push her away or Alma too will not let go. Ma's cheeks burn as though someone has hit her across the face. "Alma, my love," she says. "I'm sorry."

"Bappu," says Alma on the other side of the carriage door, when she is inside and he and Ma are still on the platform. "Bappu," she says again, and this time she almost sobs. She sticks her hand out to touch his, which she does briefly before the train pulls away, and her heart sinks for a moment to join the toast-butter-jam in her stomach. "Bappu! I forgot to water the flowers," she calls out, panic in her voice. "I'm sorry. I'm so sorry." Her words are lost beneath the screech of wheels.

The chaperone starts to shuffle and deal a pack of cards with embellished good humour. She arranges the cream horns on a china plate. The policeman looks over and salutes them. The chaperone is wearing a silver cross. It flashes holy limbs and repentance around her neck.

. . .

That evening, Pushp Vihar is unbearably quiet.

Bappu lights a row of candles and places them at the foot of the peepul where he sits with his eyes closed. He recites the kirtans he had learnt as a boy and which, to his surprise, he has not forgotten.

Ma watches him. His pressed trousers and shirt are creased and sooty. There are wet patches of perspiration under his armpits. He has not changed his shirt for days and it should not matter that he has not changed his shirt for days, not now Alma has gone, but it is all Ma can see. She will not be able to sleep next to him tonight. She will not bear the smell of him.

To distract herself, she goes upstairs into the bedroom that was once Alma and Roop's but is now Roop's only, and plays a game of jumping jacks with her youngest daughter. Roop is withdrawn, her face puffy, mouth and hands sticky with chocolate and dust and dirt. The bedroom smells of burnt hair.

"Tell me a story," says Ma. "Do you know a good one?" She wants to ask if Alma has taught her one, but the name—Alma—gets stuck in her throat.

Roop tells her the story of the churel and the tiger who liked to be called Uncle-ji. She shares her contraband biscuits and makes them a den beneath the bed.

Ma realises with a pang that she has never played with her youngest before. That night she sleeps in Alma's bed, head to toe with Roop.

Part Two

18

BAPPU STANDS AT the Hotel Shilpa at the end of Nankhatai Gali, with the other men gathered around, anxious to hear some news of what's really going on. The Hotel Shilpa is not a real hotel at all. It is no more than a patch of ground, a battered tin can for a stove, and the chai-wallah, Harish-ji, sitting cross-legged on a tatty cushion.

That the tea is weak and costly is taken as a given. Harish-ji is sorry for the rising price, but what to do? The mingled anxiety of these men, Bappu's included, stinks of dirty old canvas shoes.

By midday on seventeenth August, the results of Sir Radcliffe's Border Commission are announced. The men at the Hotel Shilpa, Bappu included, huddle close and listen as the voice on All-India Radio cuts through any delusions.

Punjab has been severed in two. East will belong to Pakistan, west to India.

"There is always a price to pay for free food and mithai. Everyone knows that," says Harish-ji, pouring dishwater tea from kettle to cup. He is morose. "I have family in the west, you know. Cousins on both sides."

The men look at Bappu. "Teacher-ji? You are wise and learned. You know things. What should we do? What will happen next?"

Bappu adjusts his glasses nervously and shrugs his shoulders. If only he knew.

It doesn't take long. By midday, alongside the official borders there are other ones too. Man-made borders with heads-on-sticks, flags stretched from tree to tree, alleys topped and tailed by men holding guns.

By the evening, All-India Radio announces an absolute breakdown of law in Punjab. All municipal corporations have dissolved. The army, in the process of division, cannot be called out. The partisan police must be avoided at all costs. Common folk are advised not to leave their homes, to bolt their doors and pile what furniture they can in front of those doors. If they can stockpile food and water, they should do that too.

Bappu, who has been at the Hotel Shilpa all day, like a wayward child banished from home, comes back at once and because he stinks of anxiety, Dilchain tells him to padlock every door and shutter.

"Call Bombay first," she insists.

"Yes," he agrees. He picks up the telephone and dials but there is no answer. He dials again and the line is engaged.

"Try every hour?" Dilchain suggests. "Keep ringing until someone picks up."

Bappu nods gratefully.

She helps him weave thick metal chains, of which she has a bountiful supply, across all the locks. When Bappu admires her foresight, her dimples flare.

"I knew," she says. "It would be our turn soon."

Bappu locks the iris-embossed padlock in the inside latch of the heavy front door and it is the dense metal, cold in his hand, that makes him stop and remember. It will be like this from now on, he can tell. Memories of her will come unexpected from nowhere and floor him, they will flood him, render him useless and wrecked.

Alma, six years old, had knotted her fist tightly and showed it to Sister Ignatius as an example of the size of the padlock on the front of Pushp Vihar. It was a tip-top Class-A lock, she had said. No one could break it. Not even a djinn. The lock had a clever catch.

Bappu's pa had insisted there should be irises embossed above the keyhole. Embossed meant stamped. Just because a thing was practical didn't mean it should also be ugly. She had looked at Bappu for the answer and he had nodded that yes, it was true. Embossed did mean stamped.

Dilchain sees Bappu staring at the padlock in his hand and she touches his shoulder lightly. Yes, she says without speaking. *I know.*

"I don't know what to do?"

Dilchain is brisk. "We will only use the kitchen door. We will need to hide it. You can use this." She fetches a sack and gives it to Bappu. "You do it," she says.

She gives him instructions on securing the haveli, and her composure reassures Bappu at a time when he badly needs reassurance.

"We are lucky to have you," he says.

"It's nothing," she says, blushing. "Hide everything valuable."

When Bappu goes to his father's safe, hidden behind the bookcase in the study, he moves Volume Four of the *Encyclopaedia Britannica* and a slip of paper—"a list of items needed to capture a djinn"—falls out. His heart lurches. She will be in Bombay soon.

He looks at the map of India on the study wall, to work out the distance between them in inches. He remembers, with his finger on Delhi, that this map of India, sketched on parchment with a fine ink pen, framed behind glass, a map that once had belonged to his father, is no longer the map of India.

At the Hotel Shilpa, the men cluster around him. He can't bear it at home, with Alma not there and Ma locked in the bedroom.

"What's new, Teacher-ji," asks Harish-ji. "What did you read in the papers today?" He gives Bappu a beedi, which Bappu accepts gratefully. He lights it and smokes.

"It is a joke," says Bappu. "In the national library the books are being separated. For every three that India keeps, one is shipped to Pakistan."

"People are dying and they are squabbling over the books that most of us don't even know how to read," says Harish-ji, lighting his own beedi and spitting on the ground.

"The government clerics are drawing up lists. Twenty-four wicker chairs from the municipality of Eastern Delhi Post Office to be kept in Delhi, and two inferior chairs to be sent over there. Paper clips, pens, staplers, staples and so on to be divvied up according to the twenty per cent rule," says Bappu, keeping as much smoke in his lungs as he can, willing them to burst. "People are dying and the clerics are fighting over paper clips," he says, finally exhaling.

Alma will arrive soon. She will be tired from her journey but she will call straightaway and they will laugh about the clerics and the paper clips. She will be eating kulfi, chocolate of course, as much of it as she wants. It is safer in Bombay than in Delhi. He did the right thing.

He coughs a dry sound and Harish-ji passes him a dirty glass of water.

. . .

In the study, Bappu calls again. The lines are still jammed. He picks up the telephone and slams it down, hard, on the table. He is ashamed at once. If he breaks the telephone, she will not get through.

In the courtyard, the air is scorched. He sits on the stone floor and even the stones are warm. He reads *The Times of India*, though he can barely focus his eyes, he is so exhausted, loses whole sentences, reads the same passage over and over, and still he forgets. The day's headlines disgust him.

When Dilchain brings him chai, he grips her hand and shows her the paper. Wordlessly she shakes her head and backs out of the room.

In Amritsar a group of hijab-wearing women are stripped naked and paraded through the streets. Once they are humiliated in memory of the ninety-three women dead in the well, they are led into a circle of turban-wearing men. Lined-up. Gang-raped. Set-on-fire. It is hardest of all for the girl at the end. She is only ten. Her naked body shudders. She has to watch her mother-sister-cousin-friend, knowing she will be next.

Like the white chickens in the cages, Alma would have said. That little girl is the last chicken in the cage, she would have said.

Twelve women at the end of the line, the girl one of them, are rescued by another group of turban-wearing men and hidden for safety in the Golden Temple. The girl doesn't look up at the gold edifice in front of her. She is so stunned, it is only days later she realises, she will never see her mother-sister-cousin-friend again. Shocked, she will climb to the top of the safe house where she is hidden and she will walk straight out into the open sky, and it will feel like a relief and falling a beautiful thing.

. . .

Ma stays in the bedroom. She reads *The Hindustan Times* cover to cover, it is the same headline and it makes her retch. She picks the silver thread on the Rabari bedspread, prises it loose with her nail and pulls each star all the way out. The next day there is an illustration in every national paper of the new map of India and one too of the day-old state of Pakistan. The borders are black ink, they cut across the land, making free less free and more restricted than ever before.

"Degrees of freedom are now judged by the soil on which you were born," says Bappu to Dilchain when she brings him some tea.

He shows her the new map. "Look," he says and points, waits expectantly. He is almost like a child in his need and this startles her.

She glances at the map, at him too for a moment, unsure how to react. That he would speak to her of freedom when she will always be a servant does not upset her, but she does wonder. There is nowhere in the world she would rather be than in his kitchen, but if there was, how would she even know how to get there?

Bappu stares at the new maps for a long time. He tries to call his twin, to speak to Alma, who should have arrived by now, but there is no getting through. Since taking Alma to the railway station, Bappu has been sleeping on the swing. He has not changed his beige shirt or washed his face for four days.

Eventually, he pushes the bedroom door open and goes in, sits unwelcome on the edge of the bed. The silver thread of the night sky seen from the desert is unpicked, discarded on the diamond-tiled floor.

"Has she called?" says Ma. She picks at a thread with her nail and wrenches it loose.

Bappu shakes his head.

"Have you tried?"

"The lines are dead," he says.

No one but Bappu has left the house since Alma left. The taps are dry. The lights and fans are off. There is a power cut that will last for two weeks and then intermittently for a month. There is no telephone. No school. No work. No post. There is only a half-hearted signal on the radio.

. . .

"How do they know?" says Ma of the black crows, when she goes up to the roof to breathe. "How can they tell?"

The black crows hop from foot to foot and smirk. Cholera-typhus-smallpox, they caw and rub their wings at what's to come. They are like blots on the skyline. Blots with cunning beaks.

"Where are the blue-grey pigeons, the diamond-shaped kites? Where is the sound of the azan? I've not heard it in days."

"There is a curfew," says Bappu. "Every night from six p.m. until seven a.m."

"I have never known a summer to be so hatefully long," says Ma. "Did you call? Did you try again?"

"I called ten minutes ago," says Bappu. He counts twenty-four gunshots. "Those are fired by men who know what they are doing," he says.

"Twenty-four people are now dead," says Ma. She looks at Bappu intently, as though seeing him for the first time in days, weeks. "Please change your shirt," she says. "I can't bear the smell."

. . .

It's not in the papers, but the news travels along the hidden byways and narrow roads, until it reaches the Hotel Shilpa. The men gathered around the tin stove for the small comfort a hot drink can bring, hear it. Bappu hears it. A few are upset, but most don't really care. News like this is old and tired already.

Twenty-four gunshots lined up in a row.

Twenty-four circumcised boys cramming for exams at a school in Karol Bagh.

"That's what we heard then," Ma says to Bappu when he tells her, "the other day. Last week."

"Yesterday," Bappu replies. "We heard it yesterday."

"Only then? When did she go? Is she there yet? She must be there?" Ma looks at Bappu as though he has all the answers. "When will it rain?" she says, wiping her face and neck with a small cotton towel. "It's so hot."

"She has arrived, of course she has arrived, but the lines are still dead."

"It will rain soon and when it rains, the lines will be fixed and the fighting will have to stop, and then she will call?" says Ma.

19

19 August 1947

THERE ARE FOUR men outside. Wearing matching uniforms and black boots, pushing against the doors of Pushp Vihar. For a moment it seems as though the iris-embossed padlock is not clever enough to keep them out.

Dilchain is quick to drape the sack over the outside of the kitchen door, to push all the copper pots against it.

The family gather in the courtyard. Fatima Begum will not come out of her room.

"What do they want?" says Ma. "Why would they come here? How are they out past curfew? It's so late."

"To loot and ransack, as they do to every other house," says Bappu. He has seen their uniforms, their badges, the slick line that parts one side of the hair to the left. He knows they are soldiers. Not trained and appointed by the government soldiers, but make-believe soldiers who have joined the HRWP. He had run up to the roof and seen them when the banging started.

The soldiers blaspheme and bray like donkeys. They laugh and giggle amongst themselves. They are young men with high-pitched voices. At night, they will go home to their mas and drink warm masala milk before bed.

Fatima Begum is in her room and she can't stand up. She can barely hold a cup of water and she is so thirsty. She clutches her grandmother's kidskin Koran tightly. In her terror she is starving but there is nothing in her room to eat. Luscious curls have sprung loose from her hijab.

Ma knocks on her door. She pleads that Fatima Begum should come out. She is family and loved, they will not give her up. "I will die before I let them have you," she says.

Roop, who has followed Ma, pushes the door open and nestles into her ayah's body. She clings on tightly. "You know, don't you, I will fight anyone who comes near you?" She holds up two small but tight fists. "I will kill them!"

Dilchain suggests they should fence themselves in, push all heavy furniture to the doors in case the locks and chains don't hold.

"We will need to hide you," she says to Fatima Begum, who has come into the courtyard with Ma. "Just in case." Fatima Begum grips the Koran as if this alone can save her. "It's too dangerous for you to leave. You can go into the water tank. There's enough air for a few days and sometimes when it's safe, you can lift the latch. We will sit with you. There is food and water, a stool, a kerosene lamp, and I'll give you some matches."

"How will she stay in so much water?" says Bappu.

"The levels are low this year," says Dilchain. "Only her feet will get wet." She turns urgently to Fatima Begum. "I am worried they will come back," she says. "People talk. Let's go now."

Ma holds Fatima Begum's moist hand tightly. "I'll take you," she says. "I'll sit with you."

With the kicking of the doors, the jasmine dead in the heat, the twenty-four gunshots to the head, the folded notes, and Alma gone, Ma

gives Daadee Ma a hard look. "If you dare tell anyone she is there . . . ,"
she says.

"What will you do?" says Daadee Ma. "You are just as much an out-
sider as she is. When they come for her, they will take you too."

Daadee Ma sits on her charpoy and accepts the weak chai. "I have
never tasted anything so disgusting," she says, taking a sip and spitting
it back, but on second thought draining the cup all the same.

"That's because I spoil you," says Dilchain. "I have to ration every
grain now."

"Where are the jalebis?" demands Daadee Ma.

"We ate them on Independence Day," says Dilchain.

"Why didn't you think to save some?"

"I did. I gave them to Alma."

"You shouldn't have had a portion yourself, then. You're a servant.
You should have kept your portion for me."

"I did save my portion for you. You ate it yesterday and thanked me
for it."

"What's for dinner?"

"Dal and rice."

"No fresh vegetables? An old woman like me will die without fresh
milk and fresh vegetables."

"I saved you the last sweet orange."

"Ah! I knew you would have something for me. Surprise me with it
later when I'm really grumpy."

"That's why I saved it."

"You are a good girl. Now oil and plait my hair."

"I'll do it now. I'll fetch the comb."

"And then will you massage my knees?"

"Of course."

. . .

It has been a week now with no electricity, no running water, no telephone line. A sweet and foetid smell lingers in each room.

All bedding is moved into the courtyard. It feels safer that way. Dilchain brings her bedding into the courtyard too. She is shy at first, to sleep so close to the family, to Bappu, the smell of his anxiety so strong, so intimate and strange, but the kitchen in the dark is a place of unfamiliar new knocks and shudders.

"The house is grieving for her too," she says one evening to Daadee Ma as she massages Daadee Ma's head, twists the white hair into a bun. "More alive with ghosts than us who are still here. Do you feel it?"

"It's him," says Daadee Ma, short-tempered and rude. "Bappu's pa's spirit. He just won't go away."

. . .

Daadee Ma is on the charpoy with Roop. Bappu is reading *The Times of India*, but Roop can see he's only staring and not turning the pages at all.

"Bappu!" Roop calls out. "Bappu? Come over here."

He looks up from his paper but doesn't move.

Roop can't stop thinking about the mouse and the cremation, and the soul of the little creature. She looks for it all over the place, had even thought it might come back as an ant. There was an ant just yesterday, looking at her from the corner of its face. It made her feel peculiar so she stepped on it at once.

"Bappu," she starts again, feeling perplexed. If only Alma were here. Alma would tell her. "What does it mean to die? Where do you go?"

"To the gods," says Daadee Ma promptly. "I went there myself when Bappu's pa died and I saw him there."

"But how did you get there? You weren't dead?" asks Roop.

"Dr. Biswas gave me a too strong sedative. He was a junior then and not very good with his measurements."

"Because you were crying so much?" says Roop, sucking on her fingers.

"Nahi. Not even crying. Screaming and screaming to find a dead man in my bed."

In her drugged-out haze, Daadee Ma had met the gods. She had bathed with them, eaten at their table, and placed garlands around their necks. In return, the gods had blessed her with lifelong fortitude. Fortitude, the gods had said, seeing where the country was headed, was the best thing they could offer.

On the same journey she had met her husband, balanced on the threshold between worlds, one foot here and one foot over there. Don't cry, he had said. If you cry, your grief will catch my soul and I will be stuck. If this happens, I will never leave you alone. She agreed at once she would not cry. She did not want him to linger. Make sure Brahma waters the flowers, he had added. At least once a day.

"Did you cry, Bappu?"

Bappu nods and he comes and sits next to Roop. "We put Pa's body upstairs. In the room that's yours now."

"In my room?" says Roop impressed. "All mine? A dead body?"

Bappu nods. "We put three hundred and sixty ghee lamps around him, on the steps down to the courtyard and then to the peepul. Cookie Auntie helped me."

"That's so many," says Roop.

"That's how long it takes for a soul to reach the realm of Yama. It would not do for the soul to lose its way," adds Daadee Ma.

She had washed her husband's body, not once flinching at his ice-cold skin. She had laughed at his shrunken so-so, and had flicked it with her finger.

"It was his wish to be cremated in Benares," she says. "So we took him there. On the train."

In Benares, at the bottom of Dashashwamedh Ghat, Daadee Ma had tied one end of her dupatta to a metal pole and the other around her waist. She had lowered herself fully clothed into the Ganga, closed her eyes. The first light of the day was tender. She had cupped her hands, filled them with water, and spoken to the ancestors. She had done this seven times, until she had said her piece, and each time she had allowed the water to trickle out of her fingers back into the river. She had held her nose and dipped herself in. She had refused to cry.

"Pa was anointed with sandalwood oil, then wrapped in white muslin and a tinsel shroud," says Bappu. "Bearers carried him through the old lanes and towards the river."

"Did you watch?" Roop asks Daadee Ma. "When they put him on fire?"

"Haan. Of course. But from a distance. Ladies are not allowed near the cremation ground. We are too emotional. We might jump into the fire and die alongside our husbands," says Daadee Ma.

"What?" says Roop, aghast. "I would never do that."

"Sati is an enlightening act. Full of honour and sainthood."

Bappu rolls his eyes at Roop and she grins, but he still reaches over and touches his mother's shoulder. She looks up at him and nods.

Daadee Ma remembers the cremation exactly. She had had no desire to burn next to her husband, having just found her voice for the first time in twenty-seven years. When dappled kids had gambolled into the air by the burning body, hot tears had sprung to her eyes, out of the blue and unexpected. Brahma's pa had loved kid goats. "Chutiya," she had said to Lakshmi standing beside her. "Curses to the sky. I'm done for now. He will never leave me alone."

After the cremation, back at Pushp Vihar, she had gathered his clothing, his good shirts, the white lunghi with the gold border, the taupe pashmina. She had stuffed these into an empty tin can, doused them with kerosene, and lit a match. He would need these where he was going. They might even make up for her tears. She had broken every earthenware pot in the house. No one had dared contradict her. The copper vessels she had passed through a dung fire to purify. I am sorry I cried, she had said. It was not to keep you here. Do not linger. There are no pots for you to hide in. Go.

Afterwards, she had stretched out on the charpoy in the courtyard, closed her eyes. She would not climb the stairs to her old bedroom again.

"Did you shave your head, Daadee Ma," Roop asks curiously, "and wear white?"

"Of course," she says.

"And what about you, Bappu? What did you do?"

"I had to set my pa's soul free," he says, his hand still on his mother's shoulder.

"How?" asks Roop, sucking the inside of her elbow, eyes wide.

"I had to smash his skull in with a stick."

"Oh my god," says Roop, clenching her fists, sitting on them in horror and delight. "Can I do that when you die, Bappu? Please?"

. . .

In Benares, it was up to Brahma to set his father's body alight. Two wax-like feet stuck out of the bundle that was once a man. The skin blistered in welts, burnished like metal dissolving. It took three hours for the body to become the ash that Brahma would throw back into the river.

Watching his father burn, he felt he had grown the roots of a tree, that the ancient wisdom of the city was feeding into those roots and into him a replenishing sort of knowledge. There he was, balanced between one world that he knew so well, and another of which he knew nothing.

It was a chosen surrender to stand like that, on a precipice, in uncertainty and stillness.

When it came to it, he smashed his father's skull without hesitation, propelled by a force beyond sentimentality.

Like that, death made sense. It was even beautiful.

20

Bappu has brought the telephone down to the courtyard. He sits close to it and he watches it and finally it rings, the line miraculously, unexpectedly alive. He spills hot tea on his leg and burns his knee.

Ma catches her breath, bites her hand.

An operator on the other end announces a connecting call from Bombay. It will be Alma. Alma, in a Sunday dress with a red apple clip on the side of her head, fizzing with news and excitement.

Ma watches Bappu's face, his cheek pressed into the hard receiver, the growing confusion. She watches him struggle with unfamiliar emotions, and he struggles so hard his features distort and his face is no longer his face.

She can't stand it, this look on his face, so she turns her head, examines a point on the wall where an insect has been squashed into stone by a child's palm. Insect blood and a wing stain the clean surface. Roop, of course. She will be six soon. Ma can't even remember when.

She tries to remember the date of her youngest daughter's birthday.

She tries so hard she forgets to breathe, stumbles off the swing, hits the floor in shock. She closes her eyes. She has hit her forehead on the stone. Whatever has happened, let it not have happened, make it un-happen. Is that even possible? Can a thing unhappen if you will it enough?

Dilchain helps Ma sit against the wall and fetches a glass of water. She dribbles the water in sips through Ma's closed mouth. "Drink, it will help," she urges.

"Why does Bappu look so strange?" says Roop, busy with a jigsaw but now staring at Bappu and then at Ma. "Why did Ma fall?"

"Go to Fatima Begum," says Dilchain. "Quickly!"

"Is it my sister?" asks Roop in a whisper. "Is she dead?"

"God no!" says Dilchain, shooing her away. "Go on now. Take Fatima Begum some rice and dal from the kitchen. You know her plate and cup."

Roop nods and gets up, curious but easily distracted.

Dilchain sits next to Ma on the stone floor and takes her hand.

Finally, Bappu puts the telephone down. There is a heavy clunk as it slots back into place. There is silence for a second, painful and brittle.

"She has not arrived yet," says Bappu.

"But where is she then?" says Ma, a hand to her chest in panic. "I can't breathe, I can't breathe," she says to Dilchain, grabbing her arm.

"I'll help you." Dilchain, herself close to tears but pushing them away, breathes with her, a slow and steady inhale and exhale that Ma tries to resist but can't.

Neither Bappu nor Ma can say her name out loud.

"Lakshmi waited on the platform, just as she said she would, and when the train arrived, it had been gutted," says Bappu.

"What do you mean, 'gutted'?" says Ma.

"Others are also missing from the train."

"Missing how?" says Ma. "Missing where? How many others?" She clenches Dilchain's hand and looks at her. Tears stream down her face.

"What does he mean? What is he saying? I don't understand." And again she can't breathe and Dilchain helps her, a slow and measured in and out.

"Half were not there when the train pulled into Victoria Terminus. Their looted luggage was still in place, but the people themselves were not," says Bappu.

"And the chaperone? Where is she? And the policeman who was paid to stand guard?" asks Ma. "And the other half, where were they?"

"The chaperone is also missing, and the other half were on the train but dead. They had been killed."

"Killed?" says Ma, and then to herself, "killed?"

She stands abruptly, stumbles for a minute, unsteady on her feet. She lurches forwards and hits Bappu on the face, on the side of the head, on his arms and body. Her fists pummelling relentlessly, the blows falling harder and harder, until she is spent, her breathing ragged.

Bappu closes his eyes and covers his face with his hands, he lets her hit him, each fist a consolation of sorts.

Dilchain grabs Ma and pulls her away. She offers soft cooing noises and strokes Ma's face and hair.

"What half was she?" says Ma, finally looking up from Dilchain's tight embrace. "Missing or dead?" If she was dead, they could grieve her. If she was missing, they would be stuck. Ma is not sure which half is better or worse.

"The missing half," says Bappu.

. . .

Ma lies down on the night sky in the desert. She wants to sleep alone, not in the courtyard with the stink of ripe bodies and the languished jasmine. Methodically, she pulls at the silver thread until the stars unravel in her hand. She uses the tip of her thumbnail to press each small, embroidered mirror with just the right amount of pressure to make it break. When a mirror breaks, she moves onto the next. She cuts her fingers on the tiny glass shards and bleeding is a relief.

A circle of nomadic tribeswomen would have sat, each one across from the other, the bedspread stretched out between them. A grandmother, a mother, a daughter, each with a section of cloth on her knees, each with a hook and a length of cotton and the precision, the in and out of the stitch. The grandmother would have sung, the mother would have copied, the daughter would have learnt the song that she would sing to her granddaughter, while going in and out of a different cloth with a hook and a length of cotton.

It is offensive to Ma, the endless beauty of the cloth, when beauty should be ephemeral and the butterfly only live for a few days. It is offensive to her, this lineage of women, when her own has been severed, topped and tailed.

She gets off the four-poster bed and walks to the dressing table. She opens a drawer and takes out a pair of scissors. She is cool when she cuts the bedspread. Neatly at first, into almost identical squares—as though neatness might be the answer—and then randomly, hacking it completely. She throws the scraps on the diamond-tiled floor. She hopes it will help, this hacking of the night sky in the desert, but it doesn't. When the bedspread is strewn on the floor, she feels heartbreak of a separate kind, for the uncle who had commissioned it, for the marriage it had been given to celebrate, for the home she had left.

She tries to close her eyes, but steel on steel of train wheels screeching and blood-soaked patches that whorl like spilt ink hurt her head. They scuff at her throat and pull until she retches, heaving herself to exhaustion and finally to sleep. She sleeps for days. When she wakes, drenched in the sweat of dreaming, she demands a strong sedative and goes back to sleep. She refuses all food and water.

"How do you expect me to eat?" she says to Dilchain when there is a timid knock at the door, a tray of food pushed through. "How can you eat?" she says, closing her eyes. "Will it ever rain," she murmurs. "I have not known the air to burn like this."

Later, days-weeks-months later, she will walk through the haveli at night and find objects here and there. A stray ribbon, an odd sock, an old exercise book filled with sums, and where there are no objects where once those objects might have been, the space itself reminds Ma of her.

. . .

When Alma was a few weeks old, Cookie Auntie gave Ma a velvet drawstring bag. "Open it," she said. Inside the bag were a pair of tiny gold bangles.

Alma. Born 2 February 1932, was etched inside each one.

"They're lovely," said Ma. She put Alma on the bed, pushed the two bangles over her wriggling wrists.

"Gold circles are a charm, you know. These will hold the secrets to her dear little soul and protect her, should she need protecting."

"Not you as well?" Ma laughed. "And I thought you were modern? All these precautions against unknown evils, and she's barely a few weeks old."

Alma stared up at her aunt with heavily lamp-blacked eyes. "Our baby looks like a ghoul," said Ma.

"Ah, that would be my mother's influence?"

Ma nodded with grim amusement.

"Make sure you keep the bangles in Pa's safe," advised Cookie Auntie, "once she has outgrown them." She fished into her purse for coral lipstick and reapplied it flawlessly with no need for a mirror.

. . .

One night, perhaps in October, Ma remembers the tiny gold bangles inscribed with her daughter's name. She unlocks the safe and sticks her hands deep into the cavity, gropes until the tip of one finger touches the edge of cold metal. The flash of yellow is bright when she draws the bangles out and presses them to her mouth.

21

Roop liked it at first, the bedroom all hers, but now she can't sleep without holding the rosebud pillow and wearing a pair of her sister's socks. It's so hot and the socks have started to stink and stick to her toes.

Pushp Vihar is spookily quiet, full of ghosts and knocks, but she knows how to be brave.

"I am a Pathan warrior," she says to herself at least once a day.

When she goes to ask Dilchain-ji and there are no snacks—only a banana with spotted black skin—and when she searches the cupboards and Dilchain-ji slaps her and there is still nothing, she goes looking for Bappu and Ma. She rubs her tummy plaintively, licks her paws, and cleans her entire face. Her plaits have come loose and no one is bothering to brush and oil her hair. She takes off all her clothes, even her knickers, and waits for someone to notice, but no one does.

She supposes there are snacks in Bombay. Kulfi and samosa chaat and popadoms. As much as you can eat. Unless you are dead, she reasons, and then there is nothing to eat at all.

The door of the bedroom is closed but she opens it carefully, peers in. Bappu is asleep on the floor in yesterday's clothes and no pillow. Ma is curled up in the corner of the bed. The room smells of soured milk. Roop scrunches her nose.

She kneels down and prods Bappu. She does not prod Ma, who is mean for not sharing the bed.

"I'm starving and bored, there's nothing to eat," she whispers in Bappu's ear. She lies down next to him, gets as close as she can, wriggles her sticky hot arms around his neck. When he doesn't answer because he has finally fallen asleep, she decides to go and look for food on her own. On her way out, she spies the scissors and snatches them off the floor.

In her bedroom, she pulls on a pair of trousers: they had been Bappu's when he was a boy and she had found them in his cupboard; they are too big so she does them up with an old school ribbon. She cuts off her plaits with two deft swipes. Hair springs up in spikey tufts, so she licks and wets it into place. She empties her school satchel and straps it to her back. She stands in front of a mirror, observes herself quizzically, bows low with a delicious sense of her own drama.

"Rajavinder," she says to her reflection. "Very pleased to be making your ac-quain-tance, sir." If only her sister were here, she would applaud and shake Rajavinder's hand and call him a "jolly good fellow." She whispers, "Bad things are happening to girls, you know. A bad thing might have happened to my sister." She cups her hands around her mouth. "She might be dead," she says in confidence and then pinches herself hard. "No," she says sternly and because there is no one else to hit, she hits herself on the head.

There is a door inside a cupboard inside the kitchen that leads directly out into Nankhatai Gali. A secret door. A door you would not know was there unless someone showed you. She waits until Dilchain-ji has turned her back, steps out into the hot air. She stands for a moment, decides to go towards the Old City. Towards the hakim, who sits on the kerb outside Best Paper Products next to Zakim the horologist, just behind the road to the left of the Jamma Masjid. She thinks she remembers the way. That's where her sister had said she would find a tiger amulet. She holds her three coins tightly, hopes and wishes the bones of the dead pig are still on the steps, covered in flies and dry blood.

Nankhatai Gali doesn't smell of dry-biscuit baking today. The grey air stinks of metal and salt. There are black crows hopping up and down, and a feeling of urgency. Roop walks quickly, looking around her as she goes. She doesn't like the crows at all. They are hateful. She throws stones at them and they caw indignantly. When she aims and hits one on the head, she whoops in delight. Caw, caw, she screams and chases the rest away.

She sees a throng of ragged bodies, small children too, so she approaches them cautiously. They're on the corner of the street, they're not wearing any shoes and some of them have boxes on their heads, others are carrying pots and pans, so she follows at a distance to see what they will do. The ragged people look lost and she can't understand the language they speak, and they all speak at once, and they all smell so bad, so she slips away. She wonders if they're beggars. She's never seen so many beggars in one place before.

She looks for markers, a chaiwallah or a sweet shop, but the kerb is bare and the shop fronts smashed so badly she can't tell if she knows them or not. She doesn't really know the way to the Jamma Masjid after all. She searches next for a weapon and finds a length of lead piping, picks it up and slips it into her waistband. There, she is ready now. Looks everywhere for soldiers with guns.

"Excuse me, Uncle-ji," she says approaching an elderly man. "Have you seen my sister?" The man looks so hungry, has so many open sores on his face, that she takes a step back. "Sorry," she mumbles, but he grabs her arm and shakes it so violently she screams.

"What have you got to eat," he demands. "Where's your money? Fetch me some water."

She kicks him hard on the leg. "Son of an owl," she shouts. She kicks him again, brandishes the lead pipe until he lets her go. "I'll kill you if you touch me again! Your mother was a dog," she adds, and runs off as fast as she can. She stops at a safe distance, makes a great show of spitting and swaggering and then runs off again.

"Why are you wearing so many clothes?" she asks a lady with a spotty face, who looks like she might be kind to children. "Aren't you too hot? It's boiling out here and there's no water. That tap there. It's broken. What's wrong with your skin, Auntie?"

The lady with the spotty face looks at her with only one eye. There is a patch of puckered skin where the other eye should be and her lips are parched. Roop stares in horror. "The sun burnt me. You would wear all your clothes too if you had to carry your home on your back."

"Where's your family," demands Roop. "I'm a boy," she adds quickly. Just to be clear. "I have a weapon and I killed a mouse with my own hands."

"Vultures ate my family."

"How?"

"Pecked and pecked with their beaks."

"Where were you?"

"In the kafila."

"What were you doing there?"

"Walking and walking."

"They must have had sharp beaks," Roop says, impressed. "How big were they? Did they peck out your eye? Where are you going now? Do you know the way to the Jamma Masjid? Can I come with you?"

"Clear off, you little frog," says the woman, not so kind after all. "Or I will eat you. You look nice and fat and I'm starving. Come here."

Roop yelps and runs. She stops for breath when she is out of sight and pants heavily, sweating everywhere, even behind her ears. She has never met a real cannibal before.

She walks quickly, slapping the flies off her face. Makes a game of counting the dead things. Sees a cow on its back, legs in the air, a dog gnawing at it, a vulture stabbing and jabbing and pulling out a throbbing vein. A horse mangled under a broken tonga. A human head on a spike, bulging eyes and matted hair, and a pile of bodies squished and squashed together, and she's not even surprised or scared, she has heard about them so often on the radio. The dead. There are black crows everywhere, hopping and digging with their beaks. Peck peck hop hop flick flick. It's actually bad manners how greedy they are, so she gathers all the moisture in her mouth and spits it at them.

When she sees a woman selling vegetables in a cart, tucked into the far end of an alley and a queue of people in front, she decides that food is more important than a tiger amulet. If she buys food and gives it to Dilchain-ji and Dilchain-ji cooks a feast, then Bappu will wash and Ma will wake up. She suddenly remembers Dilchain-ji's Philosopher's Stone, which means they will never be as poor as these people on the streets or have to wear pyjamas under their clothes. She pats her tummy, grateful for the gold lining.

When she comes home, Dilchain-ji is waiting by the door, Roop's amputated hair in her hands. Bappu is standing next to her. Dilchain-ji grabs Roop's arm and slaps her hard on the cheek. She is pale with rage.

"Don't you ever go out without telling me again," she says. "I mean it. It was stupid and dangerous. We can't have you go missing too."

Bappu shakes her fiercely. "What on earth possessed you?" he says. "You stupid, stupid girl."

Bappu has never shouted at her before. Roop bites her bottom lip. "I met a real cannibal," she says. "A one-eyed one who wanted to eat me. And I saw a vulture. And dead people."

They both look at her without speaking.

"Everyone outside is a beggar now," she adds. "So many people just sitting in the middle of the street. You should see it, Bappu."

"Refugees," says Bappu quietly. He uses his dirty sleeve to mop his brow.

"The water tap was broken, everyone was thirsty," says Roop and then, "I found food!" She takes off her satchel and throws the contents on the floor. She lines her goods up in a row. "Wheat flour and rice, dal, three potatoes, tomatoes, and four onions. A cauliflower! And malt biscuits!" She looks at Bappu, explains: "Fatima Begum is in the water tank crying for baby Azizaam. Baby Azizaam has not had her malt biscuits crumbled in milk for over a week."

Bappu and Dilchain-ji look at her, not sure what to say.

"You didn't steal the food, did you?" says Bappu finally.

"No," Roop says, wounded. "I had three coins to pay for it. They were for a tiger's claw amulet, but I bought food instead. For all of us."

"Where did you get the coins from?" says Dilchain-ji.

"They were a goodbye present," she replies, looking at the floor.

"Oh," says Bappu softly. "Oh."

"You've cut off your hair," says Dilchain-ji. She reaches across and grabs Roop's head, pulls her close. "Look at this. You little brute. What have you done?"

"I counted twenty-four dead animals and people," says Roop. She struggles out of Dilchain-ji's embrace and touches the top of her shorn head, sheepishly proud.

. . .

After days of silence, the Emerson Radio starts up again. Dilchain, who is standing next to it, jumps when she hears the announcer's voice. She calls Bappu to come at once and listen.

There is a litany of names from A to Z of girls who are missing. Another of names from A to Z of girls who have been found, but dead. Another of those who have been found but over there, across the pen-and-paper border. The names are listed once at 8:00 a.m. and once more at 8:00 p.m. On the first day, Dilchain counts twelve Almas, none of whom have pale blue eyes. On the second day Bappu will count twelve, and on the third eighteen.

"You should call the station with her name and a description," suggests Dilchain to Bappu, and she touches the edge of his sleeve when she speaks.

He looks up, surprised, doesn't notice her hand; he adjusts his glasses nervously on the bridge of his nose. "I'm not sure about that," he mumbles. "These bulletins will breed more hate."

"But what if it helps find her? Someone might recognise her and call us. You need to be practical," she admonishes, blushing at her own tone, dimples flat and confused.

There are ads too in all the newspapers.

"Missing, beloved sister of Mr. Raju Jois, Traffic Inspector, Ferozepore City. Mole on her left cheek. Loves small animals. Ample financial reward promised for any information. Mr. Jois is staying at a hotel in Delhi near the Taj Co on Macleod Road."

The litany of names starts off as a five-minute bulletin. By the time it comes round to the first week of November, there will be fourteen hundred daily messages of girls lost and found, using up three hours of airtime.

22

BAPPU SITS UNDER the peepul tree and prays, his knees scraping the ground. He can't hold the sorrow on his own, the roar in his mind, the persistent skid of the train. Sorrow dims his eyesight and pierces his brain. Simple words confuse him. Left and right confuse him.

It's not long until Dilchain approaches Bappu midprayer. "Praying isn't enough," she says gently. "We're running out of dal and rice. There's nothing fresh left, no milk and only one tin of tea."

He opens his eyes and looks at her, dazed. Her dimples are deep and lovely and it almost makes him cry that loveliness this pure should still exist. He looks at her so long she takes a step back.

"What should I do?" he says, nudging the edge of her dupatta. "Tell me what to do?"

"You need to buy food," she stammers, takes the dupatta out of his grasp. "I'll make you a list. It's not safe for me to go."

"We need jaggery," says Roop, who has come into the courtyard.

"Candles," says Daadee Ma from the charpoy. "Cotton wicks and ghee."

"Can I come, Bappu?" says Roop. "I know where to go."

"She's a boy now," Daadee Ma calls out when Bappu is unsure. "She'll be fine. If anything, she will look after you."

"I'll get my satchel!" Roop turns around and runs up the stairs before Bappu can change his mind.

"Buy what you can carry," advises Dilchain. "There might be nothing left next week? Buy tins and dried goods. Fresh will spoil too quickly."

"I know how to do it, don't I, Dilchain-ji?" says Roop, who has returned. "I've been to the market and to Chandni Chowk." She stands with spit-licked hair, trousers that are too big, and the satchel on her back. Let's go. She jerks her head. "Follow me," she says.

"Come here," says Daadee Ma to Bappu. She gives him a small silver knife and when he refuses, insists. "Take it. Tie it to the inside of your belt and come closer." She smears a stripe of ash from the pot she keeps beneath her bed, across his forehead, taps a red tilak mark into the centre. "There will be no confusion now," she says, doing the same to Roop. "Stay out of the Muslim mohallahs. If you go near them, they will cut your throat."

When Bappu stumbles through the secret door in the kitchen cupboard, and out into the hot air, he is stunned. It is one thing to read about the slide of a nation into ruin, to hear it on the radio, at a distance. It is another thing altogether to step into the innards of its gut wound. He grasps Roop's hand tightly, so tightly she yelps and wriggles free. He stands stupefied, not sure where to go, until Roop pulls his hand and says, "Here, Bappu, let's go that way," and he lets himself be led.

Delhi is shattered. Unrecognisably so. Faceless human shapes lie twisted here and there. Flies hover like mist. Bappu blinks rapidly. The clogged gutters, the coal burning white light, the shredded noise, the stench of his own body, slick with sweat, his breath hard and shallow.

It has only been twelve days since Independence, ten since the map of Partition was made public. It has not taken long at all.

They stop at the end of Prince Albert Road, now Alipur Road. A cardboard sign in crude Hindi marks the change.

Roop points to a cordoned-off lane where people are clustered. "In there, Bappu. They're selling food in there." She takes his hand, leads him in.

There is a placard by the entrance that reads "Hindu" in large letters. He stops for a moment to look at it. Roop nudges him on. "They all say that now," she says. "Even the Muslim shops."

"How do you know?"

"I saw it when I came out and then I heard a man tell his neighbour. I'm always hearing things, Bappu."

It is dark in the lane. It smells of dank flesh and rotting fruit. Housewives and uncles jostle with sharp elbows and push. Someone steps on Bappu's foot. A sly hand reaches into his trouser pocket until Roop sees it and slaps it away.

"Come on, Bappu," she says. "You have to push too, or we'll never get in."

All the vendors shout at once.

"What do you want?"

"Potatoes-onions-cabbages."

"Ghee-jaggery-milk."

"Nestlé! Nestlé! Nestlé!"

"Chainspadlockskeyscutshoespolished."

"Give me the list," says Roop, when Bappu fumbles. She takes it out of his shirt pocket. She haggles for dry goods, potatoes, tomatoes, chillies, and onions. She shouts all the prices she has heard Dilchain-ji shout and throws back a mouldy potato in theatrical disgust.

Bappu watches in mute amazement as she fills the satchel.

"It's more expensive than before," she says, counting on her fingers, looking up in dismay. "Nearly twice as much." She passes the bag across once she's done.

"You have to carry it now, Bappu. Go on. Take it then. It's too heavy for me. I'm just a child."

When they are outside again and walking towards home, she asks, "We won't run out of money, will we, Bappu?" Her face all knitted and worried, her little legs tired. "I don't want to work as a beggar with no arms. You won't chop off my arms, will you, Bappu?"

. . .

Bappu starts to go out every day. Their neighbours have gone. The gates chained and padlocked. Every day, he walks the streets and a new fragment of broken city is exposed. The fragment is always ugly, but each revelation shreds the blow of the one before, until the horrific becomes commonplace.

Every day, his mother paints his face with the ash she keeps beneath the charpoy. All men are marking themselves now, their clothes, their faces, shaving their heads with just the shikka on display. He has not known Delhi like this before.

He looks for her everywhere.

. . .

Ma doesn't come down at all. She sleeps on, yesterday's perspiration yellowish on her cheeks. When she is awake, she picks at the scabs on her fingers, pulls her hair. She pulls hard, fearless in her strength, testing and gauging the pain. The wooden shutters have not been opened for days and the poppy curtains are drawn.

. . .

"Ten thousand Muslims have been killed in Delhi over the past few days," says Bappu to Dilchain when they are at the dining table together and the tea has grown cold.

"Ten thousand?" Her features crumple and in her shock she turns to face him. "Oh," she says, bringing her hand to her mouth. Oh. "We would know some of them, friends and shopkeepers. Poor Fatima Begum. You mustn't tell her."

"No," says Bappu. "I won't tell her."

"What else have you read?"

This is the first time Bappu and Dilchain have sat at the table alone since Dilchain was a child, and having a conversation of the sort he would normally have with Ma. She is watchful of his physical closeness, the very particular smell of his animal sorrow, wary too of the helplessness behind his words, fearful of herself, of her heart. She is powerless in the moment, can't bear to break the flow of his words, and so she sits on the edge of her chair and cringes at the awful solemn things he tells her.

"All Muslims on the streets are to be stabbed and gutted," he says. "Posters saying as much are plastered all over the walls. Quicker than they can be taken down."

Dilchain glances over at Daadee Ma, who is asleep on her charpoy. The sun is low, she will have to make dinner soon. "What will we do?" she asks him.

"I don't know." Bappu starts weeping and she is thrown. It is not her place to comfort him, but she is here and must. She touches his arm. "Shh," she says. "Shh. It's good to cry. I have heard," she begins, out of her depth. "I have heard that Pandit Nehru himself has helped a Muslim family and set them up in a tent in his garden. See? There is kindness. Still."

"She despises me," says Bappu, lifting his head.

The impropriety of his comment, of his asking her—who has been a servant all her life, a widow and childless—to understand him like this, with his mother asleep behind them and his child in her room, is itself a blow of sorts. Severe and beautiful. Dilchain has nothing to offer, can't bear the feeling of sinking. "I must make dinner," she says briskly, and stands up to leave.

· · ·

The next morning Bappu goes out again. Roads are closed off with sandbags and men and boys guard them with guns. He stops an old beggar on the street and asks him where he has come from, where is he going, what he has seen?

"Don't kill me," pleads the beggar, crying wretchedly. "I don't even believe in Allah. Curses on him. I spit on him."

"I'm not going to kill you," says Bappu.

The beggar man opens an eye, regards him with suspicion. "Promise on the life of your one-legged wife?"

"I promise," says Bappu. He presses some coins into the man's hand. "Have you seen a girl with blue eyes in a lemon-yellow dress?"

"I have come from the camp at Humayun's Tomb. Oh, there are lots of girls there. They are all in lemon-yellow. How will I know who you mean? You have no idea what it's like." He holds his head in his hands and cries. "It's such a terrible place. I waited till dark and ran away. There's another camp at Purana Qila full of Muslims rounded up for Pakistan." He bends down, indicates Bappu should do the same, looks to the left and right, whispers: "I don't believe they will take them to Pakistan. They are rounding them up to shoot them." He looks at Bappu, blows his nose on his torn sleeve. "They won't take our one-legged wife, so don't worry. It is disgusting at Humayun's Tomb. The fountains are so befouled with piss and shit that the soldiers have filled them with sand. It still stinks. They promise you food and water, but when you get there, they spit in your face. There was a Nawab, head to toe in Benares silk, crying to the sky that an aeroplane should come and take him across the border. Imagine that? They say I am touched in the head, but he thought an aeroplane would fall out of the sky and rescue him."

The beggar rubs his eyes feverishly. He draws Bappu closer, as though they are comrades in conspiracy, taps his long nose with a thin finger. "My cousin is a Mughal prince. You would not think it to look at me, but my family descend from royalty." He laughs hysterically, hiccups loudly. "My great grandfather was Bahadur Shah."

When Bappu wishes him well and turns to walk in the opposite direction, the beggar begins to wail. He shakes his fist at the sky and then at Bappu. "What will happen to my pension now? What country do I even belong to?"

. . .

Although he is nervous—it means crossing a border of sandbags and armed men—Bappu promises Fatima Begum that he will take some biscuits and milk to Azizaam's grave.

He sets out at dawn. It is surprisingly easy to get past. An old colleague, Mohammed Ghualam, the one-time professor of Botanical Studies, is manning the road that he needs to cross. He lets Bappu through at once with word that no one should harm him.

"I don't even want to be holding this gun," says Mohammed Ghualam, "but I have to. You have come here with good intentions. You are an honourable man. Others will come to kill us. You can see how it is."

"Will you get word to me if you see a girl in a lemon-yellow dress with pale blue eyes?"

"Your daughter? My sister is missing too."

"Do you know Ali Abed Ahmed? The jeweller. Can you take a message?"

"I know the old man. I will send word."

"Do you know Sahib Ali, the widower and cleric from Hafiz Manzil?"

"He has left. Gone to relatives in Hyderabad. He didn't want to go, but he had no choice. He was harassed. His house smashed and raided. He had a beautiful house and they stole everything. His eldest son, Husain, was murdered. They say he was mutilated beyond recognition and thrown to the dogs. He was a good boy."

"My wife was Husain's tutor. Her heart will break to hear this."

Mohammed Ghualam looks at Bappu in his khadi trousers and sweat-stained shirt, crumpled and greasy. "You should carry a weapon," he finally says. "For your own safety. Everyone does."

Bappu finds the graves of Fatima Begum's daughter and husband. Mohammed Ghualam goes with him and stands guard at the gate. The tombstones have been smashed and the surfaces covered in excrement. Bappu does his best to wash the stones with the water that, to his amazement, he finds in a small well in the centre of the graveyard. He drops the bucket attached to the string and draws fresh water. He washes his face and drinks from it. Tomorrow he will come back with Roop, and they will fill as many copper pots as they can carry.

As instructed by Fatima Begum, there being no milk or packets of malt biscuits to spare, he crumbles a dry rusk in a cup of water. In the absence of star-shaped jasmine, he dresses the graves with the coloured confetti that Roop has made by tearing up her school ribbons. He recites a short passage from the Koran that he had once learnt by heart for a school exam, and is glad to still remember it, the words exquisite to his ears.

It is peaceful in the small abandoned graveyard. He had not thought it could be peaceful anywhere anymore.

23

Early September 1947

ONE LATE AFTERNOON Bappu finds his twin waiting on the steps of Pushp Vihar, a dupatta across her face and her head in her lap. She is asleep and there is a suitcase next to her. He kneels down and shakes her awake.

"Bhai," she says, opening her eyes. "Thank god you're here. I've been shouting and banging on the door. No one will let me in. I tried to call, to let you know I was coming, but the lines were awful."

"The haveli is boarded up from the inside," says Bappu. "How did you get here? You're alone?"

"An old business associate with a car drove me. He had pressing business in Lutyens' Delhi, important documents in his briefcase, guards in jeeps on either side, so I knew I would be safe. Husband-ji has gone."

"Let's go inside," he says, taking her suitcase. "He's gone?"

"I'll explain later." She pauses. "Dare I ask, before we go inside, how you are?"

He shrugs.

"You look awful. Like you haven't washed or changed your clothes for days."

"I haven't."

"And Tanisi?"

"She won't leave the bedroom."

"I should never have talked you into it."

"No, and I should not have let you."

. . .

Cookie Auntie sits next to Ma on the rosewood four-poster bed.

Ma looks up when she comes in, gazes with childlike wonder. "You are here. I wasn't expecting you."

"The bedspread has gone."

"I tore it up. After you called. Couldn't bear how beautiful it was."

"I would have done the same."

"I have gone grey," says Ma. She lifts up the white streak by her left temple. "See? Grey."

"Let me fix your hair? You look a mess." Cookie Auntie doesn't wait for an answer. She walks across to the dressing table, picks up a bottle of hair oil, the hairbrush, and sits by Ma. "Sit in front of me." She reaches across, pushes open one of the shutters, sighs with relief when light topples in.

Ma is oddly obedient, as if all this while she has been awaiting instructions on what to do and how to behave.

"On the way here," says Cookie Auntie, taking Ma's hair, using her fingers to untangle it, wincing at the plucked patches and the rawness of her scalp, "we drove past a hamlet just outside Bombay. It was the strangest thing I have ever seen. A rag-bag collection of men, women, and children with elaborate sandal paste markings smeared on their faces. They had erected a tatty green, white, and orange flag on a stick and were jigging around it with a desperation that bordered on full-blown insanity. If you can imagine that?"

Ma is silent.

"They were singing to the glory of Hindustan and the little ones shouting 'Jai Hind' at the tops of their voices. They were clearly not Hindus at all. I'm guessing they had been forcibly converted and were trying to prove their loyalty." She brushes Ma's hair with deft strokes.

"Do I look awful?" says Ma, her head bending with the brush. "I feel awful."

Cookie Auntie divides Ma's hair into sections, weaves gently, pulling one strand into another. "You blame him, don't you?" she says as lightly as she can, and she continues to talk when Ma does not reply. "Please don't. We are all to blame. You know, I think of nothing else."

Ma's body spasms. "She will think," tears flood her eyes, "she will think . . . ," she says and covers her face.

"We should never have let her go."

Ma turns her head and burrows it in Cookie Auntie's chest. "I will die if she doesn't come home."

"She will, she will. I know it," says Cookie Auntie fiercely, holding her close.

.   .   .

"I waited for her on the platform. The chowkidar locked the gates on Malabar Hill and came with me so I wouldn't have to stand alone. When the train pulled up, the carriage doors were hanging on their hinges." Cookie Auntie doesn't say that blood was leaking from the steel crevices of the train, or that everyone who had been left on the train was dead. "The guards searched the carriages, emptied the luggage, counted the bodies, lined them up. I went to the morgue every day for three days. I looked at each one, and not one was hers."

"Her luggage?" says Ma, her voice thin.

"The empty case was there, the address label. That's all."

"Do you think she escaped?"

"Truthfully?"

Ma nods.

"No. The women. The girls . . ." Cookie Auntie pauses. "They were taken."

Neither of them says anything for a while.

"It's so hot. Will it ever rain," says Ma and starts to cry.

. . .

"Talk about greedy fingers," Cookie Auntie tells Bappu later with an incredulous but not unknowing turn of the head, her short hair impeccably set. "One fat digit in every dish he could stuff them in. He emptied the joint bank account. Left on a chartered plane. Bhai? Don't you dare say a word to our mother," she whispers after she has told him. "I'll have to think of an excuse."

"I'm not stupid," says Bappu, also whispering.

"I was never quite sure about him, you know," says Dilchain. She comes over with two glasses of nimbu pani, hands them one each. "Not very sweet but refreshing," she says of the drinks.

"Why not?" says Cookie Auntie. She finds the one ice cube in the glass and holds it between her cheeks.

"He always ate too much." Dilchain blushes an apology. "Independence has made me bold," she adds ruefully. "I'm saying things I wouldn't normally dare."

Later Cookie Auntie hands Bappu a sari so heavy, his eyes widen.

"From the day I married him, I started to bury jewels all over the place," she admits. "I just didn't trust him. I knew he was a Class-A haramzada, but I wanted the money and the house on Malabar Hill. The jewels are buried in Bombay, an entire Aladdin's Cave, but there is gold sewn into this sari: we can use it for food. I refuse to be poor. Now Bhai, come. Sit next to me."

She puts her hand in his, tells him how the train at Victoria Terminus was emptied of passengers, how she had gone to the morgue three times.

Dilchain comes in and sits on the floor by their feet. Daadee Ma listens from the charpoy.

Hot tears drench Bappu's face. Cookie Auntie takes off her dupatta and hands it to him, just as she would when they were children.

In the silent courtyard, the heart-shaped leaves on the peepul crackle. There is a strong scent of old tobacco and bay.

"I feel Pa is here," says Cookie Auntie, startled by the leaves. "It is the strangest thing, but I can almost smell him." She looks at Dilchain. "Can you? He seems to be right next to me."

"He is always here nowadays," says Dilchain. "I hear him in the walls."

"Bhai. Look at me." Cookie Auntie is stern. She holds her twin's wet face in her hands. "Girls have been abducted on both sides. It has turned into a game."

"Is that supposed to make me feel better?"

"Listen to me. New laws are being discussed right now, in Lutyens' Delhi and Karachi. Each nation must return the abducted women and girls of the other side. It is crucial they are returned safe and well. It will become a bargaining tool. I saw the documents myself on the drive here."

Bappu looks at her with despair. "It will take them months, even years, to pass legislation like that. They will not agree on anything. They will bicker and squabble, and she will be lost," his voice breaks.

Cookie Auntie looks intently at her twin. "Forced conversions and marriages will not be recognised by either state. Bhai, she will be back in the space of a year, if not before."

"And? If she's not been converted or married, if worse has happened, what then? What if we never find out?"

"Bhai, your daughter is much stronger, much fiercer than you realise," says Cookie Auntie, taking his hand, linking her fingers into his.

"You are always so assured. You always seem to know what to do. I am just terrified," says Bappu, rubbing his face as though to flay the skin.

"It's just bravado. I am as terrified as you."

. . .

"Don't read that, Bhai," says Cookie Auntie to Bappu when he tells her the story of the girl who fell in love with her assailant. She is sitting on the swing, embroidering a cotton kurta to keep her fingers busy. Her stiches are tiny and precise. "The *Organiser* is rubbish. Why do you even have a copy?"

"I found it on the street," Bappu admits.

In the provinces, small villages are set alight and looted and the injured young girls are collected and put to one side. If the injured girl is pretty, she is put in that section of the road under the prescribed—though not said aloud—label of "good stuff." If she is not pretty, she is no stuff at all, but similarly used amongst the lesser men who are grateful for what they can get. The "good stuff" is allocated amongst the army officers and police generals and passed from hand to hand.

"Must you, Bhai?" asks Cookie Auntie as Bappu reads aloud.

"But just listen to this bit," he says desperately, and carries on.

Once the girl has been well-used and because she is pretty, an officer with delusions of gallantry will offer his coat and she will thank this man, who in her eyes has saved her modesty. She will profess undying devotion to him; her family are dead, and her home cinders. She would marry him gladly, be his slave for life, all the while forgetting that he too had raped her before offering his coat.

He throws the magazine down.

"I told you not to read it," says Cookie Auntie.

Bappu cannot sit still. "I am so useless," he says, mumbling. "I do nothing. Am nothing."

"Bhai. Stop pacing. You're driving me mad. I can't bear it. Sit down."

He glares at her but does what he is told. On the floor, his knee shudders.

"Good." She picks up the cloth and tries to sew, gives up at once, her hands unsteady. "Look at my hands. This is your fault."

"If she is dead?" he says, the words like a noose. "Discarded on the side of the road?" He rubs his eyes.

"She is not," says Cookie Auntie firmly. "She is not." She sighs, takes her slipper off, and throws it at him. "Bhai, I will kill you myself if you don't keep still."

"I think I am going blind," he admits.

"You are not. Stop rubbing your eyes."

Dilchain comes into the courtyard and gives Bappu a poultice of astringent herbs. "Put this on your eye," she says. "It will help." She sits cross-legged on the stone floor. "You could go and help at the camps?" Her cheeks redden as she speaks. "Somewhere, she is in the care of people who may or may not be kind to her. If you can be kind to someone's daughter, someone will be kind to yours? That's what my ma would say."

"And your ma was certainly wise," says Cookie Auntie.

The poultice on Bappu's left eye is calming and he touches it gratefully. "You are a gem," he says.

"Keep it there," says Dilchain. "I will make you a new one each day. She will be home soon."

· · ·

"Who are you talking to, Daadee Ma?" says Roop, just woken and sleepily squinting.

Daadee Ma is sitting by her shrine. Her deities washed and fed. The early morning light falls through the open roof and the gods glow. She opens her eyes, looks at her granddaughter standing naked in front of her. "You look taller," she finally says. "Why don't you ever wear clothes?"

"I de-plore them. That means hate. You can't really pretend to be a tiger if you're wearing human clothes. Are you talking to yourself?"

"Bappu's pa's spirit," admits Daadee Ma.

"Where is he? Why can't I see him? Ask him to make it rain. Tell him we're dying it's so hot. What does he look like?"

"He's invisible."

"What does he say?"

"Too much. Always talking, always telling me what to do, but I won't listen to him anymore. I have my own ideas now. Come, help me stand up."

Roop takes Daadee Ma's hand and walks her to the charpoy. "Daadee Ma, when will my sister come home? Ask Bappu's pa's spirit to tell you. Djinns know about stuff like that."

"Do you know the legend of Putana the dayaan?" says Daadee Ma. She sits on the charpoy and her legs dangle off the edge. She calls out to Dilchain for chai, "as much sugar as possible. Don't be miserly," she adds.

"Tell me."

"Putana the dayaan is the daughter of Bali, king of the lower world. One day she finds baby Krishna sleeping unguarded in his crib. She picks him up and puts him to her nipple for feeding."

"Poisoned milk? She wants to kill him," says Roop promptly. "I know this one."

"Haan, and baby Krishna drinks every last drop of her shaitan's milk as if it were nectar."

"Does he die?"

"Don't be stupid, child," says Daadee Ma. "He sucks at her breast and drains her lifeblood. Even a single drop of her poisonous milk would have killed a mortal infant, post-haste, but not Lord Krishna."

"He kills her."

"The land of Braj was terrified by her crying. Such a painful death!"

"Serves her right."

"Acchaa. Exactly. Now imagine that Hindustan is Lord Krishna, the shaitans will try to poison us, pollute our bloodlines, but will we let them?"

Roop shakes her head vehemently and salutes her grandmother. "No! We will not."

"Good girl. What will we do?"

"We will kill them!"

. . .

Daadee Ma is trying to sleep, but she can't. It's too hot and the thin nightdress chafing on her skin. She is sure she will have a rash in the morning. She can hear muffled sobbing from the water tank below.

She hasn't stopped crying, says Bappu's pa's spirit.

What do I care about that fatty? It's her own fault. Bad karma for praying to Allah. Bad karma for eating meat. Bad karma for making too much fuss for only losing one baby. How many babies did I lose? When did I ever make so much fuss? Crying and crying all the time. Leave me in peace, she hisses. *Don't tell me what to do. Landu! Chutiya!*

She strings together a catalogue of curses and throws them at the wall.

. . .

When Daadee Ma was married at twelve years old, she had no idea that that very night—no one had thought to tell her, why would they, what was this even called?—her husband, a gentle man, but much larger than her in size, would heave himself upon her, squash her child's body beneath his larger one, and that that would be expected every night until there was a child.

He will rip me apart, she thought the first time, in real panic. He will come out of my throat, she thought the second. I will die from this, the third. It was a disgusting thing to happen. His so-so in her private place. She had no other word for it, and if her own ma and pa had had to do that for her to be born, then they too were disgusting and she despised them for it. She refused to see her parents again. She felt they had conspired against her for the whole twelve years of her life so far, with this humiliation their ultimate goal. She hated them. She prayed diligently to Shiva that they would die. When her father first keeled over and her mother second was knocked down, within days of each other, she took mithai to the temple and declared her undying devotion to the gods for hearing her prayers. I am your number one best servant, she said.

24

Early September 1947

To DAADEE MA, Cookie Auntie reveals sparse details: Husband-ji was away on a long European business trip. Later, when more questions were asked, she would place him on a plane home and the plane would crash and she would explain this unfortunate event to her mother, who had heard otherwise from the ladies at the Gymkhana, but let it be.

"I will not shave my head or wear white," she would say fiercely to Bappu once the imaginary plane had crashed. "Do you mind?"

"You know I don't."

"You know you're my guardian now, don't you?" she would say to Bappu, flicking his nose, amused.

. . .

"Bhai," she says now. It has been a week since her arrival, a week with no news of her niece. A long week of Ma locked in the bedroom. "Everything reminds me of her."

"I have not gone into her bedroom," admits Bappu. "Not since the day she left."

"Every time I sit at the table, I see her legs kicking the chair. I see her face in her hands, listening to everything in the way that she did. That red apple clip she wore. Oh Bhai, I just can't bear it anymore. Just sitting here. Doing nothing. I know people in high places who could help us. I will start making phone calls, writing letters. I'll go to the Missing Person's Bureau, place ads, every day until we hear something. Word travels. It can cross the borders we cannot."

Cookie Auntie sets out every day with a list of places to go, letters to write, and phone calls to make when the line is clear.

"You have to get up," she says to Ma, opening the wooden shutters wide. Hot light streams in. "You have to help me."

Ma's head is heavy. Her eyes ache in the brightness. She blinks rapidly and squints. "Have you heard from my uncle?" she says slowly. "Can you call him? I want to go home. It's so hot here in Delhi."

Cookie Auntie looks at her, in pure exasperation. "No. I will not call for you. You can't go back there. You can't leave Bhai to deal with this on his own." She puts out her hand, softens the stern expression. "Come on. Take my hand. I'll help you get dressed."

. . .

When Ma was a young girl, she lived with her rich uncle in a houseboat on the edge of Nigeen Lake in Srinagar. Her pa and ma had died when she was a baby and the rich uncle, for the love of his twin sister, had brought the baby home.

"But how did they die?" she had asked him when she was ten years old, had read about death in a book. A word so unreal, absolute, and conclusive that she couldn't in her child's mind imagine it happening at all. That one day, she too would just not be there. "Does it hurt when you die?"

"They were on a boat on the lake and they rowed this boat to the middle of it, and there was a storm and the rain pulled them in, with the boat, to the bottom of the lake."

"Which lake?"

"Dal Lake."

"Oh. I was there just yesterday with Mustapha and Abdul. Did they find the bodies?"

"They had to fish them out."

"With bait and hooks and a line? Did you see them?"

"Yes."

"Did they look beautiful, like mermen?"

"No. They had been eaten by the fish."

"Oh. You must have felt so sad?"

"I will always feel sad. Your mother was my twin, you know."

"What was she like?"

"Like you."

"What am I like?"

Her uncle looked at her wistfully but did not answer.

"Dead means never coming back, doesn't it?" she had asked.

"Hindus and Buddhists believe in rebirth."

"Do you?"

"No. I believe death is absolute. Irrevocable. The end."

"I do too then," she had said.

They had shaken hands on it. Serious and grave.

When her uncle went away, as he often did, she was left with the man-servant, Abdul, and the cook, Mustafa. Both men in their seventies and as in love with their ward as you would be with a favourite pet who should need for nothing. They prepared choice morsels for her to eat. Told her stories of their boyhood days in the mountains. Put warmed stones in her bed when it was cold, and attached a fan that could be pedalled by foot from as far away as two rooms when it grew too hot.

They brought her apricots in autumn, pomegranates in winter, cherries in spring, and mangoes in the summer.

She grew older and realised something vital was missing, but for the life of her, she just could not work out what that was. Perhaps it was a need to get married? To have children? For although secluded she knew instinctively that that was what would be required. She was lonely, but because she had always been lonely, she just assumed that loneliness was part of the deal. That all humans were lonely, apart from maybe Abdul and Mustafa, who had each other and played cards every night when they thought she was asleep.

She worked her way through her uncle's library. She made notes as she went in Urdu, Hindi, and English. She put her pen to poetry and was seduced by the melodies. She was sure of it. She was a poet.

One day, the rich uncle called the young niece into the study. After a trip to Delhi, he would often come home with a new couplet of verse or a painting, and he liked to ask for her thoughts. Encourage her opinions.

There was a fire in a cast-iron burner. Orange blossom oil lit here and there.

Miniatures in gilt frames depicted scenes from the courts of Akbar and Shah Jahan. Ladies with red-poppy mouths were draped on divans. Courtiers with swords half in and half out of their scabbards lounged with intent. Where there was an embossed gold detail along a border or on a courtier's sword, the detail shone in the half-light, for though it was midday, oil lamps flickered and the heavy wooden shutters were kept closed.

The niece could tell the courtiers were eager, that much was obvious, but she couldn't tell yet what they were eager for.

Her uncle's eyes were bronze and amber-flecked. His whiskers burnt orange. Like a fox, the niece decided, standing across from him. She had seen a picture of a fox in the *National Geographic*, and even in black and white there was something in the alert eyes, in the tremble she imagined of the animal's nose, that made her think at once of her uncle's unfettered nature.

The niece sat down, crossing her legs carefully as she had been shown to do.

"Ladies of good breeding," her uncle had once said, "must cross their legs or tuck them under if sitting on the floor and in the company of intelligent men."

There was a tilt of the chin to an angle, a lift of the nose, a looking down from beneath the lashes that worked in conjunction with the crossing of the legs, and if a glimpse of ankle could be thrown in, well then, the ghost of a grin settled on the corners of her uncle's mouth, "the world as you know it is yours." He had doffed her head as he spoke, his fox paw lingering for a second at her hair.

She sat opposite him now. There was a cedarwood bureau between them, covered with manuscripts tied up with string, a quill in a pot of ink, canvases waiting inspection, a magnifying glass. There was a brass jug of water, a sprig of mint floating on the surface like a lone lily.

"There is purpose and beauty in chaos," her uncle had told her once when she had tried to tidy his desk. "Just because you can't see it, doesn't mean it's not there."

When she had confessed that she thought she was lonely, but wasn't sure because she had never not been lonely, he told her there was creativity in isolation. "Make the most of it," he had advised. "When you leave here and are surrounded by people, by your husband, your children, your in-laws, you will pine for isolation."

"I will never leave here," she had replied with scorn. "I will never leave you. I will never get married."

Her uncle untied and rolled open a large piece of canvas. She helped him place four paperweights on each corner.

"What do you see?" he asked her. "Look carefully."

She looked at the canvas in front of her. The background was cerulean blue. The exact shade of her broken moods. In the centre there was a figure, a prince or a warrior. A Mughal. The attire, the red pantaloons, the white knee-length cloak, the smallish waist and the slight standing on one hip, the delicate wrists were those of a woman. A woman loading a musket.

She had not known that women could do that. She looked at her uncle with narrowed eyes. "Is this a trick?"

He laughed at her suspicion. "No, not a trick."

She shrugged her shoulders and waited for an answer.

"You can do better than that," he said, not one to give in.

"A person loading a musket with ammunition."

"What sort of person?"

"A royal person."

"Very good. Of what league?"

"A princely league?"

"Wrong. Try again."

"A prince dressed as a princess," she said boldly.

A smile moved across his mouth. "No. Who was married to Emperor Jahangir?"

"Empress Nur Jahan? A queen loading a musket?"

"A queen who came to the Mughal courts from Persia. A queen who was a great hunter. She shot several tigers."

"This is wonderful," said the niece beaming. Why should it not be that way?

Why should women not load muskets and hunt tigers?

"Isn't it?" agreed her uncle. "One day, many years from now, this painting will be looked at by scholars and they will see how advanced the Mughal courts were and how backwards we have become."

"How are we backwards?"

"Blind faith in too many gods. The persecuting of anyone who is different, of anyone we don't understand. The leaving of women at home."

"Why does it happen?"

"The only way the favoured can rule undisputed."

"Are you different? Am I?" She hoped desperately that they were.

"We both are."

"Who are the favoured then?"

"The upper-caste Brahmins. We are Brahmins too, but of the Pir Ali caste. We are not stuck in ancient religious lore."

The ten-year-old niece was disgusted by this information, this mismanagement of power. Who had given it to the upper-caste Brahmins anyway? They had written their own texts, they had taken it.

. . .

When she was taller-stickier-sixteen, she bloomed hot blood. She examined the miniatures in her uncle's study, the poppy mouths, the swords half in and half out, with fresh understanding.

She began, hesitant at first but curious, to push her face against the stone jalis that looked into her uncle's bedroom so she might watch him entertain his guests. There were always visitors to the houseboat after dark. She pressed her eyes to the stone lace, held her breath.

She heard faint animal grunts, saw a tangle of limbs. She was momentarily disgusted, not sure why she should be and then she was thrilled. She leaked into her undergarments so she started to go without, and then she leaked all over her bare legs. Each day she promised herself that today would be the last day, that tomorrow she would stop. Each day, the climax was more sour more sweet.

She wondered if she had fallen in love with her uncle. Was that even allowed?

With her face pressed to the jalis, she taught herself pleasure of the sort that made her knees buckle. She learnt to guide her fingers inside herself. To bring them up to her mouth, to pretend her mouth was his mouth. Her uncle's mouth. Desire floored her. Any more and she would ignite.

She looked in all the books in the study to find a name for what it was she was doing but there was none. She had never considered that language might fail her.

After the first time, when he called her into the study, she was sure she would blush warm crimson, stammer, give the game away. She was cold all over and her stomach lurched. But she didn't. She was beautifully composed. The oil lamps flickered. They discussed the traveller Ibn Battuta whose journals had just been published. She had not hesitated once and had remembered all the dates.

He knew she had seen him, that she had watched him, and she knew that he knew.

Once, uncharacteristically provoking, she left her fingers unwashed. She sat as close to him as she could, waited to see if he would smell her scent with his fox nose. She wanted to make him falter.

He did not falter. Of course.

She wrote reams of poetry. Floral verse that she floated free on the surface of Nigeen Lake, and in which she thought she would die from pining.

It was hard for the uncle too. His niece's longing was so thick, it coloured the air with such dusky hues that the dust would change colour when she walked into a room.

One day, he sat her down and asked if she would like to go to Delhi. To live. To study. To be among people her own age. It would cure her loneliness.

"To leave you? To leave the lake?" She was horrified.

"I promised your mother I would give you the best of life and the best of life is not here," he said.

He gave her a pile of books to read and poems to memorise. He knew a good family she could live with. They would take care of her needs. He would set up a fund and there would be money wired monthly under her name and she would never be short of anything. Delhi was a magnificent city. He would visit, of course.

She wanted to ask him, before agreeing, if he loved her in that way. If he would ever consider her like that, but she was not as bold when it came to it, when she wasn't concealed behind the stone lace.

Her uncle pre-empted the question she could not ask. Very gently, for he could see her heart was malleable, he told her about the promise he had made her mother. Promises made to those whom you hold dearest must always be kept.

25

Mid-September 1947

T HE FIRST TIME Bappu goes to a refugee camp, he volunteers to work at the desk issuing registration cards, where he can help the displaced fill out the forms to their advantage. Most of them can't read or write, so he reads and writes for them. He guides the tired hands—calloused and half starved—to the pad of indigo ink, so they might declare their existence with a thumbprint.

"I have lost my father and my mother. They perished along the way. There was no food. I had to leave them by the side of the road."

"I am so happy to be here among my own."

"Sir, help me. I have not eaten for so long, I can't remember not being hungry."

"Sir-ji, have you seen my child? I have lost my child along the way."

"Uncle, you are a learned man, why have they done this to us?"

"Bhai, I have killed a man."

"I gave my neighbours the keys to my house. They will guard it until my return."

"I come from an estimable family. We require separate shelter. I have money. Look."

Bappu shakes his head that no, they are all in it together. There is no separate shelter.

The man from the estimable family prints out his name in angry English letters. He demands to speak with a supervisor, but there is no supervisor and he is left to work it out for himself. He swears at Bappu, slams his fist on the table and storms out.

"There is no toilet. My children have soiled themselves. There is no water. My children will die if they don't have food. Do you want them to die? If you don't help us, they will. It will be on your head when they die."

Nine filthy children with matted, sun-bleached hair and open mouths stare up at Bappu like starved baby birds. Their mother, a newborn clamped to her breast, wails with inconsolable slyness. She grabs Bappu's hand, he recoils and is immediately ashamed. She sees his shame and is quick to thrust out her palm for alms.

He empties his pockets, hands the woman every paisa he has, which is against camp protocol, but he just cannot help himself. She snatches the money and stuffs it into the lining of her torn choli. The coins sit between the fabric and her breast. She asks Bappu if he would like to fuck? Her pussy is well worn. Slick with sex. She can do that standing up and if so, she could meet him every day by the post on the right where the thoroughfare is less congested. Best morning price.

"No," says Bappu. "I don't want to fuck. Use that money to feed your children." He despises her for making him speak like that, but it's not her fault, she has nothing. She has probably always had nothing. Who is he to sit in judgement of her?

The line of migrants is long. Bappu answers their questions with as much compassion as he can. It is overwhelming and he does not have any solutions, other than to direct them to the next tent that will allocate shelter and the one after that might give them a blanket.

He stands outside for a minute to catch his breath. When a co-worker offers him a beedi, he accepts it gratefully. He smokes slowly and enjoys the bitter flavour at the back of his throat. He sees old army tents, or tents fashioned out of bamboo poles and faded saris. All of them shoddy. Washing lines and small cooking fires disclose the inhabitants within.

He can smell disease in the air. He can smell it on himself. He uses his sleeve to wipe his brow. His shirt is drenched with foul sweat.

The old and sick are spread on the floor. Where there is not enough shelter, skin blisters. A woman is making the rounds with wet compresses and balm, but she is the only one and there are hundreds of bodies laid out. There are brawls, all over the camp, that will turn into stabbings at night. Bappu can predict it already. On loudspeakers, an official voice vibrates with the names of the dead.

It starts to rain.

Finally, the rain has come.

The sky pours water. At first, it is a miracle. His co-workers come to join Bappu for a minute outside, the line of migrants scatter and everyone turns their hands to catch the precious drops, to drink them in. The joy. The rain will fix everything.

"We are forgiven," cries a man, his eyes closed in rapture, his knees in the dirt.

But in this climate, the rain will make things worse. Bappu knows that. It will not stop raining for days, for weeks, and it will be the sort of rain to soak into the bones of the half-dead, to carry infections and disease. The co-workers go back inside. The line of migrants is quick to re-form.

Outside in the rain, the woman with the nine children starts to beat them one by one, cursing god and the universe until Bappu steps forward and takes the stick from her hand. For a moment he stands with the raised stick above her head and thinks of how much he would like to hit her. He threatens to take the children if she beats them again.

The woman wails even louder. To lose her children would diminish the potential for greater rations and a bigger tent. She accuses Bappu of being a pimp, of wanting to sell her children into prostitution; she causes such a racket, that Bappu steps forwards and slaps her across the face. He hits her hard and his entire body shakes.

"Your mother is a dog and your father is a jackal. May you all burn in hell," she screams.

"I'm sorry," he says at once and drops his hand, immediately ashamed.

She doesn't even flinch. An exultant smile plays at the corners of her lips. The children, too hungry to cry, sit in the fresh mud and watch them. Like tiny animals, they nurse each other's welts.

"I'm sorry," he says again, drops the stick and walks quickly back into the tent.

"This is terrible," says Bappu to his co-workers, who have been there longer than him and are somewhat acclimatised.

"Get them in and out as fast as you can," advises a man who is missing an arm, his sleeve neatly folded and pinned to the seam of the severed limb.

"Don't listen to their stories. You are in administration, not counselling. Don't get involved. That woman has been causing trouble since the day she got here."

"Avoid skin-to-skin contact," advises a matronly woman with kind, sad eyes. She, administering medicines, has seen for herself the start of the epidemics that will soon be fatal. "I am here because I have lost everyone, it doesn't matter if I catch a disease or die."

"I have lost my daughter," says Bappu so quietly he is almost not heard. "She was taken from a train."

"Abducted?" says the man with the missing arm. "It is happening a lot. Abductions are a scourge of these times."

"She will come back," says the matronly woman with the kind, sad eyes, and puts her hand on Bappu's shoulder. The weight and warmth of her hand is achingly intimate.

"Where will they all go?" asks Bappu helplessly. "They can't stay here. They will die."

"Our leaders have failed us."

Yes, they nod, and the matronly woman with the kind, sad eyes pours the tea. She hands them each a small cup.

"I am sorry there are no biscuits," she says.

. . .

Bappu gets home around midnight. A government truck is doing the rounds and drops him off. It is past curfew and raining so heavily, he almost can't see his way to the door.

"Bhai," says Cookie Auntie, there to meet him on the other side. "Come in. There is food on the table."

"I'm not hungry." He sits on the stone floor in the courtyard, hides his face in his hands.

"How was it?" She sits next to him. "Dilchain-ji! Bring chai. He is home."

"More awful than you can imagine."

"But it is raining and cooler already, surely the rain has helped?"

"The rain will put an end to the riots, an end to the heat, but then what?"

"Stop rubbing your eyes," she admonishes him gently. "Take my dupatta."

"I hit a woman today," he says. He uses the dupatta to blow his nose and dry his hair. He looks at his twin. "I slapped her hard in the face."

"Why?"

"She offered herself up to me. She had nine children in tow and she started to beat them with a stick. For a moment everything stopped, blind fury took over."

"I bet she deserved it."

"Hunger can make a person mad. I was angry with her, but I should've been angry with the people who put her there in the first place."

"Bhai, she might have been an awful woman no matter what. The poor are not automatically saints and martyrs."

Dilchain brings them weak black tea. "There is sugar in there," she says handing him a cup. "I have some hidden for emergencies, but I did run out of powdered milk."

"Am I an emergency?"

"Yes . . . I kept this for you too," she says and hands him a sticky date.

"Can you imagine?" says Bappu, looking at them both. He drains the tea, eats the date in a mouthful, and nurses the stone in his cheek. "How difficult it will be for those who are still walking? For those who will be walking for days? They will drown."

. . .

Daadee Ma is on her charpoy trying to sleep when she hears Bappu come in.

Go away, she mutters. *Leave me in peace.* She can't understand why Bappu's pa's spirit is lingering now, more than ever. *Delhi has turned inside out. Surely you can find a better place to loiter than here?*

It is because it has turned inside out that I am here so often, he tells her each day, and each day she asks him again to go away and leave her be. *I am not alone*, he says, *the entire city is haunted. So many have died. So many are trying to get in. The line is long and the door is small, you can't imagine the crowd. The clamour! The limbless-headless-skinless, they are all gathered, pushing and shoving each other out of the way. You'd think they were waiting for a train.*

Even in death, they have no manners, tuts Daadee Ma and closes her eyes.

. . .

Dilchain sits on the stone floor, draws her legs up, puts her head in her knees. She watches Bappu drink his tea quickly and when he has finished eating the date, the stone still in his mouth, she puts her hand out. "I'll take that," she says.

He looks ashen, unwell, his skin still damp from the rain. If she were his wife, she would not be locked in the bedroom, she would be holding his hand. Dilchain's skin is calloused. She wishes it was soft and touched.

He said she was a gem. When she put the poultice on his eye. It is not much, not really, but she will have it.

"I will come with you tomorrow," says Cookie Auntie to Bappu. "Let's take what blankets and clothes we can spare?"

"I'll come too," says Dilchain. "I'll make food."

Ma comes down the stairs and into the courtyard. Her step is weightless, her arms scratched. She hasn't taken her nightgown off for days, smells of sleep and sedatives. She sits down on the stone floor, opposite Bappu, holds her hands tightly.

"I heard all your voices," she says. "I couldn't sleep."

"I'll get the tea," says Dilchain and gets up off the floor. She goes into the kitchen and comes back with a steaming cup, which Ma cradles gratefully in her hands.

"Will you come too?" says Bappu, looking at Ma, drinking her in. "I'm so glad you're awake."

"I'm not sure," she says, eyes flitting, "I am a mess."

"I will help you get dressed," says Cookie Auntie.

"You can help me cook," says Dilchain. She can see Bappu's longing, is desperate to give him something. Even this. She looks at Ma, sees too the broken woman who has lost her child.

. . .

When Ma had been pregnant, craving her body weight in sour fruit, it was Dilchain who had gone to the market for her. Dilchain, not long rescued from her dead husband's household, and not even eighteen, would never know what it felt like to be pregnant. She watched Tanisi sitting on the swing, a hand on her stomach, and it made her own womb ache. She found she had started to put less sugar in Tanisi's chai, smaller portions of kheer on her plate. This was done out of a sense of meanness which was so out of character, so impulsive, that Dilchain didn't even have time to consider what it was she was doing, until it was done.

. . .

When they leave Pushp Vihar early the next morning, Ma pulls her dupatta down to cover her face and hair completely. She doesn't look around her. Fixes her gaze to the ground, but she can feel his eyes on her back and she thinks she can smell, from a distance, the smoke from an imported cigarette. She holds Cookie Auntie's arm for support and ducks her head.

"I don't think I can walk on my own," she says.

Outside the camp, they cover their noses and open umbrellas.

The rain is unyielding and livid.

"It stinks," says Cookie Auntie to Ma under her breath.

Dilchain carries a large cooking pot, ghee, a sack of onions, another of dal and her grandmother's stone. Ma holds the firewood and matches.

The matronly woman with the kind, sad eyes welcomes them in at the gate. "There is a lot to do," she says. "Dhanyavaad. God bless you for coming."

Bappu heads to the registration tent, where he is expected. Cookie Auntie has clothes and blankets to hand out and Roop, dressed as a boy, will help. Ma will work with Dilchain.

The firewood is damp and will not easily light, the ground muddy. Ma looks at Dilchain in easy vexation. "How will we do this?"

Dilchain finds a tarpaulin and puts it flat on the ground. "You can sit on there," she says, giving Ma the onions, a board, a knife. She shows her how to peel and slice. "It will make you cry but it will clear your head."

"I'm not sure I can do this," says Ma, who has never sliced anything before.

"It will help," says Dilchain. "You're disappearing and if you go too, the grief will be unbearable."

With a lull in the rain, Dilchain builds a fire. She places the pot on the flames, and passers-by, seduced by the promise of sustenance, stop. They dawdle and wait. She fries onions in ghee. The aroma is sweet, inviting, rich. More passers-by in tattered clothing come to stand by the warmth of the fire and watch. She drops her grandmother's stone into the onions, laments the lack of chilli. If only this humble dish had chilli, how much better it would taste? She smacks her lips. If only.

When Ma has finished the onions, Dilchain gives her a sack of dal. "Pick out the grit. It will keep your hands busy, and your mind from worrying."

"Look at her. She is cooking a stone," says an old woman, back-bent. "And they say that I am touched in the head."

"You can't make food from a stone," says another, peering into the pot, worried. "I have chillies." She goes into her tent, the one closest to the fire, and brings out seven fresh green chillies. "It's not that I was hiding them, but there are so many to feed," she explains, a little shame-faced.

"It has to be like that, Auntie. Dhanyavaad. The food will taste even better now," says Dilchain. She hands the chillies to Ma. "Chop them finely," she says, "and don't touch your eyes."

The old woman goes back into her tent. She brings out a tawa and some wheat flour. "We can make roti," she offers. "For everyone, or until the flour runs out."

Again, Dilchain begins her lament. Garlic, tomatoes, salt. People come forward one by one, they give this and that, and all of it thrown into the pot. The dal is added and left to simmer.

A man in spectacles and a three-piece suit that would once have been smart and pressed but is now fraying along the seams sets up a smaller fire next to theirs and brings out his own pot and a bag of rice.

"I carried this pot from Punjab. All the way. I said to myself, no matter what happens, this pot is coming with me. It was my mother's pot. All my family meals were prepared in this," he says.

"You are a good man to look after your mother's pot," says Dilchain. "This pot was my grandmother's. She taught me how to cook in it."

"My wife and three children perished along the way. My mother and father too. They were not strong enough to walk. We were walking for weeks and the sun was burning. You can't begin to imagine how awful it was. Even the dogs on the side of the road had grown fussy about the cuts of meat they would eat. If a body was not fresh, the liver still jumping, they wouldn't go near it."

Ma stops chopping and looks at him. "You hear so many stories, you are never sure what to believe, and so you try to believe the best, but hearing you talk," she pauses, "I'm so sorry for everything you have lost. For your family. That you had to walk all this way, for this."

"I am sorry too," says Dilchain.

"This pot is all I have left from that life," says the man in the three-piece suit, his voice breaking. "There is a cousin in Delhi and I have an address."

"Show me the address? Perhaps I can help you find him," offers Ma.

"I had a good job in Lahore. I worked hard. I was a civil engineer and I owned my own house. I had Muslim friends and sometimes we would eat together. It was those friends that told me to leave. We didn't want to, but they said a mob was on its way. They could not protect us. They were too scared to hide us. I don't blame them. What could they do? We had to leave in the dark. Like thieves."

He empties the rice into the pot and tops it up with the water that Dilchain passes to him. She gives him salt and he adds that too.

There are two fires on the go. Dilchain helps the old woman with the tawa build a third. She shows Ma how to add water to the wheat flour, how to knead the dough, how to roll it into flat rounds.

"I understand now," says Ma to Dilchain. "For a few seconds, when my hands were kneading, I almost forgot." She looks at the man in the three-piece suit, says to him in a quiet voice, "We lost our daughter."

He nods with respectful sympathy. Then he sniffs the air. "The smell of roti on the tawa. There is nothing like it for lifting the spirits."

That food is cooking draws people close. There is amiable bickering. Everyone is starving. Dilchain promises she will come back tomorrow and every day to this exact spot until everyone is fed.

"Small children and the elderly first," she suggests when a surge of people with tin plates and bowls come forward.

A strong man with black eyes pushes his way roughly to the front.

"Shame on you," says Dilchain when he elbows his way in, helps himself. He sneers at her and snatches a roti off the tawa. She tries to stop him and he pushes her out of the way, into the mud. He has a rifle on his shoulder and threatens to use it, unslings it and pushes it into her soft cheek. "Not like this. I would have just given it to you," she says, putting a hand in front of her face.

He swears at her. She stares at him and refuses to look away, so he kicks her in the stomach, winds her, lifts his fist as though to strike so she curls into a ball and whimpers.

Ma flinches at the assault. She steps forward as though to help, reaches out with her hand, and when the man with the black eyes raises his fist, she hears a strangled cry. Distilled fear and animal pain.

The man with the three-piece suit comes forward. "My entire family have died," he says. "If you want to beat anyone, beat me. I don't care." He helps Dilchain stand up and holds on to her protectively.

"Thank you," she says, doubled over in pain. She turns to the man with the black eyes. "There's no salt in that. If you had waited, I would have seasoned it for you."

Kutiya! He spits in her face and walks away.

"It was like this the entire walk here," says the man with the three-piece suit.

He gives Dilchain an old handkerchief from a pocket inside his suit jacket. "It's not much, but you can use it to wipe your face."

Ma takes the serving spoon out of Dilchain's hands and guides her to the tarpaulin. "Sit down, Dilchain-ji. Let me do something for a change."

When everyone has been fed, and the pot is empty, the stone hard and grey at the bottom, Ma sits next to Dilchain. "I've not had much time for a domestic life," she admits. "I wanted nothing to do with it. I always had servants, a cook, but I was glad to help you today. Thank you for asking me. It was good to get out."

"I have only ever known how to cook, how to build a fire and hold a broom."

"The books on the shelf are my lifeblood," says Ma. "They nourish me, as your pot does you. Dilchain-ji, do you know how to read?"

Colour rushes to Dilchain's face. No, she admits with a shake of her head.

"I can teach you," says Ma. "If you want? God knows I could use the distraction."

Dilchain nods. "I would like to write my own name."

The man in the three-piece suit has finished his food, scrapes his roti against the empty bowl, and looks admiringly at Dilchain. "I don't know what you put in this, didi, but I have never tasted anything so good in my life."

"You have never been as hungry either," she replies modestly. "We have empty rooms," she adds in a low voice, looking at Ma.

"You're right. We do," agrees Ma. "Come and stay with us? We can help find your cousin. This camp is a miserable place to be when you have lost everyone."

"My name is Hari," he says with a grateful hand. "Your husband will not mind?"

"On the contrary. It is our duty."

"It will help us too," says Dilchain. "We have too many ghosts."

26

Late September 1947

DAADEE MA OBSERVES Hari from her charpoy. "I will die soon," she says to Dilchain, calling her over. "My joints are wasting away."

"No you won't. You're stronger than all of us. Who needs legs? There's nowhere to go, and nothing to see. Let me massage your knees?" says Dilchain, holding a pot of warm neem oil.

"In front of this stranger? There's no privacy."

"Shush now. Don't make a fuss. I'll hang this scarf from the beams. No one will see."

Daadee Ma grumbles silently, but lifts her sari above her knees. She moves her crooked legs into place. "Why is that fatty still here? I hear her wailing every night and it's getting on my nerves. I want to smack her. I can't sleep she's so loud."

Dilchain warms the oil between her palms and rubs it into Daadee Ma's joints. "This will help the swelling. Lie back and keep still."

"You haven't answered my question. Why is she still here? She should be with her own kind, in her own country, now that she has somewhere to go."

"Don't be unkind, Mata-ji. It's not safe for her to leave. The HRWP are everywhere. They will kill her if they see her and you know she will never go outside without her hijab. You should pity her. It's so miserable in the water tank."

. . .

At night when everyone is asleep, Fatima Begum comes out of the water tank and sits with Dilchain in the kitchen. She takes off her hijab and swigs air in grateful gulps. On the day when it rains, she puts her face outside for a whole minute just to feel the drops on her cheeks. "If it's raining over here," she says to Dilchain, "it will be raining over there. Where she is. Alma Azizaam." Fatima Begum is not afraid to say her name.

"Do you think so?"

"Inshallah. Allah is looking after our jewel."

Dilchain doesn't tell Daadee Ma about these night-time visits. She doesn't tell anyone. Her ma had taught her that discretion, when you are a servant, is a valuable thing.

. . .

The three-piece suit has been washed, mended, and pressed by Dilchain. She has folded it away, neem leaves between each layer to ward off moths, and placed it in Bappu's closet for safety. At least once a day, Hari will open the closet and look at his clothes to make sure they are safe.

"It's not that I think someone will take them, but those clothes are everything I have left of my old life. I liked that life. I didn't want to lose it," he says to Dilchain one day when she finds him in Bappu's closet, unfolding and refolding the suit. He stammers, embarrassed to have been caught, and gives her his mother's pot. "It would bring me so much pleasure to know it was being used."

Hari later admits to Dilchain that Cookie Auntie and to some extent Ma, worry and bewilder him. "None of the women in my family had ever even been to school," he tells her. "Or spoke so much and so freely, or had so many opinions." He's not sure if he totally approves.

"That's OK," says Dilchain, supressing half a smile. "You're just not used to it."

"And the young daughter?"

"Roop?"

"She's a savage. I saw her crush a beetle and gouge out the eyes with her nail."

Dilchain laughs out loud.

"When will you marry?" he asks her cautiously. "You must want children of your own?"

"I am a widow," she replies. She can see him sinking in her dimples, and it unnerves her. "I will never marry again."

. . .

Ma stands in the crocus-yellow hallway with Bappu. She presses her hands into her stomach, can feel the ribs on her waist. "I am so thin," she says. "How did this happen?"

Bappu sees the bones sharp beneath her skin. She has almost disappeared. "I have some news," he says, and despises himself that he should be the one to tell her, to hurt her like this. "It is not good news."

Ma looks up in horror.

"No," says Bappu gently. "No. Not that."

She sighs with relief and her thin shoulders sag. "Nothing you can say will make me feel worse than I already feel, if it's not that. Tell me."

"Come here," he says, and he takes and holds her, and she is so frail in his embrace, but she lets him, is even grateful for his arms. "Sahib Ali has gone to Hyderabad to stay with relatives. His house was broken into and looted," he pauses. He could almost be sick.

"Thank god, that's all. I had imagined worse."

"That's not everything."

"What else?"

"His eldest son was murdered."

Ma wrenches free from Bappu's arms, leans against the wall, slides down to the floor. She bites her hand, "No, no," she murmurs, shakes her head violently, looks up with wet and unbelieving eyes. "I don't believe you," she says.

"I'm so sorry."

Flickering eyelashes magnified behind round spectacles. The well-mannered hand raised in the air. Miss Tanisi, he would say. Miss Tanisi.

. . .

"I'm going to give you your daadaa da's old watch," says Daadee Ma to Roop. "Hand me the box under the charpoy." Roop gives her the box and Daadee Ma opens it with a key on a chain around her neck. She takes out the watch and hands it across. "Nice, isn't it?"

"Yes," says Roop. "But what do I have to do for it?" She holds the watch tightly in her hand.

"Are there soldiers outside? Hindustani boys in uniforms with shiny boots and tip-top laces?" asks Daadee Ma.

Roop thinks about it for a minute, looks at the watch again. It is a fine watch with roman numerals and thin gold hands. "Yes," she says. "There is one. At the bottom of Nankhatai Gali. I have seen him. He's there every day."

"What does he look like?"

"He has a gun!"

"Can you take him a message?"

"What kind of message?"

"A tip-top secret one. You can't tell anyone else. It's a message straight from Lord Shiva. If you tell anyone else, the gods will be angry and then your sister will never come home. They have her, you know."

"How do you know?"

"When you talk to the gods as much as I do, they tell you all sorts of things."

"Why haven't you told Bappu and Ma? They would want to know where she is. They're worried, you know."

"They haven't asked me," says Daadee Ma simply. "What can I do?" She pats the empty space on the charpoy, takes a Kwality toffee out of her box and puts it on the bed. "Come and sit next to me. I have to whisper the message in your ear."

Roop does as she is told. She listens to the message, but is not sure. "What does it mean exactly?" She takes the toffee, unwraps it quickly, and puts it into her mouth.

"It's a quote from the Ramayan. When Hanuman rescues Sita from the jungles of Lanka. The soldier will know what it means," says Daadee Ma. "You can have another toffee, after you take the message."

"Show me first," says Roop. She peers into the box. Satisfied that a second toffee does exist, she asks, "Do you mean Fatima Begum? Because no one's supposed to know where she is."

"Pinky-shake on it that you will never tell anyone else?" says Daadee Ma, offering out her hand.

"No," says Roop. She puts her hands behind her back. "I'm not sure."

Daadee Ma shrugs. "What do I care. Give me the watch back then." She puts out her hand. "Come on. Pass it over. Spit out the toffee. I saw you kill the mouse," she adds, sly.

Roop looks at the thin gold hands moving across the face of the watch and shakes her head. No. "Why do you want me to give him that message? It wasn't me anyway, the mouse died from a heart attack."

"Your ayah wants to leave. She wants to go to her uncle's house and the soldier can give her safe passage. He can take her there and no one would stop them. That's all," says Daadee Ma.

"But she lives here."

"She won't be gone long. Just a few days."

"Promise?"

"If you must know, the water tank is directly under my charpoy and I can't sleep at night for all the crying. Like a baby. She makes such a racket. You would think it was the end of the world. Anyway, it's been raining so much the tank will fill up with water soon and then she will drown. Do you want her to drown?"

Roop looks horrified. "No!"

Daadee Ma holds out a wizened finger. "Good. I promise. Let's shake on it then."

"With spit?"

"Theek hai with spit. It doesn't count otherwise."

. . .

The next day, Roop goes to find the soldier at the bottom of Nankhatai Gali. When she sees him, nonchalant against a brick wall, she walks over and pulls at his sleeve. He looks down at her.

"Yes?" he says. "You come from that haveli, don't you? The one over there? I've seen you before."

"Yeah." She looks him up and down, impressed by his rifle. "Do you have a pistol as well?"

"Do you want to see it?" He moves his coat to one side and pulls a small pistol out of the holster attached to his belt. "And a knife." He lifts up his trouser leg and shows her.

"Can I hold it?" she says, looking at the pistol.

"If you want?" He gives her the gun. "It's locked anyway. What's your name?"

"Rajavinder," she says carefully, and holds the gun in her hand as though the gun is the most precious thing in the world.

"I'm Arun."

"It's heavy," she finally says of the gun and then, "can I shoot something?"

Arun laughs. He lights a cigarette. "Are you really a boy? I thought she had two girls."

"Yeah. I'm the cousin," says Roop, thinking quickly. "I'm on holiday. That means I don't have to go to school."

"How is she then? Auntie with the blue eyes?"

"Mostly sad."

"That is a shame." He drags on his cigarette thoughtfully. "Where does she go every day?"

"To the refugee camp. To volunteer."

"Good as well as beautiful," says Arun to himself. "Here," he holds out the cigarette. "Smoke? You'll have to give me the gun back so you can hold it."

"Yeah, OK." Roop takes the cigarette, puffs frantically until she coughs and splutters with a mouthful of smoke. "I've never done that before," she admits, handing it back, standing on her toes for extra height.

"It's easy. Watch me." Arun takes a slow drag, inhales, exhales. "Try again."

Roop tries again, better this time. The smoke makes her feel blowsy, light-headed, a little bit queasy. Very grown-up.

"Are you allowed out by yourself?" says Arun. He looks down at her with interest. "I've seen you coming and going. Where do you go every day?"

"Yeah. I can go out whenever I want. It's because I'm a boy. If I was a girl, I wouldn't be allowed." She looks longingly at the gun. "Go on, Mister-ji. Let's have a go?"

Arun looks round him. "OK," he says. "Only because I like you. You're funny." He picks up an empty soda bottle off the floor and places it on a nearby wall. "You can shoot that if you like. Three goes, OK?" He shows her how to unlock the gun, how to cock it and aim. "Hold it like this." He guides her hand around the weapon and helps her aim it at the soda bottle on the wall. "Now, pull."

She pulls and fires. The strength of the shot knocks her backwards and the bullet hits the wall with a loud boom of gunpowder. She falls to the ground but stands up quickly, dusts herself off, eager to try again. She doesn't hit the bottle once but applauds and whoops loudly when Arun takes the gun, aims, and fires. The bottle explodes.

"It's just practise, that's all," he tells her. "Come back tomorrow, if you want? You can try again."

"Are you in the Indian Army?" she asks. "Are you a real soldier?"

"Not exactly the army but, yeah, a real soldier. We're recruiting, you know. Always on the look out for lively young boys." He passes the cigarette back to her and she puffs at it quickly, proudly, and hands it back. She wobbles, unsteady on her feet, and laughs.

"Yeah," she says. "Could I join? Would they give me a gun?"

It starts to rain. Small spits at first but then bigger drops.

"You better go inside," says Arun. "I'm going to stand under there," and he points to a nearby shelter.

"I have a message for you. It's from Daadee Ma. It's a secret, so I have to whisper it into your ear."

"Quickly then before we get wet." Arun bends down and Roop tiptoes up. She cups her hands and tells him.

"OK?" she says and he nods, thoughtfully, OK.

A slant of rain pelts down and peppers her face in chastisement. Roop puts her arms over her head and runs quickly back into the house.

. . .

When the six soldiers arrive days later, smart in their uniforms and sturdy boots, they bang on the door with fury, scream for the whole street to hear about the Muslim ayah hiding in the water tank.

Daadee Ma, who hears them from the charpoy, is ashamed at the racket. "Now everyone will know our business," she grumbles to herself. "These badmaash goondas. No sense of decorum or subtlety."

Bappu, Ma, and Dilchain are at the camp. Cookie Auntie is at the post office.

Roop is upstairs, playing cards against herself. She hears the noise outside and stops playing at once. She puts on her trousers, goes half-way down to listen. The banging and kicking is so loud, so spiteful, she knows exactly what it means. Knows too, with a sharp wrench in her gut, that if the soldiers break in it will be her fault.

In the water tank, Fatima Begum clamps her hands on her mouth, rocks backwards and forwards, drenched in cold sweat, and begs Allah for mercy. She knows that bribes don't work, but she can't help herself, she promises everything she has in exchange for her life. Who would give Azizaam her malt biscuits in milk, she says, if I were to die? Fatima Begum's nose starts to bleed.

Roop, crouching on the stairs, does the only thing she can think of do-ing. She runs swiftly down to the water tank and yanks open the hatchet.

"Come on," she whispers to Fatima Begum in the dark. She holds out her hand.

"We have to go right now." She grabs her ayah's hand and pulls her out. "Stop crying. Hurry. Let's run." She leads Fatima Begum by the hand, up into the kitchen and through the secret door.

Fatima Begum protests at being led like this. She trips up over her own feet and falls over. "I can't go anywhere without my hijab," she says. "I have to get it. I have to get my grandmother's Koran." She stands still and holds her head, breath rising in panic. "I can't leave without my Koran."

"No," says Roop. She stamps her feet impatiently. "Hurry. They will break the door down any minute now." When Fatima Begum tries to run back into the water tank, Roop pulls her arm. "Fatima Begum! They will kill you if they find you. They know where you are. I told them. We have to go. We have to leave right now."

"No."

"Now!"

"I can't leave without my things."

"Yes you can. I know where Bappu is. Let's find him. Nobody will know who you are without your hijab."

"I can't go out without my hijab."

"Let's pretend we're Pathan warriors. We have come from the Afghan Mountains and we are here to save these stupid people. We have to be brave."

Roop drags Fatima Begum through the courtyard and into the kitchen. She pushes her into the cupboard and pulls her through the secret door. Roop peers outside and around the corner. If only her sister were here. She can see the men pounding on the front door with their rifles, kicking at the wood with their boots. She sees Arun. She so wishes it wasn't him. She'll never be able to join the army now or practise with his gun. "If we creep down and go this way, they won't see us," she whispers. "This door leads out to the back alley."

"Where are we going?"

"Shh. Stop talking." She thinks for a minute and then claps her hands as quietly as she can. "I know!" she whispers. "Let's go to the graveyard to see Azizaam! Bappu goes every week. He says there is never anyone there. I know the guard. His name is Mohammed Ghualam-ji. Follow me. I know where it is. I went there with Bappu to fetch water from the well."

"Are you sure?"

"I'm sure, but you have to stop crying. You have to stop. Real Pathans don't cry. If you cry, people will look at you."

They walk together, quickly, hand in hand, away from Pushp Vihar. They disappear into a crowd and let the mass of other people's bodies carry them. Fatima Begum has never had her hair out in public, not for as long as she can remember, and the air is fresh on her scalp.

"It will be winter soon," she says to Roop when they are some distance from the haveli and it is clear the soldiers have not seen them, are not following. "If it is winter soon over here, it will be winter soon over there."

"Where my sister is?"

"Yes, where Alma Azizaam is. The cold on my face and yours will be the same as the cold on hers."

"Fatima Begum. I have to tell you something; it's all my fault. The soldiers."

"Of course it's not, ladoo. You saved me."

"But I told them where you were," says Roop. She starts crying miserably. "I'm sorry. I didn't know. I made a bad mistake."

"Shh now." Fatima Begum bends down, clasps Roop to her chest, wipes her wet face with the hem of her kameez. "Everyone makes mistakes. It's what you do after that counts."

27

ONCE SHE HAS left Fatima Begum with Azizaam in the graveyard with strict instructions not to move, Roop runs to the camp to find Bappu. She runs until she sees a bullock cart going in the right direction and pleads with the driver to give her a lift.

"Please, Mister-ji. It's life or death," she says, flushed with urgency.

At the camp, she pushes her way through the line of migrants, punching and kicking, until she reaches Bappu. She clamps his legs so tightly he can't walk. In her childish agitation, she talks quickly and out of breath.

Bappu shakes her gently. Slow down. "What's happened?" he says kneeling, his eye level with hers. He holds her by the shoulders. "Tell me."

"It's all my fault. I didn't know. I don't want to go blind." She doesn't tell him about the watch or the toffees or even about the secret message. "Now she will never come home," she says in a small voice. *I am a brave Pathan. I am a brave Pathan*, she whispers to herself, shaking, almost crying again.

When Bappu finally understands what she's trying to tell him, he grows cold all over. "I need to go home," he says to his co-workers. "They have broken into our house." He tells Roop to go back to the graveyard and sit with Fatima Begum. "It is safe there, and I will come as soon as I can."

"We'll come with you," says Dilchain, who, seeing Roop run through the crowds, has followed her. Ma is with her.

"We need to get word to Ali Ahmed Abed," says Bappu. "She won't be able to come home after this."

"I can help," says the matronly woman with the kind, sad eyes. "I have good friends on the other side. I can easily get a message across."

. . .

By the time Bappu gets back to the haveli, the soldiers have left. The front door has been kicked in and the iris-embossed padlock lies wrenched on the steps.

"I never thought this would happen. I thought, no matter what, Pushp Vihar would always be safe," says Bappu. He rubs his left eye in quiet agitation, bends to pick up the padlock. It is heart-shaped and heavy. It could almost beat.

"How did they know she was here?" says Dilchain. "We've been so careful."

They walk into the courtyard. Afternoon light pours in and is strong. Pots of star-shaped jasmine have been kicked over and smashed, their roots upended.

Ma picks one up. "They were just starting to mend. Oh, your pa!" She looks at Bappu. "How he would have hated this. His flowers. His home."

Bappu straightens a chair. The British Burmese teak Made-in-India table has been pushed over and two of the legs kicked off, as if it were a toy and not solid wood at all.

Daadee Ma sits on her charpoy with a bruised cheekbone and a bloody nose. She makes low wailing sounds, like an old museum puppet with a mechanism that has run itself down to the ground. "Scoundrels and goondas," she grumbles and shakes her head. "I'm sorry," she whispers to the eaves, to the ceiling, to the new fissures that run up and down the walls. "I'm sorry. I never thought they would break our home." She sees Bappu come in and calls him to her. "Your pa will never forgive me," she says.

"Look at your cheek," says Bappu, seeing the high colour on her face. "And your eye. What happened?"

"This?" She touches the bruise gingerly. "This is nothing. They weren't interested in me. I'm just an old woman. What good am I to anyone? I shouted and cursed so much, your pa told me to mind my manners. When I wouldn't be quiet, one of them hit me."

"Who were they? The police?" asks Bappu. "Militants?"

"HRWP soldiers," says Daadee Ma in a low voice. "Our own boys, and us a Brahmin household and your pa so esteemed a gentleman all his life, and you a teacher at the university."

"These pretend-soldiers, they have no shame," says Dilchain, bending down to pick up a broken pot.

Ma picks up a cigarette butt flicked carelessly to the ground. She can see him standing there, smoking it down to the tip, giving orders, smiling. He would not care. Her stomach sours. It's too late now to wish she had said something. Told someone.

"Come on now," says Dilchain. She picks up her broom. "We haven't been forced to leave. Our home hasn't been burnt down. We are still alive." She goes to Daadee Ma, uses the edge of her dupatta to wipe Daadee Ma's bloody nose. "I'll boil some water. Open a tin of tea."

"The emergency sugar?"

"I'll put an extra spoonful in each cup."

Hari inches down the stairs. "Oh," he exclaims when he sees the mess, hangs his head in shame. "I was so frightened. When I heard the soldiers break down the door, it reminded me of the kafila. HRWP soldiers had patrolled there too. Kicking their way down the line. Looking for Muslims. Trampling on arms, legs, even heads. I ran upstairs and locked myself in your cupboard. I'm so sorry."

"It's OK," says Bappu wearily. "You had no choice. Of course you were frightened. They would have hurt you too. I am glad you hid."

Bappu stands in the middle of the courtyard. All colour is drained and the walls are cold to touch; a low whistling pierces the air, it rustles through the leaves of the peepul. He can smell old tobacco and bay.

. . .

The hatch to the water tank is flung open. Bappu stands in front of it. He can't stop thinking about Roop, her agitation, her rushed disclosure of blame.

He climbs down into the tank. Everything has been pushed into the inch of now murky water. Fatima Begum's hijab floats face down, billowing among the streaks of gasoline from the shattered lamp.

Her grandmother's Koran has been ripped and the paper scattered. Ma fishes a few pages out, tries to retrieve them by smoothing them flat, but they are bloated and skin-like, so she pushes them to one side, can't bring herself to touch them.

"Months ago, Ali Ahmed Abed asked me to promise we would send Fatima Begum back to him if she was ever in any danger, and we didn't. I didn't." Ma looks at Bappu. "I didn't want to lose her, so I said nothing. I just assumed she would be safe here. That no one would dare threaten her whilst she lived with us. I was so naïve."

"We were all naïve," says Bappu. "We were not prepared for any of this." He bends down to smell the water in the tank, scoops a little into his cupped hand and brings it to his face. He throws it back at once. "They have urinated in here. Like dogs," he says with disgust.

Upstairs, Bappu and Ma stand outside the bedroom. The heavy wooden door has been kicked off its hinges.

Inside, Ma walks to her closet. It has been emptied. Torn clothes are strewn across the floor. "They have taken my shoes," she says in a flat voice. "Why would anyone want my shoes?" She knows it is a warning. That he has taken them.

Bappu picks a piece of wooden shutter off the floor. A wedding present shutter, its intricate lace kicked in, torn muslin poppies littered across it. "What's the point of destroying things like this? It's not even for the money, or they would have taken the wood to sell. I would have preferred it if they had. Then at least I could have thought to myself, yes, however brutal the soldier, his children will eat well tonight."

He walks across the room to the jewellery box, upside down and plundered of its treasures. A trail of neatly folded paper leads from the box to the four-poster bed. One of the notes has been opened. The careful creases of its folds laid bare. He reaches down to pick it up, brings it closer to his face so he might read it. His left eye throbs so he stops to rub it.

"Don't touch that," says Ma. "Don't." She walks across the room and picks up the notes, holds them in her fist. She grabs the one in his hand before he can protest. "This a warning," she says quietly. "A warning to me."

"What do you mean?" says Bappu. "What does any of this have to do with you? Let me see the note."

"No," she says. "I will burn these. I should have burnt them in the first place."

"I don't understand."

"When those women jumped into the well, when we heard it on the radio, I thought to myself, I would never react like that. Lose my life to protect my honour, my husband's honour, the family name. My sense of worth is greater than that."

"I would never ask you to, you know that. We are not that kind of family."

"I thought I was better than that, than them. I was too sophisticated, too cultured. But I am not you know, when faced with it, the threat of it, I just crumpled."

"What do you mean? You're not making any sense."

"Read the notes and you will see. Go on, take them if you want?" She holds them out. "I'm so tired."

Bappu can see the notes in her hand, can read the one word "whore" in cursive script across the top. He steps back in confusion. "Why do you have that?"

She meets his eye. "Now you know," she says, defeated and small.

He stands for a minute in stillness and shock, on the verge of speaking but backing away too, shaking his head, blinking rapidly. It is all too much. "I just, I can't right now. I have to go. Fatima Begum is waiting for me. This, these notes, will have to wait."

"Of course, you must go to her at once," says Ma, sitting on the edge of the bed, her hands feeling for the bedspread that is no longer there, her face burning.

. . .

Dilchain picks up and dusts, arranges into piles what can be saved and what thrown away. She straightens the copper pots in the kitchen. Everything tipped over. Flour-rice-dal trodden into the floor. All of it a spiteful mess.

She takes a strand of saffron from the jar on the slate shelf, dissolves it in warm water, bright yellow and fragrant. She opens the pot of unrequited love and inhales deeply. Unrequited love still smells like a too-ripe Alphonso mango. It makes her dizzy so she closes her eyes and pulls herself together. *Shame on you*, she says. She closes the lid. She will not open it again.

She is a servant. It would not do to forget her place.

She stirs a spoon of sugar into the saffron water and pours the mixture into a small copper vessel. She takes it to the peepul tree and offers it up. *I'm sorry for your loss*, she says. *I'm sorry I wasn't here to look after you.* She tips the golden liquid into the roots.

Dilchain makes a simple dinner and sets it out on a mat on the courtyard floor. The swing has been pulled loose from its chains and hangs lopsided like a fallen grin. She will fix it in the morning. She is too tired to do it now.

No one is hungry. She sits on the mat with Hari and they drink some tea, wait for Bappu to come home.

"I had no idea there was anyone in the water tank," says Hari. "How would the soldiers have found out?"

Dilchain looks at Daadee Ma. Daadee Ma is under the peepul tree, she is praying and her eyes are closed. "Someone would have told them," Dilchain finally says. "Someone who knew."

"A neighbour perhaps?"

"No. Our neighbours left long ago. Their houses are full of refugees who are too hungry and tired to meddle. No. It was someone who knew her," she says, watching Daadee Ma.

"I was fond of my Muslim friends. I would never have betrayed them."

"If you had met Fatima Begum, you would have loved her too."

. . .

Cookie Auntie comes home and when she sees the gutted house she cries. She walks from room to room, touching broken objects, bits of wood and crockery, picking them up in disbelief. The cerulean blue and white

coffee pot, the porcelain cups and porcelain saucers are in a pile of fragments on the floor.

They are only things, she tells herself as she walks upstairs to see
Ma. Things can be replaced.

She holds the broken porcelain in her hands and shows Ma. Look. "The
cerulean bold blue ache of loss. That's what you used to say, isn't it?"

"Yes, back then when I didn't really know the meaning of loss. It
came from a painting I saw as a girl: the Empress Nur Jahan loading a
musket. The background was cerulean blue too." She puts one hand on
a pillow, motions nervously with the other. "Come and sit next to me? I
want to show you something."

On the bed in front of her, the notes are laid out in a row.

She tells Cookie Auntie about Arun. "I'm sure it was he who destroyed the house. Read them."

Cookie Auntie picks up a note and inspects the handwriting, the
words, the in-between-the-lines intentions. She reads each threat out
loud. "Why didn't you tell me? To think you kept this to yourself. To
have a secret like this on top of everything else." She looks at Ma. "It
started with the Supervisor, didn't it?'

Yes.

"It's because of your friendship with Sahib Ali, isn't it?"

Ma nods. "It's just been so awful. I felt, so . . ." She grapples for a
word, shakes her head weakly. "I don't know anymore."

"God, I feel sick. Have you shown these to my brother?"

"He saw. The notes were on the floor when we came home."

"And?"

"We haven't talked yet. What if this is also somehow my fault?"

"You know it's not, Tanisi-ji."

"I want to believe you."

"It's lucky we don't have a well in the courtyard, isn't it?"

Ma smiles weakly. "You know, I used to hope, when she had just been born, that by now, our India would be different. How stupid I was. I thought Democracy would bring so much, but it has given us nothing."

Cookie Auntie leans against the wall, legs stretched out on the bed. "Come sit next to me," she says to Ma and, when she does, holds her close.

"I would like to tell you something, Tanisi-ji. Something I have not told anyone before." She chooses her words carefully, wants to reveal a more truthful version of herself and perhaps in doing so to ease, somehow, the shame. "Twice, I have been used by a man."

Really she would like to call it by its name. She would like to say out loud, "I have been raped" and "I was not to blame." "It was a business associate of Husband-ji's," she says instead.

Ma looks up at her in shock. "What happened?"

"The first time he pushed me into a wall, in my own house at my own party. He followed me up to the bathroom. I even tried to joke it off, thinking to spare him the humiliation. I'll never forget how sour his breath was. He held my throat." She shudders now to remember it. "I fought him, you know, but he was strong. Kicked me in the stomach when he was done and left me winded on the landing. 'Your husband is a good and fine man,' he said. 'So generous with his goods.'"

"Oh," murmurs Ma.

"I started to carry a small knife in my brassiere after that, and come the third time I was ready. I held it to his throat and threatened to kill him. He spat in my face and told me I was soiled goods. I picked myself up, cleaned off the sticky mess—god, men are messy—and when I came to speak about it, I found I couldn't. I blamed myself each time. You know, I still carry the knife with me everywhere I go."

Ma nods slowly. "I'm so sorry, Lakshmi-ji, that this should have happened to you."

"I knew Husband-ji would brush it off in the name of a good business deal. Each time I wondered if he were somehow complicit."

"I never knew," says Ma.

"That was the man I married," says Cookie Auntie. "I made that choice. See, even now, I blame myself. It is the same logic, you know, that made those ninety-three women jump into the well. The same logic where a woman will allow her husband to behead her before she is defiled by another man. Honour."

"I deplore that word," says Ma.

"As do I." Cookie Auntie takes off her dupatta and wraps it around Ma.

. . .

"Fatima Begum," says Roop when she's back at the graveyard and finds her ayah, sitting by her real daughter's grave. "Let's go home. The soldiers will have gone by now," she adds with a twinge of childish possessiveness.

Fatima Begum looks at her with surprise. "I can't go back," she says, "it's not my home anymore."

"But, Fatima Begum, it will always be your home."

"Ladoo, they will only come back for me. When your Bappu gets here, he will know what to do. He will send for my uncle and then later, when I have passage, I will leave for Pakistan."

"But what about me. You can't leave me," says Roop, stunned. "Who will look after me?"

"Your ma and Dilchain-ji of course."

"But they don't know how."

"I will visit. Once this is all over and it's safe. I promise. Every week."

"But you won't, will you? If you leave, you will never come back. Pakistan is a different country. Bappu said so. It's not India anymore. He said there are borders."

"Let's say goodbye now? Your Bappu will be here soon."

"No. I'll come with you. I'll become a Muslim. That's what I'll do. I know how to pray. I've watched you."

"Come and sit with me. Let me hug you."

"No. You shouldn't make promises you can't keep, because I know you won't come back." Roop looks at Fatima Begum and then, not knowing what else to do, she hits her, kicks her, punches her on the arms and then on the legs, until she's sobbing. "It's all my fault. It's all my fault. I don't want the nasty watch anyway."

Fatima Begum takes each blow. She waits for Roop to exhaust herself, grabs and pulls her in. Holds her. "Shh," she says. "Come on now. Only babies cry. You're not a baby, are you?"

"No," says Roop, allowing herself to be pulled in, hysterical now. "You can't go. You can't."

When Bappu arrives, Roop jerks herself free and runs to him. "Don't let her leave," she pleads. "Bappu, make her stay. Force her. I didn't know."

For the second time that day, Bappu kneels down to face his youngest daughter, holds her shoulders. "What did you say? Who did you tell?"

Roop hangs her head in disgrace. "I can't tell you," she mumbles, looking at the muddy ground. "If I tell you, my sister will never come home."

. . .

Roop pulls off her bedcover and drags it under the third long-legged bed. She holds the rosebud pillow tightly, crawls under the bed frame, pulls the blanket over her head like a cowl. She holds her daadaa da's watch in her sticky palm, winds the dial and brings it to her ear.

She listens.

Tick-tock.

I'm here, she says in a whisper to the ghost of Bappu's little brother, *if you want to come and talk to me? Or to play? You can have this watch if you want? It's your pa's.*

She sits hidden in the silence for a minute. *Do you know*, she asks, still whispering, still clutching the watch, *where my sister is? Ghosts know that sort of thing, don't they? Maybe, if you do and you want to tell me, give me a sign?*

She waits and there is nothing. She sighs. There's not even enough sugar to offer a bribe.

. . .

They sit on the edge of the rosewood bed, not talking, backs turned, each facing a stone wall. The room feels oddly empty. It is empty.

"Is she with her uncle now?"

"Yes," says Bappu. "Mohammed Ghualam escorted her. She will be safe now."

"I burnt them," says Ma after a while. "The notes. They were from an old student, Arun. He threatened me the day I lost my job, and then when I came home, a note, pushed through the door . . ." She pauses for a response, but there is none. She can't see Bappu's face, can only imagine he is pale and hurting and confused. "I'm sorry I didn't tell you. Really, I am."

"I wish you had trusted me to help. I feel so useless. So spare."

"I never encouraged him, you know."

Bappu looks up, pulls her arm so that she is forced to turn and face him. "Is that what you thought—that I would blame you?"

"I don't know. I thought perhaps that I would eventually mend. That I could do that on my own. That I was strong enough. I am not."

He looks at her for a long time. "I have always known," he says, carefully, quietly, "that I loved you far more than you did me. But I thought my love would be enough for us both."

"It is," says Ma. His honesty, its precision, strikes her to her core. "It is. I have let you down."

"I used to catch you dreaming, looking out into the distance with an expression on your face, and I would think to myself, my beautiful wife, what could be on her mind that excludes me so completely."

"I never wanted to hurt you," says Ma. She weeps quietly into her hand.

"Tanisi-ji, I am many things. I am not stupid."

They sit quietly for a while in a shared sort of loneliness, no dull epiphany, just a gradual awareness, a sense of meaning like a sense of place, an unfamiliar land they will learn to navigate.

"What will we do?" she asks, drying her face and her eyes. She is surprisingly humbled, in awe of his clumsy kindness.

"Let me undo your hair?" he asks.

She sits closer to him and bends her head.

He unties the band and uses his fingers, and they tremble so, to unweave her hair. It is thinner than it used to be, almost completely grey; she whimpers from the shame, from the loss of her beauty. She was so beautiful once.

He presses his face into her hair, her scalp against his skin, "You are still beautiful," he says. "Will you lie down, next to me?" He moves his mouth through her hair, finds her ear.

They lie, heads on the pillow, shoulders touching awkwardly until Ma reaches out for his hand and threads her fingers, hot and sticky, through his.

. . .

When Brahma had proposed to Tanisi, she had hesitated before saying yes. Just for a second, but it was enough of a second for them to both know her heart was not in it, not burningly in it, not the way Brahma's was, so torched and true.

On their wedding night, once the lengthy ceremony was over and they were giddy from the whisky Lakshmi had smuggled into the room in a silver teapot, leaving them giggling and rejoicing at her audacity, they stood face to face.

Alone. Married.

"You smell of cigarette smoke and jasmine."

"So do you," he said, lifting the edges of the sheer wedding veil. Blood red unspooling gold.

"How was your day?"

"How was yours?"

"Middling-to-fair," she replied teasingly. "Definitely not the best day of my life. Not even close."

"Really?" he said, so easily hurt, pretending not to be hurt. "Really?" he repeated, as if he couldn't quite believe her.

"No, of course not," she laughed. "I'm only teasing you. The whisky has made me bold and you are always so serious. So sensitive."

"Hello, wife," Brahma said, relaxing at last, taking her face in his hands. He kissed her tentatively. His fingers through her hair.

"Husband," she replied, letting herself be kissed, slowly at first and then with urgency. Where he hesitated, inexperienced and timid, she took over. She had seen her uncle. She knew what to do. She had spent years practising on herself.

She pushed the tip of her swollen tongue into the edges of his lips and opened his mouth. "This is how you do it," she said with whisky fire and daring. "Stand still."

She knelt down and slowly, carefully unbuttoned his trousers. She unrolled and unravelled the cloth, pleating it as she went along, tracing the soft of her cheeks and open mouth across his skin and he shivered, goosebumps on his stomach, his thighs, every hair standing on end. She took him whole in her mouth and he gasped. She liked him being in there. She liked the erotic anonymity of it.

28

30 January 1948

DILCHAIN GOES INTO the kitchen and lights a candle. She bathes Annapurna in cold water, rubs turmeric on the goddess's face, pushes a nub of emergency sugar through the goddess's lips. Kneels in prayer. *Please let Gandhi-ji live.* She prays for so long, she forgets to make dinner. Dilchain has never forgotten to make dinner before.

When Hari comes into the kitchen and sees Dilchain crying, he is immediately awkward. Dilchain knows he would like to reach out and take her hand, show his support, but it would be inappropriate, her being a widow, so instead he will watch her cry and feel suitably hopeless.

"At least pass me a handkerchief," she says, her nose and eyes blocked. This he does as graciously as he can.

"I can't believe it," he says in a sad voice after she has blown her nose.

"Nor I," she replies. "I heard the news on the radio. Gandhi-ji shot in the chest."

"They say it was a Maratha from Poona. He shot him twice."

"We are done for if he dies," she says, pulls her cardigan closer. "It is so cold today."

. . .

Bappu is home from the refugee camp and the house is quiet and dark. He sits down at the teak dining table, switches the Emerson Radio on.

"Please, let him live," he says to the empty room. "He, of all people, should not die."

White noise sputters and the announcer's voice rings tin. "All other programmes to go off air," it says.

Bappu listens.

The news is repeated four times in Hindustani first and then in English. Four times so that, in the midst of the confusion of who belongs where and to whom, this at least should be heard loud and clear by all.

Mahatma Gandhi has been shot and killed.

Bappu reaches, pulls the plug out of the wall. He snaps the antennae in two. Pushes the radio off the table. There is a crunch as it hits the stone and lies on its side, cracked and crackling. He rips *The Times of India* in half.

"What else?" he says. He says it again and louder. There is no one in the courtyard but he has to say something out loud. He goes into the kitchen to tell Dilchain, but the kitchen is empty.

"Gandhi-ji is dead," he says to the indigo walls.

Back in the courtyard, he puts his head on the table, glad the table at least is solid and strong. He smells old tobacco and bay, his pa's scent rises in the room. He closes his eyes and falls asleep at once.

. . .

Cookie Auntie and Ma are out walking on D Block in Connaught Circus. Cookie Auntie has persuaded Ma to come with her, so they can peer into the shops and drink coffee at the United Coffee House.

"For one minute, let's try and remember how things were? Just while we drink our coffee? Please? It will do us good. Though where they have managed to procure the coffee is a mystery to me."

Ma, reluctant to stray too far away from home, is not convinced. She has not left the haveli since it was broken into.

"When was the last time you drank real South Indian filter coffee? From the Coorg Valley, with real sugar and real milk?"

"Independence Day," says Ma.

"Six months ago."

"That long? I have lost all track."

"That is exactly why you have to come with me," says Cookie Auntie firmly, taking Ma by the hand and leading her out the door.

Once they are outside, Ma has to admit it feels good to have the cold air on her skin. "It's bracing," she says, and then, "look how old I've become?" She covers her hair with a headscarf, ties it beneath her chin.

She is nervous he might be there, loitering on the corner of Nankhatai Gali, but he isn't. "Can you smell it?" she says.

"Smell what?"

"I think someone close by is smoking an imported cigarette."

"No," says Cookie Auntie, "but it does stink out here." She holds her pashmina shawl to her nose as they walk past the gutters, notices Ma's worried glances. "He hasn't been there for weeks now. I've been keeping an eye too," she says.

"I can't sit still sometimes for fear of another note, another break-in."

"He is gone, Tanisi-ji. He won't be back. Bhai made sure of that. They had to listen to him. His words count." Cookie Auntie takes Ma's hand and pulls it. "Coffee!"

They are outside the United Coffee House when a wedding procession goes past. The shy bridegroom, the white horse decked out in tinsel, the bride held down by her body weight in gold brocade. A small band trumpets and drums around them, children in tulle party frocks, thick cardigans, and woollen bonnets throw confetti and firecrackers into the air.

"This is so odd," says Ma, transfixed. She pulls her shawl closer and shivers.

"The wedding?"

"It seems absurd, the old traditions continuing when the old world no longer exists."

"It could be the last day on earth and people in India would still be getting married. Don't you know that a good marriage is everything? It is the pillar to all our beliefs," says Cookie Auntie, freshly widowed and carrying off the farce with as much dignity and good humour as she can.

The band stops midtune. A passer-by is talking to the conductor and showing him the day's newspaper headline. The wedding party stand in the middle of the road and whisper amongst themselves. The newspaper circulates. The bride sobs hysterically, the elder women in the group, also crying, comfort her.

Cookie Auntie turns around. There are other passers-by now, standing still, shocked expressions on their faces. She slips her hand into Ma's and holds it tight, feeling the weight of something important and devastating. She grabs a paper from the hands of a gentleman walking past.

"Take it," he says. "Read it aloud. I need to know it's real. That it's not just my eyes playing tricks on me."

She reads it. "No," she says slowly. She hands the paper back. It is dated 30 January 1948. Today's paper. "Your eyes are not playing tricks on you."

"I don't believe it," says Ma. She lets go of Cookie Auntie's hand. "I don't believe it," she says again.

. . .

They walk into the courtyard. Bappu is sitting beneath the peepul tree and his face is wet. The Emerson Radio 517 is on the floor, woefully

267

cracked on its side. Fragments of *The Times of India* are strewn all over the place. There is a cup of cold black tea on the table.

"Bhai. We just heard the news." Cookie Auntie kneels beside him and puts a hand on his back. She tells him how they sat with their feet balanced above the gutter, and how so many people, all types of people, sat down next to them, and how the entire pavement was covered with passers-by, too striken to move.

"I cried," she admits to Bappu. "I didn't cry when my bastard husband left me, but this . . ."

"I'm just so relieved," says Ma, "that he was not shot by a Muslim." She sits next to Bappu by the tree, places her head in the hollow between his face and shoulder, offers what broken comfort she can.

Even Daadee Ma recognises the enormity of the crime. She lights and places seven candles in a circle around the peepul tree.

Daadee Ma has been quiet since the break-in. She is not sorry at all that the fatty ayah has gone. She did what she had to do. She is actually quite proud, but the fact that the house was broken into, the pots of star-shaped jasmine smashed and the roots upended, has caused her no end of anguish. Her joints ache more than ever and she feels a slight roughness now in Dilchain's hands when Dilchain oils and plaits her hair.

. . .

One day, it's not cold anymore. It is spring.

There is a telegram from Kashmir addressed to Ma on the table.

"You read it," she says to Bappu.

He opens it and scans the words. He looks at her, at the crease on her forehead, at the grey hair that she tries so hard to pin back and hide. He shakes his head.

"I know what it will say," says Ma. "I have known for months."

"Let's sit down then," he says.

They sit on the swing. One on either end. Ma in her shawl wrapped tightly across her hair and face with only her eyes watchful. She nods, go on.

Her uncle is dead. He was tortured and left to die. He was too ahead of his time, too open, too free.

"Too free?" says Ma.

The telegram was sent by the old servant, Mustapha, who thought his niece, their little pet, should know. It is March 1948 and the telegram is dated December 1947 so that Ma, even if she could, even if transport to Kashmir was possible, could not attend the funeral—a ceremony that probably never even took place.

"They would have thrown him off the side of a mountain and spat on him like he was a dog," she says.

She lets Bappu embrace her, hold her tight and firm, and it feels good and right that she should be held like this, comforted like this; there is no shame to it, and his smell so familiar, his skin so warm, and there is the scent too of jasmine rising, the blossoms tended and alive again, but then she can't breathe, and she is frightened she can't breathe so she moves to the floor and sits with her face to the wall. "I want to be alone," she says to Bappu. "Please?"

She does not cry and it is odd that she does not cry. She wants to cry, her head to pound, and her body to slacken and fall.

"When will my child come home?" she says to the wall, to the fissures that run up and down its spine. She clamps her eyes shut and sits like that for hours.

. . .

The next day, before light, Ma goes down into the courtyard in her nightdress. She needs to feel the cold morning air on her skin. She peels off her dress and stands in her undergarments but they cling to her so she peels them off too and the fabric petals to the floor. She stands naked, starts to weep with loud choking sobs until she is hoarse, until she folds over on the stone, holds her face with her hands, rocks backwards and forwards, curled into herself like a shell.

Cookie Auntie brings a shawl and wraps her into it, holds her and does not let go. Dilchain comes in with hot tea and sits on the floor next to them both.

Ma is shivering, her teeth chattering, muscles jumping.

"Drink this," says Dilchain, hands her the warm cup. "Let me do your hair." She sits behind Ma, untangling and twisting, gently pulling her head this way and that.

Cookie Auntie picks the nightgown off the floor. "Let me dress you," she says, "before you freeze."

. . .

Ma stands by the sink, pours water from a jug. She uses a shard of brown soap to wash her hands, her face, her neck. She scrubs until she is raw. The water is cold. She washes her face several times a day now. Clean is never clean enough.

One day soon, Cookie Auntie will tell her that what feels like joy, is actual joy, and she will say this to her on a clear day that is spring, in all its perfection, and Ma will listen, nod even, smile, but she will not believe her. She will look instead for comfort in distractions. She will leave the taps open and watch the water flow. She will wash her face again and again and then her hands and feet.

29

Spring 1948

ONE MORNING, A blue airmail letter with red go-faster stripes is dropped through the letterbox. Dilchain, in agitation, knowing the letter to be important, seeing the stamp from over the border, hands it to Bappu straightaway.

The letter has been opened and retaped, the green-and-white stamps in fresh circulation.

"I can't open it," says Bappu staring at the letter. "I can't."

"Don't give it to me. I can't read," Dilchain stammers.

She leaves Bappu standing in the courtyard. She takes the stairs two by two and yells out.

Cookie Auntie is plaiting Ma's hair and Roop is lying across the bed, bicycling her legs in the air.

"I'm going all the way to Pakistan," yells Roop, pedalling furiously.

"A letter!" says Dilchain. She stands in the doorway, waves the paper in her hand. "A letter from over there."

Part Three

30

Lahore, August 1947

THE WOMEN ARE very kind. Their gentleness bewilders her. They smell of almond oil and stewed mutton. They hop on flat feet like crows, whispering from inside their black veils. They think because they speak Urdu, she can't understand them but she can. They are talking about her.

Little moosh, she hears them say. *Little mouse. So far away from home, her bones so brittle we could chew them, pick our teeth with them. Her marrow would taste so good in a stew. Look at her eyes! Have you ever seen such a colour?*

They want to eat her eyes.

The girl closes them at once, not wishing to be seen.

She slips in and out of a heavy consciousness. Colours are muted. Sound is stifled. She will feign stupidity. When she is awake, she will refuse to talk.

The four kind women worship Allah. She can smell their faith. It sticks to their glistening pores. She can see, when her eyelids flicker, that she is bound in black cloth. Head to toe. Shrouded like them.

She does not move. It hurts to move. One of the women sits beside her and with great care, as though the girl is a child, begins to spoon thin dal through her lips, which she purses until another kind woman pinches her nose, softly, so the girl opens her mouth—it does not feel like her mouth—and the dal trickles in and is good. The dal is different here. Darker, spicier, thicker.

It hurts to eat.

She remembers with a jolt that she bit her lip. The enamel of the tips of her two front teeth, top and bottom, met and tore a hole in her mouth. She marvels she did that. If she could do that, to herself, there are other things too that she can do.

Anything you want, says a voice. A female voice, a voice in her head, resoundingly omniscient and endlessly deep. *There is nothing to dread. Everything that could happen, has happened.*

She doesn't know that voice but she does remember that someone once said: rat poison works best.

She doesn't smell of her own defecation anymore. Someone has cleaned her, bathed her, scented her. There is a whiff of talcum powder on her skin.

One of the four kind women mashes something into a bowl and pushes it through her mouth. It is disgusting. Whatever it is smells like them: almond oil-sweat-mutton. She gags at once.

Everyone knows that humans should never eat or drink from the fairy kingdom. If they do, they will never be allowed to go home. Not. Ever. Never. Someone once told her that, but who?

"She's not used to it."

"She's not had it before."

"She must eat it. It will nourish her. Fatten her in time for the wedding."

"Little moosh so far away from home."

Wedding? Her wedding. She had always wanted to get married. There was a pair of silver shoes with pearl buckles and a so-fair-boy on a distant shore.

They caw around her. The crows. Flap their arms, billowing black, gently pushing the puree through her mouth and she is too weak to protest, her stomach too empty and eventually some of it sticks, and what does not stick they clean with a damp cloth from around her chin.

She doesn't know where she is, can't move her head yet to look around. She hears servants moving outside. Three times a day they knock on the door and bring in the food.

At night she wets the bed. She dreams of steel screeching on steel, a plate of cream horns, a djinn inside her ripping through skin-muscle-white bone. Her white bone and a blood-soaked lemon-yellow dress.

Her dress.

She had always wanted to see a djinn. There was a girl called Mary once too. Mary had a halo. Mary was good.

When she wakes up, she can't remember. She sees whorls of red like ink in water.

She feels that someone might be watching her. Not the four kind women, but someone who might be kin.

Are you real or have I made you up? the girl whispers in the dark.

I'm real for you, replies the voice.

Are you my kin?

I will be if you worship me.

The girl, herself, is not good. She forgot to water the flowers. The star-shaped jasmine is dead. Even the roots are dead. He will never forgive her, the person whose flowers they were. There was a distant cousin who loved pineapple jam. A red apple clip. Ninety-three women dead in a well and the two that floated. It was a nursery rhyme, she thinks, sung to frighten small children into going to bed. There are child-size fingerprints on her arm. Indigo sky and plum. Compared to the rest of her, these bruises are delicate, faded now, pretty even.

She has not moved for days. She can't move. Has tried to lift an arm or a leg but is pinned by an invisible vein to the bed. Every morning, a fissure inside her leaks hot blood on the mattress. The four kind women move her and change the sheets. They use damp towels to clean in between her legs and when they do this, they do so with sorrow, and the fourth kind woman, the youngest, always cries. The other three comfort the fourth. They bring hot tea and stroke her head.

It is as if the girl's wounds are not her wounds alone.

It annoys her so much. This sharing of the wounds.

The four kind women love talcum powder. The girl's skin has taken on a ghostly pallor from all that talcing. They talc themselves too. Constantly and under the arms, in all the creases between the flesh and on the soles of their feet. They sit on the floor, fresh from bathing, and douse the fine white dust all over themselves.

They pray-eat-sleep in one room in a big house. It is an empty room. A not-lived-in-long room. The four kind women sleep on rolled-out mattresses on the floor and the girl has the only bed.

The four kind women pray five times a day. She watches them perform their ablutions with half an eye. They wash their hands, the soles of their feet, their faces and necks, their arms and legs, their white-grey-black hairlines. Even inside their ears. They mutter and lay prostrate on bright pink prayer mats that face the same way.

They are so clean from their ablutions five times a day, the girl wonders where all the pollution is. Under the skin, no doubt.

When she can move her head to see the entirety of the room, everything looks unfamiliar. Not just to her but to them too, as though they too are in a new and uncomfortable place. When they are not tending to her, the four kind women sit in a circle and the youngest, the only one who can read, recites quietly from the Holy Book. They take it in turns to sit by the girl's side, so she is never alone.

She is not stupid. She knows it's not company on offer. It is a keeping an eye.

The eldest of the four kind women, the one with the whitest hair, speaks Hindi the most fluently. She translates each passage as it is read. "Allah is great," she says with bright and shining eyes.

The girl pretends she is deaf and mute. She will not talk to them, no matter how kind they are. She will be stupid. Stupidity is her saving grace and the rain is her friend. She knows she has a name. She could say it if she wanted to but somehow to say it would make over there seem even farther away.

Hello, she says to the rain one night when everyone is asleep. *It's very hot. Surely you should be here by now?*

I am late, says the rain in a whisper of mist. *I will be even later still. It's not that I don't want to come, but mankind must atone for his sins.*

Well, I'm here, she says, *when you are ready.*

The mist settles on the girl's cheeks for a minute and cools her down.

· · ·

One day, a man comes into the chamber and because a man has entered into a chamber meant only for women, the four kind women flap nervously, even though they are covered head to foot.

"We should hide her eyes," says the eldest, the wisest. "It's that colour. Unearthly. Unreal. It will give the game away."

They cover her eyes with a cloth so diaphanous it might almost not be there at all. If the girl could move her mouth to laugh at their foolishness, she would.

When the man, a mullah with a trim and henna-dyed beard, stands in front of the bed, she closes her eyes. He reads from the Holy Book and instructs the fourth kind woman to place the girl's hands on the pages. He doesn't touch the girl and she is so glad not to be touched.

"Do you have faith?" he asks, not looking at her face.

No. I curse all gods to the sky.

Not all. You worship me. That imagined voice again. A fork-tipped-tongue-licking-its lips-blood-smeared-mouth sort of voice. Resoundingly omniscient and endlessly deep.

Are you a djinn?

I'm Kali.

Are you real?

I'm real to you.

"Yes, she has faith," the eldest kind woman answers for her. "She is a mute," she explains. "I will read the Shahada on her behalf. La ilaha illallah muhammadur rasulullah."

She is converted. She is a Muslim now.

Is that it? Is that all it takes to switch allegiance from one faith to another? All that effort, all that blood, for this: a human hand on a sheaf of holy paper and a line of man-penned verse.

"Little moosh, you are one of us now," the eldest kind woman whispers as she strokes the girl's hair and kisses her cheeks, her forehead, with such tenderness that the girl who has been renamed as a mouse, thinks she will cry.

Bit by bit, she starts to heal. One day she can move her arm and the next she can move her leg and then one day, she sits up in bed. The four kind women are so pleased they coo like pigeons, warm-throated and round, and bring her a dish of sweetened cream.

The girl's brain is full of tightly lidded holes that she knows she could open if she wanted, but she won't. She learns by listening to the four kind women that she is in Lahore, which is in Pakistan, the Independent and newly formed Land of the Pure. She had not thought it would ever actually be real, or a space on the map of the world. That she would be here and not there, which is home.

. . .

"It's a pity she is mute."

"It is appropriate."

"Anything else would be difficult."

"It is a blessing."

Oh. She had not wanted to make it easy for them. She has landed her-self in a bind. She will have to find another way of inflicting harm. Does she really want to harm them? Yes. Yes. She does.

"It will suit Baby Bhai perfectly, him being so simple himself."

"Sisters, she has been sent to us from Allah."

"She is a gift."

"A miracle."

"You will be married soon, dear child," says the eldest kind woman. "A small wedding. A modest wedding. Just us and your husband-to-be. He saw you when you were sleeping, loves you already."

"A small, almost-not-there facial disfigurement, but such a pure soul! You will never meet a soul so pure."

"Mashallah, little moosh."

She looks at them, does not blink. She will do what she is told and when she is strong enough, she will open the tightly lidded holes in her brain and work out how to get home. This, here, this is not her home.

. . .

One day, it rains.

You are here, she says to the rain with a touch of joy. She feels the moisture in the air and hears the pelt against the window frame. The heat lifts. *You have come.*

If it is raining here, it will be raining over there.

. . .

"Today is your wedding day," says the eldest of the four kind women, envoy for the rest.

Of course she knows their names by now, but she will not acknowledge them.

She lets them help her off the bed. Her mouth has healed but is still swollen. She can feel the fullness of it with the tip of her tongue. The bleeding fissure inside still gathers on her thighs, and she still dreams of screeching steel on steel and in dreaming wets the bed.

They put her in a tub of warm water and bathe her. Soap her with rose-scented soap, wash and oil her hair, dress her in silken undergarments and while they tend her, sing in rounds and harmonies beautiful to hear. Beauty hurts her. She sobs inconsolably until she is sick and dry. The four kind women, ever patient, bundle her in towels and wipe her mouth, they talc her as though talcing is the cure to all grief.

Some of the holes in her brain have opened.

There was star-shaped jasmine in the courtyard.

A cook with dimples.

An ayah who smelt of cake.

A sister who suf-fo-cated flies.

A clever Ma.

Bappu. She turns her head to the wall.

The four kind women fuss over her. Dress her in imitation finery five times her weight, place gold earrings in her lobes.

"Pretty one."

"Jewel-of-our-hearts."

"Allah in his greatness has blessed us."

"You are one of us now."

The curdled words scream in her brain.

They guide her. They help her stand. She has not left the bed in days, weeks, perhaps even months, has almost forgotten how to walk. The four kind women lead her into a garden and the air is cool on her face.

It must be the end of summer. If it is the end of summer here, it will be the end of summer over there.

She is led into a room with two ornate chairs backed with red bows, and she must sit on one. She does not want to sit on one, knowing what it would mean to sit on one, but gentle hands push her gently down and keep her gently in place.

Almond stuffed dates are fed through her lips.

"A wedding is not a wedding without delectable morsels to sweeten the heart."

The mullah who converted her stands to attention, eating a date, sipping hot tea. He is so polite, doesn't look at her once.

Two men enter the chamber. The first man is shy. His mouth is twisted out of shape. He looks down at the carpet fixated by the peacock blue.

The second man looks straight ahead and, when she looks at him, prodded to look at him by the fourth kind woman, because one must respect one's elders, she smells him like a bottle of vinegar pushed to the nose before she catches his eye.

Do you remember, now?

She remembers.

Every hole in her brain opens and the shock of the flood is caught in her throat. Her knees collapse. Her stomach heaves like dry rot pickling and all along her spine ice-cold sweat stinks. She vomits at once. Her skin blanched and peeled, ligaments-muscles-white bone exposed.

Almond stuffed dates are all over her dress and the fourth kind woman is quick to clean her up.

Alma for soul. Alma for apple. She has a name.

The man with the vinegar smell, they call him Eldest Bhai, catches her eye for a second and then he looks away. He will never look in her direction again.

She stares at the peacock blue carpet for ages.

There is rat poison in the kitchen. Rat poison is best.

When she looks up from the carpet, she is married to the man with the twisted mouth and simple brain. He sits next to her, blushes damp scarlet. Her husband.

Don't fret, says the rain just come in a soft mist that settles on her raw skin like a balm.

White chicken flesh is mashed into spiced rice and pushed into her mouth. When she purses her lips in defiance, her nose is gently pinched and the food forked with cupped fingers into her mouth and it is done with such love, this forking of the food into her mouth, this pinching of the nose between forefinger and thumb, this keeping of her in the bow-backed chair, that she is overwhelmed-confused, full of something like hate. She has not felt revulsion like this before.

The four kind women, having eaten their fill, help her to her feet and guide her elbows.

She is trembling like a struck thing as they take her into a chamber she has not seen before.

"This is your marital chamber."

"Where you will lie with your husband."

"He blushed when he saw you!"

"You will still sleep with us in the zenana."

"We are always separate to the menfolk. Allah requires it."

"But for an hour each day, you will lie here, do your duty by your husband."

"Sisters? Does she know?" asks the fourth kind woman, the youngest, who is more cunning than the rest. Her face is round like the moon, her cheeks full, eyes dark and green.

The other three are silent. They look at the floor. The eldest gives the youngest a look, and there is something in that look that fills them all with shame.

The four kind women guide her, still trembling, silently to the bed and lay her on it. They remove her garments and massage her feet. They wipe away the hot blood from her thighs and dust them with talc. So much talc. The fine white powder lifts into the air and they sneeze.

She does not sneeze. She will not. She holds it in her nose and the fourth kind woman watches her do it.

They place a brand-new cotton sheet across her naked body. Admire her with adoration, with envy.

The eldest kind woman uncorks the top of a small dusty vial and feeds her drops of bitter liquid. She has been holding the vial in her hand all this time, hiding it in the clench of her fingers as though it were a dirty secret.

A dusty vial from the Jadoo Wallahs Lane behind the Jamma Masjid bought from a dusty hakim with a tangled white beard no doubt. She knows about vials like that.

"This will help."

"It will be over before you know it."

"It is never enjoyable."

"But it is a duty."

"And then there will be a child."

"A child will bring you joy."

What is joy? she asks the rain. *What is joy?* She falls asleep at once.

She comes to with a thick head. The man with the twisted mouth and simple brain is next to her. Her husband.

She tries not to look at him, but there is an unfamiliar movement and her eyes are drawn across. His hand is in his pyjamas and he is frantically masturbating. He heaves release, leaks a patch of moisture in the cotton seam of his crotch, grunts like a baby pig snuffling for food, and falls asleep. He snores.

Oh, that's it? Oh, thank you, she whispers to the rain, to Kali. *Thank you!*

Of course, says the rain with a single drop of water to her swollen lip.

He will not bother you, says Kali, fricative and slow.

This, the daily act of her husband masturbating, too shy to look at her or touch her, becomes the pattern of her marital bed.

This is joy. It is small joy, but Alma will take what she can get.

. . .

She starts to heal. She learns to walk in slow steps. To go to the toilet by herself and feed herself. She collects as much of the grey meat fat as she can in the corners of her cheeks and spits when no one is looking.

She learns that the four kind women are the wives, mother, and sister of the man with the vinegar smell. There are other women too, servants and cooks who flit around like vagrant spirits and never once catch her eye or even look up from the floor. They are always cleaning, dusting and mopping, sweeping with a twig broom, mending and sewing. Sometimes there are guests, but she doesn't see them, she only hears them. She smells the saffron tea. When the guests call by, she is kept in the bedroom and then she knows she is not free. She is a secret and the door is always locked.

Her nipples and belly swell. The four kind women examine her with shrewd sideways glances.

"Is she?"

"Praise be to Allah for his mercy and wisdom!"

"She might be!"

"It is too early to tell yet."

One day she is allowed out into the garden. The garden is full and rich with shrubs and flowers in bud, desperate to bloom. She digs her hands into the earth, gets as much of the soil beneath her fingernails as she can, like a starved seedling she turns her face towards the cooling sun.

The four kind women watch her with pleasure. When they talk she listens to every word and when they stand or sit at a distance she has taught herself to read the movements of their lips.

"We should let her sit outside for an hour a day."

"I have not seen her so happy."

"She has lost so much."

"Sun spots will stipple her complexion," says the fourth kind woman with a sly upturn of the mouth.

There is a mali who tends the trees. He lives in a small hut at the bottom of the garden. Alma sees him from the corner of her eye, looking at her, trying not to look at her, trying not to be seen looking at her, as she sits on the ground beneath the guava tree.

The four kind women watch closely. They have never seen little moosh so at peace as she is now sitting beneath the tree.

"Soon there will be a child."

"Until then we should give her this small pleasure. An hour or two beneath the tree each day."

"She has suffered so."

. . .

She knows they are as new to this as her. There is an anxiousness to their movements, a desperation to the constant reading of the Holy Book in search of succour.

When she can stand, they teach her to pray. They show her the ablutions, how to raise her hands and cup her ears, when to bend, when to prostrate. One day, she does not know what day, only it must be autumn for the air is cooling and dry, they give her a pink mat. A mat like theirs. A gift. They line her mat against theirs.

She had an ayah once. Her ayah had a pink mat too. When she was small, she would watch her ayah pray and copy the movements.

She refuses to pray now though. She turns her head, clenches her fists, imagines she will hit the first woman to touch her. She would like to hit them, to kick and scratch them.

Wait, murmurs Kali. *Patience. Your time will come.*

The eldest of the four kind women pushes her gently forwards, and then shakes her, still gently, still full of love and when that doesn't work, reprimands her with a hard pinch on the arm.

Alma is surprised. She was not expecting to be pinched at all.

In the end, she prays alongside them five times a day. The eldest of the kind women prays out loud and the others repeat and follow after her. Instead of the sacred verse Alma mumbles profanities under her breath. Each day she makes these profanities coarser still, inventing phrases she didn't even know could exist.

She curses god in all his forms. She curses tin Jesus on the wooden Cross, blue-skinned Shiva beneath the peepul tree, the prophet and his wife. She wants to scourge out all their brains, and as for the man with the vinegar smell, she curses him—cross my heart, hope to die, stick a needle in my eye—the most.

She smiles so serenely while she curses, that the four kind women rejoice at her compliance. They select the choicest morsels of oily mutton fat to put on her plate, which she duly eats, and regurgitates as quietly as she can when no one is watching.

The four kind women instruct the mali to stay in his hut between 3:00 and 5:00 p.m., so their little moosh can sit outside and put her fingers in the soil. They would like to give her something. She has lost so much. He is not to approach her or look in her direction. It would be a sin. Punishable by flogging. They are stern about this, and of course he agrees. He has no wish to be flogged.

They dress her head to toe in a billowing veil several sizes too big. They remove all garden tools and sharp objects out of her way. They watch her carefully at first—unsure-suspicious-afraid—but it's boring watching little moosh sit under the guava tree, and after a while the four kind women grow sleepy. They yawn loudly, indulgently, and go inside to nap.

These women are ridiculous.

Alma sits with her back against the guava tree, eyes closed, face towards the sun.

Hello, she says when two drops of water hit her eyelids.

31

THE FOUR KIND women have not always lived in Lahore. Alma, with a head turned to the wall, feigning sleep, listens to them chatter. They are like birds. They never stop.

They have not long been in Pakistan, having crossed the border in a jeep, boxes on laps, at the hour of its inception. In Lahore, they have no dhobi women to sit and gossip with, no first or second cousins twice removed, no aunties popping by, no Kasai Chacha hand-delivering the choicest birds straight to the kitchen door with mutton cheeks thrown in for added melt-in-the-mouth richness.

They all agree, that the rosewater in Lahore is not as rose-scented as the rosewater in Ahmedabad. There is no kebabwallah here on Friday nights, behind the Jamma Masjid, grilling, lemon juice and chilli pepper adding, rolling the meat of the new-born kid into the pliable naan and twisting it up in newspaper. A roll that to bite into, they all agree, juices on the edge of the hijab, was the closest thing to paradise, as they knew it.

They had not necessarily wanted to cross the border. They were just told that moving to Lahore was what was going to happen. Eldest Bhai knew best.

Before they were nicknamed the four kind women, they had their own names. Zainab, Nubila, Nilufer, and Mojghan. Mother of, sister to, first wife, and second wife of Eldest Bhai.

In Pakistan, Land of the Pure, they are not allowed out at all. Not yet. The streets are awash with unrest.

"Do you think we will ever be allowed to go to market?"

"Inshallah."

"Do you think we will ever make friends?"

"Allah will provide."

"Did you hear the gunshots last night?"

"Yes. They say it is worse across the border?"

"What kind of border is it?"

"A line on paper and men with guns."

"I'm not sure I like it here."

"It was better over there."

"Our house was nicer. We had furniture."

"For shame. This is Allah's chosen land. When matters settle, we will send for our things. Our home will be beautiful again."

"I am worried about Eldest Bhai," says the fourth kind woman with a hand held over her mouth. She looks at Alma often, when the others can't see. Her eyes as sharp as glass.

"Slowly slowly, time will heal."

The wall is the colour of cream. The dark night a soft creature around her face. Alma likes the dark now—the dark is for Kali—though she still dreams of steel screeching, and in sleeping wets the bed.

"I wish little moosh could speak. Tell us what happened."

She turns her face towards them in feigned sleep. Through a sliver of open eye, a haze through which the four kind women are huddled by a kerosene lamp.

There is pig blood all over the steps of the Jamma Masjid. This is what Alma likes to imagine at night. It lulls her to sleep. On Friday, the four kind women going to pray, step in pig blood and walk it up and down, all around the courtyard, and then into their house, dragging it on the soles of their feet all through their carpets.

"No. It is better she doesn't speak," says the eldest of the four in a low voice, slick with meaning.

"Do you really think she has been sent as a gift?" asks the fourth kind woman, eyeing little moosh up and down.

"Of course. A gift from Allah to reward our faith and appease our troubles."

The fourth kind woman, the second wife of Eldest Bhai, likes it best when they cover little moosh's face with a veil. A bud of envy curls and unfurls at the backs of her eyelids, like a bright green fern in the monsoon rain.

Alma, always eavesdropping, what else is there to do, looks at the yellow-backed spider, building with extreme skill and dedication, a gossamer web in the corner of the room. When the four kind women are asleep, she sticks her finger in the middle of the web. Jiggles and jiggles and tears it.

. . .

One day when the air inside and out feels crisper, the eldest of the four kind women wraps a light shawl around Alma's neck and over her veil and while doing so feels each of her breasts. She takes one in each greedy hand and squeezes. Alma's breasts are swollen and sensitive, she flinches in discomfort, fingers itching to slap the hand away.

Bide your time, murmurs Kali.

The eldest of the four kind women looks up in pleasure. "Daughter! Daughters-in-law! It has happened."

"What?"

"What?"

They crowd round.

The fourth kind woman puts a hand on her own stomach, "A baby," she says softly.

A baby?

Alma goes into the garden and her legs give way so she sits on the ground. A new kind of bitterness rises to her throat. She puts a hand on her mouth, swallows the rise of rajma and rice until she can't swallow anymore. She spits and retches into the nearest bush.

A baby?

In *her* stomach?

The bush is dark green. It will flower red hibiscus in the spring. The petals like bloodied mouths a warning she will not heed.

The mali is in his hut as instructed between 3:00 and 5:00 p.m. but nevertheless, like all people who are told to do one thing but are then, on account of being told, compelled to do the other, he stands half in and half out of the door.

He watches her vomit into the bush. He has only ever seen slivers of skin in the gap between her eyebrows and the bridge of her nose, her smooth hands, the lilac around her eyes. Her eyes are pale blue. He had looked at them twice and then once more to be sure. He takes a faded handkerchief with a leafy embroidered edge and places it by her small hunched body.

She hears his footsteps. She retches again into the bush. When she turns around, throat dry and belly emptied, ears burning, she sees the handkerchief folded behind her and a steel cup of water. He was standing so close! The handkerchief smells of brown soap, the cheap kind shaved off a larger block and sold by weight at the market. She almost doesn't want to use it or put her mouth to the cold of the metal cup and really how dare he approach her with such stealth when he has so specifically been instructed against approaching her at all?

She is angry, and then she is not. Hot disdain rises and falls. She is no longer the girl in the lemon-yellow dress sitting on a long-legged bed, feeding kheer to the ghosts of her bedroom, her ayah oiling and plaiting her hair. In the carriage of the Bomaby Express, on the upper berth, he had—she stops, chews the soft inside of her cheek, tastes blood. The salt and mineral ooze is calming. She puts her face in the soil. The soil, too, is calming.

She is a Muslim, now. In word and deed. In the mutton fat she is forced to eat. If she went home, would they even want her? She sits back into the earth. Thinks of the diagram of the human heart. Puts a hand on her chest, on her stomach, feels it drop.

There is rat poison in the kitchen but she will not drink it. She will heal. She will find her way home. She will ask Kali, she will ask the rain.

She gulps the water and rinses her mouth out, wipes the faded cloth across it. The cotton is soft from having been washed so often. It might have belonged to his mother, or his sister. She doesn't suppose he has a wife. Perhaps he is lonely?

She is lonely.

She tucks the handkerchief into her sleeve. Leaves the empty metal cup on the ground.

. . .

She goes to his hut at ten past three the next day. The four kind women stuffed full of stewed chicken, are napping. The handkerchief is clean. She woke up in the middle of the night and washed it under the pump in the outdoor latrine, pulling it flat against that corner of the ledge where she knew the sun would shine first. It had to be clean when she retuned it. It could not smell of her.

Sometimes, in the morning, early, before the stench of mutton rolling to a boil takes over, she smells it, sharp like asafoetida in her pores. The vinegar. The train. It is under her armpits, in between her legs. The talcing does not help. Will the mali smell it too, this new feral stench, because if he does, he will surely know. There is no attar of roses in the big house to daub on her neck or the insides of her wrists to hide it.

She imagines the mali is kind. Not kind like the four women, choking and smothering, too sweet, like jasmine decaying, but that he is gentle and true. She does not know this for a fact, but she imagines it so.

She places the handkerchief on the ground by his door. The door is made from tightly woven palm fronds and is closed. She wonders what kind of a hut the mali lives in, whether it would be bare like the big house and what kind of a charpoy he would sleep on and what sort of possessions he might own, if he owned any at all?

The mali has dirty skin and fine features. He is barefoot most of the time. His eyes are black-coffee-coloured and almost opaque. She had not thought, is surprised, that someone as poor as all that could have such fine features. Had always presumed the hardships of poverty pared out pockmarks and crookedness as part of the course. She doesn't suppose he owns any good shoes but the arches of his feet, when she looks from beneath her veil, are deep and beautiful.

. . .

That evening at the allocated hour, in the marital bed, her husband one hand in his pyjamas as is his way, the four kind women with an ear pressed to the door as is theirs, she looks at the ceiling and thinks of the mali. Would his skin feel as rough as it looks? Like the earth in her fingernails, would it feel like that? It is only right that dirty hands should touch her, she is stained after all. And his hands, what would he do with them, where would they go?

They would touch her face very softly. That is all.

There is shame but there is something else too. Each so tightly bound with the other, she can't tell how to unpick them. She is not sure what to call the something else, the heat fluent and hot inside her, but she does know it is absolutely-not-allowed.

She supposes it has something to do with Krishna playing the flute and the gopis in the water enthralled and the cows in the paintings she has seen, looking up at the blue god with adoration in their bovine eyes. Or with Mary Magdalene washing Jesus's feet.

She has a husband. She is a wife. She has a baby in her belly. She doesn't hide the vomiting anymore. She can't. It comes up so fast, knocks her over. The four kind women nod sympathetically, all but one having been there before. They put a pot by her bed and instruct a servant girl to empty it each night.

. . .

There is a guava tree in the garden. She likes to sit beneath the tree and smell the fruit. If she sits beneath the tree for days in a row, the mali will know that that is where she will be. He will watch her and she will possibly like being admired so long as he doesn't come too close. She is not sure by what logic or sense she has worked this out, but somehow she knows.

Just after three in the afternoon is a propitious time. Just after three in the afternoon, the four kind women grow drowsy and doze on their mattresses on the floor, all in a row. Each day she hopes that, by wishing it, she will return to the house at five and find them dead, on the floor, in a row, soaked in pig blood, but of course they never are.

The days are too long. They stretch and stretch. There is nothing to do but sit and pretend to pray. She counts the seconds one by one by one.

Days of vomiting pass. She sits beneath the guava tree with her fingers in the soil and she waits. She waits, but she does not pine. Home is an endless distance away, a non-possibility by virtue of geography-politics-transport. Delhi doesn't even exist. There is no Bappu, no Ma, no sister, no ayah, no cook. There is no star-shaped jasmine to water. No hand-stitched silver shoes to wear. If they do not exist, she cannot miss them. If she cannot miss them, she will not break.

There is however, a guava tree, a mali, and a mud-lined hut. So, she longs for him instead, to defy the promised flogging, approach her and invite her into his hut.

Her cheeks flush. To be invited into his hut, unchaperoned, shrouded as she is, married, what would that mean? Friendship, she hopes.

She sits on her knees, straight backed and alert. She waits.

One day, she builds a palace from a pile of stones that she polishes on her shawl. The next day, twigs and leaves that she plants as the palace grounds. The one after that, she writes her name on the ground in seeds. The next, she writes Kali's too, embellishes the letters.

She thinks to herself, on her bed at night, that Kali, like Mary's djinn, will surely want a sacrifice?

There was a Bappu in that place called home. She used to ask him questions and he always knew what to say. Bappu said, Kali destroyed life in order to make way for rebirth, that there was beauty to it, a release—the old for the new.

She writes other things too with seeds. Places leaves in height order, petals in a mandala, and then she scrunches them all up in disgust with an angry sound. If only the mali would approach, she would have someone to talk to. She looks at the zenana and then she looks at the hut.

This restlessness gets the better of her. One day she stands up, props herself up with encouraging words, and walks to his hut, one eye on the big house to make sure she is not being watched. She stands outside the palm frond door cheeks-on-fire. The palm frond door is ajar.

"The guavas are pickling on the tree," she calls out in English. The absurdity almost makes her laugh. That this should be the first sentence she has spoken in weeks, perhaps months. It feels good to talk.

"I don't speak English," says a voice in broken Hindi. A boy's voice. A normal voice.

She repeats herself in Hindi. "No one has thought to pick them. They will ferment up there. Spoil and turn into toddy."

The mali laughs, catches himself laughing and stops.

"They drink toddy in the South of the country," she says, talking too quickly, encouraged by the sound, his laughter but also the sound of her own voice. She has not heard her voice for a while. "They're mostly Christians in the South. They drink toddy and tell each other jokes. They don't kill each other in the South. Well, maybe they do but it's not as bad as the North." Her words tumble out and she stops, self-conscious. She is talking too much.

He laughs again. A warm full-throated sound.

She pushes the door open and goes in. It is a dark but not unpleasant hut with a narrow bamboo bed in the corner. Pale light is scattered through the cracks in the thatched door and roof.

The mali looks at Alma, and Alma looks at him. Neither is sure what to say.

He has nothing to offer. No tea. No chair. No light conversation. She has never been in a room alone with a boy before.

"OK," she says awkwardly in English and then switches to Hindi. "Can you pick some guavas from the tree, and put them under it, so I can eat them tomorrow? I'm craving sour fruit." And because she is already in the hut and the four kind women are still dozing, though unfortunately not dead, she may as well go and sit on the edge of the mali's charpoy.

He is surprised and then he is not surprised. There is safety in the black shroud.

"What's your name?" she asks him.

"Bhaumika," he says.

"What does it mean?"

"It means from the earth."

"Where are you from?"

"From the South, where they drink toddy," he says with the hint of a grin. "Kochi."

She sits on her hands and reddens. She likes his grin. "Why is your Hindi so bad?"

"We speak Malayalam in Kochi."

"Oh. Why are you here?"

"To work."

"Wasn't there work in Kochi?"

"In Kochi I had to follow my father's business. I am not restricted here."

"Your skin is very dark," she says, staring at him, a little dazzled to be so close. She had not thought anything would dazzle her again.

He averts his eyes, unnerved. "I'm outside all day."

At the back of the hut, half concealed behind a dry palm leaf, she sees a small statue. "What's that?" she asks.

"I don't know. It was here when I came."

She stands up to leave, goes to the statue instead. She kneels and uses the hem of her shroud to wipe the stone clean, licks her fingers and rubs them along the contours of the goddess's face.

"It's Kali," she says in a whisper.

There you are, says the goddess, nodding, pleased. *You took your time. I've been waiting for you.*

"Will you clean her?" she asks the mali. "And burn a candle by her feet? It's important."

He nods that he will.

"The women will wake up soon, I must go. Don't tell them I can talk. OK? They think I am mute."

"Even your husband?"

"He is not my husband!" She flashes. He is her husband. Chastised, she looks at the floor. The floor is mud, smooth and hard.

"Does he think you are mute? I'm not going to tell them. They'll blame me that you're here."

She flushes crimson beneath her shroud. "He is worse than a stunted child. I did not choose him."

The mali nods sympathetically.

. . .

The next day, there is loose fruit in a pile beneath the tree. She lifts the fruit to her nose and inhales the heady perfume. Guavas. Pale green, pale yellow. Almost, but not quite ripe. She holds them close to her chest and takes them to the hut at the bottom of the garden. The palm frond door is ajar again.

"I have guavas," she calls out. "Do you have a knife? I'm not allowed sharp things. They think I will kill myself."

She hears him laugh. He comes out and pushes the door behind him. Puts an old sack on the ground that she might sit. On a scratched tin plate, he slices the fruit into quarters with a paring knife.

"Would you try to kill yourself if you had a knife?" he asks.

"I might have done, when I first got here, but now I would take the knife, hide it, and think very carefully about how best to use it."

Rat poison does not always work best.

"Really?"

"Really." She means it too.

He waits for her to eat first. He is very careful not to touch her.

"Are we to eat from the same plate? At the same time?"

He nods. "I only have one plate."

She reddens then is ashamed of herself, so she nods that she will share. She lowers her veil to eat. Removes the top half and rolls it down to her waist. Beneath it her kameez is plain brown cotton and ugly. She turns her face to the sun.

She has blue eyes like Ma. Drowning in a Kashmiri lake sort of blue. The mali has not seen eyes like hers before. She can tell.

Not sure where to fix his gaze, he stares at the tin plate and inspects the freckles on the pale green pale yellow skin of the fruit.

He waits for her to pick up the first quarter and when she does, she waits for him to pick up the second. They eat at the same time, each acutely conscious of the other. She makes a soft appreciative sound and because she makes a sound, he mimics and makes one too.

The guavas are sour and sweet. Sweet and sour.

"How old are you?" she asks, wiping the juice off her mouth, licking her hand.

"I'm not sure," he replies watching her lick her hand. "How old are you?"

"I can't remember either," she lies.

"Have you forgotten everything?"

"Not everything. How long have you worked at this house?"

"Since I came to Lahore."

"Why would you come here if you didn't have to?"

"My family are chamars."

"Oh," she says looking at him, and then at the ground. She is about to shift back, stops herself and looks up. "I am a Muslim now," she says carefully. "A mullah converted me."

He can tell, by the way she sits, stands, commands with few words his attention, by the way she picks the fruit between forefinger and thumb and lifts it to her mouth, that she is a high-caste Brahmin.

Before they have finished, she wraps the last slice in a leaf she finds on the ground, he brings water and she washes her hands. Dries them on the hem of her veil. Her palms have cooled so she presses them into her hot face.

"This is for Kali," she says, picking up the leaf wrapped parcel. "She will grant me release." She stands, pushes the door open, and places the offering by Kali's stone feet.

"You should go. They will wake up soon," he tells her.

"Perhaps they are dead?" she says with a smile. "If I could poison their food, I would."

"You don't seem that type of person."

"Everyone is that type of person now."

"For someone who has forgotten everything, you seem to know a lot about a lot."

She thinks he admires her. "When I was over there, across the border, I liked to read. I read all the time. My brain is full of useless information. For example, did you know that rats will eat their own tails before they die of starvation?"

"No," he says. He laughs. "I didn't."

"Would you eat yours?" She widens her eyes. He frowns, considering it.

"No. Would you?"

She thinks of the tiny life inside her. "Yes," she says, "I would. I had a little sister once, who stabbed a mouse with a knife. It was for a sacrifice. She wasn't afraid of anything."

"My sisters are brave too."

. . .

Alma sleeps. She dreams. The mali's dark arms from fingertip to elbow are covered in grime that is not the soil of the earth, but the mucus, the

blood and guts of a human. Cockroaches scuttle across the yellow carcass. Her carcass. She wakes up, freezing-cold all over.

The chamars are the lowest of the untouchables. That's what Daadee
Ma said.

. . .

It is the start of winter. There is a chill in the air and the sky is thick
with fog. Her stomach when she prods it is doughy. She tries to poke the
baby's head, to find it, but it's not there, not big enough yet. She is pos-
sessive over her body, every day inspects the changes, the skin that she
imagines is stretching and giving to accommodate.

She is hungry all the time. Ravenous. Even the mutton fat, if she
holds her nose, tastes good. She licks her fingers after every meal as if to
eat her own hands.

The four kind women watch her and whisper among themselves.
They are pleased she is eating, pile up her tin thali.

"Is it normal to sit outside in the cold?"

"Should we stop her?"

"How can we deny her? She has suffered so much."

"I will ask the servant girl to keep an eye," says the fourth kind
woman.

A few days later, when a servant girl is sent to keep her company,
Alma, furious at the intrusion, stands on the garden path and hits her.
She slaps and pushes her to the ground. Go away! The servant girl cries
out in pain as her small body is pummelled and kicked.

She is *their* servant. Beating her is like beating them.

Alma marches back to the big house, shaking with indignation, and
stands in rigid fury above the four kind women who are dozing. She
tenses her broken body.

She screams.

She was on a train. She had a tiffin tin of lunch, a red apple clip in her hair, glass bangles on each arm. She was raped. She was left for dead. A curious contrition must have got him in the end, because he came back and fetched her. The man with the vinegar smell. Bathed and talced, patched and stitched, she was the perfect gift. A girl-bride for his baby brother: the man with the twisted mouth and simple brain.

All the prostrations in the world will not save him now, says Kali in her ear. *Guilt will make fine work of him. He will hang himself soon.*

And them? The four kind women?

Don't worry. Guilt will devour them too.

The four kind women flap in agitation.

"What has happened?"

"What shall we do?"

"Calm her quickly."

"The baby."

"The servants will hear. They will tell the neighbours."

"The neighbours will tell their friends and relatives."

"They can't!"

"Shh. Little moosh. You shall have your heart's desire."

"We are indulging her," says the youngest kind woman, the fern beneath her eyelids spooling its bright green existence. Now that little moosh is eating, little moosh is radiant.

Alma is quiet now. She has stopped screaming, is listening with renewed interest to the panic. The neighbours will tell their friends and relatives. Of course they will. Neighbours talk, servants talk, they excel at spreading tales. The four kind women can't keep her here for ever, against her will, and this fact once gleaned, is an extraordinary thing. A gift from Kali.

Thank you.

Alma sits on her raised bed and refuses food or water. She wonders what it would feel like to have calloused hands on her skin and she is sure she would like it. Let them panic. She is so grateful they are stupid.

When they bring the servant girl in and question her, she exaggerates so much they don't know what to believe, only that no matter what, there can't be screaming of this sort again.

The four kind women whisper, worried. *The baby.*

32

THE OTHER SERVANTS refuse to chaperone her. They say she is touched in the head, that she will bring bad luck to them all.

The four kind women whisper, watch, quarrel.

"Does she understand what we say?"

"No?"

"Poor little moosh, she has suffered so."

"Her eyes move when we talk."

They lower their voices, let her sit in the garden and although they take it in turns to watch, they soon grow tired of watching and anyway do not much like the cold.

She goes to the mali's hut every day now, takes a flower or a leaf and places the offerings by Kali's feet.

She sits on the edge of the mali's charpoy, tells him her name.

"Alma," she says. "My name is Alma. Alma for soul, but depending on where in the world you stand, it could also mean apple."

She likes that. Alma for soul, Bhaumika for the earth.

"Where are you from?" he asks.

She shakes her head swiftly then, trips up over the one false word. No. She is not ready to tell him that.

She rolls her black veil down and it folds over her stomach. It is not obvious she has a baby in her belly, but every now and again there is a tiny somersault. A ripple and it always surprises her. She wonders if the mali can tell.

In an old condensed milk can balanced on a metal grill, over a small twig fire, he puts tea and crushed cardamom in boiling milk. Because sugar is still so heavily rationed, he uses local honey purchased on the black market, and two thimble-size earthenware lamps cleaned of the ghee and wicks, and in these he pours the chai in two sip-size portions that he refills again and again until the tin can is empty. The last cup, the sweetest cup, the honey having sunk to the bottom of the tin, is always for Kali.

"I heard you scream," he says handing her the chai. "Alma," he says.

"I shocked myself," she replies with a wry rolling of the eyes that makes him laugh.

"I saw you hit the servant girl."

"I was angry."

"It wasn't her fault."

"They sent her to spy on me."

"When you're a servant, you have to do what you're told."

"You don't do what you're told," she points out. "They don't trust me."

"Should they trust you?"

She smiles at this, relishes the forbidden place she inhabits on the mali's charpoy. She almost wants them to find out, to be stung by her duplicity. What would they say, those four kind women? Would they still be kind, feed her sweetened cream? She thinks they would not.

It would seem, in this strange new place where the dal is thicker and spicier and talc is used every day, that it is more sinful for a girl to sit on a mali's charpoy than it is for a son-brother-husband-and-soon-to-be-father to rape. She has an awful feeling, a sinking feeling, that it will be the same across the way, in that other place, the one she calls home.

. . .

"Do you think I smell strange?" she asks, sniffing her wrists, looking up in sudden panic. "Like asafoetida? Do I smell like that?"

"No."

She nods, relieved, drinks her chai. The chai is delicious. It tastes like the chai over there and it makes home seem much less far away.

"Our cook," she says, blushing at the word, "Dilchain-ji, made chai like this. She would pound the spices with her grandmother's stone."

The next time she goes to his hut, she tells him about the baby growing in her belly.

"I know," he says meeting her gaze head-on.

"How?" she asks, flustered, armpits sweating mutton fat, pores glossy. She wipes her hands on her shroud to dry them. "How do you know?"

"Servants talk."

"What do they say?"

"That you are with child."

She looks at the ground. Exposed-embarrassed-ashamed.

. . .

It's cold outside.

Her lips and nostrils chap. On the soles of her feet too, in between her toes, the skin flakes. Sometimes, her feet will swell and the four kind women take turns slipping greased fingers in between her toes, cracking her joints, and it tickles so much but she clenches inside, refuses to stir. Even her eyelids she keeps steady.

Her limbs are heavy, a new heft to her body. The baby is lazy. In the mornings, she opens her eyes and her eyelids are stuck with sleep. The eldest of the four kind women brings a compress of cold tea leaves and presses it to her sockets.

Every day she must stand at the head of the pink prayer mat, lift her clean hands to her clean ears, to her clean temples with holy susurrations. She talks to Kali instead. *What can I give you?* she says.

And Kali replies, *What is it exactly that you want?*

. . .

In the mali's hut there is a newspaper fire and an old hand-stitched blanket folded on the charpoy, his ma's blanket, which Alma wraps around her shoulders.

She likes talking to him. Likes watching the shifting colours on his face, the gleaning light when he learns something new.

"Do you know," she asks him one day, "the story of the churel?"

"No," he says.

"The churel is the djinn of a woman who dies while she is pregnant. From the front she is fair, the fairest you will ever see, but it's the feet that give her away. They're turned inside out and back to front."

"Inside out and back to front?" He has not heard of this sort of djinn before, the djinns of the South are different to those from the North.

She nods solemnly. It's true. "The churel uses her charms to seduce those young men who have nothing better to do than loiter on street corners or play cards. She takes them back to her kingdom, offers them all sorts of tasty treats, and there she keeps them until they are old and ugly. That's what happens if you eat or drink in fairyland."

"I promise I will never talk to a girl whose feet are back to front."

"Good. Let's pinky-shake on it."

"What's that?"

"Put out your little finger." She puts out her own. Spits on it. "Spit on yours too. Go on."

He hesitates. He has not touched her yet. He thinks about touching her every day, her ear lobes, her fingers, the crook of her arm, her knees, the lilac skin beneath her pale blue eyes, but he has not dared. He looks at her little finger held out, a request, and proffers his own. OK.

She nods, cheeks on fire.

They link spit-moistened fingers and shake.

. . .

"Do you know about the tiger in Kashmir who likes to be called 'Uncle-ji'?" she asks him another time.

He laughs and shakes his head no.

"There was a young boy walking on the edge of the forest when a tiger came out of a bush and opened his mouth wide—such terrible teeth! So sharp and yellow—he wanted to eat the boy but the boy was not scared. No! He was very brave. He put out his hand as his grandfather had taught him to do and said 'Uncle-ji, let me pet you.'"

"What happened?"

"The tiger let him of course. He rolled on the ground and nuzzled him."

The mali laughs. "I'd like to meet a tiger like that."

She likes making him laugh, so she tells him about the village in Punjab where snakes are so revered, when they die they are dressed in fine clothes and cremated with rites and a wake. "Like humans," she says.

"No?" he replies with a grin.

"Yes," she says with an earnest nod of her head. "They're Naga worshippers. You don't read much, do you?"

"I don't know how."

"Oh! Didn't your ayah tell you stories at bedtime, at least?" she asks in a sweet conciliatory voice.

He laughs. "We didn't have an ayah. Sometimes my sisters sang to me."

"I suppose it doesn't really matter." But it does, she thinks. These things matter, unfairness matters. "Do you know about equality?"

He shakes his head.

"All humans are equal. Gandhi-ji said so."

Alma can tell he doesn't believe her, and she is not sure now if she even believes herself, so she asks him a question—"Have you seen a real tiger before?"—in the hope of distracting them both.

"No, have you?"

"Only pictures in books."

She thinks she would like a book. A storybook. If she had a book, she would read each word twice, so slowly, and then she would read it again, roll the letters around her tongue and after that? She would memorise it. All of it.

. . .

He tells her about Kochi. About the gossamer nets and the boats on the sea.

"When you are on a boat on the water, the wind whistles in your ears and you can taste the salt on your lips. All this talk of freedom," he says, "and until you are on a boat on the sea, so far in, there is only the horizon and you, you can't even begin to understand what freedom really means."

"I've only seen the sea once," she admits, "at Chowpatty Beach."

"Only once?" He tells her about the catching and slicing of a fish. "Using a sharp knife against the backbone and the meat translucent, so fresh that to eat it is to eat the sea."

"To eat the sea?" she marvels at the thought. It makes her squirm and her toes curl, this raw eating of the flesh, but she craves it too. Suddenly, she is starving for the fish, for the sea. Her body tilts forwards; she pulls a face but her eyes are bright with curiosity.

She thinks if she could eat the sea, she might be free.

Two days later, he brings her a gift. A small fish wrapped in a sheet of newspaper. She can hardly take her eyes off the damp paper it has been so long since she last had something to read. She drinks in the Urdu script of last week's news, looks with baffled eyes at the date.

"I have been here for nearly six months," she says. "The news here is as bad as the news was over there. It's almost like Independence never happened."

"Partition happened."

"To divide-separate-divvy up," she says, eyes wet, throat thick and sandy.

The Viceroy was a charming man. He rode a Sunbeam-Talbot, a white-gloved hand always in the air, that royal wave. He had come to save the Indian people. He had failed.

Cookie Auntie said that it rained in England all the time and that the food was bland. So there.

He unwraps the damp paper and shows her the fish.

"I bought this in the market," he says. "They caught it in the Ravi, but I have salted it and we can pretend it's from the sea."

She stares at it with interest and revulsion. She prods the fish with the tip of her finger, strokes the scales so they prickle sharply before falling back into place. The fish is iridescent and it has a glass eye.

"I've never seen a real fish before," she admits.

He shows her how to sharpen a knife against a stone, how to feel for the vertebrae, how to slide the blade along the thin frame and cleanly cut the fillet away from the bone. The long thin skeleton is delicate and the cut so sharp there is no gut wound, no bleeding of the organs.

She observes him in awe.

She had not known death could be so clean.

The mali spears a flake of fish on his knife and holds it out. Go on.

She accepts the knife, though she pulls a face, stands, and places it, an offering, on a leaf by Kali's feet.

The mali spears a second slice and holds that out too. "This one's for you," he says.

"I can't," she says. "It's not cooked. I'm a vegetarian." She turns her head away.

"You're a Muslim now," he says grinning. "And you eat mutton, lamb, and chicken."

"Only because they force me. Not through choice."

"This is different." He holds out the speared knife. "Try it?"

She tries it. She closes her eyes, pretends she is on the seashore. The fish tastes like sea salt on her lips.

On Chowpatty Beach in Bombay. She is eating bhel puri from a paper cone. Wearing silver shoes. Her dress is like the sapphire sky and it spills from her hips as she walks. Her heart is the moon. Cold and bright.

She opens her eyes. "I like it," she says. Salt on her sentences from having tasted the sea.

. . .

"I'm worried," he says one day. "That we will be found out and punished. I don't care about the flogging. The flogging is nothing. That you might be prevented from seeing me is not."

"The four kind women are fools," she says, blue eyes flashing. "Let them try their worst."

"You're fearless. I like that about you."

"You would be fearless too. If what happened to me had happened to you."

"What happened?"

"I don't remember," she stammers, not ready-not yet-caught out.

. . .

The fourth kind woman dawdles often by the bed. She leans right in, her round moon cheek flush with Alma's growing stomach. She wants to press her ear to the stretching skin, to the new marks that move like silver fish, the belly button that has turned inside out, but she doesn't dare. Alma watches her rock a little, on her bare heels, staring, always a hand stroking her own flat belly. The fourth kind woman is very good at not blinking.

She stares and Alma stares right back. There is something between them now. A feeling, an understanding that Alma can't put into words but a feeling like scratches all over her face. They might even be the same age.

If Alma could talk, she would ask the fourth kind woman if she has ever seen a djinn. Alma believes that she has.

. . .

"If I tell you a secret, will you still be my friend?" Alma says to the mali one day after she lights a ghee candle and places it with a briar rose by Kali's lotus knees.

"Yes."

"No matter the secret?"

"Yes." He spits on his little finger and holds it out. She spits on hers and they shake.

"Cross your heart, hope to die, stick a needle in your eye?"

"I don't know what that means, but yes," he says.

"It means you will go blind if you tell?"

"I won't tell."

She tells him her secret and then she waits, head hung, to be banished. He will ask her to leave like any decent boy would. She lifts her veil back over her head. She never imagined she would be grateful for it, this black shroud, this border between her and him, but she is.

He does not interrupt. Does not look away.

"It happened to my mother," he says in a low and steady voice when she has finished. "It happened too to each of my five sisters. Our landlord took his property as he wanted. In my village, the Brahmin landowner could not be hanged whatever he did. In fact, it was considered an honour our women were beautiful enough for him. My father tried to stop him each time. It is strange to see your father beg and plead with another man when you are just a boy. It makes you think that you too will spend your life begging and pleading for things that you should not need to beg and plead to protect."

"Oh," she says and looks up. "So, you know?"

"So, I know."

Alma looks at him for a long time. She doesn't speak. The mali's eyes are black-coffee-coloured. His skin is dark wood, like walnuts in their shell. Of course he is beautiful.

She thinks of how much she would like to kiss his eyes, forehead, cheeks, nose, and mouth. The top of his dark head. She has a baby in her belly, but she has never even kissed a boy.

. . .

Another time, she asks about his caste.

"When you are an untouchable," he says, "there is no value to your life. Growing up, I had to stand by the Ashoka tree at the fork of the road every morning with my sisters, and wait for the landlord to pass by after his puja. We would wash his feet in bowls of water for our mother. She would make our chai with it in the morning, our rasam in the evening. When I asked my father, he said I had to accept this way of life, that no other was possible. He told me it was noble to be a servant."

"That's what Gandhi-ji says too, but there's nothing noble about being treated like an animal."

"Our landlord was kinder to his animals than he was to us."

"Bappu is a Brahmin. He cares about existence. He cares about everyone's existence, no matter the caste or what god they believe in. I am a Brahmin too. It is nobody's fault what they are born into."

Bappu. In pressed khadi trousers and a matching shirt done up to the top, buffed brown shoes and all the right words in his head. She can't imagine how he must feel not knowing where she is, wondering perhaps if she is dead. If he thinks she is dead, he will be mourning her. Grief can undo a person. It can unspool the intricate mechanisms of their heart.

She puts a hand on her stomach, on her throat.

It is her fault. His grief. She had insisted. Shouted. Stamped her foot in spoilt rage. He had been so thoughtful, so kind to hide a bar of Cadbury's chocolate in with her lunch.

She had tried to share the chocolate with the chaperone, but the chaperone had refused.

She longs for her sister now. Roop, crawling into her bed, winding her skinny limbs into the folds of Alma's Sunday dress, pleading for a story, face sticky with sugar. Ma on the swing reading from a book of Shayaris. Dilchain-ji stirring kheer, talking to the rain. Fatima Begum plaiting her hair for school. Even Daadee Ma, cross-legged by her shrine. She longs for her too.

"I have to go," she says, though her time is not up. She pulls the black shroud over her head.

She runs back up to the big house and sits with her veiled face to the wall where she pretends, by placing the Holy Book on her lap, to pray. She stays indoors for a few days, a week. The air is colder, her chapped lips and nostrils cracking, and the eldest of the four kind women rubs coconut oil on her face. She can feel the raw peel of her skin, the exposed muscles-ligaments-white bone, the scuttle of cockroaches along her scalp.

Every tightly lidded hole in her brain is open. The stitched and patched-up wounds unravel. She wants to go home again and again.

Is that what you want? says Kali. *More than the rest?*

The rest?

Vengeance and love. Your pick.

She has to pick? *I am your kin,* she says. *I want it all.*

The four kind women are worried. They fuss around her. They take turns to oil and plait Alma's hair. She hates it when they touch her hair, but some days, she is too worn out to protest, grief exhausts her, though she will twist away feebly, and her hair is too long now, anyway, not to be tended with care.

Little moosh, they say with imploring words, pushing milk-soaked halwa through her closed mouth.

She pretends she can't see them. Lets herself be turned this way and that. She knows it's not her they care about now. It is the baby.

. . .

She sits on the ground beneath the guava tree. A thick shawl on her head, around her shoulders and neck. She almost can't breathe the shawl is so heavy. She tries to dig her fingers into the soil, if she touches the soil, the soil will help but the ground is hard. It might even be frozen.

One day, she thinks she smells him near, the man with the vinegar smell, and this terrifies her and because she is terrified, the baby too must be terrified because it swims and swims and she imagines she can see it flailing against the dome of her skin.

The next day, she finally goes back to his hut. She knocks once and the mali lets her in.

"I had to close the door to keep out the wind," he says, and bundles her up in another, heavier blanket that scratches her new sensitive skin.

"I missed you," she says.

He nods shyly, pleased.

He builds a newspaper fire, puts the tea in the tin to boil. He gives her a pencil and a blue airmail envelope with red go-faster stripes along the edges. When she unfolds the envelope it turns into a sheet of paper with faint grey lines all the way across and to the top.

She looks up at him.

"To write a letter," he says. "I got it yesterday." He crouches by the tin of tea over the newspaper fire, busies himself. If she writes a letter, if he sends it, she will go home. "I'll post it for you. There is a new post office near the market. It opened a few days ago."

"Write a letter home?"

"Yes."

"But what would I write?"

"They are saying, at the post office, that letters are travelling between the borders now, even if they are taking a long time to arrive. Write to your pa."

"Bappu?"

"Tell him you're safe."

She is so startled, she stares at the blue paper for ages.

Finally, she writes in awkward English letters, in a script she doesn't recognise as her own, a letter.

Dear Bappu and Ma, dear Cookie Auntie and Roop, dear Dilchain-ji (and Daadee Ma),

I am in Pakistan.

I am fine.

Don't worry.

The women here are very kind.

Please come and get me. I am in a house in Lahore, but I don't know the address only there is an iron gate and a long garden with a guava and a mango tree.

"Husain Zakir Road," he says, when he sees her looking around, confused. "That is where we are."

She looks up at him, "Thank you," she says.

33

T HE FOURTH KIND woman, being the second wife of Eldest Bhai,
and them just wed a few months before moving to Lahore, has
started to watch little moosh closely.

The curling green fern behind her eyes is brighter, now that there is
a baby in the belly, when she so wishes there was one in her own. Eldest
Bhai no longer comes to their marital chamber at the allocated hour.
Eldest Bhai ignores her, despite the morsels she fans out on his plate. Despite the orange-blossom water she has started to bathe in. The fourth
kind woman is not sure why she blames little moosh for the cooling in
the husband that is hers, she just does. She can't take her eyes off the
girl's stomach.

When her sisters lay down for their afternoon nap, she cannot sleep.
The bright green fern pricks her eyelids each time she tries to close them.

One day, when her sisters are snoring, she goes and stands by the
jalis looking out into the garden and she watches little moosh through
the stone lace. Little moosh sits beneath the guava tree and tries to stick
her fingers into the hard winter soil.

The fourth kind woman can't see past the guava tree, no matter how she twists and cranes. The garden is too long.

Prurience proves stronger than faith. She follows little moosh to the end of the garden, at enough of a distance not to be seen, and watches her go into the mali's hut. That the girl doesn't knock, that she pushes the door open with implied familiarity, shocks the fourth kind woman the most.

She doesn't tell her sisters what she has seen. She doesn't tell them because she has never had a secret of her own before. In fact, she has never had anything of her own. Even her husband she shares. That she might admire little moosh's daring—pretending to be mute when she can so obviously speak!—is something she keeps concealed, even to herself.

The fourth kind woman supposes that little moosh must always have been this way, as some girls are known to be. That she knows how to talk, how to lie so well, is further proof of her wickedness.

This would absolve Eldest Bhai of blame, her sisters of culpability and hang the noose in its rightful place. She is so relieved with this deduction that the food on her plate, which had started to stick in her throat, is delicious once more.

The secret gives the fourth kind woman daring. A thrill in an otherwise dull existence—sleeping-eating-praying—and because it is a thrill, albeit a slow one, she cherishes it all the more. She will wait to see what happens next, and once clear, well then, it will be her duty to share the knowledge with her sisters.

In telling them she will assume she has only now, by chance, found out. She will be appropriately shocked. She practises widening her eyes and the round O of her mouth as she catches her breath.

Oh! Sisters, I am shocked-appalled-disgusted!

They will not have the heart to beat little moosh, who was delivered to them half-dead and pulped, they are god-fearing women after all, compassionate and kind, but they could banish the mali. They could take the baby.

She wonders briefly about timings, about the early pregnancy and the wedding night, but only briefly. Numbers have always confused her.

It is not that she has actually seen anything incriminating, but even the going into the hut uninvited speaks of gunah. Sin. Gunah is a strange and frightening word made less strange and less frightening when someone else is doing it.

When the fourth kind woman goes to sleep at night, she dreams of limbs. Her limbs, Eldest Bhai's limbs, and those of little moosh all entwined. She wakes up oozing white milky fluids all over the mattress, which she strips and washes at once.

"Forgive me, Allah, in your greatness, forgive me," she says and, one eye on little moosh, pinches her breasts until they bruise.

. . .

The baby is growing. Alma can feel the weight of its heart beating next to her own. It is a drowning feeling. There is revulsion, choking and pungent, but there is an unfamiliar longing too, an endless devotion for the life inside her.

She is no longer queasy every day, is instead crying with emotions that consume her in tides. All of a sudden she is crying over nothing. Like the lack of sugar in her tea, or the wilt of a flower, and it is so odd this crying over nothing when she did not cry over the heart-wrenchingly important, that she is confused. The confusion makes her cry even harder.

The four kind women bring her sweetmeats for breakfast every day now and clay cups of lassi and she eats and eats. Eveything they put in front of her, she gorges on. It is still never enough and there is no point, not now, in resisting.

She relies on them completely, their loving-kindness a surfeit that will surely block her gullet, suffocate her child, but still she eats and she no longer fights them, not with a look or a flinch at least.

Her child. Not theirs. All the fussing in the world cannot change that.

. . .

"I don't know what's happening to me," she says to the mali when she eats a guava and cries because the fruit is not sour enough, sourness having by now bloomed into lush ripeness.

"The mangoes on the tree will be ready soon," he tells her. "They will be so sour your eyes will water, and then they will be so sweet you will want to eat them until you're sick."

"But I want to eat them now," she says sobbing. "Why aren't they ready now?"

"It's the baby inside you. It was the same with my sisters. First you are sick, then you cry, and then you are full of joy. The more you swell, the happier you will feel."

She looks him up and down. Full of doubt.

"I have sent the letter," he says to brighten her mood.

. . .

She sleeps. She dreams of ninety-three dead babies, mottled blue-green-purple, bloated like toads and risen to the top of a village well. She pokes each one with her toe. When she wakes up, she has wet the bed.

She wets the bed often now and the four kind women ever patient, change the sheets. They give her a towel to slip into her underwear and the fourth watches her position it with intrusive eyes.

She gets bigger every day. "Look how big I am," she says to the mali crying. "How fat?" Even in despair, she is vain.

. . .

One morning, she looks up, curd on her bottom lip that she collects with her tongue, and she almost speaks.

The yellow-backed spider is back in his corner building his web. Three of the kind women are facing the other way. They are sewing small sweet clothes for the baby, cooing with admiring sounds.

Bring me some kheer. I am craving kheer, is what Alma almost says. She would do anything just now for a spoon of the cardamom-infused cream, jaggery, and rice, cooked by Dilchain-ji in her daadee ma's pot.

But it is not the kheer she wants so badly, the milk condensing and the jasmine soaking the courtyard air, it is Dilchain-ji herself.

The fourth kind woman, always attentive and alert, sees Alma open her mouth and catches her eye. Alma closes her mouth quickly. It would not do to talk so late in the game.

"Can you speak," says the fourth kind woman coaxing, "little moosh? Tell me what you want to eat and I will ask cook to make it." She comes up to the bed and presses her side into Alma's. She smells of powdered milk and chapatis but her breath, so close, is clotted. "I could be your friend," she says. She wheedles.

Alma baulks, shakes her head, moves away and turns to the wall. They could never be friends.

. . .

It is deeper into winter now. The grey fog almost opaque. When she stretches her arm out in the garden, her fingers disappear.

The fog in the winters in Delhi was thick too. She would stand next to her sister, whisper about the witch and the djinn and the ghouls that were hiding ahead. "You can only hop on your left foot," she said. "If your right touches the ground, the witch . . ." She growled and her sister shrieked and they laughed and fell against each other in the cold, which suddenly didn't feel so bad.

The cold is always bad here. Even by the mali's fire, there is always a draft.

She no longer has to lie in the marital bed for an hour a day, but she is still a wife and one day there is a husband to tend again. In a room in the big house, the peacock blue carpet, those same bow-backed chairs she was pushed into, held down in, food stuffed into her mouth, nose pinched—her wedding day—she sits and waits. The chairs are plain now, the bows have been stripped away, and she is no longer feral with vulnerability.

There is a stain on the carpet, where she had vomited. They have not managed to clean it completely, those servants with their twig brooms, and she is glad about that.

The eldest of the four kind women sits with her on this occasion. They drink saffron tea and there are butter biscuits on a plate.

The man with the twisted mouth and simple brain giggles foolishly, drools, he reaches out, tries to caress the baby inside her body, and the eldest kind woman, who is after all quite shrewd, stands up and holds Alma gently in place.

. . .

In the mali's hut, she pulls the blanket around her and nestles into the rough softness. She kneels by the small shrine she has built, uses her sleeve dipped in milk to clean the goddess's face, rubs a little honey around the goddess's mouth. She has smuggled a square of halwa out of the zenana and she places this by the goddess's feet.

They drink the chai quickly, savour the hot burn, until there is none left, so the mali lights the small fire once more and boils the water.

Sometimes, they will sit quietly and cherish silence by the warmth of the newspaper fire. Sometimes, she will fillet a fish as he has taught her to do and they will eat it in bite-size pieces pretending it tastes of the sea. Once or twice, he brings her dates from the market and these she likes best, the sticky sweetness. She eats one as slowly as she can and licks her fingers to clean them.

"They're so sticky," she laughs when she sees him watching. "Go on. Give me yours. Your fingers!" She reaches out and takes them, marvels that skin as brown as his can redden so.

He gives her his sticky hand and she licks it, laughing, embarrassed herself, trying not to be. "Even your ears have gone red," she says.

"So have yours," he replies, and laughs with her. "It tickles."

She has told him all the stories of djinns and jadoo that she can re-member and he has told her again and again of the sea.

"Did I tell you?" she asks him one day, boldly mocking, cruel even, "that my husband with the twisted lip and simple brain has not yet spo-ken a single word to me? He just grunts like a baby pig."

"He is afraid of you. He thinks you don't exist. He thinks if he touches you or speaks, you will vanish."

"Does he?" she says thoughtfully, drawing the blanket closer. The blanket smells of wood and smoke, like the soil after the rain. "What makes you think that?"

"His mind is simple. I feel sorry for him. None of this is his fault."

"Did you know he has never once touched me? Not in the way a husband should touch his wife? I don't think he knows what to do. Every night I lay next to him and every night I was so grateful for this small mercy. I thank every god there is, that my husband is a stunted idiot." She lingers on idiot and smiles.

"I did know that," says the mali quietly, deep pity in his eyes. He does not smile.

She does not like the pity in his eyes. The pity is misplaced. So she says, "He touches himself instead."

The mali does not reply.

"You must know then that the baby isn't his?" She is pushing now, won't drop her gaze, forces him to look. She wants to see how far she can take it. She is cruel today. She has a plan, an inkling of a new idea, avaricious, taking hold.

A plan? It's the rain come as a light mist that settles on her face.

Yes, a sacrifice! She will do whatever it takes to be released. Surely with a sacrifice of this magnitude Kali will see her home?

Be careful, says the rain.

"Yes, I know," the mali says in a quiet voice. "I have always known."

He is so gracious, the mali, so wise, she is at once ashamed, absorbs his goodness like a shove.

. . .

One day, when she is sitting in the hut, the baby inside her kicks. She is so startled, she yelps. Somewhere in the back of her mind, she had hoped the once-cashew-size child would stop growing and disappear. Now that her plan is cruel, it disquiets her, that she could do-feel-think this even as the baby moves inside her, so she pushes the disquiet away.

"Feel this," she says, lowering her shalwar and moving aside the folds of cloth that engulf her, so that her stomach, round and big, is on display. She is self-conscious but she does it anyway. "Put your hand on here."

And although he is hesitant, she takes him by the wrist, moves his palm onto her full belly, and positions it a little to the left, so that he too may feel the full force of the baby's foot.

"Would you marry me, if I were not married? If I were like you?" she asks, emboldened by the weight of his hand on her stomach, the pressure of her own longing pinning her to the bed. There is a creaminess in her lower belly, a spreading expanding tingling fizz of heat.

Is this desire? she thinks. There is a recklessness to it, as if she would do anything, fear nothing, bury herself in the dark soft soil, a whoosh that would carry her with it.

"You are like me," he says.

"No, I mean, if we were the same caste. If we lived in the same village. If it could be different?" Head to one side, she observes him, deliberately scents her voice.

"I would marry you anyway, if I could." He lowers his head and kisses her stomach and in kissing her stomach, longs to kiss her mouth, to put himself inside her, to reach up and feel the wet warmth of her. He doesn't know how he knows she will be wet and warm, having never touched a girl before, he just does.

The fourth kind woman, finally bold enough to walk, in tiptoe steps, up to the mali's hut, peeks in through a gap in the mud and straw wall. The gap is barely a gap at all but it is enough for her to see the dark hand on the milk belly, to guess the baby is kicking and rather than the rage or resentment she had expected to feel, she aches with such sadness she hardly knows where to put it. That evening when a plate of laal maas, steaming red and rich, is put in front of her, she pushes it aside.

"I'm not hungry," she says. Tears gather in her eyes and to hide them, she pretends a headache, covers her face from the light.

Alma watches her, pretending not to notice at all. She knows she is crying for the baby and a husband who does not want her.

34

31 January 1948

IN LAHORE, THE dhobi kneeling by a bucket in the kitchen, hitting and slapping the clothes against a stone, tells the four kind women the news.

They clutch each other, clucking and fussing.

"Who do you think shot him?"

"Was it a Muslim?"

"One of their own, I think."

Serves them right, thinks the fourth kind woman and is ashamed at once. *Allah, in your mercy absolve me*, she prays with her face to the wall.

"He was a good man."

"Yes."

"Yes."

"Yes."

"Perhaps we should not tell little moosh?" suggests the eldest. "It might be the sort of news that would distress her? She must not be distressed."

"No."

"No."

"No," says the fourth kind woman grudgingly.

"It might be bad for the baby?"

"The baby," they coo in gentle harmony. A baby in the house will bring them delight.

. . .

She sits on the edge of the mali's charpoy. He is making chai in the tin can over the twig fire. She is imagining they are married. Him and her. They live in a simple hut on the seashore, somewhere where caste and religion do not matter. She wonders if she could really live like that, eating fresh fish and coconuts from the palms, and she thinks that yes she could.

Since writing the letter, Alma has started to remember more and more what home was like. And, because she remembers mostly when she is in his hut—the tea boiling, his presence close, the dark walnut skin, the black-coffee-coloured eyes—when the memories come they are not so sore.

She finds that, in telling him, she is not even wistful anymore. For two hours each day, the mud hut is her home.

She tells him next about Dilchain-ji's kheer. "Close your eyes," she says. "Imagine this," she says and pretends to put a spoon into his mouth. "Cardamom simmered overnight with ghee-jaggery-milk and rice and left to set so it crumbles like soft toffee in your mouth. Have you even tasted anything like that?"

"I have not," he said.

Later, when he hands her the small clay cup, there is a different sort of gravity to his movements. In fact, she notices he has hardly spoken and wonders if he is bored of her prattling on and perhaps bored also of her talking so often of home?

"No," he says in a low fierce voice. "It is not you at all." He tells her the news of Gandhi-ji's death. "He said poverty was a gift from god, worthy and romantic, but to be poor is to be hungry all the time. He was still a good man though. A saint."

"How did it happen?"

"A Maratha from Poona shot him twice in the chest."

She puts her clay cup of chai on the ground. Her hands are shaking.

In her distress, she only wants Bappu. She looks across the small mud-lined hut at Kali, her red mouth, the un-blink of the painted eyes. She stares at the goddess for a long time.

What should I do, she finally asks her. *If only you would come to life and tell me?*

The goddess does not reply.

. . .

That evening, Alma sits on her raised bed and faces the wall. She can't look at the four kind women, can't bear to hear their chattering, or to see her own expanding belly, what that means. A vinegar baby will change everything. How would she go home with a baby strapped to her back? She blinks the tears away, digs her nails into the soft of her palms. She hides her face in the pillow. She refuses to eat.

"Perhaps she knows?" they whisper, worried. They try to push the food through her lips, as they would have done when she was weaker, but she gives them a look so severe, they stop. Sometimes they are afraid of her. Now that she has almost healed there is a grittiness to her. An unpredictability in the way she sits-moves-tilts her head they have not encountered in a girl before.

"How could she know?"

"Who would have told her?"

The fourth kind woman knows that he would have told her, but she does not tell her sisters she has seen them drink chai and talk. Not yet. She watches them every day now. She sees intelligence flicker behind the pale blue eyes. Sometimes little moosh and the mali sit next to each other, sometimes their shoulders touch and it is this intimacy, the thick innocence of it, seen through a gap in the wall, that shakes her the most.

The mali will be flogged of course, to a state of near unconsciousness but not to death, her sisters are so kind after all. Eldest Bhai will commend her bravery. Thank her. He will invite her to lay with him. He will sow his seed in her. The seed will be a boy. Two boys. Twins with hazelnut eyes.

She will tell her sisters soon. She must.

. . .

It is warmer. There is a light sun that teases the ground. Crocuses push through the soil. They keep chickens behind the kitchen now; nervous chickens that squawk and shriek loudly and a cockerel that breaks the dawn.

Alma would like to take Kali a chicken, but how would she catch it, kill it. She asks Kali again and again, *what can I give you*, but there is no reply. Would a chicken do, she wonders, and if not that, then what? She has an idea. A terrible, awful idea. One that reeks of vinegar, that she keeps locked in the back of her mind.

. . .

Will they even want her when she goes home? She wonders that too, knows that they will. Is ashamed of it.

She is enormous now, breasts are ripe and so tender. Like the how-now-brown-cow, she is full of milk.

The baby has strong legs and kicks, somersaults with such gusto that the four kind women, who are kinder than ever, so excited by the prospect of a baby, are sure he is a boy.

"Mohammed," says the eldest of the four, "after the Prophet. That is what we will name our little jewel."

"Are you thirsty? There is cold soda in bottles and fresh lemons."

"Are you hungry? There are hot pakoras in the kitchen."

"Look. Halwa! Cook made it especially for you. Not as sweet as it should be, but still so good."

So they continue, three of the kind women addressing her every unspoken whim. The fourth has grown sulky.

The more they fuss, the more Alma scorns them

. . .

One day, Alma asks the mali if he knows what a human heart looks like.

No. He does not.

"I think," she says, "the doctors in their white coats have got it wrong. I think the heart moves around the body. Sometimes, it might be here," she reaches over and touches his chest. "Sometimes it might be here," she touches his head, then his stomach, "and sometimes when you are very scared, it's here." She touches the smooth hollow of his throat.

"Where is it now?"

"Everywhere," she says and giggles softly with a hand held up to her mouth.

"Let me kiss you?" she says impulsively bold, and just as suddenly, "no!" She covers her face with her hands, blushes crimson-ruby-rose. "I've changed my mind. Tomorrow?" She opens two fingers and observes him through the gap, her pale blue eyes aglow. "Can I kiss you tomorrow?"

. . .

"I was almost married," she tells him the next day. "To a boy who had a fair face. He wore shoes with laces. He was going to be a doctor."

"What happened?"

"Daadee Ma rigged my horoscope and his family found out."

"Your horoscope must have been bad, if she had to rig it?"

"I never saw the real one, but I heard it was awful. There is an evil eye above my head."

She looks at the flame of the ghee candle flickering by Kali's knees, tells the mali she does not want the baby growing inside her.

"People kill babies all the time," she says, the fact like an illumination; it takes hold as she speaks, the words burrowing into the dark, surprising herself. She had not thought she would have it in her. She is thrilled and devastated at once. "Especially if the baby is a girl." She prods her stomach, emboldened by her own words. "She is a girl. I will sacrifice her."

The mali does not answer. Does not look at her. Does not say goodbye when she leaves.

"Look," she says the next day, because she would like him to understand, this boy whom in her mind's eye she has wed several times over. "I need to pull it apart before I can make it whole again. Don't you believe in rebirth?"

He stares at her, still speechless.

"Look," she tries again. "This baby will stink of vinegar. It will look like him. How can I love it?"

. . .

"I have something for you," says the mali. He reaches over to the corner of the room and pulls out a small tube folded down and creased flat. His face is damp and flushed.

The fourth kind woman is watching. She will tell her sisters today. It is her duty.

"What is it?" says Alma.

"You will need to give me a patch of skin? Somewhere, that you can hide, that no one else will see," he says. He is shy.

"I will give you my swollen knees," she says. She rolls her cotton shalwar up to sit on her thighs. Her legs are bare and that he should see her legs, makes her fidget with quiet pleasure and shame, her ears grow hot. "She is almost here," she says of the baby.

"I'm going to draw on your knees. Keep still. It will tickle."

"As if we were getting married," she says. "Do you know how?"

"I have five sisters. They taught me."

He bites off the tip of the tube with his teeth, pushes the thick brown paste up towards the nozzle. He draws henna patterns on her knees. He draws swirls that turn into lotus flowers, roses in full bloom, peacock feathers, the moon, the sun, the stars.

"Stop moving," he says, because she can't keep still.

"It tickles!"

The fourth kind woman watches in silence. She sees the drawing of the mehndi on the knees and has to look away. The bright green fern curls and unfurls so quickly she has to close her eyes.

When he has finished, he tells her to sit still and wait for it to dry.

"Have you ever seen snow?" she asks, looking admiringly at her knees.

"No."

"Neither have I but I have read about it, seen pictures of it, imagined it. You are like snow."

. . .

When the mehndi is dry, she pulls her cotton shalwar down and goes back to the big house. She is on the path, when a hand reaches out and pinches her, sly and sharp, tugs at the long plait beneath her veil. She turns around at once. Stands with one hand on her hip, defiant and angry that someone should dare touch her.

"Whore," hisses the fourth kind woman in Urdu, full of a spite she cannot contain, the green fern curling and unfurling so quickly, she almost falls over.

Alma in her shock stands still. She places a protective hand on the round of her stomach. She had not realised she was being watched, but when faced with it, she is surprised it hasn't happened sooner. She has almost willed it.

"I know you can talk. I have seen you go into his hut each day. I have seen you sit on his bed."

Alma looks at the fourth kind woman carefully. Slowly. The fourth kind woman is no bigger than her. She is no older than her. She would not dare harm Alma while there is a baby in Alma's belly.

"Talk," says the fourth kind woman, "say something."

"If you shout any louder, your sisters will wake up," Alma replies in perfect Urdu.

"I will tell them. Today. I will tell them everything I have seen. Shame on you. Shame!"

"Allah does not like girls who spy. He does not like men who rape."

The fourth kind woman stops and stares.

"Allah," says Alma, careful, "does not like women who imprison another of their kind against her will."

"You dare use his name in vain? You are not imprisoned," says the fourth kind woman, astonished. "You are not here against your will. We have cared for you. We have fed you and loved you. We were kind to you."

"That was not kindness, covering up his tracks. Shall I tell you what he did to me? Your husband? Have you worked out the dates yet?"

The fourth kind woman trembles and sways on her feet on the path. "He did nothing," she says in a whisper. "You lured him," she says with doubt.

"I was only fourteen. Guilt is a funny thing, don't you think?"

The fourth kind woman reaches out as though to push her to the ground.

Alma takes a step back. "If you push me, you will harm the baby," she says in a cool voice. "Your sisters will be awake soon. Shall we go and tell them? I remember everything now. I have sent a letter home. They will come for me soon."

"No one will believe you," says the fourth kind woman, breathing so fast she might almost run out of air.

"Allah in his wisdom and grace. In his mercy, he will believe me."

The fourth kind woman who is not a woman at all but a girl, young and small, sobs and her entire body convulses.

"Imagine," says Alma, holding her stomach, feeling the little foot kick its way into life, the clenching wet running down her legs, saturating her pyjamas as she moans softly, crumples into the earth on the path, "if it had happened to you?"

35

May 1948

THE BIRTH IS so hard, she thinks she will surely die. She was on the garden path when they came to fetch her. Three kind women in a flap and a fourth in silent sorrow. They helped her back up to the big house.

The four kind women are frightened—little moosh has enormous pupils and yellow skin—but the eldest is practical too. She calls out instructions. Hot compresses, cold compresses, blankets and towels. A bucket of boiled water. Scissors. She has done this before. She teaches Alma how to pant, to push through, how to crawl, how to bite on a rag.

When it is time, Alma lies on the bedroom floor, teeth bared, skin pale dripping ice-cold sweat. There is a raw animal noise, a moan that begins in her belly and rips up through her throat. She urinates and defecates all over the floor, all over herself.

The neighbours will hear. They will tell their relatives and friends.

Two of the four kind women hold her arms and stroke her brow. They pray. The eldest delivers. The youngest, moon-faced and green-eyed, backs herself into a corner.

Alma closes her eyes and imagines Kali. *Help me*, she pleads. *I will die if you don't.* The old stiches are unravelling, the baby is pushing against them desperate to live and suddenly she wants her baby to live no matter the inkling of a plan, or the promises made, or the dark soft soil against her skin.

On the seashore she walks with the mali. They live in a mud hut, eat fresh fish and coconuts from the palms.

What will you give me, Kali finally replies, cool and unruffled as is her way.

Alma's legs are spread so far apart, they could snap. With every push, the baby is closer; her own body expanding, contracting, and the eldest kind woman is saying, "Yes yes, like that, little moosh." Her body arches. The room is hot-white and sound curdles, the bloodied tip of a round head poking through her, tearing.

But the head is stuck, and there is panic in the eldest woman's instructions now. Panic that she tries to still.

What will you give me, says Kali again.

"Will she die?" asks the fourth kind woman. Her voice from the other side of the room dislocated and hopeful.

Alma does not want to die. *You can have her*, she says to Kali. *Is that what you want?* She can hear steel on steel of train wheels screeching, the starched white sheets of the upper berth, now befouled, cling to her sweat. *I will give you my baby*, she says. She would do anything to go home, to Delhi, to not die in this horrible house all alone.

She is delirious now, skin scorched, hallucinating. She thinks, Kali is in the room, imagines it, wills it so. Kali reaching into her womb with a long tongue, coaxing the baby out with a flicker.

. . .

When she comes to, the four kind women are gathered around the screaming baby, milky in grey fluids. They are cooing and drooling, as though the baby is theirs, it makes her sick to see them. She checks her own feet first, then her daughter's. They are the right way round and they have the same long toes. They have Bappu's toes.

The fourth kind woman is tongue-tied for days. She watches the baby at Alma's breast and pinches her own viciously, pummels her empty stomach when no one is looking. When they pass her the child to hold, cooing and mewling, she refuses but the little girl is so sweet, and her own arms ache with desperate longing.

The four kind women name the baby Khadija, after the Prophet's first wife.

When the baby is a few weeks old, and the fourth kind woman's mood is still saturnine, the others question her.

"What is it?" they say. "You will have a baby, one day too," they say.

The fourth kind woman looks at Alma. "She can talk. She has been mocking us all," she says. Her rage is quiet but spittle sprays out of her mouth.

The other kind women stare, incredulous. "Sister, are you sure? How do you know?"

"Yes, I can talk," says Alma in perfect Urdu from the other side of the room. She knows they will not harm her. Not whilst there is milk and the baby clamped all day to her breast. "So?"

Kali has made her bold.

"She has been going to the mali's hut," says the fourth kind woman. She tells them everything she has seen, embellishes, of course.

"Would you believe me anyway," says Alma, "if I told you he never once touched me?" She does not care. "Will you strike and punish me? Flog me? What can you do that has not been done already?"

The four kind women dither in panic around her. Like black crows billowing from inside their black veils.

"We must punish her. Cut out her tongue."

"It is only right. We should put out her eyes. Cut off her breasts."

"We cannot be mocked."

"Eldest Bhai will know best."

Alma is afraid then, when she hears his name.

"You will not go out."

"Never. We will build locks on every door."

"You will not leave this room alone—we will always be with you."

"He will be punished, you know. Your lover. Beaten and thrown out of the house. When Eldest Bhai comes home, *my husband*, he will do it. Allah has no mercy for those who sin."

Alma is watchful then, quiet, keeps her tongue. She can see the spite in the fourth kind woman's eyes. Does not trust it at all. She doesn't care what happens to her, there is nothing they can do, but she cares what happens to him.

. . .

The four kind women leave the bedroom door open at night. Alma's bladder is weak and she often needs the latrine.

"She would not dare," they murmur. "Eldest Bhai will be home soon," they say.

There is a skinny servant girl, outside on a thin mattress to keep an eye, but she is always fast asleep. The women are as stupid as ever.

Tonight? Shall I do it tonight?

Tonight, Kali agrees.

And she will be reborn?

Of course.

To a better life than this?

To comfort and riches and safety.

When the four kind women are asleep, she creeps out of the room and stands in the dark corridor. Her daughter, swaddled against her chest in a sling, moves her mouth in quiet sucks keen for her ma's milk.

Two heartbeats and Alma can feel them both, like a thud-thud, in her throat.

She has a steel paring knife hidden in the sling, a vial of rosewater and a newspaper twist of turmeric. She touches each one, holds her breath—that same thud-thud. The baby is warm against her breast and lately the child has learnt to watch her mother's movements until Alma is overwhelmed with a love that cuts it is so exquisite to behold.

Alma clutches her closer and walks outside, stands on the garden path. It is raining. She holds out her one free hand and the water splashes on her palm and that too is exquisite.

Thank you for coming, she says to the rain. *Thank you. I will need your help*.

Mud swells in every crater and dent and she slips a little as she walks, clutches the baby tighter.

The red hibiscuses are flowering.

The rain pushes her forward. She lets it take her by the hand, by the elbow.

Will you show me how to do it? she asks the rain.

I will.

The wind arrives next and is gentle on her face.

Sing, says the wind and the rain too, says: *Sing. It will help with the rebirth. The melodies will guide her way; the gods love music.*

So, she presses her mouth to the baby's head and sings. When she was young Ma would sing to her, poems and ditties that she put to playful verse, and then later, Alma would sing the same to Roop.

Yesterday, she told the mali again what she would do, a stolen five minutes in the dark. The last time she had seen him, he had painted her knees.

"You don't have to? Please, don't." He was almost begging, almost even crying.

"I do."

"Crumble this then," he said, the crook of one elbow wiping his eyes. He gave her a small lump of opium. "Feed it to her in a drop of milk."

She nodded, could barely speak her throat was so tight. There was a mossy quiet in his eyes that struck her. His hands were shaking violently.

"I stole a knife from the kitchen," she whispered.

"This will help," he said. "Ease the suffering." He gave her a vial of rosewater and a newspaper twist of turmeric. "To do it right," he said.

"And you must leave," she replied. "When he comes home, he will punish you. They are not kind. They will hurt you."

"And leave you?"

"Yes."

She walks past the guava tree now bereft of fruit. The leaves are whispering and rustling, a forewarning, that she will not heed.

She walks past the dark of the mali's hut. The palm frond door is closed. There is no light creeping out through the cracks in the weave.

At the end of the garden she crouches down, sits in the wet earth beneath the mango tree. The fruit is sour and dizzyingly fragrant already. She unties the sling and places the swaddled child on the wet earth. The sleeping baby is unusually still, the rain seems not to disturb her.

Alma uncorks the vial of rosewater, sprinkles it over the tiny face. Sweet and musky, the scent lingers. Next, she dips her finger in the powdered turmeric and smudges it across her daughter's forehead.

Yellow to repel the evil eye, rosewater to please Kali, beg for her grace.

Yesterday, she had picked yellow marigolds from behind the mali's hut and threaded them into garlands. The eldest kind woman watched her, was appeased when Alma offered her one.

She sticks her hand now into the hollow of the tree's bark and pulls the other garland out, places it, sodden, around the baby's neck.

The baby is still sleeping, still soundless and there is something about the small cheek blue-grey and cold that frightens her.

She thought she was done with fear, she is not done with fear. Fear swallows her whole.

Will the sacrifice count if the child is already dead?

I think I gave her too much opium, she says to the rain.

Slit the throat first, then break the skull to release the spirit, suggests the rain.

She does what she is told. Holds the steel against the wet throat, pushes in. The tip of the blade nicks the skin.

She has a Bappu a Ma a sister an ayah a cook.

The baby, blue-grey and cold, awake now, whimpers and mewls.

I can't, says Alma, looking down at the baby, choking on her sobs. *I have never killed a thing before.*

Alma stands up quickly, holds her daughter tighter, shelters her from the wind and rain.

She walks across to the mud hut and stands outside the palm frond door. She hits it once, twice with the flat of her hand. The rain has stopped, but she is cold in the wet and shivering. The baby is screaming with a pitiful hungry howl. Shh, she says, shh, and holds her tightly to her breast. She is such a tiny animal. A real human mouse.

When the mali opens the door, sleep stuck to his eyes, Alma thrusts the baby to him and he is confused, not knowing what to say or do, but she pleads, "Take her?" She does not trust herself anymore. Besides, how would she ever go home, to Delhi, with a baby? What would she say?

"But what will I do with her?" He takes her, of course.

"Keep her warm and dry. Wrap her in your ma's blanket. Feed her milk with a spoon and at dawn, before they wake up, take her to the Kali Mata temple across the way. It is not far. A day's ride on a bicycle. You have a bicycle."

"I have a bicycle and I can ask the way."

"At the temple, give her to the priests. They will care for her. Pinky-shake on it," she says and holds out her wet finger.

He links his own and they shake.

"Please, don't come back," she says, and even as she turns, he reaches, pulls her closer, and he is awkward—the baby between them—so she stands on her toes, presses her face to his face, to her daughter's face, until she twists free with a cry and stumbles back out into the dark.

She stands on the garden path in the wind and the rain. She cuts her hand from little finger to thumb, gasps at the bloody gash, it opens like a grin and she lets blood drip to the ground. It is only right she should bleed after what she tried to do tonight. If she had done it, the sacrifice, how would she have explained it to Bappu?

Back at the big house, she leaves the door ajar. Trails mud along the corridor, throws leaves on the floor, and into the cot. In the morning, it will look like a wild dog has broken in and stolen the child. It is not uncommon for wild dogs to steal babies for food. She had heard the four kind women discussing it last week.

In the indoor latrine, she doubles up over the hole in the ground and retches until she is dry. Places a hand on her cheeks for a minute. Washes her face but she still cannot stop the cries that come from nowhere and wrench her senses apart.

In the distance the cockerel behind the kitchen crows.

· · ·

In the morning, she is asleep when rough hands jostle her awake, demanding and loud.

"Where is she?"

"What have you done with her?"

"Our jewel. Where has she gone?"

"She is not yours," says Alma, her hand throbbing so she is almost dizzy. "She is not."

"The mali will know," says the fourth kind woman, reaching across and yanking Alma's hair.

"Eldest Bhai will know," says Alma. This is all she has left. "Ask him. Call him. His child." And then it comes, as she knew it would, the swelling ache, the easy tears of vexation, her grieving breast leaking milk on her skin.

They spit on her now as though she has taken the name of god himself in vain.

They kick and slap, claw and scratch her. They scream in her face. They are not kind women at all.

She kicks back this time, hits back, until her hand where she had cut it last night, bleeds across the sheets, across her nightdress, across the hands that pull and pinch her. So much red blood and they stop at once. They stare, whimper. It wasn't them, was it, this awful frightening thing?

"The baby has gone," says Alma, pale, holding her hand, wrapping the sheet around the wound and pressing to stopper the flow. She knows they will not look after her anymore. "A wild dog took it. Snatched it for food, bit my hand. See?"

Four hands slap her face.

"Liar."

"Why did you not scream to wake us? Liar."

"How did you sleep with your baby gone? Liar."

"Whore!"

"Leave me alone," says Alma. "I am telling the truth. You will see. Allah knows." She closes her eyes and lies down in pain. They leave her in the room and lock the door.

The four kind women stand on the garden path.

"What should we do?"

"We must go to his hut. Punish him."

"Sisters, he is stronger than us. He is a man."

"But we are four," says the fourth kind woman pining for the baby she had named Khadija.

Outside the mali's hut they flounder and flap some more. They call out but there is no answer. The palm frond door is closed.

"Push it," says the fourth kind woman. When they stall, she does it herself, the weight of her shoulder and body against it. There is no lock and the door swings open so easily she falls.

Darkness and damp. The ash of yesterday's incense on the ground. The whites of the goddess's eyes smirking. *Come in if you dare,* she says.

There is nothing else there. No man. No child.

. . .

"That's what happens, you know," says the fourth kind woman to little moosh, when they are sitting in a circle and reading from the Holy Book, because now they must pray all the time, "when there is gunah. Allah punishes. He sent the dog to eat your child. You will have to do your duty now and bring us another baby. A boy this time."

Alma says nothing. She watches the yellow-backed spider build with such care its web.

. . .

Little moosh is no longer allowed to sit on the ground beneath the guava tree.

Nor is she given tasty morsels to eat. She's not even allowed to leave the room except to piss and shit and even then she is escorted by them all, two on each side. Their hands are rough and firm now.

She can hear them at night, with her face to the cream wall pretend-ing to sleep. They have no idea what to do with her, how to chasten her. They are as stupid as they have ever been. They pray for the baby all day long. Cry and wail with misery, beat their breasts with hard palms. She is glad.

She has started to pray too.

When can I go home?

Soon, says Kali. *Soon.*

36

December 1948

WHEN THEY COME to take her, she is not totally willing at first. For a whole minute, as her rescuers, one man, one woman stand expectantly, the jeep door open, she does not know how she feels.

"The mangoes are not ready yet," she says, not knowing what else to say.

. . .

In the beginning, the four kind women don't open the door. They sit and rock and push their beads.

"They will go away, if we pretend we're not here."

"Keep praying, sisters."

"They cannot just take her. She is our brother's wife."

"She belongs to us. By law."

"Who?" says Alma. "Who is here?" and when she realises with a sudden blow, she runs and kicks at the closed door until they restrain her, shove a pillow on her face. All four of them hold her down, sit on her.

Shh, little moosh, shh, they coo so full of misplaced love.

Her rescuers come back with police who are really soldiers, who are not soldiers, who are only young boys with stolen rifles and a pocketful of baksheesh. There is no choice in the end. The laws are changing anyway. They have official documents to prove it. The neighbours have been talking and there are hefty fines now for disobedience.

. . .

"Have this," says the lady, the neat and tidy volunteer who has come to travel with her. There is a man with them too, but he stands aside, watches from a distance. Alma cannot look in his direction, had not realised she would be so afraid. The lady passes Alma a samosa hot from a vendor on the platform, wrapped in newspaper. "Eat," she says, "you are all skin and bone. Don't worry," she adds, tracing Alma's look with her own. She pats her arm. "He is a good Hindu and a family man. Very kindly and honest."

Alma accepts the offering and holds it in her hand. She does not eat it just yet.

"You're lucky. Your family have high connections. Other girls are left where they are for now."

Alma looks at her blankly. "My letter," she says, finally understanding.

"Perhaps, beta. There will be new laws soon, to bring back the rest of the girls, but they are still squabbling. The new governments can't agree on anything. Marriages that were forced will be annulled," she says carefully, curious but knowing not to pry.

"No," says Alma in a weak voice, and then, "yes."

The lady pats down the creases of her uniform, points to her badge. "This is my job," she says. "To help the new nation. I work for Lady Mountbatten's Corps. I've been trained. We can talk. I know what to say. I met her, you know," she adds brightly. "She shook my hand."

Face pressed to the bars, restless, Alma stares out of the train window. She holds the paring knife in her hand. She had been on a train when it happened, had not wanted to be on a train ever again but there is no choice and this train will take her home.

. . .

She had shared her lunch with the chaperone. They had played cards and eaten a plate of cream horns. The bar of Cadbury's chocolate, miraculously not melted in the heat, had fallen out of the cloth bag.

There was a policeman outside and he had a gun.

It was the hottest summer she had known and the rain was late.

At night, they made the beds with starched sheets and white pillowcases, IRC embroidered on one corner. They pulled the sheets and tucked in the sides. Alma had the upper berth and the chaperone helped her climb up. They were both asleep when it happened.

The train skidded to a halt. There was screaming and gunshots. High-pitched sounds that tore at her ears. She thought she was dreaming. Curled into a tight ball and tried to go back to sleep. *Go away, go away*, she whispered to the dream.

It was only a bad dream. It was a nightmare. She would wake up. Any minute now.

Tommorow she would be in Cookie Auntie's bathroom with the rose-embossed tiles and the taps that ran water, hot and cold.

Someone opened the door, she heard the hinges creak so she clenched her eyelids so tight, tiny red slits swam against the skin. There was a scuffle below and terrible words, snarled, words she had never heard before and she could feel the berth rocking as the chaperone was hauled out of her bed, squealing like a butchered pig. It was a horrible noise, the worst sound, and then the chaperone was a silent heap in the corner. Alma forced her face and ears into the pillow.

Was she a white chicken in a cage?

Go away! She was screaming now. *Go away!*

Her legs were warm and sticky. She had wet herself, all over the starched sheets and her new white knickers with the love-heart motif were sodden.

Was it a djinn? It must be a djinn. She did not know djinns could smell so human.

It was not a djinn. It was a man. A huge man. And she watched him through her gritted eyes as he reached up and pulled her down by her arm, her hair, her shoulder, to the ground. She fell and the ground was hard, a shock. She heard her bones break, her head crack.

He was on top of her then, this man. His entire weight and she thought he would crush her to death.

When he looked at her, on top of her, holding her down, she bit her own lip and ripped right through it.

He must not have liked the colour of her eyes because he punched her in the face when he caught her eye. She blacked out at once.

When she came to, he was holding her hands with one of his own and he was kicking her and hitting her and ripping right through her. She could not open her eyes. They were glued together. Her lips were also glued. Someone had glued her and her throat tasted of bile-vomit-some other foul thing.

Was the chaperone dead?

Later, in the daylight, in the back of a car, her mouth stuffed and tied, she would unglue her eyes and look down at herself. The lemon-yellow dress, the Sunday dress, the dress she wore to parties, was crimson-scarlet-red.

.   .   .

There is a line of sweat, like hard beads, sticking to her back and behind her ears.

"I want to stand by the open door," she says, standing up in a hurry, thinking she might be sick. "I need some air."

"Oh no, beta, ladies don't stand by the door."

Alma gets up anyway, ignores the tuts and the tugging of the hand on her dupatta. She pushes her way to the open door and holds the bar, leans her face into the warm wind. She is more fortunate than all those other girls, who will get home and be unwanted all over again. She will be homeless only once. She has a Bappu, a Ma, a sister, an ayah, and a cook. An Auntie who lives in Bombay.

She thinks of the mali, decides she will never marry. In her mind's eye she touches his mouth with her mouth, his black-coffee-coloured eyes watching her, the rise of a blush on his face. On hers too. They are walking on the seashore, the baby she has named Usha on her back and the sun low and kind. Perhaps she will take his hand.

The train speeds on, forwards forever forwards. She sees bony cows weaning their calves. Ebony buffalo lolling in shallow waters. Tents set up by the side of the road, refugees squatting by the plume of a cooking fire or hanging torn washing on stunted trees to dry. Naked children with sun-bleached hair shriek and run alongside the train waving manically.

She can't take her eyes off the landscape. The endless sky: she had almost lost herself in it but is now at the other end, a different person altogether. She sees miniature shrines hidden in trees. The heart-shaped leaves of a peepul fluttering with no breeze. Flaxen fields burning gold in the lonely midday sun. Water flowing.

Usha is on her back, and the sand is soft on her feet. She links her little finger to his and they walk.

Wife-mother-sister-daughter-niece.

This is India, her India and she is nearly home.

ACKNOWLEDGMENTS

I SPENT A SUMMER at the British Library working my way through history books, Partition fiction, newspapers, and compendia of Indian folktales and myth. The recordings and legacy of the Partition voices stayed with me long after I heard them. The statistics of human lives reduced to numbers, of women raped and abducted, of women whose only voice was their silence, kept me writing and imagining, desperately hoping I had the skill to pass on the information, to create lasting empathy, to be as truthful in my narratives as possible. I believe, truly, that the telling and sharing of stories, oral and written, is our route to salvation.

I am forever grateful to the British Library for its selection of audio recordings, "Partition Voices," and the many copies of *The Times of India* and *The Hindustan Times* that I was able to so easily access and work through.

To Caroline, my brilliant agent at Felicity Bryan, for having infinite faith when my own had run out. For her incredible editing skills, sense of humour, and the phone calls when I most needed them. Thank you, Caroline, for not letting me kill the baby.

Acknowledgments

To Erin, my wonderful, insightful editor and the rest of the team at HarperCollins. Thank you.

To Stephanie Cabot, at Susanna Lea Associates, for taking *Moth* to the US. Thank you.

To my Birckbeck writing group, Clare, Kate, Vanessa, and Martin, who read those first three chapters when I was in India and came back to me with valuable and honest criticism. Sometimes, you just have to cut and start again.

To Tam and Cee, thank you for reading that first 200,000-word draft, and the unwavering belief, when I had none.

To my sister, Maryam, who also tackled that first heavy draft with a red pen and helped me tighten it all up. Thank you. I can honestly say my grammar has much improved since then.

To Tiger and Pippin, for teaching me how to play, for giving me Roop.

To my mother, for sharing her home when I needed one.

For treacle&co. Thank you, from the bottom of my heart, for letting me go.

FURTHER READING

BOOKS

Twilight In Delhi by Ahmed Ali*

Annihilation of Caste by B.R. Ambedkar

The Other Side of Silence by Urvashi Butalia

The Age of Kali by William Dalrymple

City of Djinns by William Dalrymple

Nine Lives by William Dalrymple

Handbook of Hindu Gods, Goddesses, and Saints
by H. Daniel Smith and M. Narsimhachary

Clear Light of Day by Anita Desai*

Ants Among Elephants by Sujatha Gidla

---

*denotes work of fiction

Further Reading

Midnight's Furies: The Deadly Legacy of India's Partition
by Nisid Hajari

The Great Partition by Yasmin Khan

Manto: Selected Short Stories by Saadat Hasan Manto*

Folktales from India: A Selection of Oral Tales from Twenty-two Languages
by A.K. Ramanujan

Midnight's Children by Salman Rushdie*

Indian Folklore by Sanyal and Co.

Modern Hindu Thought by Arvind Sharma

Train to Pakistan by Khushwant Singh*

Indian Summer by Alex von Tunzelmann

The Long Partition and the Making of Modern South Asia
by Vazira Zamindar

Partition Voices by Kavita Puri

POETRY

Selected Poems by Rabindranath Tagore

ARTICLES

"The Great Divide: The Violent Legacy of Indian Partition"
by William Dalrymple (the *New Yorker*, June 29, 2015)

---

*denotes work of fiction

ABOUT THE AUTHOR

MELODY RAZAK started writing *Moth* while studying for her MA in creative writing at Birkbeck. Previous to writing, she owned the café treacle&co and more recently worked in the kitchens of Honey and Co. in London as a pastry chef. Melody has been awarded distinctions for her short stories, and has also written articles for the *Observer*, *Food Monthly*, and the *Sunday Times*. *Moth* is her first novel.